THE FAN OF RYL

A CORELLE OF DUR NOVEL

HAYLEY PRICE

HAYLEY PRICE
BOOKS

A catalogue record for this book is available from the National Library of Australia.

National Library of Australia Cataloguing-in-Publication entry

Author: Hayley Price

Title: **The Fan Of Ryl**

ISBN: 978-1-7637998-2-0 (Print)

ISBN: 978-1-7637998-4-4 (ePub)

ISBN: 978-1-7637998-3-7 (PDF eBook)

❀ Created with Vellum

This book is dedicated to the marginalised everywhere. You are seen.

———

At times this book will change point-of-view. Please note that each new scene does not always follow the same timeline as the last.

———

A note for my American readers. This book is written in UK/Australian English. Many of the words will be spelled differently from what you're used to - realised, colour, centre etc. We pronounce the "h" at the start of "herb", so we preface it with "a" rather than "an."

In addition, we do not share your fondness for the letter 'Z'. I realise you may find this difficult and offer my humble apologies. We make up for this by using a plethora of "L's where you would make do with one. Marvellous.

———

All the writing and artwork in this book was created by a real person. No AI was used at any time.

ALSO BY HAYLEY PRICE

The Vermilion Saga

The Vermilion Ribbon

The Vermilion Cross

The Vermilion Triangle

Corelle Of Dur

The Blade Of Ryl

THE BLADE OF RYL RECAP (SPOILERS)

In The Blade Of Ryl, Corelle sailed south to live out her banishment from Dur with Pettra, Raolos's wife, as her lover. A cruel fate lay in wait for Pettra, but Corelle managed to kill the former Bailiff of Dur, Glailam. Corelle became more and more dependent on wine as a salve for her shattered self-esteem.

A letter from Dur summoned her home to avenge the murder of Klordia, Wilash's wife. With Synna's aid, she learned elements of the Guild still lived and were holed up on a farm in the Eastlands. Despite their best intentions and efforts, Corelle and Synna could not take the Guild's new leader, Krage, captive, and he fled south.

In the Eastlands, Corelle met a woman named Vamma. Their relationship caught the attention of the Guild, who tried to kill her. Vamma left for safety in Ort, and Corelle followed her later when she accepted the Guild had escaped.

Synna told Corelle Arella had been with child when she had urged Corelle to kill her in Zhanghar, and Corelle wavered between leaving Dur or pressing Wilash, who knew the full story, to tell her the truth.

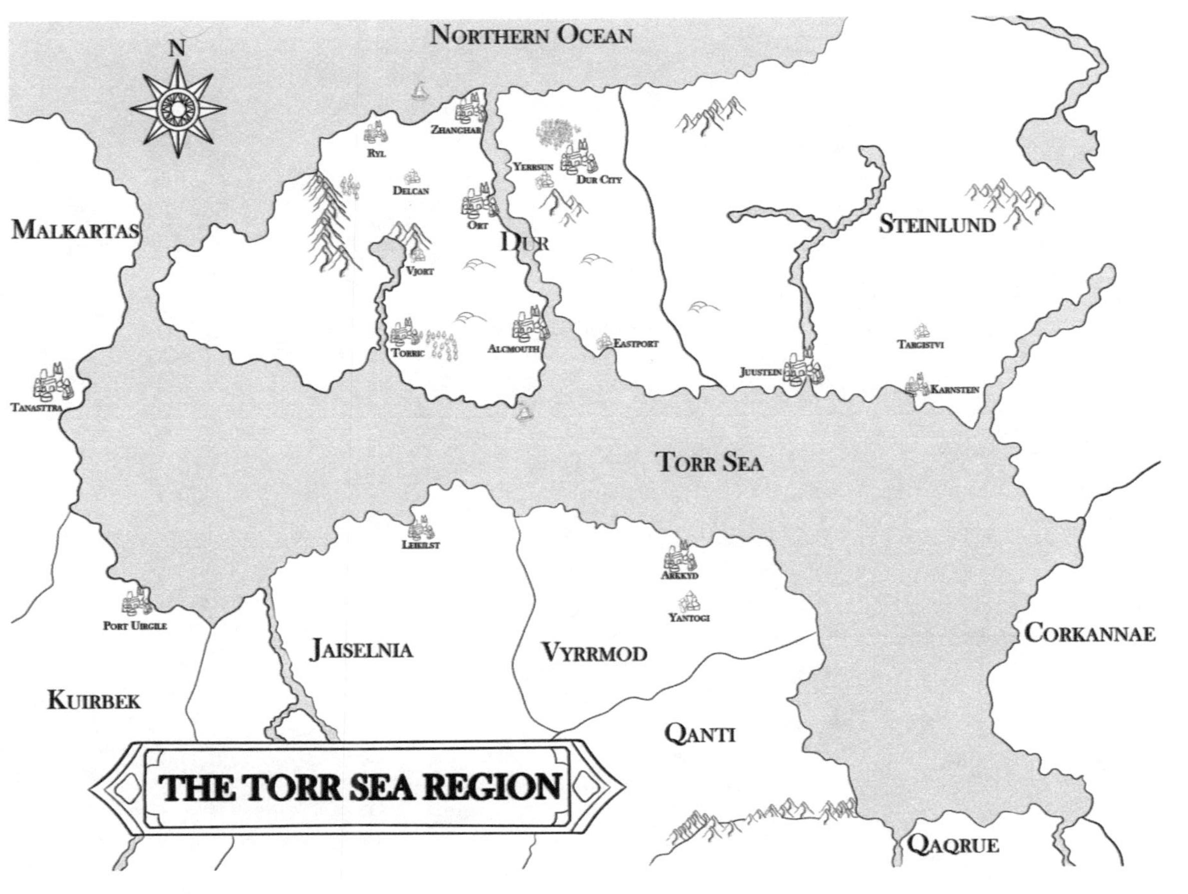

N
NORTHERN OCEAN
MALKARTAS
RYL
ZHANGHAR
DELCAN
ORT
DUR
VJORT
YERRSUN
DUR CITY
STEINLUND
TORRIC
ALCMOUTH
EASTPORT
TARGISTVI
JUUSTEIN
KARNSTEIN
TANASTTRA
TORR SEA
LEIKELST
ARKKYD
YANTOGI
PORT UIRGILE
JAISELNIA
VYRRMOD
CORKANNAE
KUIRBEK
QANTI
QAQRUE
THE TORR SEA REGION

Dur
Northern Ocean
Northlands
Zbangbar
Forest of Dat
Dur City
Taro's Farm
Ort
Eastort
Yerrsun
Solgarn
Ryl
Delean
Ortlands
Mount Belram
Eastlands
Wantu Mountains
River Alc
Vjort
Wantu River
Freelands
Alcmouth
Eastport
Torre
Torr Sea

CHAPTER 1
CORELLE

The beam of sunlight through the window scooped one corner of the bedroom into the comfort of its embrace and drove away the night with its nightmares and darkness. Later in the morning, that sun would share its light and warmth with the entire room, but at this hour, it still scrambled into the blue sky of a perfect day. The shutters stood open; Corelle had neglected to close them the previous night, consumed with desire. Vamma slept beside her, her soft, rhythmical breaths the only sound in the house.

If angry disappointment had a taste, Corelle would be tired of it by now. She had swallowed its bitter seeds daily since she had met Arella as a girl of seventeen years. The latest, when she had failed to apprehend Krage and kill him for all the wrongs he had inflicted on her even though his men might have struck her down in payment for the deed, opened deep cuts in her none could see, but Corelle felt them, felt the sting of each one as it carved her failings into her. Krage had escaped and had paid no price for Klordia's murder.

Corelle had spent a great deal of the last three days in bed with

Vamma. They had slept little as they enjoyed each other's bodies often. Whenever she had time to ponder, such as now, Corelle tried to decide whether to sail south to Alcmouth, driven by a desperate need to confront Wilash and learn the truth about Arella and her unborn child. She had stumbled on the tale courtesy of a casual word from one of Raolos's men, and Synna had confirmed it outside Yerrsun. Styrrach shrouded Corelle, sold her to the authorities in Zhanghar, and with the Portreeve's men on the way to capture and hang her, Arella had intervened, had begged Corelle to leave before she could be taken. Corelle had urged Arella to flee with her, but the unborn child had driven Arella to urge Corelle to kill her. Arella felt unable to flee with the child in her belly and could not bring herself to tell Corelle the truth. She chose a swift death from Corelle over the Guild justice she earned once she had told her lover the Portreeve's men were on their way. Corelle had seen an example of Guild justice in Yerrsun. Arella had made the correct decision.

Corelle knew no more, but Wilash did; Arella had confided in him even as she would not confide in Corelle, her own lover. Styrrach had forced himself on Arella, and when he learned of the child, had shrouded Corelle and marked her for death at the Portreeve's hand. He would then have been free to raise Arella's child as his own. No child could ever have been cursed with a more despicable father than Styrrach. The child had been fortunate to die with its mother.

Corelle sighed. Such a judgement had not been hers to make, and she would not think it again. The nature of the father could not be laid in blame at the door of the child, who had no say in how it came to be. She longed to speak with Wilash and learn the full details, but his words would open old wounds. In recent years, Corelle had visited terrible retribution on those who wronged her, but she had already killed Styrrach, and more information about the events in Zhanghar would not make him any more dead. She should sail away from Dur. The Duke's banishment still applied, and she had failed to bring to justice those who had ordered the death of Wilash's wife, Klordia, which left no reason for the banishment to be lifted, and no reason for her to remain in Dur even if it were.

Beside her, Vamma stirred and mumbled something Corelle did not catch. Corelle turned on her side, slid an arm around the sleepy woman next to her, and whispered, "I did not hear you. What did you say?"

Vamma's teeth on her nipple drove the unheard words from her mind, and Vamma's hand between her legs pushed all thought of Wilash from her. She gasped as Vamma's hungry fingers teased at her nipple, which hardened under the attention. Corelle abandoned herself to the touch of her tormentor and moaned as her desire mounted until Vamma coaxed her to a peak of satisfaction.

Vamma spoke at last, a breathy whisper. "No more than that."

Corelle turned to her, confused, filled with the warm glow of fulfilment. "What?"

"This is what I said. I wanted you."

Corelle smiled. "You always do, it seems."

"You would prefer I did not?"

Corelle laughed as Vamma teased her. "That I would not." She did not lie. Vamma's touch brought her to swift and complete fulfilment. Vamma demanded little in return, but she remained an enthusiastic woman to make love to. Nonetheless, over time, she appeared content to give pleasure without any obligation she be pleasured in turn.

Vamma snuggled closer. "That is good. Your body excites me. I cannot help but touch it."

"It has been ill used." The weight Corelle had gained in Vyrrmod still lay upon her. "I must work to return it to its former glory."

Vamma's laughter filled the room. "Glory, you say? It is glorious now. I fear to imagine it when you would describe it as 'in its glory.' I could not be pried from you, day or night."

Corelle laughed again. Vamma made easy company, intelligent and thoughtful, never moody or argumentative. When asked a question, she pondered it before she gave a response, doubtless to see all angles that might weigh on the answer. She would talk even when Corelle had nothing to say, a trait that endeared Vamma to her. Despite this, questions ate at Corelle, and the answers would not be found here in the bed in Ort. Three days ago, she had thought she might sail south again and ignore the issue of what had turned in Zhanghar, how Arella had become with child. Now those questions burned in her mind once more, and if she did not find the answers, she would forever ponder what lay behind the tale

Vamma snuggled closer to Corelle. "What is on your mind?" Corelle did not reply straight away, concerned at what she must say. "Corelle?"

The three days in Ort had been an agreeable distraction, but the time had arrived. "I must sail south."

Long moments of silence passed before Vamma spoke again. "The day has come. I must return to Yerrsun now the danger is behind me."

Corelle doubted the danger had passed. "Krage may still return, and you may not be as safe as you believe."

She felt Vamma shrug beside her. "I will take my chances. My stall, home and family are there. My friends also. I am from the Eastlands. I am not Westfolk, I am happy to say."

Corelle pushed at her and laughed. "You tease me." Heartbeats passed, and without thought, she blurted out, "Come away with me." The idea had not entered her mind until this moment, but after all else, why not?

Vamma raised herself up on her elbows, and her earnest gaze remained locked on Corelle's eyes. "Where?"

"I know not, in truth. Wherever the wind blows us. Wherever the tide carries us. Who cares?"

"I care." A soft, wistful tone had crept into Vamma's voice.

Corelle gazed at her. "You do not wish to be with me?"

Vamma fell back onto the bed and gazed up at the ceiling. "That is a harsh way to describe it. You are a remarkable woman, and our time together, brief as it has been, has been a delight to me, and not without incident." Corelle guessed she referred to the moment Vamma had almost been killed by the Guild, saved only by fortune; Corelle had been at hand to intervene. "I crave many fruits and have never hidden this from you. Never have I been bound to one person. I have never contemplated I would abandon all others and settle with one, man or woman."

Corelle frowned, uncertain of what she had meant. "You tire of me?"

"That I do not. But I cannot be bound to you, and you alone. If we returned to Yerrsun together, I would make no promise I would never lie with another. I take my pleasures when, and with whom, I wish them."

"You are unfaithful?" Corelle could not comprehend why anybody could profess to care for one person yet seek pleasure with another. Raolos had strayed, and rumours suggested he strayed more than once. Corelle could never live with such a choice.

"I do not call it 'unfaithful.' I could build a life with you, but at times I would desire other pleasures. I could not promise to ignore those desires."

Corelle could not understand the concept, and it did not appeal to her. Guilt gnawed at her. *"You betrayed Deineike with Pettra,"* it whispered. Still, in the soft light of this early morning, Corelle could not imagine a life with somebody who might leave her bed to lie with another, as Pettra had done in Arkkyd. She could not be with Vamma in those circumstances. It would be easier for them to part and would also avoid any deeper connection between them, something she dreaded. At that, she wondered whether Vamma could ever love somebody if she desired others at the same time. "So, you could not fall in love with me? To say, 'I love you,' is an inconceivable notion to you?"

Vamma gave a short laugh. "I did not say that. I have not professed love for another, ever, but I would not say I could not love you. Even if I did love you, I still could not confine myself only to your bed."

"This is a mystery to me." Corelle had mumbled as much to herself as to Vamma.

"I am sorry I am contrary to the things you desire."

"You should not be. I pass no judgement. Your life is yours to live, and after all else, you must find your happiness. I am banished and must sail from Dur. Meanwhile, your heart lies in Yerrsun. Your outlook on life is your own to craft, and I wish you happiness."

Vamma moved and kissed Corelle's stomach. "If you find yourself in Yerrsun, even if I am married with eight children, I would always welcome a night with you."

Corelle could not suppress her ironic laugh. "That is one advantage to your attitude, after all else."

"That it is."

They fell silent for a time, and Corelle considered all that had been said. In truth, it meant Vamma would not utter the three words that would damn her and write her an unkind fate, as it had the three women who had said those terrible words to her before Vamma. Much of what Vamma had admitted to, she could not understand, but she had no right to understand how another person's mind worked. Part of the conversation came back to her, and she sought to lighten the dusky mood that had settled on the room despite the sun's efforts to brighten it. "Eight children?" Vamma pushed her from the bed onto the floor.

After they had broken their fast, they each packed up their

belongings and made ready to leave. Now the decision had been made, Vamma seemed as ready as Corelle to part ways with no further delay. Corelle locked the door behind her and slipped the key into a pocket in her trousers. They walked together in the warm sunshine of a late summer day and discussed the town and the weather, the conversation now that of friends, not lovers. Their time together had come to an end, whether for a brief period or for all time. Corelle felt comfortable in the moment, and Vamma appeared content with it.

Corelle waited with Vamma until the rowboat arrived, then sat on a bench and watched as it rowed back across the river. The journey seemed gentle today, with little wind and a benign, friendly river. As the rowboat grew smaller and smaller, and she could no longer identify Vamma's light brown hair, Corelle rose and moved off the bench. She eyed the ships moored at the dock in search of a three-master, but doubt blew on the embers within her, and her need to know the full story of Arella's abuse sprang into a great blaze. Its hungry flames licked at her curiosity and burned her resistance to ash. She would head for Alcmouth first, then travel south, far from Dur and the terrible memories it held. As luck would have it, a two-master would sail for Alcmouth within the hour on the new tide, so she paid for passage from her reduced supply of coins and threw her pack into the cabin provided for her.

She went onto the deck and watched the mariners make the ship ready to leave. They pulled and coiled ropes and drew cork fenders up from the ship's side as the dockworkers untied the lines that had secured the ship to the dock. The mariners hauled on more ropes, and the sails climbed the masts and billowed as the wind filled them. The ship moved out into the river, and Corelle settled at the bow to endure yet another voyage on the River Alc.

Throughout the uneventful trip, Corelle would not permit the crew to bring food to her cabin. She insisted she would eat in the common room with them. Most of them came from Dur and told her the ship sailed to and from the cities between Torric and Ryl, from one dock to another as the cargo dictated; hard work, they said, but they all seemed content with it. They pressed her to tell them what work she did, and she lied and told them she had run a market stall in the Eastlands. They did not show enough interest for her to need any elaboration of the tale.

She sewed the key back into the seam of her pack, although she felt some guilt she had kept it. If she could have talked to Raolos, she might have raised the issue of the house with him. It had not been his, in truth, but it did not belong to Corelle either. Pettra had said nothing about what should happen to it, and it had proved useful as a place to stay on occasions. Now she intended to leave, she did not know what to do about it. She resolved to talk to Synna about it in Alcmouth.

Most days she sat at the bow, but she now faced the rear of the ship and watched the mariners. She observed the duties they carried out and soon learned what formed part of their routine and what tasks they undertook less often. She listened to the way they spoke and how they referred to items of equipment and parts of the ship, and she resolved to try to become a mariner once she left Dur. Such a life would keep her occupied and would require no decision about where to set up home.

Unfavourable winds lengthened the voyage. The way the ship could sail into the wind enthralled her. It swung across the river from one side to the other as the crew pulled on ropes to change the angle of one or other of the sails, which caught the wind and used it to push the little ship forward even as everything Corelle understood should have seen it pushed backward by the wind.

Five days later, they docked at Alcmouth, and Corelle bade the crew farewell as they waved her off the ship. She headed for an inn, took a room for one night, and borrowed parch and scribing tools from the innkeep. She scribed a hurried letter to Wilash and asked him to meet her in the tavernroom that night, then she delivered it to the nearest courier office. She walked around the poor quarter for a time and passed the house in Torric Street where she and Synna had apprehended Priu. She wondered whether Wilash felt justice had been served, since she felt it had not. Krage had ordered Klordia's death, and he had evaded their clutches.

CHAPTER 2
CORELLE

Corelle grew tired of the aimless walk and returned to the inn to find a table in the tavernroom. She chose a table in a quiet corner at the rear, far from the door but with a good view across the room so she could see all who came and went. She ordered a cask of wine and filled her goblet. She suspected she might need all the succour the wine could bring her before she had heard the tale she would insist Wilash tell her.

He arrived as she poured her third goblet. He waved at her as he saw her, made for her table, and paused to order a tankard of ale as he passed the counter. He smiled as he took a seat opposite her. "It is good to see you again. Synna brought news of all that turned in the east."

"Synna brought us both news, then." Corelle battled to keep the anger from her voice.

Wilash frowned and tilted his head to one side. "I do not understand. What news did he bring you?"

"I will come to that in a moment. First, I wish to know whether the justice we delivered for Klordia satisfied you."

He sipped at his ale, and his eyes never left hers. "Raolos hanged her killer." He sounded guarded.

Corelle's words shot from her lips like small stones cast into the wind; they might yet come back to harm her. "He did not hang the man who ordered her death."

"Corelle, what is wrong? You sound angry. Is something awry?"

She lowered her voice to a whisper, too furious to hold her rage inside any longer. "That it is. That it is, for I did more than kill Arella that night in the The Ship's Yard. I killed her child also."

He had been about to lower his tankard to the table, but he froze, the tankard suspended a span from the wooden surface. He stared at her without so much as a blink of his eyes. Corelle took a sip from her goblet and slammed it down onto the table, which slopped some of the wine out of it. Some heads turned in her direction, but Corelle's vicious stare ensured they returned their attention to their own affairs without hesitation. She must take care not to raise her voice. These people need not learn of the matters they discussed.

Wilash had not replied, and she snarled at him, a quiver in her furious lips. "You have naught to say on the subject?" It proved difficult to keep her voice quiet as her rage boiled within her.

"Corelle..." He seemed to have no words.

She waited moments, but he said no more. "It seems you will not speak of it now any more than you would then."

He sighed and looked away for a heartbeat. "Corelle, I am sorry. Arella swore me to secrecy. She could not tell you. She feared what you would do, afraid you would go to your ruin because of her."

She growled through tense lips. "I would have been happy to do so, Wilash. I would have done it, because I loved her."

"I am dejected you have learned of it in this way. I could not tell you. She would not permit it."

"That did not prevent you from..." Corelle took a breath as her efforts to contain her anger appeared futile. "You blurted it out to all and sundry in a tavernroom, I hear. I am the only one you did not tell; the one above all who ought to have been told."

A tear formed in his eye, and he wiped at it with a sleeve. "Arella did not want you to know. She knew you would try to kill him and would be struck down."

"She had the right of it. I would have tried to kill him, and if it brought my ruin, then a fair price had been paid. His deed would have been avenged. Instead, I killed him here, long years later, though I did not know what I avenged."

He looked puzzled. "You have killed him?"

"You know this. I killed him for Deineike, when I should have killed him long before for Arella. Deineike would still be alive, and Arella also."

Wilash gave her a blank stare. When he replied, he sounded confused. "You killed Styrrach."

Corelle tutted at his response. Had he turned simple? She already knew she had killed Styrrach. Unless… "Then who should I have killed, if not Styrrach?"

He threw his head back, anguish scribed across his face. He seemed to struggle to speak. He stared into her eyes as he replied, though it seemed he had to force the words from his lips. "Styrrach did not father the child. He arranged it, but Krage violated her."

The room swam before Corelle, and Wilash blurred in her sight, even though she could have reached out and touched him. She swayed to one side and placed a hand either side of herself on the settle to steady her body. Krage, not Styrrach, had forced himself on Arella. She could find no words to reply. Her mouth had turned as dry as a stone left in the sun for days, and her tongue had turned to dust. Tears streamed from her eyes, and she threw her head back in a silent scream. It had been Krage, and she had abandoned her pursuit of him. She had allowed him to escape, who had raped the woman she loved and given her a child she had no desire to bear.

Dizziness overwhelmed her, and she fell forward. Her head hit the table, and she heard voices but could not discern the words they spoke. A familiar coppery smell told her blood came from her forehead, but she could not feel the pain of the blow over the agony Wilash had laid on her heart.

A vague, distant voice echoed in her ears. "Corelle, Corelle. Are you all right? Sit up and let me see you." A hand rested on her back, but she brought an arm up to swipe it away.

After moments too numerous to count, she found some strength to push herself upright, leaned back against the settle, and gasped anguished words. "How? Why?" She kept her hands on the settle either side of her for support as dizziness threatened to cast her to the floor.

Wilash had moved around the table and now sat beside her, but she could not bring herself to look at him. He spoke in a voice so quiet, she could scarce hear him. "It will do you no favours to hear more of this."

Corelle tightened her lips into a snarl. "I will hear it all, and you will tell it." She must know how it been allowed to happen. Arella had been violated, and he who had done the deed had lived to tell the tale.

He sighed. "Krage had become attracted to her in Ryl, but she had rejected his every advance. He had thought it strange and believed she would succumb because of the position he held. Arella suspected he saw the two of you together."

They had been so careful, yet not careful enough, it turned. To Corelle's utter devastation, Arella had died not only at her hand, but in no small part because of their relationship.

Wilash continued the dreadful tale. "At some point, Styrrach summoned Krage to Zhanghar. Arella had returned from Ryl, but he had not forgotten her. It seems they discussed you and Arella, and Krage learned you had joined the Guild. Krage knew you were more than friends and must have told Styrrach. You know how Styrrach despised your… No, I will not say the word. You know the word I refer to. He summoned Arella to the Guild building and confronted her with Krage's accusations. Then he ordered her to lie on the floor of his office as Krage ravaged her."

Numb from the story, Corelle longed to reach for Wilash, to squeeze his neck and stop the words that dripped from his mouth, tore her heart to shreds, and scattered them in the breeze. She did not trust herself not to fall from the settle if she did so, and the story went on. "He told her you would receive Guild justice if she did not comply. She did not wish that fate for you, so she endured it." He paused, and Corelle glanced at him. Tears ran down his face, his eyes swollen and red, and he wiped at them every few moments. He looked broken, and his utter dejection stilled her temper. "When she realised she had the child inside her, she told me, in search of advice. A poor choice, for I know nothing of children or childbirth, but she had nobody else to turn to."

Corelle gasped as another barb of agony pierced her heart. "She had me." The tale had left her so bereft, the breath to form words had to be dragged from her lungs.

"That she did. She longed to tell you but knew it would be your ruin, and she loved you…" He choked on the words and sat in silence, head bowed, for a time. The story had not yet ended, and he drew in a sharp breath. "Somehow, Styrrach learned of the child; not from me, I swear it. She may have confided in another, one she thought she could trust, and they betrayed her confidence. I know not. I believe Styrrach became so furious Krage's child might be raised by two women who lay together, he ordered you shrouded. I confess, I speculate on some of these issues. I do not know the full truth of the final days."

Corelle's heart ached, and her devastation left her drained. Her lungs betrayed her and would not draw air into her body, though she fought to gulp breaths enough to survive the utter desolation Wilash's tale had left where her heart had once been. Styrrach had known about them? They had tried so hard to cover the truth and had even rented two rooms at the inn to allay suspicion, yet they had been uncovered. In truth, their only crime had been to love one another. What could be so shameful in their love? She hated Styrrach even more now, and Krage too. She hated herself also; she had not noticed as Arella had endured so much, and Corelle had allowed Krage, Arella's abuser, to escape unpunished. She filled her goblet and threw it down her throat in one swallow.

After Synna had told her his version of the story, Corelle had guessed why Arella refused to travel with her. Arella had preferred death to the birth of a child conceived in so brutal a manner. She had remained focused on Corelle's safety. Corelle's heart had shattered. She could no longer stand to live, forced to carry this extra burden around with her. She would end her life this night.

She turned to Wilash and became furious again. "You knew, and yet you said nothing. You should have told me. We could have fled long before that night. You could have saved her and spared me all the grief and guilt that have been mine to bear since then."

He opened his mouth to answer, and a snarl came to his lips, but he seemed to battle to control his emotions. "I could not tell you, as I have said already. Arella did not wish you to know, for she knew it would lead to your death. She swore me to secrecy, and I loved her and would not betray the promise I made." He held up a hand as Corelle drew a breath to continue her tirade against him. "I know I betrayed her memory that night in the tavern when I told Synna and Raolos. They would have said naught, after all else, but other ears must have overheard, and the cat was out of the sack. Grief had destroyed me. My wife had been murdered. I had become intoxicated and angry at you for all that had turned, the deaths of Arella, Deineike, and Klordia." He stared in her eyes, and his own eyes blazed with fury before he spat, "You brought this destruction into all our lives."

His words stung Corelle, but she could not deny the truth of them. She had brought everything upon them all—death, heartbreak, and disruption, and she hung her head in shame.

After a moment, Wilash went on in a softer tone. "Corelle, I am sorry. I should not have said those words. I care for you. I always have. You cannot be blamed, in truth. You were nothing more than a piece in a tragic game."

She thought back to his claim Styrrach had known for some time she lay with Arella. "You told me he became angry because you had kept our love from him. Why, if he already knew?"

"I have never met such a vile, spiteful man. I believe he despised me because I kept it from him. In truth, I suspected he knew, even on the night Arella died. It pleased him to hurt people, and I believe he intended to hurt me the day he told me he knew about the two of you. He loathed you because you escaped his justice. I suspect Krage hates you because you killed his child. That may be why he had Klordia killed and wished with such fervour to have you in his clutches."

"Why did Styrrach shroud me and not Arella?"

"I imagine Krage played some part in the decision, but I confess I do not know."

Corelle shook her head. Wilash's argument carried more weight now she knew more of what had turned between Krage and Arella, but she remained convinced more lay behind Klordia's murder. He could have fled with his wealth and not risked his life. Instead, he had risked all for nothing more elaborate than revenge. It made no sense.

Wilash reached out as if to take her hand, but she kept them pressed on the settle at her sides. "What will you do now? Where Krage has fled to, nobody knows. I do not see how you can pursue him now."

"That I cannot. You are correct. But what can I do, Wilash? I cannot stay here. I am banished. I have no wish to live, in truth. I have been a terrible storm of devastation that has blown through all your lives. Four women are dead because of me, your wife among them. I do not deserve to draw another breath."

His stern reply rebuked her. "Do not say that, Corelle. You have much to offer to this life. You are a warm-hearted woman with many skills. You could—"

She cut him off. "Even you can find few enough good words to say about me. I am nice, and I can sew, is that it?"

"Corelle. Do not do anything rash. You believe four women are dead because of you. Remember, I knew them all. Do not add another Pyre to my life, I beg you."

She could not admit she intended to end her life once he left. "I am banished from Dur. Tomorrow I will leave this land and see where the wind blows me. If it takes me to the bottom of the Torr Sea, then so be it." He looked so unhappy, she abandoned her fear of a fall, laid a hand on his arm, and gave him a warm smile.

He would not meet her eyes but muttered into his tankard. "I should go home. I have brought you more unhappiness with my tale."

"I asked you to tell me. Do not blame yourself."

"It is late, and to relive these horrors has wearied me. Good night, Corelle. Please, do not do anything foolish."

She found a smile of reassurance deep in her battered self and dragged it, reluctant, to her lips. "I will not. Goodbye Wilash."

He half rose, then paused. "You mean good night."

Corelle maintained the smile but did not correct herself. She sipped at her wine as he stood. He gave her a sad smile, then disappeared through the door. She raised a hand to her forehead and squeezed at her temples. Her heart felt like a rock in her chest, the tale hurt her so much. Her head swum from the blow and the wine, and she could not unravel the implications of all she had heard.

How had she not realised Arella had fallen with the child? Arella must have known when she missed her moon cycle. Had Corelle been so self-absorbed in her own misery about the deadly work she performed for the Guild, she had no longer noticed the woman she loved had missed her cycle? She poured another goblet of the wine and stared into it, her elbows on the table and her head in her hands, but she found no answers there. She drank it back, then poured another. More answers lay in the story, and she longed to reach for them. She would stay her own hand until tomorrow in the hope everything would make more sense in the morning.

It made no more sense in the morning, but her head ached, her mouth felt as dry as sand, and her stomach roiled. After she had consumed the contents of the cask, she had staggered to her room, as far as she could recall. She still wore her trousers, but her tunic lay in the vanity bowl. One of her boots lay in a corner, and the dagger protruded from it. She could not see the other boot from the bed.

For some time, Corelle lay there half-awake and reflected on the story she had heard last night, but she felt so ill from the wine, she could not focus her thoughts. She dragged herself from the bed and wrung the water from her vanity bowl out of her tunic. She mopped her face with it, threw it into her pack, and took out a replacement. A short search revealed her other boot beneath the bed. Dressed, she went downstairs, paid for her room, and walked out into the sunlight. The glare hurt her eyes and her head, and she squinted as she trudged toward the dock.

Every voice on the street pummelled her head; the hooves of every horse deafened her. She could walk until she reached the edge of the dock, then continue to walk into the river. The wine had left her so ill, it would be a relief to drown in the Alc. As she approached the moorings, however, she spied Rakulaj's sigil on the rear of a ship, so she changed direction and boarded the ship to seek out the master.

Once he realised who stood before him, he urged her not to travel to Vyrrmod. The Upholders sought her in connection with the mysterious death of Pettra, and Corelle's disappearance had not cast her in a good light. She feared he would order her off his ship, but he went on to say Rakulaj had heard of the murder of a stall-holder whose reputation suggested Vyrrmod had been left no worse off by his death. As a result, word had been sent throughout his fleet; respect remained due to Corelle of Dur. The ship would sail for Arkkyd on the next tide, but he again suggested she seek a ship that sailed to a more hospitable destination. Corelle insisted, however, and he ordered her shown to a cabin.

In truth, if the Upholders apprehended and hanged her in Arkkyd, it would be an appropriate fate. She had more than earned an early death. She lay on the bunk in her cabin, unable to venture out onto the deck as she battled the after-effects of the wine. Exhausted, she dozed as often as not, and as darkness closed in outside the small round cabin window, she felt the ship move out into the river as it set sail for Vyrrmod.

Throughout the voyage, Corelle talked to the master at length about the prospect that a woman might become a mariner. Despite his initial scepticism, she persisted until she persuaded him to let her work alongside one of the crew and learn some of the skills. She threw herself into the work and paid attention to everything the mariner told her. He taught her the types of knots, the names of the sails, and when and how they were deployed.

The work satisfied her, and she took to it well. The mariner told her there should be no reason she could not fulfil the deck duties, but at each dock, the cargoes must be loaded and unloaded, which involved the hardest physical labour. She climbed the mast without difficulty and had no fear of the height, to her own surprise. At the top of the main mast sat a barrel known as the nest. A mariner climbed up to the nest to keep watch during difficult conditions such as heavy seas, fog or narrow inlets. Corelle enjoyed the solitude at the top of the mast, and the mariners soon learned to trust her eyes and directions. The phys-ical work had a beneficial effect on the weight she had gained in the last year, and she craved wine less at the end of a strenuous watch.

A day out from Arkkyd, the master summoned her to his cabin and complemented her on her performance. He revealed the other crew members had made fun of her at first, amused she had wished to learn their trade, but she had won reluctant respect for her abilities and her eagerness to learn. He suggested she should seek out another of Rakulaj's ships when they reached Vyrrmod, one which sailed to Qanti or some other land. If she could persuade the master of that ship to permit her to continue her training, she might become a reasonable mariner. It would be a first. He had never heard of a woman who became a mariner. His words made her more determined than ever to pursue the goal, and as Arkkyd drew close, she felt she might have found work that could bring her some peace. She thought Deineike would be proud of her, and she allowed herself a contented smile.

CHAPTER 3
CORELLE

A YEAR LATER

Corelle pushed the heavy cork fender over the rail and re-checked the clove hitch in the rope that held it to the ship. She moved aft to the last of the fenders, lifted it to the rail, and pushed it over. She re-checked the knot to ensure it would hold fast, then heaved a sigh. The fenders had to be thrown out each time the ship docked, and the hard work satisfied her. Sweat glistened against her dark skin in the early summer sun, and she wiped her brow as she picked up the roving fender and carried it to its station midships. She checked the knots, then nodded at the young lad who would watch as the ship came alongside the dock. He must stand ready to throw out the roving fender if the ship threatened to impact the dock with some part of its hull not already protected by the fixed fenders.

She moved aft to the stern line, which she had already coiled and checked twice, but she checked it again. As she gazed at the western bank of the river, her heart raced in her breast. It always beat faster as the ship came into a dock—one bad throw from her and the line might fall short of the dock, and the stern could swing out into the current. That would require a dangerous and lengthy manoeuvre to turn the ship and bring it again into the dock. Worse, they might sail past their own dock and strike another ship—a disastrous outcome. Today, her heart pounded faster than normal as she gazed on familiar buildings and recognised the dock that drew closer to them with every rapid heartbeat.

It had been certain they would carry a cargo to Dur at some point, and so it had proved. Their hold filled with rich spices from Qanti, the ship drew alongside the dock in Alcmouth. She had not seen the city for more than a year.

After she had sailed from Ort to Vyrrmod, she had found another of Rakulaj's ships. It made for Kuirbek, a land she had never heard of before. The master of that ship also agreed to continue her training, and her skills developed until she felt confident she could obtain work aboard a ship on her own merits as a mariner, rather than as a favour to the strange woman who carried Rakulaj's button. She left the ship, since any vessel that called Vyrrmod its home would carry her to jeopardy on every home-bound voyage.

Despite her skills, it had been difficult to find a master who could be persuaded to take her on. No woman had ever been a mariner on the Torr Sea, and Kuirbek resembled Dur in its view of women. Other lands might view women in a more favourable light, but she found herself here. She had been laughed off many vessels before she encountered Legorant Sugallia, a Kuirbekian master who, after much argument and persuasion, agreed to take a chance on her. He needed crew for a cargo to Qanti he had not expected or been prepared for. The cargo had not yet been loaded, and her first task had been to help load it into the hold. The crates of Kuirbek ore, used to fashion the elaborate jewellery of Qanti, had been heavy and awkward to lift. Corelle's short stature compounded the difficulty, and the other mariners made no attempt to disguise their laughter as she struggled to carry each one aboard. Undeterred by either the difficulty or the laughter, she carried every crate allocated to her onto the ship and down into the hold. By the end of the process, sweat and grime coated her, and she panted, exhausted but exhilarated. Her arms were cut and bruised from the cases, and they shook from the unfamiliar effort of the work, which had taken a dreadful toll on her muscles.

She leaned back against a mast and gulped down drafts of air to slow her heart, which pounded from the effort she had expended. One of the mariners spoke to her as he passed, and others around her laughed. Corelle did not understand his Kuirbekian language but guessed he had insulted her, and she saw her chance to show she would not tolerate any disrespect. She launched herself off the mast, landed on his back, and slapped at his ears as he yelled in surprise and clawed at her. He bent forward and threw her off his back, and she crashed to the deck. She had drunk no wine since she boarded the ship in Ort, lost in the rigours of her training as a mariner. She had lost weight, grown fitter, and become lithe and fast again. She regained her feet before the kick the mariner aimed at her connected. She crouched down and sucked in large draughts of air as she stared into his eyes. He moved forward on the balls of his feet, but shouts came from behind Corelle, and the mariner stood upright, still and silent. A man in the coat of an officer forced his way between them and yelled something she could not understand. Corelle remained crouched and ready for an attempted attack, but the mariner stared past her at some point in the distance and said nothing.

The officer turned to her and yelled again. She glanced at him before she looked back to the mariner whom she had fought, who looked into her eyes and flicked his head upward. It seemed he had suggested she stand upright, so she abandoned her crouch, stood, and glared into the eyes of the officer.

"What has turned here?" Legorant's powerful voice boomed

from behind her, and she turned to face him. He wore a look of anger and tapped the fingers of one hand against a thigh.

Corelle gave a terse response. "This man insulted me." Better to take the position of victim early in her justification for the attack.

Legorant flicked his eyes to the mariner, who said nothing. "What did he say?"

"I confess I do not know. The others laughed, so I guessed it had been some comment about my performance with the cargo."

Legorant spoke to the mariner in their language, listened to the man's reply, then turned again to Corelle. "He says he did not insult you. He claims he said you had performed well, for a woman."

She blinked in surprise. "Then why did the others laugh?"

Legorant spoke to the mariner again, and he paused before he answered. Legorant's lips turned up at one side, and he raised his eyebrows. "They laughed because he did not say 'woman.' He used a term that is less… complimentary. This could be perceived as an insult, had you understood it." He leaned closer. "I realise you wish to make an impression. You are but a woman, and a small one, but I will not have fights among my crew. Do you understand this?"

"That I do." Corelle softened her tone and gave a nod of her head for emphasis. She did not want to be cast off from the crew before the ship had even set sail.

"You are new, so I will not punish either of you this time. You will make our gesture of friendship with this man and go about your duties."

She turned to the mariner, who had his hand raised before her, palm toward her and fingers to the sky. Unsure what to do, she raised her own hand in the same way. He tutted and moved his hand so their palms touched, then interlocked his fingers between hers and folded them down against the back of her hand. She repeated the gesture, he nodded, then pulled his hand loose.

She looked behind her, but Legorant already ascended the stairs to the aft deck. The officer remained, however, and spoke to her in Dur. "I punish. Scrub deck."

Corelle nodded and he moved off. The other mariners drifted off about their own duties. As some of them passed, they held their hands up toward her and repeated the gesture of friendship. It seemed the fight had achieved its intended result. Some of the crew might now treat her with respect. She smiled and searched for a mop and pail.

As the ship sailed on and the passes went by, she earned the full respect, confidence, and friendship of the crew. She worked non-stop and never complained, learned fast, and soon became competent at any new task given to her. In every port, she drank with them and brawled alongside them if things turned awry. The hard, arduous work kept her mind occupied, and she volunteered for extra watches whenever the need arose. The officers and Legorant grew to trust her and treated her as they would any of her crew-mates.

She never forgot any of the pain that had plagued her life before she joined the ship, but some of it eased as the time passed, her agony over the death of Deineike in particular. The crew were rough and ready, and in the early days, some attempted to cajole her into a dalliance. None of them tried more than once, and she drew and lost much blood in fist fights she almost never won, but in which she never gave up. She slept, ate, and worked alongside them, and she became one of them. They would tolerate no unwanted attention toward her from any man when they were in a tavern somewhere ashore. Many of the brawls they found themselves in ashore started after a man pestered her to lie with him. Her crew-mates would order him away without ceremony, and her would-be suitor's friends would often take offence.

She revealed she had some skills at making, and before long the mariners asked her to repair their clothes for them. Her superior making exceeded by some margin the crude attempts they made to fix tears and the like. They used the large loop stitches that repaired the sails but were unsuited to clothes. At first, their clothes smelled so terrible, she insisted they wash them before they brought them to her for repair, but over time she smelled as bad as they did and no longer noticed. They continued to wash their clothes before they asked her to repair them, nonetheless, and they paid her a few coins for her work. Her repairs lasted longer than their own had, they told her, and the coin represented good value.

Corelle soon learned the Kuirbek language in an environment where little else was spoken much of the time, so different from her experience with the Vyrrmod language in Arkkyd. After a few unpleasant attempts that almost sent her down to Helchik's treasure, she learned to swim and often worked on the removal of the barnacles from the hull whenever they were in a dock. The crusty animals attached themselves to the hull in huge numbers, and they amazed Corelle. The crew faced a constant battle to remove them, but they slowed the ship, so she volunteered to dive into the water and scrape the hull at every stop. She wished she had learned to swim while she had been young, and she treasured her time in the water.

She learned to row the small boats the crew sometimes launched from their davits to venture ashore if shallow water made it difficult for the ship to dock. The crew claimed the two little boats hung there in case the ship sank, but to be far out in the middle of the sea in such a small boat seemed no escape to her.

After a year, they had come to Dur at last. The coppery taste of blood in her mouth surprised her. She had bitten her lower lip harder than she realised, and she shook her head to dispel her nervousness as the ship drew closer to the dock. As far as she knew, she remained banished from the land on pain of death. She threw the stern line to the dockhand. As ever, she made a faultless throw, and the dockhand tied the line to the cleat on the dock. She allowed the line to play out until the aft of the ship passed the cleat, then tied it off to another on the deck of the ship as other crew members adjusted the fenders to the height of the dock and made fast the bow line. It had been another flawless arrival at the dock; she could no longer recall a time when her throw had been short of the mark and, in truth, the stern line had become her permanent station these last few passes when the ship had docked.

The crew unloaded the cargo once the ship had been secured at the dock. They carried the crates of spices down the ramp and left them for the dockworkers to move on to whichever tally houses awaited them. The master and one of the dockworkers completed some parch, and the dockworkers moved the crates away from the ship. Corelle saw no cargo nearby as she worked. Unlike most masters, Legorant operated as a freesail—he owned his own ship, and he had no connection to any one merchant or union of merchants. He took contracts anywhere he found himself and went wherever that contract took him. He often obtained work from regular sources but could also pick up a cargo wherever they had sailed to. Wherever the new cargo needed to go would be their next destination. He paid well and relied on a hand-picked crew, whom he trusted and treated with respect and a firm hand. The day she had been taken on, it seemed she had been fortunate. The cargo had been unanticipated and needed urgent transportation. To her good fortune, some of his men had taken lengthy shore leaves after they had been away from home for an extended period.

Once they had unloaded the Alcmouth cargo, the crew gathered on the main deck as usual, and Legorant addressed them. He had no return cargo arranged and would head ashore to track one down. He gave a shore leave to every mariner other than three who would stay aboard, as always, to watch the ship. To her relief Corelle escaped selection to remain aboard, and she joined the boisterous, noisy crew as they headed for a nearby tavern.

CHAPTER 4
CORELLE

The sun sank toward the skyline of the city as Corelle's feet stepped onto Dur territory with her crew-mates. Evening would soon cloak the docks in darkness, but for now, Alcmouth lay before Corelle, resplendent in her bright summer dress. The sun glinted on windows and reflected from shiny metal flashing on roofs. No smoke drifted up from chimneys, the hearths below cold and black, fast asleep until the wet season disturbed them and brought the bright red of fire to them once again. She smiled at the familiarity of the skyline and wondered how Raolos, Wilash, and Synna fared. It seemed unlikely she would see them; doubtless Legorant would have a cargo for them to load in the morning, sore heads from the night's drink no excuse for them not to load it aboard and make the ship ready to sail away to their next destination. She had sailed to Arkkyd twice aboard The Salty Home, a poor translation of the ship's Kuirbek name into the language of Dur, but she could find nothing closer. Both times she had approached Arkkyd, she had been anxious, but if the Upholders still sought her in connection with Pettra's death, she had evaded them.

In truth, they would have been hard pressed to recognise her. She had become lean and muscular. The sun and sea breezes had burnt her skin a deep brown. She wore her hair cut close to her scalp and covered it with a deep blue kerchief, knotted at the back of her head.

They crowded into the tavern, eleven of them, and they all shouted orders at the innkeep at once. The men all drank ale, but Corelle still favoured red wine. She had discovered many fine quality wines in various lands but had also found some that tasted worse than the way they made her feel the next day. She helped two of the crew push three tables together and drag settles over while the others ordered and carried drinks to the table. As they always did, they paused and fell silent with their drinks held out before them for a moment, to pay respect to the sea and all whose lives those waters had claimed. Then the noise began again as they all spoke at once and laughed at each other's mistakes and misfortunes on the last voyage.

They dropped an agreed number of coins into a hat one of the crew always brought ashore and sat it in the middle of the table. Anytime one of them went to the counter, they would take some of the coin and return with several tankards and, every so often, a goblet of wine. Frequent squabbles broke out over the ales as hands pushed into the collection of tankards in search of a fresh one to replace another. Corelle laughed as they fought over the tankards. They cursed each other and threatened death until smiles split their faces, and someone went to the counter for more tankards.

She felt comfortable here among these rough, simple men. They never questioned her about her past and judged her only by the standard of her work and how well she drank with them ashore. All were equal among the regular crew, and if one became embroiled in any difficulty, they all did. At one time, one of the men had incurred some gambling debts on a lengthy shore leave, and two burly men came to the ship one night with stout wooden clubs to ask for him. Corelle unlocked her trunk, took out her dagger and joined the others at the top of the ramp. One of the debt collectors walked part way up the ramp and slammed the club against it as he tried to intimidate the crew. Corelle skipped down the ramp, pressed her dagger to his throat, and warned him not to take another step if he valued his life. The debt collectors left, Corelle replaced the dagger in her trunk, locked it, and from that day forward, the entire crew, even Legorant, looked on her with renewed respect. None of them asked how she had wielded the dagger in such a calm, collected way, nor why she kept it in her trunk.

Here in the rough Alcmouth tavern, they were all well on their way to sore heads the next day when a chant went up for her to visit the counter for a fresh round of drinks. They would bring her wine, but they did not afford her any other different treatment. She must take her turn to go to the counter with some of the coin and return with as many tankards as she could carry, and woe betide her if she dropped one.

While the innkeep filled the tankards, she gazed around the room, a smile on her face. She reasoned Deineike would have enjoyed this life. Deineike's tall, muscular body would have been better suited to the work than Corelle's, but they would have found joy in it together. A brief sadness washed over her at the opportunity missed, but she dismissed it before it could drag her down into melancholy. Nearby, some men spoke together. They looked like dock workers finished for the day who enjoyed a drink together after work. She thought she heard Raolos's name mentioned and strained to catch the conversation.

One of the men seemed to be in the middle of a tale. "Took his son, the word is. Raolos is behind it, as I heard it."

She took a curious step closer as another stepped in to defend the Bailiff. "Raolos is a good man. I doubt his involvement."

Another seemed to have no doubts about Raolos's character. "He has no part in it."

Corelle had to know what they discussed, so she pushed toward the middle of the little group and addressed the one who had mentioned a son. "Tell me what you speak of." As she glowered up at him, one of the others kissed her on the cheek, a clumsy, intoxicated action that caught Corelle by surprise. She often endured the attentions of men in taverns across the lands, but she had not expected the kiss. She pushed at the man, a reaction borne out of instinct, and he lost his balance, then fell to the floor. His ale sprayed around him.

One of his friends grasped her arm above the elbow, but before he could say whatever he intended, the crew of The Salty Home leapt from their seats. Tankards and ale scattered across the tavern-room as they yelled at the local men and pushed them away from Corelle. The locals bristled at the rough treatment from the mariners. Somebody called Corelle a courtesan and his friend a potential customer, which inflamed the already angry mariners. Corelle tried to push the men apart and yelled for everybody to calm down. She wished above all else to learn the story she had overheard a small part of, and a fight would not bring her any useful information.

Some punches were thrown, but as normal in an inebriated brawl, many of them missed their marks. The incident ended in little enough time, and the local men left with many glares and muttered insults for the mariners. The crew bought more ale and returned to their tables. Corelle drank another goblet of wine and wondered about the snippet of gossip she had heard. It might mean nothing, some petty event exaggerated by men with tongues loosened by ale, but part of her wanted to know nothing more lay behind it. She worried for Raolos if he had become involved in some unpleasant incident. She imagined Synna still guarded him, and he would have his men, but if he had become embroiled in some complication, it would be hard for her to board the ship and sail away in the morning unless she knew what had turned.

Her crew-mates prepared to move to another tavern. She told them she came from Dur and knew of a dalliance here in Alcmouth that awaited her, and the men all yelled and clapped their hands. On occasions, she had enjoyed some dalliances with courtesans in various cities who were open to such experiences. The men all knew she lay with women rather than men and were unconcerned by it now she had been accepted as one of them.

Corelle made her way toward the square, but darkness had fallen, and it had grown too late for either the Portreeve's or the Bailiff's Offices to be open. She stopped a man and asked him what he had heard about a scandal that involved the Bailiff. He gazed at her in astonishment, but she could not tell whether her less than feminine appearance surprised him or whether he thought her from another land because of her darkened skin. He seemed unprepared or unable to answer, and she pressed him. "Have you heard anything?"

He blinked, then seemed to compose himself. "Rumours fly. It depends on who you speak to, but you will hear different versions of the tale. It seems Peben, the Duke's son, has disappeared."

"Disappeared?" Did he mean wandered off, or some darker explanation?

"That he has. He vanished one day a while back, and nobody has seen him since. The Bailiff searches for him, so I hear. Others say the Bailiff has killed him and burned his body. As I say, it depends who tells the tale. The boy has gone, the sole thing everybody agrees on, it seems to me."

Corelle muttered and shook her head. "This is dreadful news." Why would somebody take the boy? She did not believe Raolos played any part in it but could not unravel how rumours had spread that he had some involvement.

"That it is. The people are unhappy. Durfolk dislike this sort of thing. Durfolk are people from Dur."

It seemed he thought she came from another land, and she did not care to disavow him of the idea if it meant a lengthy explanation. She nodded instead, already lost in her own thoughts, and he walked on. Corelle stood and pondered the story. It matched the pieces of conversation she had overheard in the tavern, but the man had shed no new light on the matter. Rumours always abounded whenever anything out of the ordinary came into people's lives.

She could achieve nothing tonight. It would be best to return to the ship for the night and attempt to find some better answers in the morning before the ship set sail. With any luck, she could meet with Wilash or Synna tomorrow. Resolved, she turned, hurried back to the ship, and headed for her bunk. When the crew returned to the ship, their boisterousness woke her, and they asked about her dalliance. Had she been successful, she would be gone longer than she had tonight, and she told them she had been rejected. They laughed and teased her, inebriated and rowdy. In jest, two of them offered to take the place of the woman who had rejected her, and she laughed along with the men and insulted the two who had offered with a complaint they could not sustain her enjoyment for anywhere near long enough. The others laughed even louder and pushed the two around in some good-natured rough and tumble. Soon enough, they all lay in their bunks, and the sounds of their snores filled the cabin. It took Corelle a long time to get back to sleep, and her mind refused to abandon the turmoil of the night's news.

She woke early the next morning and rose from her bunk. The smell of ale filled the cabin as she rose, and one of the crew had fetched up on the floor through the night. Corelle avoided the pile of vomit and went up to the deck. She ran up the stairs to the aft deck, and relief washed over her as she saw Legorant near the wheel. He shuffled parch, but he looked up as she approached, and she gushed out a hasty lie about a sick relative she had heard about in the tavern last night. He seemed sceptical, but she begged him for some time to visit with them. Anger tinged his tone. "We have a cargo to load, and the goods will arrive within two hours. We sail for Steinlund on the midday tide." It seemed he did not wish to excuse her from her duties.

"I have been on your crew for over a year. Have I ever failed you in that time?"

"That you have not." He sounded unhappy, reluctant. "Be back as soon as you can."

She thanked him and ran from the ship, headed for the square. The square lay some distance from the docks, and she had no more than two hours, but she must find out what lay behind the rumours. Her work aboard The Salty Home had improved her fitness, and these days, she found she could hurry through the empty streets quicker than she could ever recall. She was twenty-four years and had never been so fit in body or mind. It took her less than an hour to reach the square, but neither the Portreeve's nor the Bailiff's Offices had yet opened their massive Ortwood doors, so she sat on the step outside the Bailiff's Offices and waited.

She watched the city awaken as the deserted square came to life. People hurried across it bent on whatever activities awaited them this day. Stallholders arrived at the market area to set up their stalls. A familiar figure strode across the square toward her; Wilash, although he appeared to take no notice of her. He reached the door and pulled out a large ring of keys. He fussed with them as he sought the one to open the doors, and still he had not noticed her.

Still seated nearby, she felt she must say something. "Is this how you treat old friends?"

He looked down, confusion on his face. "Who might you..." Realisation spread across his face, and a huge smile sprang to his lips. "Corelle?" He sounded uncertain.

"That it is." She rose to her feet.

He swept her into his arms and squeezed her so tight, she felt he might crush her ribs. "It is good to see you again, although I took you for a boy."

She gave his back a playful slap but could not keep the laughter from her voice. "That is not the welcome I anticipated."

"What brings you here? Why do you look so… different?"

"That is a lengthy tale, and I am short on time. I came to discover the truth behind some rumours I hear about the Duke's son."

He released her from his grip and his eyes clouded over with sadness, but before he could speak, a carriage turned into the square and made for the Bailiff's Offices. The Bailiff's crest on its door left no doubt about who rode within it, and Corelle tutted. "Raolos comes. He must not see me. My life is forfeit here, as far as I know."

He sighed. "That it is, although it need not be so, mayhap. Synna has said more than once he wishes you were here to help with this mystery. Hurry to the back alleyway, and I will send Synna out to you as soon as I can."

She kissed him on the cheek and ran off along the front façade of the building. Synna still served Raolos, which pleased her, but her brief meeting with Wilash had told her nothing more than she had heard the previous night. As she entered the alleyway where she had saved Klordia's life some time ago, she reflected on the inglorious end Klordia had endured. The Guild had taken her life from her and abandoned her body in the very alleyway where Corelle had first met her.

Corelle ran to the rear door of the Offices, where she waited, impatient and flustered. The sand fell, and she needed to be back at the ship soon. At last, Synna came out of the door. He stopped when he saw her, and his mouth dropped open in apparent surprise. "He said you looked different, but I had not expected this." She looked down at her calf-length trousers and the leather shoes she always wore on the deck of the ship, her tunic stained with sweat, food and other unidentifiable matters as he continued. "Where is your dagger?"

It could not be kept in the leather shoes, and she never carried it aboard the ship, after all else. "Locked in my trunk. I do not kill any more. Enough idle chatter. What turns?"

A look of sadness flashed across his face, but anger soon pushed his unhappiness to one side. "The Duke's son has disappeared. He left the house of a friend after a visit, but he did not arrive at the Highhome."

Corelle could not disguise her surprise at the apparent lack of security. "Did he not have guards? Why did he walk, rather than ride in a carriage?"

Synna sighed. "He did have a guard, but somebody killed him."

"Then he has not 'disappeared,' he has been taken."

"Things have been peaceful in Dur since you left. Nobody would have anticipated such a brazen act. Nobody quite knows how to react or how much to reveal. Where have you been, after all else?"

She sighed, impatient. "Everywhere, but there is time for that later. What followed his disappearance?"

"We searched the city for him once word came to us but could find no trace of him. We questioned the parents of the friend at length, but they could shed no light on the matter. Two or three days ago, a parch arrived at the Ducal Highhome. It said the boy would be returned when the Duke granted a city charter to Ort."

The twist mystified Corelle. "Why Ort? What significance does Ort's status have for this lad?"

"Because Raolos had argued for some time for Ort to be granted a city charter. He had argued the town pays substantial levies, and Ibie is a popular Portreeve. The town prospers under his leadership, in truth. Raolos is desperate to find the boy. Word of his disappearance has already gone abroad, and rumours spread like spilled water. The people are unhappy the Duke's heir has disappeared. If the truth emerges, that he has been kidnapped for ransom, such a brazen crime would outrage the Durfolk."

Corelle had no doubt about who had kidnapped the boy. "It is the Guild."

"Oh? And how have you come to this determination?"

Synna appeared sceptical, but in Corelle's mind, everything pointed to them, and to Krage. "They killed Klordia and made a clumsy attempt to position me as the culprit. We had them in our grasp, but I made a mistake, and they fled. Now the boy is taken, and a crude attempt is made to lay the blame at Raolos's door. It is the same game, played by the same players. It is Krage. I do not doubt it for a heartbeat."

Synna nodded. "I see your point, although I feel less certain than you. Why do they have any interest in Ort? What do they stand to gain if Ort is made a city?"

Corelle tutted with impatience. "That is a distraction. They do not care about Ort. Their one wish is to spread anger and division. The more important question is how they came to know Raolos had made such fervent attempts to have Ort granted the charter. It gave them the opportunity they sought. Somebody must have told them."

"Who would tell them? Nobody but the Duke and his Senior Aides would know, other than Raolos. Even I knew nothing but sketchy details of what they discussed."

"One of those Senior Aides cannot be trusted, my guess." Corelle's head reeled as she tried to piece the mystery together. It might be another ruse to flush her out, but she had no connection to the boy, and there would be no guarantee she would take any interest in it. Indeed, she had learned of it by the merest chance. Something more must be at play, as she had protested a year ago. None believed her then; doubtless none would now. She adopted a more forceful tone. "It is Krage."

Synna nodded but appeared reluctant to embrace her explanation in full. "We need more help. We need help from a mind that understands the players and the game. We need you."

Corelle could not catch the derisive laugh before it burst from her. "I know nothing of this game. It is politics, my guess, and it could not interest me less."

Synna persisted. "You have skills we could use. You can find people. If you are right, and it is Krage, who can think the way he thinks better than you?"

She laughed at the compliment even as she felt her cheeks burn. "You, for one."

"I am nowhere near as good as you. Your skills exceed mine by some margin. I have always said this."

"They may have exceeded yours at one time. I have not used them since I left Dur." Her Guild skills had been neglected as a mariner other than in the brawls aboard the ship and ashore, and the time the men had come in search of her crew-mate. She doubted she could depend on her training any longer.

He seemed to sense she had rejected his request for help. "What if I gave you an incentive for your help?"

Something in the tone of his voice put Corelle on her guard. "What manner of incentive?" She strove to keep any hint of interest from her voice.

"What if I could arrange a full pardon for you? Your banishment lifted. You would be free to return to Dur. Vamma may still be in Yerrsun. The two of you became close, did you not?"

A grim chuckle, laden with irony, burst from her before she could suppress it. Corelle had thought of Vamma no more than once or twice in the last year. Deineike and Arella occupied her thoughts most of the day, but Vamma had become a distant memory for her. "I have no wish to return to Dur. Had you considered that? For all you know, I have a new life I love, and someone who warms my bed as much as I desire. I have not killed since

Yerrsun, and the nightmares do not plague me as they once did. I do not know what would happen to me if I killed again, and the prospect does not appeal. I am sorry."

He had more cards to play, it turned. "What if you are right, and Krage is once again in Dur? Have you forgotten your wish to avenge Klordia? If you have, then what of Arella, and her child?"

Most people would have withered before the stony stare she gave him, but Synna held her eyes. He had played a hand as high as it had been dishonourable. Arella's face filled Corelle's mind, and the nightmares inhabited by the unborn child were like fresh scars on her memory, even though she had not dreamt them for some passes. She replayed the moment her fan ended both their lives. She imagined the humiliation, the full horror of what Arella must have endured at Krage's hands in the Guild building as Styrrach watched.

She set her jaw in an angry scowl. "I will be at Raolos's office soon after the midday, as will my dagger. If I find myself unwelcome in Dur, I will leave again and may never return. Those are my terms. Do the best you can with them."

She did not wait for his answer. She turned and walked away furious, unsure she could trust her temper not to aim a punch at his face for the underhand way he had cajoled her help from her. She raged inside, and she felt prepared to let the Five Cities run vermilion with blood if she encountered Krage and any who still served him.

CHAPTER 5
CORELLE

Corelle hurried back to the ship. To her dismay, her crewmates already worked to load the cargo into the hold. She joined them and tolerated their banter about her tardiness. Beneath the warm summer sun, Corelle toiled up and down the ramp, drenched in sweat. It took until almost the midday to load the ship. As the crew prepared the ship to put to sea, Corelle skipped up the steps to the aft deck. She told Legorant she had not concluded her business and begged for two more hours.

His face turned red, and his lips pressed tight together. "You have been a good worker, but we sail on the next tide. If you are not aboard, we will sail without you. You will be denied pay if you are late and cannot perform your duties as we cast off." He turned his attention back to his charts, a blunt dismissal. Corelle ran down to the bunk room and unlocked her trunk. Little enough sat in the trunk; her old pack, some boots, her dagger, a pouch of coin, Deineike's tattered sketches, and some spare clothes. She left the clothes, swapped her leather shoes for the boots, and pushed her dagger into one of them. She dropped the shoes into the trunk, shoved the pouch of coin into her pocket, then grabbed her tattered pack and thrust the sketches into them. With one last wistful glance around the room, she locked the trunk and ran up to the aft deck again.

"Legorant, it has been a privilege to sail aboard your ship for this last year, and you have my thanks for the chance you took on me. I may be back, but if I am not, take this coin and give it to the crew for the hat next time you dock." She handed him half the coins from her pouch.

Misery cloaked his face. "Something important calls you, I see this. We will miss you. I will miss you. You are one of us. I wish you fortune."

She turned away and wiped at her eyes. "My thanks. Sail well. May the breeze be always at your stern." With no time to wait for a reply, she ran down the ramp and ignored the shouted questions from her crew-mates. Although she ran all the way to the square, the midday had long passed before she arrived, and she panted from the exertion, her clothes soaked in sweat, which dripped from the tip of her nose and ran down her arms and legs.

An ornate carriage stood outside the Bailiff's Offices, and men in yellow tunics stood guard at the door. She wondered why the Duke would be there, but she could gain nothing from speculation. When she rushed into the building, she spotted Synna in the lobby. He paced back and forth and did not stop until he saw her. "You come at last. Your terms are met. You will be pardoned, and the banishment lifted. Will you stay and aid me?"

Before she answered, Corelle needed to understand the Duke's visit. "The Duke is here?"

"That he is. Wheels have turned since our conversation this morning. You are to be a citizen of Dur again. Raolos and the Duke await you with little patience. You are late." He smiled, and she guessed he had teased her.

She laughed at his jest. "I have done more work in the time I have been gone than the Duke will do in his entire life."

Synna lowered his voice so she alone could hear him. "Please do me a favour."

Now Corelle teased him. "Another favour? What is it?"

"Please call him 'my Duke.' Do not antagonise him again."

The Duke's stubborn insistence on the formality had irritated Corelle before, and a spark of ire ignited in her stomach again at the reminder. "We will see. He is no longer my Duke, in truth. He banished me."

Synna looked as though he had more to say on the subject, but he gestured at a large Ortwood door and indicated she should precede him through it. He then led her through a great many corridors until they stood before another Ortwood door with a sign that read, "Bailiff of Dur," in bold golden letters.

Synna looked her up and down, then shook his head. "What they will make of this new look of yours, I cannot guess."

"Let us find out." She pushed him aside and opened the door. Beyond it lay a large office with several people seated behind Ortwood desks. Corelle guessed the inner sanctum of the Bailiff's Aides would once have been staffed by men alone, but now two women sat behind the desks. Raolos, it seemed, had brought about some change in Dur's attitudes.

As soon as she entered, one of the Aides stood, a look of alarm on his face, but when he spotted Synna enter behind her, he relaxed. "The Duke and his Bailiff await you." The Aide pointed to double doors to one side of the office.

Synna tugged at her tunic and pulled her backward. "I will go first." His firm voice brooked no denial. She shrugged, and he pulled open the double doors. He announced her by name, and she followed him into the room. Raolos, Wilash, and the Duke stood near an enormous Ortwood desk, along with two men in the Duke's yellow tunics, still with the foolish hats on their heads. A woman with parch and scribing tools before her sat at a smaller desk to one side. Corelle wondered if every word the Duke uttered became scribed onto parch. He had once wished to have Corelle's confession scribed, but she recommended against it due to the nature of the revelations she had been about to make. That day seemed so long ago now.

Everybody in the room stared at her open-mouthed. She waited for one of them to speak, but nobody said anything. Their eyes travelled up and down her body, and it seemed they could not decide what those eyes beheld. She flashed them a victorious smile. "What? Have none of you laid eyes on a mariner before?"

Wilash seemed to regain his composure first. His voice full of confusion, he spluttered, "A mariner?"

She laughed and snapped her fingers in the air to draw their attention away from her appearance. "Enough. Tell me what I must do."

The Duke shook his head as if to clear his muddled thoughts. "Corelle of Ryl." He still sounded as pompous as she remembered from their previous encounters. "I remind you; you are banished from Dur on pain of death." She shot Synna an inquisitive glance, but he shook his head and flicked his eyes to the Duke as though he suggested she hear him out. "I hear you rendered aid in the unfortunate situation with Klordia, despite my banishment. Raolos has pleaded with me to lift your punishment and has made a strong case for a complete pardon. He insists you can be of assistance in the search for my son, whose fate we cannot guess. If you are instrumental in the safe return of my son and the capture of the despicable miscreants who have carried him off, I am disposed to grant my assent."

There had been more difficult words in the short speech than Corelle could fathom, but of them all, the last one baffled her the most. "Assent?"

The Duke gave his Bailiff an exasperated glance. Raolos smiled, glanced down at his shiny, polished shoes, and left it to the Duke to explain the unfamiliar word. "It means I am inclined to agree with his request. *If* my requirements are met."

She balled her fists. Her ire at his long-worded blather remained as volatile as it had ever been. "Duke—" Synna gave a discreet cough, and she corrected herself even as she heard the tension in her own voice. "My Duke. I have always believed former members of the Guild lay behind the death of Klordia for reasons I could not fathom. This latest outrage follows the same pattern, and I fear some of them may have returned to Dur."

A lack of comprehension clouded the Duke's eyes. "Why have they returned? There is nothing here for them but the hangman's noose. What is the significance of Ort? What are their designs?"

Corelle did not understand "designs" in this context, but the question about Ort seemed clearer to her. "Ort is a distraction, I think, unimportant. They have learned of Raolos's attempts to have the town granted a city charter, and they saw an opportunity to draw him into the plot and cast him in an unfavourable light."

The Duke gave a slow, sombre nod. "It is true Raolos pressed me to grant the charter. I felt inclined to assent before this unpleasantness."

Corelle glanced away at the woman who scribed at a small desk. Her scribing tool made rapid scratching sounds as she scribed the words onto the parch. Corelle wondered if she scribed the conversation word for word. The Duke's choice of words confused Corelle. The "unfortunate situation" with Klordia, when "death" would have sufficed. He had described the abduction of his son, the heir to the Duchy, as "unpleasantness" when stronger words were needed. He spoke unlike anybody she had ever encountered.

At that, an idea pushed its way into her brain, and she muttered aloud. "Words." She waved away the quizzical expressions of the men in the room. The woman scribing did not look up from her parch. Earlier, Corelle had wondered whether every word the Duke uttered must be captured on parch. Synna had said only the Duke's closest Aides knew of the arguments between him and Raolos about Ort, but after all else, what if every word had been scribed? If so, it would mean people other than the Aides would know of the dispute between the two most senior men in Dur.

"Duke." As she rushed to get the words out of her mouth, she did not care whether she had once again offended him with the incorrect title. "Is every meeting between Raolos and you documented like this one?"

His mouth opened, then closed. He tilted his head to one side and knitted his brows. He seemed to struggle to understand what point she tried to make with the question. "That it is. Why do you ask?"

"Then your Aides were not the only people who knew of these debates between you." The Duke wore a confused look on his face, but behind her, Synna gasped. "Those who scribed the records of those meetings also knew what had passed between you. They may be less scrupulous than your Senior Aides, and coin may have been used to pry loose a tongue to spill such knowledge into hands that now seek to turn it to their advantage."

"Ridiculous." Even as the Duke snapped the word out, a dark look of doubt crossed his face. Corelle glanced again at the woman, who had stopped scribing and stared at her in disbelief.

Corelle crossed the room and stood before the woman, who flinched backward as Corelle spat a question at her. "Have you scribed at the meetings we discuss?"

The woman spluttered as she replied. "That I have. That is, not I alone. Others. But I am loyal to my Duke. I would never betray him. I am fond of Peben. He is a sweet child." She sat up straight and stared back at Corelle.

Corelle turned again to the Duke. "Synna and I need to talk to all who scribed at any of these meetings. We will attend to it in the morning if you can make it so."

The Duke gave a thoughtful nod. "The prospect of betrayal

from within my own staff horrifies me, but I will arrange it. All who scribed the records about the city charter will be made available to you."

Corelle drew a breath to thank him when a thought struck her. "Ort is not a city, yet Dur City is, though it is all but impossible to reach. Why does it retain its charter? It must serve little enough purpose in the great affairs of Dur. The people of the Eastlands have little love for any who live west of the Alc."

The Duke gave a low chortle. "You desire my knowledge of the history of this great land? I recall you had no patience with it on a previous occasion."

Corelle could not deny the irony of her question. "I apologise." She forced humility to her voice. "I used to be ignorant. I have since travelled to many parts of Ictharelian, and I have changed my views on many things."

Everybody appeared baffled, the Duke among them. Raolos knitted his brows as he repeated the name. "Ictharelian?"

He had not spoken a word until now, and Corelle addressed her answer to him. "Dur is a land, but it exists in a greater collection of lands." All eyes were on her, and everybody paid rapt attention to her words. Even the scratch of scribing tool on parch ceased. "It seems our lands rest on a globe, though none have yet sailed far enough to prove it." There were gasps of astonishment from some. "Not yet, at the least. In the land of Malkartas, to the west of Dur, Ictharelian is what they call the globe on which all the lands sit. That is how they name it in their tongue. I have not found any other name for it that comes with ease to the tongue of a simple girl from Ryl."

A heavy silence settled on the room as they all seemed to try to comprehend the concept she had laid before them—so few words for such a vast new prospect. After a while, the Duke, frustration in his voice, muttered at her. "You know more than I on this matter, after all else. If word gets out this simple girl from Ryl, as you call yourself, knows more than her Duke, you will be banished anew." Everyone laughed at his words, even Corelle. In truth, his words amused her almost as much as the fact the stuffy Duke had made a jest at all. "To return to your original question, though it seems as dull as an old rock in a box of bright gemstones in comparison to your tale of lands and globes, Dur City used to be the seat of the Duchy, and the capital city of the land. As you have observed, it is a difficult place to reach, and it became so hard to rule or do business from, the Duke of the time decided to move the capital city to the river. He settled on Alcmouth, had the Ducal Highhome built here, and named it the capital."

"It kept its charter in spite of this?" The Duke's words more often rankled her, but, to her embarrassment, Corelle found the tale of Dur City fascinated her.

The Duke smiled. "It is, in essence, the home of Dur. Its charter will never be revoked, though it sends little enough in the way of levies, and news of events there come to us only on rare occasions. It takes three tendays for a replacement Portreeve to be appointed when one dies or tires of the role, or the excitement grows too great for him." More laughter followed this latest jest.

Corelle laughed along with everyone at the jest, but her laughter died in her throat as a thought occurred to her. "Dur City." All eyes once again turned to her in curiosity. "It is a terrible place to reach, which makes it the perfect place to hide out. Or to hide the kidnapped son of the most powerful man in the land."

"That is a guess." The Duke did not sound convinced. "If you are wrong, much time would be wasted. Besides, how would you find them there? It is a large city still, despite its decline into virtual insignificance."

Synna leapt to her defence. "She reaches for shadows, but her guesses have often proved reliable before. This is why we sought her help. More than any, she can think the way they think."

Corelle looked to Raolos for support, but he shook his head.

Nobody seemed convinced. She decided to change tack to ground she felt more confident in. "Will Synna work with me to unravel this puzzle?"

Raolos turned his gaze to Synna. "If he wishes it, he will be made available." Synna nodded his head in agreement.

It would be good to work with Synna again, Corelle felt. "The sand falls. Tomorrow morning, Synna and I will speak with the scribes at the Duke's Offices. That may yield more information we can use to further our theories."

With one sharp nod of his head, the Duke replied. "Very well. I will take my leave. The scribes will be available in the morning. Do not be too hard on them, I beseech you. None of them may have played any part in this heinous deed."

Corelle strove to keep her face neutral. None of them may be involved, but somebody must be, and she would trust nobody until she had unravelled the mystery. Raolos and the Duke would expect nothing less, or they would not have asked her to help.

# CHAPTER 6
CORELLE

The Duke and his entourage said their farewells and swept from the office to leave Corelle with Raolos, Synna, and Wilash. She felt more comfortable in their company. Her entire body relaxed as he left and took her crippling tension with him. Her fingernails had dug white, semicircular marks in her palms. She turned to Raolos. "I am sorry about Pettra. A terrible fate was written for her, and I regret my part in it."

He gave a sombre nod, as though he wished to copy the Duke's self-importance. "You owe me no apology, though I appreciate your compassion. I begged you to take her, and you did so against your own wishes at my insistence. I blame nobody but myself. I heard you took justice on the one who abused her."

"That I did, though it brought me no satisfaction to do so." Her sorrow threatened to choke her voice in her throat.

He crossed the room and swept her into his embrace. "By the Five Cities, it is good to see you again, nonetheless. The Corelle I knew was different from the one I see before me." He smiled, a twinkle in his eye. "It is odd, but I think I like this Corelle more."

She heard no hint of mockery in his voice. "As do I."

He smiled. "That cheers me. You were troubled beyond help, and I hoped you would find some redemption before your guilt and self-hatred led you to your ruin." She wiped at the tears that pooled in her eyes. "Come, let me buy us all dinner tonight. We are all that remains of the original cast of this tragedy, after all else."

Corelle held up both hands in caution. "I have no clothes for fine cenacles. I own nothing but what you see me wear, and these are clothes better suited to deck work and brawls in taverns."

"Nonetheless, if these two are not as curious as I am to know all that has turned since we last gathered together, then I know naught of the nature of Durfolk." Wilash and Synna nodded in agreement as their smiles threatened to split their faces in two. "I know of some places less salubrious than a Bailiff might be found in as a rule. Pettra would be horrified to visit them, I am sure. There is an inn on the edge of the commercial quarter called Inn Of The Stranger. Your clothes will look acceptable there, but the fare is most agreeable. Where will you stay?"

"At that inn, my guess, if it is not too expensive." She had given no thought to accommodation; she had grown used to life aboard The Salty Home.

"Nonsense. You are about to undertake important work for the Duke and his Bailiff. You will stay at The Alc's Mouth. It is a fine establishment here in the square. Your room will be charged to the city, and all you require also. Even a change of clothing, since the ones you wear bear an aroma not all would appreciate."

She hid her smile. A change of clothes would do nothing to improve her smell unless she also had a long soak in a deep tub. "I would feel out of place in so fine an establishment. The Inn Of The Stranger will suffice, my thanks. If you wish to pay the bill for the lodgings, I will not object."

He seemed about to argue but appeared to think better of it. "So be it. We will give you some time to settle in and meet you there later."

Synna guided her out of the room and along the maze of corridors until they stood in the early evening sun in the square. "It is good to see you again." He laid a hand on her arm.

She smiled at him. "You also."

"I will meet you later. I am beside myself with impatience to hear all your tales, but I will endure the wait."

She laughed. "I hope they do not disappoint." He told her how to reach the inn, and she set off. Grateful there were no longer any time constraints on her, she sauntered through the busy streets of the city. As she walked, she imagined the ship as it headed down the Alc and turned east toward Steinlund. The voyage would not take long compared to most, and she imagined the crew would soon enough have the chance to throw her coin into the hat in some tavern. They would laugh and jest until one of the other patrons let slip a slight, real or perceived. A brawl would erupt, they would all be cast into the street, then head to the next tavern to repeat the entire process. Corelle's faint smile carried all her sadness. She would miss life aboard ship, and she hoped the work the Duke required of her would not return her to the despondency she had known before the Torr Sea had foamed, thrashed, and wooed her into the life she had walked away from earlier in the day.

Once she arrived at the inn, she arranged for a room. When she said the Bailiff would visit later to arrange payment and to eat in the tavernroom, the innkeep laughed and handed her a key. He must have believed she had made a jest about the Bailiff, but she said no more and went up the narrow stairs to the room. Plain but clean, the simple room suited her more than she felt a fancy room at The Alc's Mouth would. A bed, a vanity stand, a trunk she had no need of, and a chair were the only contents. She removed the kerchief from her head and decided to eat dinner without it.

She would take Raolos up on the offer of some clothes. She had brought her pack because it still had the key to Pettra's house sewn into it, but she had left behind the few items of clothing she had in case she needed to return to the ship, although they would not have been suited to life in a city, after all else. Once she had decided to buy some new clothes as soon as she could, she wandered back down the stairs and into the tavernroom. She ordered a goblet of red wine, and to her surprise she had a choice of two. She chose the more expensive of the two. She had made do for a year with food and drink of ordinary quality at best, and for tonight at the least, she would enjoy the somewhat finer things life could offer.

She found a table big enough for the four of them. It faced the door, and Corelle slid onto the settle with her back to the wall. Without her crew-mates, it seemed the old Guild training still drove her choices. Wilash arrived first, ordered a tankard of ale, and came to the table.

He sat opposite her. "You still drink red wine, I see. I would have expected mariners to drink ale."

She pulled a disgusted face. "I have never acquired the taste for ale. Under sail, they drink a spicy brew that reminds me of a drink we used to take in Ryl, in a shop owned by a woman called Orgel. I first met Arella there." She paused, and it seemed Wilash's head bowed a little as if he shared the moment of sadness at the mention of Arella's name. "It is an acquired taste. It is strong enough to kill a horned hog if enough of it is drunk."

"Horned hog?" Wilash's face became a picture of confusion.

She laughed and reached across to brush his cheek. "Horned hog is not its real name. I saw the animal once, in a carnival in Qagrue. I did not learn its true name, and that is the best way I can describe it. It is enormous, the size of many hogs, in truth. It has two fearsome horns on its snout and short, thick legs, not unlike yours." He laughed at the jest and took a swill of ale. His face betrayed his fascination with the story, and he leaned toward her as though that might urge her to continue. She smiled and continued. "It has a hide so thick, I swear no crossbow bolt could pierce it. But it smells, Wilash. It smells so bad, I almost fetched up. I have never seen a creature look so ferocious."

He laughed again and shook his head in apparent wonder. "A horned hog. You have seen much you would never see in Dur, my guess." He paused, then reached into a pocket in his tunic, produced something wrapped in cloth, and placed it on the table before her. "Here is something you have not seen before, though it may be familiar to you."

She frowned and gave a quick, inquisitive smile. He pushed the item closer, and she picked it up. It had been wrapped in cloth, which she pulled away. Shocked, she hesitated when she saw a fan, and she glanced up at Wilash, who watched her with a contented smile on his face. Breathless, she held the fan up before her and admired its beautiful craftsmanship. He had once made a fan for her, but it had been a weapon rather than a fan, and it had not been as big as this one. She snapped it downward, and the two sides parted to reveal the pleated half circular fabric leaves attached to the guards, with a bright pattern of red and blue lines dyed into the fabric. "It is beautiful." As she whispered the words, she waved it before her face and enjoyed the cool breeze it generated.

"My thanks. I began some casual work at a friendly smith soon after they killed Klordia. I had too much time on my hands after work and wondered if I still had the skills of old."

"That you do. There can be no question."

He did not acknowledge the compliment. "I began work on the fan to test myself on something I had created before. It brought me some pride to find I could re-create that work. I wish you to have it now you have returned."

"It is a wonderful gift, and I will treasure it. My thanks. But it is not like the other. The other had no function other than to steal life. This brings relief from the warmth of the air. It is a better use of your skills, in truth. Though the making in the fabric could be better." She winked and favoured him with a mischievous smile.

He laughed. "I did not have one as skilled as you available to complete that part, alas. After all else, you are wrong about its functionality. Press the rivet."

The smile ran from her face and took some of her joy with it. Deep within, she had wanted the fan to be nothing more than a fan. His words implied it had a weapon concealed in it like the one she once had him make for her. That weapon had claimed many lives. She squeezed the rivet as she had squeezed the other years before, and a concealed blade sprang from it. She studied the blade, in awe of Wilash's ability to craft the perfect edge. It had been impossible to detect until she had squeezed the rivet. With the fan open, it felt unwieldy, but when she folded the ribs closed, it had perfect balance in her hand, as the other had. The blade gleamed in the soft lantern light of the tavernroom, and she brushed a finger along its edge. Blood oozed from the tip of her finger. The sharp blade had been honed to perfection, as sharp as, or sharper, than her old one.

Corelle looked up at him as tears pooled in her eyes. "My thanks. The dagger you gave me in this city long ago has seen much work. There are some nicks in it, and the blade is stained and refuses to be cleaned any further. This will prove a magnificent replacement." She blinked away her tears, and her eyes bored into his. "I hope I will have no use of it for the work the old one performed, but if that is the fate written for me here, then I see it will be more than capable."

"My thanks." Wilash stared down into his drink and seemed embarrassed. "If you tire of death again, do not cast it into the ocean. I have made it functional in other ways, and you may remember me by it."

She nodded, but before she could reply, Raolos and Synna entered the tavernroom, accompanied by several men in the yellow tunics of the Bailiff. A hush descended on the room, and all eyes turned to the new arrivals. Raolos cast around until he spotted

Corelle, and he waved. All eyes turned to her, and she returned the wave, uncomfortable at the attention.

Raolos strode over and sat beside her while Synna took a seat next to Wilash, and Raolos waved the innkeep over. He came to the table and bowed. "Welcome to my humble inn." He wore a servile smile. Corelle could not guess whether he recognised Raolos as the Bailiff, but he recognised that guards in the Bailiff's tunic meant his guests deserved respect. "What service can I offer?"

"A bottle of your best red wine, if you will." Raolos sounded authoritative and resolute. Corelle could not recall if he had been this way before he became the Bailiff, but it seemed he expected his wishes to be met without question. "Ale for those who do not wish wine, and plates of your best fare. We celebrate tonight, and I apologise if we become boisterous. An old friend has returned, and we have missed her more than I have words to explain."

The innkeep beamed at Raolos. Such important custom intent on spending large sums on revelry must be unusual in his inn. Once he had bustled off to arrange for the food and drink, Raolos turned to Corelle, a huge grin on his face. "Begin."

She stared at him in confusion. "Begin? What do you mean? I already have wine."

Raolos shook his head. "We are not interested in your wine. We want to know how you became a mariner. We want to hear about all the strange places you have been and the things you have seen. Above all, we wish to hear more about this theory that Dur sits on some sort of globe."

They all stared at her as though determined to hear every word. Even the guards had pulled chairs up close to the table. If Krage wished to kill them all, none at the table would even notice him enter, she guessed. She recognised two of the guards from Ort, she thought, and felt pleased they had remained loyal to Raolos.

She told them how she had learned the basic skills on the journey south to Vyrrmod and ended up aboard The Salty Home, then she took them with her across the Torr Sea. They dodged blue giants, arrived at docks in mysterious cities from Corkannae in the east to Malkartas in the west. She held them spellbound with tales of strange animals she had seen and rare items she had loaded aboard the ship. Food and drink came, and they picked at it as they hung on her every word, distracted by the tales she spun. None of them had ever been out of Dur and they begged for more stories even when she protested she could add nothing to all she had told them. They appeared unconcerned when she repeated some of the more outrageous sights and adventures she had been through over the last year.

Raolos insisted once she had completed her current assignment, he would employ her to seek out some of the spices and goods she had mentioned. Most had never been seen in Dur, and he wanted her to broker trade agreements with new lands that did not yet sail to Dur. She could find no jest in his eyes, and she settled on a non-committal nod of her head.

Synna wanted to know if she had spoken the truth when she told him she had not killed in over a year, and Raolos pressed her to confirm she would still be capable if it proved necessary.

She gave a guarded reply, and her eyes never left Synna's. "I am unsure. We will find out, if it comes to it."

Synna shook his head. "I do not doubt it. The training will never be forgotten, after all else. I notice your choice of this table seems familiar." He smiled encouragement at her. She gave another non-committal nod.

All present had eaten more than they should have, and Corelle felt uncomfortable with so much food in her belly. The four of them had become the worse for drink also, although the guards had taken no ale. The time had come for them all to part for the night, and there were many embraces. At one point, Raolos embraced Synna, and Wilash laughed and pointed out how inebriated he must be to mistake his closest Aide for Corelle. Intoxicated laughter rose to the beams of the tavernroom, and soon enough they had gone, a large pouch of coin handed to the innkeep by one of the guards. It seemed Raolos did not deign to carry coin anymore.

They shouted their final farewells from the door and left the inn, and the quiet that descended on the tavernroom must have been enjoyable for the other patrons. Corelle sat at the table again, thought back over the evening, and smiled at their childlike fascination with her tales.

With a contented smile, she stood, said goodnight to the innkeep, and walked up the narrow stairs to her room, where she fell into her bed with a happy sigh. As she drifted off to sleep, a thought came to her. They could check whether any of the Duke's staff came from Dur City. They may have some insight into where in the city an organisation like the Guild might hide. She knew she reached for a straw when she had speculated the Guild might have taken the lad to Dur City, but they had no better idea to work with at this point.

That night, she dreamt Raolos and Pettra walked toward her, hand in hand. They smiled at her before they both spoke together. "We love you." They turned and walked away. No monstrous killer appeared to strike them down, although Corelle waited with bated breath for some horrible death to visit itself upon them. They stopped and turned to her. "We forgive you." They disappeared.

CHAPTER 7
CORELLE

Corelle awoke, rose from the bed, and wondered about the dream. Could it mean any who said they loved her might be spared the fate of the three women who had said it so far in her life? She dared not hope for such redemption after no more than a year.

Once she had tied the kerchief on her head, she gazed at herself in the reflecting glass. At sea, the sun bounced from the water and had increased the lines on her brow, around her eyes, and at the corners of her mouth. Those lines had already been there for many years, and she could not blame the effects of too much sun for the imperfection of her skin. Her face of twenty-four years resembled that of one much older. The others had struggled to recognise her, and in truth she could scarce recognise herself. Her life had taken its toll on her appearance, and the shadows around her eyes remained a constant reminder. Even though she had not brooded overmuch on her past as she threw herself into the physical work of a mariner, the cost of those years could still be seen, etched into her face. The damage caused in places where it could not be seen, such as her heart and her mind, would doubtless be far greater.

She had arranged to meet Synna in the tavernroom this morning, and she wondered if he would remember the arrangement. She had never seen him drink as much ale as he had consumed the night before, and he had been deep in his cups by the time they left. She asked for some bread and meats and took them to the same table they had occupied last night.

The door of the tavernroom opened and Synna walked across to her table. He looked the worse for wear, and when she opened her mouth to tease him, he silenced her with his hand, palm toward her. "I know. You need say nothing." He slumped down into a chair and tore off a piece of bread.

She faked a stern scowl. "Yet you told me off time and again about my alcohol consumption a year ago."

He stared at her for some time, then seemed to have no retort. "Silence, vixen."

She laughed. "We had a good night, and I enjoyed it."

"As did I, at the time. This morning, I pay a terrible price."

"Then I will torture you no more, for I know how you feel. Come, let us be away, if you are up to it." She stood, anxious to be about their business, and watched in amusement as Synna dragged himself to his feet.

While Corelle enjoyed his discomfort, she sympathised with how he must feel. She led the way out of the inn into a bright, sunny day. The day already felt warm despite the early hour, and she turned her face to the sun, closed her eyes, and enjoyed the warmth on her face. She missed the sea spray already, and it baffled her how life aboard a ship had taken such a hold on her after only a year.

Synna pulled her to two horses tethered to a rail and mumbled, "It is too far to walk to the Highhome. I brought us horses."

The walk would not have been lengthy, and she had looked forward to it. She had not had sufficient time in cities over the past year to take long walks and listen to the rustle of the wind in the trees, the sound of her feet on the street, but Synna refused to walk, so she pulled herself into the saddle and tried to recall the fancy word the Duke had used yesterday. Askisent, or something similar. She would askisent to Synna's desire to ride rather than walk.

If she had been a poor horsewoman at best a year ago, her life at sea had done nothing to improve her abilities. Indeed, she felt she might be worse than ever. Synna watched as she laboured to control the horse, and he asked why she had not ridden on her time off from her work on the ship.

"We received nothing more than a night or two off before we would set sail again the next morning. We only had a lengthy shore leave when the ship returned to its home in Port Uirgile, in the land of Kuirbek. That has been no more than twice in the last year."

"How did you come to Kuirbek in the first place?"

"I told you. I learned my skills on Rakulaj's ships as I sailed from here to Vyrrmod, then on to Kuirbek. Last night, I told you this."

He looked over at her, surprise on his face. "You did?"

Corelle laughed, amused by the effects of excess drink, effects she had once known all too well. "That I did. The ale has driven it from your memory. I had been in Kuirbek a few days. I spent them in Port Uirgile and pondered my future. One night in a tavern, I fell into a conversation with some mariners. I told them of my ambition, and they laughed, as all had done to that point. I drank with them for a time, and when a brawl broke out, I aided them. I impressed them enough, and they told me the name of their ship and its master, Legorant Sugallia. They had returned to Kuirbek a day to two earlier, and many had headed off for some shore leave.

"I thought no more of it at first, but the next day I sought out The Salty Home. That is not its name—its name in Kuirbek is Cahjekki Vigharti. The Salty Home is the best translation I can make of the name into the language of Dur."

Synna made a half-hearted attempt to pronounce the ship's

name, but he mangled the effort so much, it sounded closer to "Tired My Door." She laughed, he joined in, and he enjoyed the jest when she told him what he had said. She continued her tale. "I found the ship, and after much discussion, Legorant took me on. He had picked up a cargo he had not expected and could not contact all his usual crew. He needed more hands aboard—my good fortune, my guess. He runs a good ship, and he is a good master."

Synna nodded. "You got into a brawl in a tavern?"

"Every time we docked, or so it seemed."

"You were never a brawler. You always relied on stealth and cunning. I find it difficult to accept you are now a skilled brawler."

"I did not say I am skilled. I said I brawled. I almost always lost and suffered frequent injuries." She shrugged. "I had to take a stand. I could not let them think less of me because I am a woman."

"If they had known how deadly a woman you are..." He gave a small chuckle but winced at whatever it cost him in his sorry condition.

"We brawled often, as I said. The ale would flow, and somebody would say something amiss. The tavern would become a wild, chaotic brawl. Nobody ever used weapons. It seemed to be some sort of unspoken rule. In truth, we almost always fought the dock workers."

He snorted. "That must have made the following day difficult."

"The next day, everybody forgot the disagreements. Mariners and dock workers alike would appear with cuts, bruises, blackened eyes, and scraped knuckles, say good morning to one another and carry on with the day's business."

Synna said he found such attitudes remarkable. They rode on and agreed the first order of business for the meeting with the staff would be for Corelle to address them all together while Synna observed them and said nothing. He would look for any reactions to Corelle's words that might suggest some involvement in the disappearance of Peben.

Synna turned to her at that point. "As a friend I must tell you this. You smell terrible. When did you last bathe?"

With an embarrassed laugh, Corelle promised to bathe that night to avoid further offence to his delicate nostrils. He asked where her long hair had gone. "At first, I tried to tie it back and keep it out of the way, but it interfered with my work too much. One day, I caught it in a coil of rope, and it hurt so much, I cried, even though I strove never to cry in front of my crew-mates. I cut it off and have kept it short ever since."

Synna studied her for a time, and she became uncomfortable as he looked her up and down. She tutted, and he seemed to realise he had stared. "I do not care for this new look. I preferred your hair longer. You could almost be mistaken for a boy if not for your large…"

His face reddened, and she glared at him in anger. "You should keep your eyes on women who might show some interest in you. My appearance is my business and mine alone."

He seemed surprised by her response but made no reply. They rode on in an awkward silence for a time until he muttered an apology. When Corelle turned to look at him, he seemed downcast.

She wished to lighten the mood, embarrassed by the testy outburst. Synna had been a good friend and had provided invaluable help since the night they had fought one another outside Raolos's house in Ort. "As for my size, I have always been this way, since my teenyears. Deineike found it enjoyable." She gave him a sad smile. "I miss her."

He sighed. "As do I. I miss her humour. Her speedy retorts could cut a grown man in half."

"That they could." She brightened her smile. "We are almost there."

They turned onto the Duke's Highway. The Highhome stood

before them, imposing, and its bright, painted roof shone in the sunlight. Its many windows glistened and reflected the sunshine out into the landscape all around the Highhome. Banners waved a playful greeting in the gentle breeze. Corelle had never noticed the banners before, and she did not recognise any of the sigils displayed on them. She imagined one of them must be the official banner of Dur, and one must be the Duke's own sigil. What the others might be, she could not guess.

They rode through the archway into the courtyard, and the hoofbeats of their horses resonated on the stone of the pathway and echoed from the walls. Guards approached them and took the bridles of their horses as they dismounted.

"I am Corelle, and this is Synna. We are expected."

One of the guards nodded in acknowledgement. "That you are. My colleague will attend to your horses while I take you to the Duke's Secretary. Please follow me."

They walked behind him into the Secretary's Offices, which were as splendid as Corelle remembered. The walls had been panelled with Ortwood, and many paintings adorned the walls. Most of them were portraits of men she guessed were previous Dukes. She saw no women represented among them and guessed there had never been a Duchess. A pang of guilt hit her when she recalled the time Pettra had told her about the difference between Duke and Duchess. The shame of her actions could be buried within her, but they remained ready to surface at the least provocation, even after the passage of years.

The Secretary sat behind a large desk when they entered his office, and he looked up as the Duke's man introduced them. He rose and greeted them like old friends long parted. Corelle asked him whether any of the Duke's staff might have originated from Dur City. He did not know but promised to investigate. He had assembled the scribes whom he believed might have been on duty during the Duke's discussions with Raolos about Ort, and he had gathered them in a room where Corelle and Synna could talk to them. He had also arranged a smaller room to be available if any discussion needed to be more private in nature.

He led them to another room where five nervous women sat. Corelle recognised the woman from yesterday, and even though the scribe knew the purpose of the meeting, she looked as anxious as the others. Corelle expressed her surprise there were no more than five, but the Secretary confirmed no others had taken notes in the meetings. One other worked at the Highhome, but she had started work there no more than a sevenday ago. As a junior, she had not gained sufficient experience to scribe conversations between the two most important men in the land.

The Secretary scurried off to seek out any staff who might have lived in Dur City before they arrived in Alcmouth, and Corelle and Synna closed the door behind him before they turned to face the group. Corelle turned her gaze from one face to another, slow and measured. None of them held her eyes for any length of time. "My name is Corelle. This is Synna." She did not point to or look at Synna as she introduced him but switched her gaze from one pair of eyes to another and never looked for long on any of the women as she spoke. "I seek Krage and Sisnop."

She paused, and after a few moments, one of the women said, "Who?"

"They are the men who kidnapped the son of the Duke. They have crossed a line I hold sacred when they involved a young boy. The price they will pay now they have crossed that line will be terrible. I will kill everybody who had any involvement in the abduction, without fear or favour. If I grow too weary to wield my blade to take their life, Synna will hang them as the Bailiff's representative." She paused again. A deathly silence had settled on the room. It had been her intent to shock them, and she believed she had succeeded. She meant to ensure that if one of them had given the Guild any information, they would be under no doubt the repercussions would be dreadful. Fear could be a powerful motivator, and she needed one of them to be motivated to help them find the Duke's son.

"If one of you knows anything of the whereabouts of Krage, speak now. Yours will be a swift death. I promise you this. If you withhold that knowledge, then your death will be far more unpleasant once I do learn your name. No matter what you believe or have been told, I will learn it." She wanted to stare them in the eyes again, but they all looked downward and would not meet her stare, fiddled with their hands, and said nothing. "In a moment, we will speak to each of you, one at a time. Do not leave."

She turned and walked into the side room. Synna followed and closed the door behind him. He gave a low chuckle. "Most effective. I almost doubted myself; I confess it."

She smiled her thanks at him. "Did any of them seem unusual, after all else?"

He nodded. "They were all distraught, and could not meet your gaze, but one seemed more ill at ease throughout, and she shuffled about more than the others. When you mentioned you would learn the name of any involved in the crime, she snapped her head up and her jaw dropped. She regained her composure soon enough, but that threat frightened her. I suspect her more than the others. Your threat sounded so terrible, in truth, it could have been every one of them. They all seemed frightened beyond words. This one though; something is awry with her. I am sure of it."

Corelle pursed her lips as she pondered the outcome of the meeting. Unless the women had been members of the Guild, they would all be easy enough to break if they were involved. None of them had belonged to the Guild while she had been a member, and she doubted any of them ever had, since a Guild member would have stood out from the others. They would not have allowed their fear to control them as the scribes had. "We will see her last, then.

Let her think on the fates that may be written for her and wonder what her colleagues might tell us."

One by one, Synna led the women in. Despite Corelle's ruthless questions, often accusatory, it became obvious that none of the first four had any involvement in the disappearance of Peben, unless Corelle had been fooled to such an extent, she could never trust her own judgement again.

Time at last for the fifth woman, the one Synna most suspected. Corelle grimaced at him as he prepared to lead her in. "If you are wrong about this one, we are back at the place we left from. I do not suspect these others."

"I agree. They seemed genuine to me. Let us hope I did not misread this last one."

Corelle pondered his words. "With luck, we will learn where the boy is before it is too late to save him." She doubted Krage would spare him but could not abandon hope until she saw it dashed to pieces before her.

Synna called the woman in and stood behind her. Corelle guessed she could not see him from the chair, and she said nothing. The woman fidgeted on the chair and half-turned now and again as if she tried to see Synna.

The silence had endured long enough, and the time had come for Corelle to break it. "Do you know me?" The woman nodded, silent. "Were you present the day I told my tale to the Duke?" She nodded again. "You know Glailam?" The woman nodded her head once more. "Speak when you answer me." The woman started at Corelle's harsh tone. Corelle repeated her last question. "You know Glailam?"

"That I do." A quiver in her voice suggested tears lingered nearby. "He used to be the Bailiff, before Raolos. He met with the Duke often. I scribed their meetings many times."

"He sends his regards."

The woman's eyes widened. "Why would he have any interest in me? Besides, is he not dead?"

"Is he?" Corelle had been away from Dur for a year and had no idea how much of what had turned in Yantogi might be known here.

"People say he died, somewhere to the south." The woman wiped at her brow with a small kerchief.

"Who says this?"

She looked down at her feet and gave a slow shrug. "People. It is the rumour around the city. It has been for some time."

"He did not die." Corelle leaned forward, grasped the woman's chin, and tilted her head up so she could stare into her eyes. "I killed him." The woman gave no sign of surprise to hear Corelle had brought about Glailam's death. "Krage. Sisnop. Gillar. You know these names?"

The woman blinked and looked confused. "Who are these people? Are they others you have killed?"

Corelle straightened. "You know who they are, I think. Which of them paid you for information?"

Outrage crossed the woman's face. "How dare you suggest—"

Corelle grabbed the arms of the chair and shook it. "You are mistaken. I do not suggest. I accuse." The woman flinched backward, although Corelle could not decide whether from fear or her own rank smell. "Where are they? Where is Peben?"

"I do not know what you mean." The woman struggled to hold back her tears.

"I think you do." Corelle took a step back. "How many years is Peben?"

"I believe he is nine years."

"Nine years. I do not know Peben, but I do know these men. They will kill him. His blood will be on your hands. Do you wish this?"

She raised her hands to her face and broke into convulsive sobs.

Corelle stayed silent as the woman cried. At last, the woman stared up at her again, steel in her gaze. "My own son is eight years. Eight years. They said they would kill him if I did not help him. How else could I have chosen? How would you have chosen?"

Corelle nodded her head. The woman had decided to tell the truth at last. "How do you know them?" She softened her tone to sound less confrontational. Behind the woman, Synna loosed a loud breath, as though he had held it for some time.

"I do not know them. They came to my house, two of them. They told me I must pass any information I had from the Duke's Offices to them, or they would kill my son. These names you mention, they did not speak them. I do not know these names, I swear it."

Corelle glanced over the woman's head to Synna, who spoke his first words for some time. "They may have followed her. They may have followed them all. They are patient, as you well know."

Corelle returned her attention to the woman, who had begun to cry again. "How did you pass this information on to them?"

"A man would come to my house from time to time. I told him of the things I had scribed. I do not know them, I swear it. I tried to protect my son, nothing more."

"You told him of the arguments about Ort?"

She nodded. "That I did." Misery dripped from her voice.

"You sought to protect your son, but you may have killed the son of the Duke."

Her sobs intensified. "I did not know they would take the boy. I did not know." She buried her head in her hands again.

Synna intervened. "Do they still come?"

"That they do not. Nobody has been to my house for many days. More than a tenday, my guess."

Synna spoke to Corelle, one corner of his mouth turned up in disappointment. "They learned enough to cast doubt on Raolos."

Corelle shook her head. Doubt still filled her thoughts. "I cannot accept that. To kidnap the Duke's son is a risky venture. The noose awaits at every turn. If they wished to bring down Raolos, a simple scandal would suffice. They used the ploy once before with great success. More is at play here; I am certain of it."

In a tired, meek voice, the woman asked, "What of me?"

Corelle's emotionless reply could not have brought the woman any comfort. "That is for the Duke's Bailiff to decide." She did not care what fate was written for the woman. As naïve as she may be, she had endangered the boy. How Corelle might have acted, she could not guess, but the woman played a part in the crime and must answer for her actions. "Do you know where these men are now?"

"That I do not. I am sorry."

Corelle asked Synna to bring the Duke's men and the Secretary. She spoke no more to the woman, who sat in the chair and sobbed. Corelle turned the tale over in her mind and attempted to unravel some sense from the tangled skein of words the woman had poured out.

The Secretary returned and apologised; he had been unable to find any staff who came from Dur City. Corelle told him the story and suggested he should apprehend the woman and hold her until Raolos decided her fate. Synna reappeared with some men in the Duke's yellow, and Corelle and Synna followed one of them out of the building to their horses. They rode in silence, the sun high in the sky and warm on their faces, although it could not touch the icy dread in Corelle's heart. She felt certain Peben had been killed in Dur City or at Estway Farm. The woman had been a piece in their game and had given them what they had sought. What they would do next, however, she could not guess. She sighed in frustration often and wondered whether she should abandon the task, sign on to another ship, and leave Dur.

None of this concerned her, other than for the impact it might have on Raolos, Wilash, and Synna, but in truth they were men full-grown who could take care of themselves. Against her wishes, she had become embroiled in something she had no wish to be a part of. Then she saw Arella's face, and the image of Krage as he writhed atop her while Styrrach watched. Corelle's knuckles whitened. Krage's blood would serve as payment for what he had done. Whatever other plans he had need not trouble Corelle, but if by coincidence it served Dur for her to exact her revenge, then so be it. She would kill Krage and sail away. She hated him, she realised. She had once said she did not hate, but that had not been true.

She glanced at Synna. "Krage is behind this. I hate him. I will kill him."

Synna's lips tightened, and he nodded.

She whispered it again. "I hate him."

CHAPTER 8
CORELLE

Raolos hung his head in disappointment when he heard the news. "I had hoped none who served in the highest offices of the land would betray Dur. Such a thing is almost unheard of. Curse this Guild. They corrupt at every turn." His intense gaze burned into Corelle. "What do you propose?"

"I believe our only option is to ride for Dur City, or at the least the farm near Yerrsun, and trust to luck we find information."

Synna remained unconvinced. "It is a risky move. It wastes valuable time if you are mistaken and could be the very thing they count on. If you and I are far from Alcmouth, we are in no position to offer counsel or our blades if something turns awry."

Corelle turned to him. "Something greater is at play, I have long been convinced of this. Ort is a distraction, an attempt to split the leadership of the land, to drive a wedge between them. The Guild do not know I am here and may not suspect I would come. We cannot be certain how much they know about you. I do not believe they expect you to sail away in search of the boy. This is all a carnival trick. Ort is nothing to them. There is no Guild there, and there never has been. There is no Guild anywhere. It is destroyed."

She knitted her brow as a thought came to her. In a soft voice, she repeated her assertion. "It is destroyed. Or is it?"

"What do you mean?" Raolos sounded anxious. "Do you suggest the Guild has not been destroyed?"

Corelle's mind churned as she sought to form a rational argument from the thought that had come to her. If the Guild did still operate, few would know. They had always concealed their operation from unwelcome scrutiny. There would no longer be any benefit to them from Raolos's trade system, but these were bitter, angry men. They might now kill for sport rather than profit. Did that sound feasible? She could not help but doubt it and could find no reason they might do so. She shrugged her uncertainty. "I do not know. They may seek to re-establish the Guild for some other reason we cannot see."

Synna added his own thoughts on the matter. "They might try to restore all they lost. All the more reason to remain in Alcmouth. If they try to move against the Duke or Raolos, we must be here to defend them."

Corelle's ire boiled, but she strove to remain rational. "They have already moved against the Duke, and all those yellow tunics could not prevent them. They still have ten or more Guild members with them, my guess. None but you and I could stand against them, and there are too many for two of us." Synna looked chastened, and Corelle laid a hand on his arm. "Do not blame yourself. My words were harsh. We know nothing of their plans. All we know is they have taken Peben, and we must attempt to save his life, if we are not already too late."

"And you are no closer to a solution on that matter than you were yesterday." Raolos sounded angry, and Corelle wondered whether he felt some disappointment in her. "All that has changed is you have been proved right about the Guild, and I must decide what to do about a woman who has betrayed her Duke and the Duchy to an end that might be disastrous for Peben."

He had the right of it, and it irritated her as much as it must do him. She clenched her teeth as she fought to control her emotions. "You are correct, and worse. I did not prove anything, because I already knew beyond doubt Krage lay behind it." She tightened the muscles in her thigh against any pain from the frustrated fist she pounded into it. "Very well." She felt unsure of what she would say even as she said it. "I will ride alone to Dur City. If they plan some further treachery here in Alcmouth, they will not have factored me into it, for they do not know I am here. My presence will not make any substantial difference. Synna will stay and protect you as best he can." Synna nodded, his lips drawn and little hope in his eyes. "He may yet uncover more information that may guide you in the matter. I will do all I can to save the boy, although my heart tells me he is already dead."

Raolos looked contemplative for some moments, then the uncertainty fled from his face. "Very well. Leave as soon as you can and return unharmed. I hope you will bring back good news."

Corelle nodded. "What will you do with the woman?"

Raolos threw his head back and stared at the ceiling. "I must hang her. I see no alternative." Corelle and Synna both protested the punishment did not fit the crime and asked him what he would have done to protect Raopul. He gazed at each of them, and tears pooled in his eyes. "I know not, in truth. Help me with this. It is beyond all my knowledge to resolve."

Corelle imagined he battled his sense of duty as Bailiff with his love as a parent, a terrible dilemma, and she grasped some of the agony the woman must have endured. Synna suggested she be placed in the stocks, but Corelle resisted the idea, fearful the woman might be attacked by the Durfolk if they learned the reason behind her containment.

"She cannot continue to serve in her role at the Highhome." She thought aloud rather than talked, but Raolos paid her rapt attention. "It might be time to create a gaol." Synna snorted in derision.

Corelle did not doubt he remembered her humiliation that night in Ort when all had laughed at her belief in such things. "I am serious. The old Dur ways may now need to be swept away. Recent events have been unprecedented. Once infection takes hold, it can spread if it is left unchecked. Gaol might be the threat that maintains order."

Raolos smiled despite the intense atmosphere the conversation had created. "How do you know so much of infection?"

She gave an embarrassed laugh. "Deineike suffered an injury, and a chirurgeon in Torric educated me on the horrors of infection in the body."

Raolos gazed at her in respect. "You give me an idea. I will confine her to her home. My men will guard her night and day, and she will not be allowed to leave. Any provisions she needs will be brought to her. It is a gaol, of sorts." Corelle approved of the idea. "I will give further thought to the other things you have said about our people's corruption at the hands of the Guild. It may be possible to stop the spread of this infection." He smiled.

Corelle drew in a sharp breath. "I will leave as soon as possible. I will take ship to Ort as soon as I can find one."

"Do you have coin?" Raolos seemed ever anxious to provide help, despite all Corelle had laid at his door since they had first met.

"Some." She felt the weight of her pouch in her pocket and realised all Styrrach's hoard had gone.

"I will provide coin, as much as you feel you need, and letters to declare you my agent. Save the boy if you can. Hurry back if…" His voice trailed off. It seemed he could not bring himself to voice the thought the boy might be dead.

Corelle accepted the offer with a slight nod. She waited while he scribed letters and called for an Aide to bring a pouch of coin. Once she had both, she said a simple farewell to each of them, and with their good luck wishes in her ears, she turned and headed for the inn to collect her pack. She had not kept her promise to Synna. She had not taken a bath, and she doubted she would have the opportunity now for some time.

The docks were a hive of activity. Several ships were tied up, and men bustled up and down the ramps to load and unload cargoes. The scene looked so normal, she found it hard to imagine foul deeds took place in the land at Krage's instruction. She might be mistaken, and he played no part in any of it. She had never doubted he had some scheme in his mind, but what if her conviction misled her? What if he had tried one last time to kill her in Yerrsun, then fled Dur to live out his life somewhere far away, wealthy and content? She shook the thought from her head. She must believe in what she set out to accomplish. Her life had taught her that all too well. Never doubt and never question, for down that path lay failure, brought undone by lack of resolve to see the thing through.

She thought it best to try the two-masters rather than the three-masted southern vessels if she needed to sail to Ort. Three two-masters stood at the dock, and the first two were both headed to Torric. The last one intended to sail to Zhanghar, but Corelle persuaded the master to put in at Ort with the help of Raolos's letters and some of his coin.

As the crew made the ship ready to sail, she stood on the deck to watch and felt excitement grow in her. She longed to help, to be involved. She watched a mariner coil a rope and knew she could have done a better job. Another lost his grip on a line as a sail unfurled. Once under way, she thought the crew were too slow to haul in the fenders. On the river, they should not lose a fender to a large wave, but if they sailed to sea and had not hauled them in, it could cost the ship one.

She smiled to herself. Not much more than a year ago she would not have spotted these things. Although she did not profess to be an expert, this crew seemed inexperienced. Once again, she pined for a return to the mariner's life.

Why did she pursue the boy? Of course, she wished Krage dead, but she believed the pursuit of the boy would turn into a lost cause, since she believed they had already killed him. Did she hope to find some of the Guild members still at the location they had taken Peben to, or had she sought an excuse to visit Yerrsun and see Vamma again, after all else?

She had been fond of the stallholder but saw no future in any relationship with her. By her own admission, Vamma did not seek a commitment with one person, and she might be married by now, in truth. Corelle had not seen her in over a year and anything might have turned. It would be pleasant to see her again and ensure she had stayed safe. That excuse would serve, and she felt more comfortable to sail north in search of Peben, or his body.

Corelle spoke to the crew often but never revealed herself as a mariner. She spent less time seated at the bow on this voyage, although she did pass some of her time there. Most of the journey, she watched the crew work or spent time on the aft deck to observe the navigation of the ship along the river. Where possible, ships sailed a direct line through the deeper waters. Under calm conditions at sea, the helmsman's job seemed simple enough. He held the large wooden wheel steady unless the ship needed to tack or change course.

On the river, the helmsman needed to turn the wheel more often, so the ship followed the course of the water. He must find the easiest path he could between the features of the land. Water could not flow in a straight line if it had obstacles to negotiate such as high cliffs or large bodies of land where it could flow past one or both sides. As she watched, she thought the position of helmsman might interest her at some point. What would she be called if she were to obtain the position? Helmswoman? She needed Deineike or

Pettra to answer such complicated questions, and she had neither of them.

CHAPTER 9
CORELLE

The days passed as the ship furrowed the river on its journey north. The winds appeared to have taken a dislike to Corelle, but at last Ort came into sight on the fifth day. Corelle hoisted her pack and thanked the master for the cabin and for the unscheduled stop in Ort. He seemed happy to help the Bailiff, and as soon as the ramp had been pushed up to the ship, Corelle ran down it. To the apparent surprise of the dockworkers, the crew called down for the bow and stern lines to be cast off from their cleats and pushed the ramp back onto the dock. The ship returned to the river, and Corelle sat on the bench to await the rowboat from Eastort.

She watched it cross the wake of the ship as it departed, and the little boat bobbed in the disturbed water behind the larger vessel like an insect as it crawled over a discarded, crumpled parch. Thanks to nothing more than luck, it had almost reached the western side and had not condemned her to a long wait if it had set off on its eastward journey moments before she ran down the ramp onto the docks. She longed to complete her task, kill Krage if she could, and return to Alcmouth. If she found the boy, she would be free to return to Dur and live out her days here, but she felt no joy at the prospect and doubted she would take advantage of the opportunity.

The little rowboat made land, disgorged its few passengers, and Corelle took a seat at the front. The middle would pitch less, so she left it for any whose stomach would tolerate the voyage less well than her own. They set off, and she watched the eastern shore draw closer. Eastort had nothing but a small jetty, and she wondered why nobody had ever built a dock there. The transportation of people and provisions would be much simpler and safer if there were a proper dock a ship could tie up at.

She left the rowboat even before the crew had it tied to the jetty and hurried to a nearby stable, where she rented a horse and tack and soon rode into the Eastlands. As evening fell, she rode on. She could rest at the same inn she had visited with Synna on their way to Yerrsun, The Eastlands Inn, although the inn had no stable, and she might encounter Bushy and Sparse again, which she would prefer to avoid if possible.

Darkness had fallen before she saw the familiar lights of the inn, and no horses were tethered to the rail outside it, to her relief. She entered the tavernroom and gazed around. An old couple sat at one table. They talked to each other in low whispers and did not look up at her. A man sat at the counter with his back to Corelle, and behind the counter, the innkeep wiped at a tankard his daughter seemed ready to put away. No other patrons sat in the inn, and she wondered how the inn ever made enough coin to remain open.

The innkeep smiled at her but seemed not to recognise her as she approached him. The girl, however, gestured at her father, who gestured back at her before he turned to Corelle. "I recall you now my daughter has reminded me. Some time ago you passed through, and you travelled with another. Your appearance has changed somewhat in that time."

"That it has. I have been at sea for over a year since then."

The man seated at the counter turned toward her. "At sea?"

Her heart sank as she recognised Bushy, his beard as prominent as ever, if not more so. She explained the reason for her time on the water. "I became a mariner."

Both men raised their eyebrows as though somebody co-ordinated them. It came as no surprise when Bushy had a ready answer. "A mariner? A slip of a girl like you? What turns over in the west?"

Bushy laughed, and his brother joined in, as usual, before he asked, "Need a room, do you?"

"That I do, please." In truth, she fought the urge to turn and leave. Her back would thank her in the morning if she stayed at the inn, but her temper would need a close watch kept on it.

Bushy's next words surprised her. "They were not together, by the way."

Corelle stared at him in utter confusion. Had he addressed her, or had he continued some conversation he and his brother had been engaged in before she arrived? He held her gaze until she felt compelled to speak. "What?"

"They were not together, them as rode through here that time. You asked about them."

She cast her mind back but could not make any sense of his comment. "I did?"

He glanced at his brother and made a face that suggested amusement. "That you did. My brother told you they all rode through together, headed west. But I remembered they rode through in two groups. Big groups, lots of men."

"You remembered?" Corelle guessed he meant Krage's men. She now recalled one of them had told her they had all ridden through the village together. She could not believe he had remembered such a trivial thing, much less felt it worthy of mention a year or more later.

"That I did. About four passes after you left, in fact. Glad I got to put that straight."

Corelle lied. "As am I." The girl had come out from behind the counter, and she smiled at Corelle and held out a hand. Thankful for the chance to escape the two brothers, Corelle took it and allowed the girl to lead her to the rooms at the rear of the inn.

She took the first room again, the one the innkeep had called the Duke's room, and laughed to herself. "I might as well have the best." She headed back to the tavernroom to ask if the innkeep had any food available. She felt hungry, and even though it had grown late she hoped she could obtain something to eat.

"I can find you something, I reckon. Might not be much more than tubers and a bit of meat, if that suits."

"It suits me well, and my thanks."

He gestured at the girl, who disappeared through a door at the rear of the counter area. "I still have some of that wine, I think." He ducked down behind the counter.

Corelle could not imagine how they remembered such small details for so long a time. "My thanks." No better response came to her befuddled mind.

He came up with the cask and poured a small amount into a tankard. It seemed he had not invested in goblets since her last visit. "Best you check it. Might not be any good anymore." He winked at her for reasons she could not fathom.

She sipped at it and found it still drinkable. "It is fine." He topped her tankard up.

Bushy spoke again. "He died." Corelle's bemusement grew. "Our brother, Budlic. Him as told you they rode through here together."

He meant Sparse, she realised. "I am sorry." She strove to sound as remorseful as she professed.

"Not as sorry as him." They both laughed at the innkeep's jest.

They baffled Corelle. Why did they tell her Sparse had died, then laugh about his death? Nothing had changed. They remained as unfathomable as the first time she had met them.

"Fell off his horse, intoxicated. I do not know how he got so inebriated. We had only been here three days." Bushy shook his head as he spoke and seemed confused as to how somebody who drank without pause for three days could be so in their cups, they would fall off a horse.

The innkeep corrected him. "Four."

"Do not argue with me, you irritable buffoon." Corelle turned away from them in annoyance as they roared with laughter.

Once they had controlled their mirth, the innkeep returned his attention to Corelle. "The fall did not kill him."

Bushy agreed with the claim. "That it did not. As I sat there and laughed at him, and he laughed right back up at me, a branch broke off a tree and landed on his head. Killt him outright."

Corelle guessed she had misheard. "Killt?"

Bushy drew his brows together in a question. "What do you Westfolk say when you mean something killt a person then?"

"Killed?"

The innkeep seemed unconvinced. "Sounds like fancy Westfolk language to me."

Bushy's response seemed unconnected with the debate about the correct word. "It were a windy night, right enough."

The girl appeared with a plate of food that steamed and smelled delicious. Corelle could have kissed her, delighted the girl had saved her from the inanity of the brothers' chatter. She followed the girl to a table, sat down, and gave her a grateful smile. The girl flicked her eyes to her father and uncle, and she made a face that suggested she understood Corelle's frustration.

Corelle took her time to eat the meal, the simple fare substantial and tasty. The innkeep came to her table and upended the cask to pour the last drops of the wine into her tankard, and she smiled up at him in thanks.

The last mouthful of the wine contained small pieces of something she could not identify, and she pulled them off her tongue with a finger and thumb. They were the same colour as the wine, small lumps of some substance that must have fallen into the cask or her tankard, she imagined.

With the food and wine gone and no desire to join another strange conversation with Bushy and his brother, Corelle bade them goodnight and headed for her room. She lay awake for a time and pondered the strangeness of the men and the ailment that did not allow the young girl to speak. Sleep took her after an hour, and she woke to the sound of a soft drizzle outside the room.

Bushy and his brother were both in the tavernroom when she emerged from her room, and she had to endure their conversation a while longer as she settled the bill and requested some meats for the road. She had no cloak, so she left the inn, climbed up onto her horse, and kicked it east. With luck, she would reach the Belram's Shadow inn that night, where she would attempt to make good on her promise to Synna and take a bath. A bath at The Eastlands Inn would have carried with it the risk Bushy might have burst into the room to regale her with one of his inane tales about his late brother, and she had not risked it.

Nothing marked the passage of time as her horse plodded east. The rain petered out soon after the midday, and the sun broke through the clouds. The steady drizzle had soaked both Corelle and her mount, and as the sun's warmth dried them, steam rose from the neck of the horse. By the time she reined to a halt outside the Belram's Shadow, Corelle was almost dry.

After she had obtained a room, she luxuriated in a bath for some time. She had still bought no new clothes despite her earlier promise to herself, so she washed her trousers and tunic in the left-over water from her bath. She requested some food and wine be delivered to her room, so she did not have to sit in the tavernroom in her wet clothes.

Determined not to loiter the next day, she retired early. A long ride to Yerrsun lay ahead of her, and she wanted to arrive before dark if possible. She had no idea how she would feel if she saw Vamma again but felt she could not ride through without a visit to see how she fared.

As Corelle set off from the Belram's Shadow, the sun peeped above the horizon ahead of her. It looked like the top of someone's bald head as they peeped over a wall. Her horse trudged along at a steady pace, and the featureless Eastlands drifted past. Corelle took little notice, consumed by thoughts of the last time she had taken this part of the journey. Synna had revealed he had known about Arella's unborn child, and it had all but destroyed Corelle to hear the story. She passed the farm trail she had turned onto as she circled back to Estway Farm, but today she rode on toward the town. As the skyline of Yerrsun came into view, her thoughts went back two days. She pictured an inebriated Sparse as he fell from his horse, lay in the road, and shared the customary mindless laughter with his brother. She imagined a branch as it snapped and broke away from a nearby tree. It struck him in the head, and he lay still, his head split open as blood pooled around him. It must have been quite a shock for Bushy.

She laughed out loud as she recalled the story. "Killt." The word made her laugh so hard, tears ran down her face.

She stayed at the same inn she and Synna had used a year before, The Market Inn. The long ride had exhausted her, and she ate a quick meal before bed.

When she left the inn the next day, the mid-morning sun warmed the air and brightened the streets. She had tarried over-long in bed as she turned her options over in her head. It made sense to call into Estway Farm and do a more thorough search in case she had missed anything last year. She would also check for evidence the Guild had been there since her last visit. They might be there with the boy, and she would need to be cautious and inspect the farm from the corner before she approached. As the morning had already moved on and her caution would delay her further, she would return to Yerrsun afterward rather than ride onward. Dur City would be many days' ride, and to her surprise, she wished to see Vamma now she had come to Yerrsun.

She had eaten in the inn, and she made her way across the square toward the busy market. People bustled around the stalls, and Corelle fancied it might have grown since last year, with more stalls and even a small group of minstrels who performed at one edge of the square. It seemed Raolos's new Portreeve had performed well, and the town had thrived under his leadership. She hoped so.

She saw Vamma from a distance, busy with one customer while another waited to be served in turn. Corelle watched Vamma place tubers and vegetables into a wicker basket. The stallholder chatted and laughed with the customer as she worked, and the second customer joined in with the laughter at one point. Corelle imagined Vamma had made some jest.

Vamma still wore her light brown hair long, although today she had piled it into a bun atop her head. The first customer left, and Vamma served the other. Once the woman had gone, Vamma wiped her hands on her tunic and moved some fruit from out of sight on the floor behind her stall up to the display area.

She had her head down as she fussed to arrange the fruit, and Corelle moved forward. Her shadow fell over the stall and Vamma looked up with a warm smile on her face. The instant she saw Corelle, Vamma gave a squeal and ran from behind the stall to pull Corelle into a tight embrace. "You are back." She nuzzled into Corelle's neck, and her warm breath carried the whispered words into Corelle's ear.

"You recognise me?" Corelle stroked the back of Vamma's head and luxuriated in the softness of her hair and the smell of her, a mixture of soap and the sweat of an honest morning's hard toil.

"I could never forget you." Vamma moved her head and kissed Corelle's lips. "Where in the Five Cities have you been since we last saw each other?"

Corelle kissed her again. Her lips tasted sweet, as though Vamma might have eaten some fruit or a sweet treat. "That is a tale for another time. I am in Yerrsun overnight, no longer. I travel onward to Dur City in search of a lost boy."

Vamma wore a curious look. "You are still banished, are you not?"

"That is a long tale to tell. Do you know if anybody is at the farm?"

Vamma's eyes bored into hers in search of answers, Corelle guessed. "Your visit here is related to those people, the Guild?"

Corelle chose careful words that did not convey any real meaning. "I am not certain." She did not wish to reveal too much, since she acted on nothing more than guesses, in truth.

"I believe it is empty again, although I heard some people were out there a tenday or more ago. Nobody asked for food deliveries, and I have not noticed anybody suspicious. You should ask Minarko. He will know, the old busybody. How long will you be in town? We could meet later tonight."

Corelle's heart leapt in her breast. By now, Vamma might be married or in some permanent arrangement, but the tale she had told in Ort still appeared true, if so. She would not be constrained to one person and would go her own way if she wished. Corelle smiled and nodded. "Shall I meet you in the tavern or come to your home?"

"Time is short, it seems. Let us waste none of it. Come to my home when you can." The way she breathed the words aroused Corelle, who reasoned it would be a busy night.

She kissed Vamma again and headed for the stable to collect her horse. As she saddled the animal, she pondered Vamma's advice but decided she would rather avoid further humiliation from Minarko, who had despised her the last time they had met and had no reason to have changed his opinion. She rode out along the eastern road toward the farm at an unhurried pace. She did not hurry, since Vamma had not believed anybody would be at the farm. If somebody had indeed visited within the last pass, she hoped to find some evidence to suggest who it had been.

She passed the copse, the trees filled with leaves and the grass longer than last year. As on previous occasions, she concealed her horse among the trees and crept forward to the corner to peer at the farm. She saw no sign of movement, no guards, and no horses. She had never seen their horses, in truth, and reasoned they had kept them in the barn where the unfortunate man whose name she could no longer recall had met Guild justice. The barn door had not been closed and banged in the breeze.

Corelle rolled the dice, returned for her horse, and rode toward the farm, wary of detection. She reined the horse to a stop short of the door and pulled the fan from her boot before she dismounted. She stood motionless beside the horse and listened for any sound from within the house. She heard nothing other than the barn door as it banged, and she approached the door to the farmhouse. When she tried the handle, it turned and had not been locked, so she pushed the door open and stood to one side of the doorframe. Nobody came out, so she bent and peered around the door. With no sign of movement inside, she ducked into the scullery.

A tattered cloak lay across the back of a chair, and an empty pack lay in a corner. Some clothes lay on the floor of the parlour and a mouldy, half-eaten loaf stood on the scullery table. Some of the items had not been there a year ago. Somebody had visited the farm since her last visit. A quick search of the house revealed nothing else. Corelle returned to the horse and placed a foot in the stirrup, determined to return to Yerrsun. The barn door caught her attention, and she paused. She decided to inspect the barn before she left in case they had left some clue inside it.

The smell of rotten flesh assailed her before she reached the door. They may not have given their former colleague a Pyre, and he still lay in the barn where she had left him a year ago. He would be little more than bones by now, his flesh long eaten by wild animals or rotted away to nothing. That could mean only one thing. Her eyes smarted as tears threatened.

She pulled the door open, and her tears spilled down her cheeks. Suspended by a rope from a rafter hung a small, naked body, that of a young boy. Flies flitted around his decomposed flesh. He had the same colour hair as the Duke's son, but his purple face had bloated beyond recognition, even if she had known him.

It must be Peben. Corelle collapsed to the ground and sobbed. She covered her face with her hands and cried into them for some time. After many moments, she rose and walked into the barn, each dejected step a greater effort than the one before. The boy's body rotated in the breeze, and she spotted some words carved into his back by a dagger or some other pointed instrument. She made the words out as, "TO LATE." How could anybody be so evil they could do such things to a young lad? She overlooked the misspelled word. She had become so filled with revulsion, it seemed petty to be annoyed by it. A crate lay nearby, so she stood on it and used her fan to cut the rope that held the body before she lowered it to the ground with as much reverence as she could. She might have stood on the same crate when she had cut down the body of Krage's last victim in this barn, and her temper got the better of her. She kicked at the crate and sent it end over end to the wall of the barn.

Corelle ran to the house and found two ragged, threadbare blankets. She took them out to the barn and covered the boy's body. Then she mounted her horse and turned it toward the road.

Tomorrow she would bring a cart and carry his body into town for a Pyre. The Portreeve would need to arrange it and say the Sending, while Corelle rode back westward. No purpose could be served if she rode on to Dur City. She had been sent to save the boy, and she had failed. She cried all the way back to Yerrsun.

CHAPTER 10
CORELLE

By the time she reached the town, the sun sat on the western horizon, ready for a night's rest before another day's work. The market had closed, and she guessed the Portreeve's Offices would be also. She returned her horse to the stable and willed her body to ignore the distress that coursed through it, to place one weary foot in front of the other until she reached Vamma's house. Vamma tore open the door in response to Corelle's knock, and the huge smile on her face vanished, replaced by a look of concern and a furrowed brow. "What is wrong?"

"He is dead." Corelle struggled to push the words past the grief and dejection that lay on her like a heavy blanket whose weight pushed her to the ground.

"Who is dead? The young boy you sought?" Corelle nodded, loath to speak any further confirmation of his death now it came to it. Vamma wrapped her arms around Corelle and pulled her close. "That is tragic news. Come inside and tell me about it."

Vamma seated Corelle on the couch and left the room. She carried two goblets when she returned. "Some wine may be needed. Did you find him at the farm?"

Corelle took the proffered goblet and took a hearty drink from it. "That I did. They hanged him. They have fled, and I have failed. Again."

Vamma sat beside her and took a hand in her own. "That you have not. They were bent on his death, my guess. You came all this way to seek him. You cannot be blamed for his death. How long had he been dead?"

"Some time. His skin had rotted. They scratched some words on his back, 'Too late,' although they spelled it T O."

"Then you cannot be blamed. They must have killed him before you even crossed the Alc." She pulled Corelle's head toward her and stroked the side of it. "Poor Corelle, forced to see such a thing."

"I have seen worse, and in that very barn." Fresh tears sprang to Corelle's eyes as she remembered the Guild member's body suspended upside down, mutilated by Krage's cruel Guild justice. "Everywhere I go, everything I touch—all turns to dust and ruin."

"Not everything." Vamma sighed as she slid a hand up Corelle's stomach beneath her tunic.

Corelle stopped the hand. "I cannot. Not after this. I am distraught."

Vamma nodded. "I understand. Tell me what happens next, then."

Corelle sighed, unsure of anything beyond her responsibility to bring the lad's body into town for a Pyre. "I will borrow or rent a cart in the morning and drive out there. I will bring his body back, so the Portreeve can arrange a Pyre and a Sending for him. I cannot take him back to Alcmouth. His father will not wish to have a blackened, rotten thing in his mind's eye as his last memory of his son."

"That is understandable. Who is his father? A friend?"

Corelle frowned as fresh disappointment washed over her. She had not told Vamma the worst detail of the search for Peben. "Not a friend." She doubted she had ever been so miserable as she breathed the truth she wished she could bury deep inside herself. "The Duke."

Vamma covered her mouth with a hand and stared at Corelle in disbelief. "The Duke?" Corelle struggled to hear the whispered words. It seemed Vamma also feared to admit to the horror of what she had heard. No words of Corelle's could lessen the atrocity of what had turned, and she gave one glum nod. Vamma blinked several times before she asked, "How did the Duke's son come to be in Yerrsun? How did his guards allow the boy to be killed?"

"The Guild, I suspect. They took him from Alcmouth and killed his guard in the process. Those men are no match for the Guild. They brought him here, and here they ended his life for no good reason."

Vamma's confusion seemed to grow. "Why? Why did they do this heinous thing?"

Corelle did not know how to respond. In truth, she did not understand why the Guild had kidnapped the boy. Some motivation must lie behind it, but she could make no sense of it. It could not have been an attempt to take some perverse revenge on her, since they could not have known she would ever hear of it. "I do not know, in truth." What more could she say?

Vamma sat in silence for a time, and Corelle lay down with her head in Vamma's lap. As Vamma stroked her cheek, Corelle gazed up into her face. She saw concern and anxiety, which did not surprise her. Few in Dur would ever consider the abduction of a young boy. To learn the Duke's own son had been kidnapped and murdered would lead every citizen in the land to question all they had ever believed. That might have been Krage's intention; to so disrupt the accepted pattern of Dur life, the Guild could once more begin its operations.

Raolos would not stand for it. If Krage meant to drive a wedge of distrust between the people and the Bailiff, he would not succeed. The Durfolk must realise Raolos's fine character and qualities. He would never relinquish the trade arrangements back into the hands of cruel killers, not while breath remained in his body.

Vamma interrupted her thoughts. "I will go with you. We will collect him on my cart in the morning."

Corelle half rose to protest, anxious to protect Vamma from the sight of the dead boy. "You ought not to see these things. I will take your cart if that suits. You should work at your stall."

"I cannot work while my cart is employed in such a horrible task. I will come with you."

Corelle remembered how difficult it had been to persuade Vamma to leave Yerrsun a year ago. It had taken a direct attempt on her life to convince her. She had a stubborn streak, and Corelle had no energy for an argument over whether she came to the farm with her. She slumped back into Vamma's lap. "Very well. It will not be pleasant for you, but if you are determined, you may come."

"I am determined, and you are weary beyond mere tiredness. Come to bed. A new day may be kinder to you."

They climbed the stairs, closed the shutters, and took off their clothes. Corelle lay on her back, and Vamma lay on her side to face her, her arms wrapped around Corelle, warm, comforting. Vamma smelled familiar, and Corelle traced the line of the stallholder's thigh and hip, down into the valley of her waist and up toward her breast. Vamma smiled in the soft light of the room, and the smile warmed Corelle's heart.

Corelle turned her head and Vamma kissed her on the lips. Vamma's hot breath brushed her cheek, and Vamma's tongue dived into her mouth as slid she a hand between Corelle's legs. She parted them, and Vamma's fingers teased and aroused her. Those fingers drove Corelle's misery away, although she knew it would return. For now, she gave in to the pleasure and bucked her hips upward to thrust herself against Vamma's fingers and urge them to enter her.

Corelle gasped as Vamma's fingers drove into her, lifting her to dizzy heights of sensual pleasure, and the first wave of satisfaction crashed over her body. She snarled for more, and Vamma redoubled her efforts to pump her fingers in and out, in and out. Corelle cried for her to go deeper and opened her legs wider to accommodate further penetration. She became lost in her ecstasy and stared at the ceiling while guttural sounds she did not recognise clawed up her throat and out through her mouth. Wrapped in the smell of her own sex, she begged for more until she could resist no longer, and she arched her back as her body shook with the culmination of her frenzied lust. She groaned; a long, deep animal growl of carnal fulfilment, and fell back onto the bedsheet as she reached for Vamma and pulled her on top of herself. She slid a hand along Vamma's stomach, palm upward, until she could flick and caress Vamma's swollen nub.

Afterward, they lay in a sated jumble of bodies, arms, and legs, breaths heavy, while sweat ran in rivulets over their bodies as though small insects crawled across their skin. Corelle held the back of Vamma's head against her neck, and delicate kisses sent trembles through her.

After some time, Vamma rolled away onto her back with a contented sigh. "You could be distracted by pleasure, after all else."

"That I could. I confess I cannot resist you."

Vamma gave a short laugh. "Those words come to your lips with such ease. I am certain I am not the first woman to have been told this."

"You may be, I cannot remember. You have taken me to a place where I have no memories." Grateful Vamma had driven away the horrors of the day, Corelle smiled into the stallholder's brown eyes.

"No memories? Not even of Deineike?"

Corelle exhaled, a long breath of frustration, remorse, and disappointment. "I can never forget her, though I find I can tolerate my memories of her these days. If I could rewrite the fates, I would. She is gone, and I go on." Vamma reached out a hand and touched

Corelle on the leg—the merest touch, but it carried hope, assurance, and support. In that moment, Corelle felt happy. "Arella also, although the child still grieves me at whiles."

"Who is Arella? And what child? The boy at the farm?"

Vamma's bewilderment showed on her face like a reflection in a pool of still water, and Corelle nipped at her tongue with her teeth. She had let slip some things she had kept hidden from Vamma until now. "Vamma, there is much I have not told you. You know this, I think, for I have mentioned it before."

"Will you tell me now, then?"

Corelle sighed. "I would like to tell you, if for no other reason than to unburden myself of the horror. But tonight… Not tonight, I beg you. I spoke out of turn, nothing more. In truth, it is your fault. You took me to this wretched place beyond contentment." She smiled, and she had spoken the truth.

Vamma's thoughtful reply soothed Corelle's anxiety. "I understand. I do not comprehend all you say, but you do not wish to bring further pain into this day. I cannot blame you for that."

Corelle's heart skipped a beat. "You are a good woman, Vamma. Tell me, has nobody swept you up while I have been gone? Have you married? Do you lie with somebody who brings joy into your life?"

Vamma gave another short, sharp laugh. "I have not married." She gave Corelle's nose a playful flick. "But I do lie with someone whose company I enjoy, and whom I crave whenever I am not with her."

Corelle squinted to see Vamma's face as the darkness intensified in the room. She did not know whether Vamma had meant her, and it seemed vain to think it. She kept her voice noncommittal. "Tell me about her."

"I need not tell you about her, for I am with her."

Corelle blinked in the gloom, unsure how to respond. "This does not sound like the same woman who professed she must be free to lie with whomever she wanted, whenever she wanted, that day in Ort."

"That woman was younger than me by a year and more." Vamma had laughter in her voice. "I might have spoken in haste."

Corelle had not foreseen any of these revelations. "You are a stallholder, and I am a mariner. What future could we have?"

"A mariner? You are a mariner?" Vamma moved, and Corelle felt her turn onto her stomach and prop her chin in her hands. She guessed those brown eyes stared at the dark shape Corelle had become as night cloaked Yerrsun in its black embrace.

"That is how I have spent this last year. I have sailed all over the Torr Sea."

"You have?"

Corelle recounted the tale she had told Raolos, Synna and Wilash a sevenday past. Vamma listened in silence as Corelle revealed the journey she had taken aboard The Salty Home. The story left Vamma breathless. She fell onto her back and repeated small pieces of all she had heard with undisguised wonder in her voice.

As sleep overcame Corelle, Vamma muttered, "A mariner is a better profession than a killer."

"That it is." The instant Corelle spoke the words, she fell asleep.

CHAPTER 11
CORELLE

Vamma shook Corelle awake in the morning. Sunshine crawled around the edges of the window shutters and squeezed through gaps between each one. Sleepy, Corelle complained. "What hour is it?"

"Not late, but there is much to do. I left you to sleep for a time, but now we must be up and about the day's grisly business."

At the mention of what lay ahead of them, Corelle's mood darkened. She recalled the previous day and the miserable moment she had discovered Peben hanged in the barn. She dragged herself out of the bed, and despondent arms tugged clothes onto a body reluctant to face that dreadful reality again. Vamma asked if she had any different clothes she could wear, and Corelle confessed she had only the one set.

Vamma folded her arms and drew her eyebrows together. "We shall have to remedy that later, if there is time."

Corelle had not followed up on her intention to buy more clothes, but that could wait. More serious work lay ahead of them this morning. They ate some meat and bread, then headed for the Portreeve's Offices. The letters from Raolos ensured the new

Portreeve saw them without delay. He promised to help the Bailiff's emissary in any way he could and agreed to arrange a Pyre and Sending for Peben. He requested his condolences and deep sorrow at the tragic turn be conveyed to the Duke.

Corelle and Vamma collected the cart, and Vamma drove it out of the city toward the farm. The atmosphere on the cart was sombre, and Corelle tried to lighten the mood. She expanded on some of her tales and mentioned the horned hog. Vamma laughed at the description of it, and a vague memory returned to Corelle. "I saw it in Qagrue. That is the land your friend… what is her name?"

"Zui."

"Zui." Corelle repeated the name, which felt easier on her tongue since her time aboard The Salty Home. "That is where she is from, is it not?"

Vamma hesitated before she replied. "That it was."

Corelle could not miss the sorrow in Vamma's voice. "Was? Has something turned?"

"She did come from Qagrue, but she is dead. Her husband killed her. He came home inebriated, they argued…"

"I am sorry." Corelle caught Vamma's hands in her own. The reins dangled from the mass of fingers as their hands entwined. "Did the Portreeve punish him? He should have been hanged."

"That he did not. Her husband claimed she struck him, and he pushed her in his own defence. She fell and struck her head, so he said. He lives on in the house and still works. He fells trees for a local lumber seller. She has travelled wherever she went to afterward, and he has not been held to account."

Corelle turned the situation over in her mind. "Did her injuries match his story?"

Vamma looked at her with tears in her eyes. "Her eyes were blackened, blood ran from her nose, she had marks on her neck, and many scratches on her arms and legs. Her injuries did not match his story." She spat the words out with a vehemence Corelle had not heard from her before.

After a short silence, Corelle replied. "I did not care for Qagrue. I found the people short on friendliness, and the men were disdainful of me if I spoke to them. I am sorry about your friend. It seems all is sadness." She did not mention Styrrach, nor that he had come from Qagrue.

They rode on in silence for a time before Vamma spoke again. "Do you imagine you could kill him?"

Corelle sighed as old sensations of violence embraced her. She travelled with death, but she loathed it. "I could, my guess. Doubtless, he is little more than a bully who could not defend himself from me." She paused and watched the horse's head bob up and down as it pulled the cart along the dusty road, heedless of the horrors they discussed. It knew nothing of murder and treachery. She envied it. "I will not kill him. Not for this."

"I did not ask if you would. I asked only if you could." Corelle raised a hand to placate Vamma, who had sounded angry. After a moment, Vamma pressed her. "How then do you decide who you will or will not kill?"

"I have not killed since the two men who tried to take your life, in truth. I hope I do not have to kill again, ever."

"Then how did you decide, when you did kill?"

"If they threatened me, or owed me vengeance for hurt done to someone I cared for, then I would kill." She did not admit she had killed her own lover, and her unborn child also, to save her own worthless life.

"Vengeance is owed, is it not? He killed her." Vamma sounded more flustered.

"That it is." Corelle forced her voice to remain calm. "Not from me, however. I did not know her or care for her."

"You do not kill for others, for coin or some such, in cases of this nature?"

Memories of the Guild crowded Corelle's mind, and an instinctive sigh escaped her lips. "I did, at one time. I killed on the orders of others, for coin. I have left that part of me behind, and it might destroy me to return to it."

"Would you kill for love?"

Corelle recalled the man outside the tavern in the Torric docks. As he relieved himself and fetched up on himself, her hand had slipped around his neck from behind, and the warm vermilion spray of his blood had poured onto the street. The wrong blood, spilled for love. "That I would not." She had lied, and could not explain why, even to herself.

Vamma fell silent, and the horse plodded onward. It did not carry the burden of the deaths of unborn children, or the wrong man, or the man who had killed one it loved. It pulled the cart and ate when it could, and it knew no other concerns.

The blue sea, white foam-capped waves that lapped at the bow of a ship, the salt smell in the spray; they all called to Corelle and urged her to leave Dur and return to them. She had never served a more reliable and honest master, and it did not ask her to kill for it. It might claim her life with the same ease with which she had slain others, but if it did, it would take her into its bosom and nurture its own from her remains.

They passed the copse, turned the corner, and saw the farmhouse ahead of them. A terrible remorse settled on Corelle as they turned into the lane. Vamma stopped the cart outside the barn. "Did you leave him in there?"

"That I did." Corelle climbed down from the cart. "You need not come in. I can bring him out alone. He is but a boy."

Vamma nodded and remained on the cart. Now it came to it, Corelle imagined Vamma did not wish to look upon such a desperate sight, and who could blame her? When she entered the barn, Corelle found Peben's body undisturbed. She had closed the door yesterday by luck rather than judgement, but as a result, no animals had entered the barn and pulled his body apart in search of food. She sniffed back tears as she picked his lifeless form up, so small she could lift him with ease. With the blankets tucked tight around him, she carried him out and laid him in the back of the cart. Vamma pulled out a kerchief and fastened it around the lower part of her face. How could it be that this smell no longer unsettled Corelle, this repulsive odour of old death?

They drove back to the town, and the shadow of the boy's corpse prevented anything more than cursory conversation between them. They delivered him to the Portreeve, who had kept his Offices open beyond the normal hour to await their return. He accepted the remains of the Duke's son in sadness and watched one of his men lift the boy onto a smaller cart. Corelle watched it depart, consumed by misery.

The Portreeve turned to Corelle. "He will have a Pyre at the sunrise tomorrow. I will speak his Sending. Will you attend?"

"That I will."

Vamma corrected her. "That *we* will."

Corelle raised a foot to the step of the cart. "I will leave after the Pyre." She pulled herself up into the cart, and Vamma drove it back to the stable.

When they reached the house, they sat at the small table in Vamma's scullery. They pushed some bread and cheeses around plates, unable to eat even though they knew they should.

At last, Vamma asked the question that had hung between them for some time. "Will you leave tomorrow, as you said?"

"That I will. I can do nothing more for Peben, or for Dur, I fear. I may as well return to my work. Join a ship's crew, sail again until the sea takes me, or I find some other thing I would rather do."

Vamma held her gaze. "Until you find love?"

Corelle smiled, surprised by the question. She had not considered the option. "If that is the fate written for me."

Vamma nodded in a way Corelle could not interpret. "Will they return, do you think?"

"The Guild? They may already be in Dur. I do not know what turns, in truth."

"Am I in danger?"

Corelle doubted it. If the Guild had known of their relationship at any stage, it seemed unlikely they would now recall it. Vamma represented no threat to them here in the Eastlands where they would not operate. "I do not think so." Corelle affirmed her response with a shake of her head.

"I am safe then?"

"Are any of us ever safe? You are as safe as you could be, my guess." Corelle sensed something more lay behind the questions, and it would be revealed when Vamma judged the time to be right.

Vamma again gave a nod. She appeared thoughtful. "Could you keep me safe?"

Surprised again by the question, Corelle took a small bite of the bread before her. She needed time to unravel the implication hidden in the question. "That depends on what it is you wish to be kept safe from." She measured each word, careful not to imply anything she did not mean. "There are things in my past it is safer for you to know nothing about. You have a stall and family here, and you would miss them if you were with me. I could not keep you safe from that. If the Guild wants to kill you, nonetheless, you would be safer with me than alone here."

"Where will you travel when you leave here?"

"I am obliged to return to Alcmouth and report the death of Peben. After that task is performed, they are sure to ask me to avenge him, as you wished me to do for your friend. I do not want to do so. I risk too much if I kill again. It has taken me a year to find a way to live with myself. I am not at peace, but I am at a truce with myself. I do not wish to break that and descend again into the woman you knew a year ago."

"Will you take to the seas again?"

Corelle sighed. "Vamma, what is it you ask me? These questions must lead to some point you wish to make. Please, make it, and spare us this dance."

Vamma sat upright and fixed Corelle with a proud, determined stare. "I wish to travel with you."

They had come to the point at last. The six words Vamma had spoken had implications and consequences too numerous for Corelle to count. She could see no way for Vamma to be with her if she returned to the mariner's life. She had no home and shared a bunk room with the crew. That would be no life for Vamma. If Corelle remained in Dur to help Raolos avenge the death of Peben, they might have some life together, but the prospect of death would hang over Corelle if she went up against the Guild. Worse than either of those outcomes, what if Vamma fell in love with her? Once Vamma told Corelle she loved her, her fate was written, and her fate would be an unpleasant death at too young an age. Corelle could not take on that responsibility.

In Alcmouth, before Corelle became a mariner, she had asked Vamma to travel with her. Now Vamma offered that outcome, but Corelle no longer desired it. The revelations about Vamma's preference to lie with anyone she chose even though she loved Corelle, together with Corelle's new-found joy as a mariner, combined to leave her reluctant to take Vamma with her now the opportunity had presented itself.

Corelle enjoyed Vamma's company, nonetheless. She was funny, compassionate, and considerate, an energetic lover and an attractive woman. Corelle believed she and Vamma were around the same age. Arella and Deineike had both been older than her, and Pettra also, by some margin. None of those considerations would matter if Corelle somehow brought about Vamma's death. What depths of despondency that fate would cast Corelle down into could not be guessed. She dared not take the risk.

With a sad smile, Vamma interrupted Corelle's thoughts. "You take a long time to respond. I had hoped for a more enthusiastic response than this dark, gloomy face I see before me."

Corelle huffed a small laugh and pushed a smile to her lips. "I apologise. Your words took me aback, nothing more. If I return to sea, I can see no way you could accompany me."

"Then do not return to sea." Vamma reached across the table and took Corelle's hand. "Stay here with me."

"I do not think I wish to stay in Dur. I cannot explain it. The sea calls to me now, and there is much still to see."

Vamma's smile may have hidden disappointment. "Then let us travel to Alcmouth together. I have never been there and would like to see it. I would have you for a while longer, at the least."

"What of your stall?"

"It will not open for a time." So simple an answer for what must have been a far more complex decision.

Company on the journey to Alcmouth would not be altogether unwelcome, and company that provided satisfaction in bed would be most welcome. To have another person to talk to might prevent Corelle's descent into despair as she thought about the ill-fated outcome of her quest to rescue the boy. "Very well." She leapt to a decision before her fractured mind could fill the canvas of her thoughts with dark sketches of doubt and denial.

"It is agreed then. Beyond Alcmouth, we will make no commitment at this time. We will see." Vamma pulled Corelle's hand to her mouth and kissed her fingers.

"We will see." Corelle smiled as Vamma pulled her from the chair toward the stairs.

The next morning, Corelle left Vamma to pack some belongings for the road while she ran to the inn, collected her pack, and paid for the room. Together, they dragged themselves to the Portreeve's Offices, where the Portreeve led them to a square field that seemed dedicated to the town's Pyres. The Pyre had already been prepared, with Peben's body sewn into a white sheet, doubt-less so the few attendees need not see its advanced state of decom-position. The Portreeve said a short Sending and invited Corelle to light the wood piled up around and beneath the young lad's body.

Corelle had not had the strength to light Deineike's Pyre, she remembered, but would do Peben better service. She took the lighted torch from a man nearby who had held it throughout the Sending. She thrust it deep into the wood. The torch spluttered for a moment, then the wood around it caught fire, and soon it crackled as the flames sated their hunger on the logs. Smoke plumed into the air as the fire reached the boy's body, surrounded him with its heat, and devoured him with its appetite.

Nothing more could be done. Corelle thanked the Portreeve, and she and Vamma headed for the stables. They saddled Vamma's horse and led it to the inn's stable where they collected Corelle's own mount. They climbed into their saddles and pointed the horses west. The sun had not yet risen far into the sky and Corelle thought they might reach the Belram's Shadow that night if they rode at a steady pace.

Vamma rode better than Corelle and did not find it difficult to maintain a good pace as the sun rose into the sky and pursued them across the bleak, featureless Eastlands. It passed them and left them in its wake as the day wore on. Vamma badgered Corelle to reveal more of the things she had hinted at since they had first met, and she worried at Corelle's resistance like a hungry animal will gnaw at a piece of meat.

Corelle relented and told Vamma how she had met Arella and joined the Guild. She told her about the shrouding, how she had been selected and sold to the Portreeve. She stopped, unsure whether she wished to continue with the next part of the tale.

Vamma reached over and touched her shoulder. "Why did they wish you dead? It seems you were good at this dreadful work."

The tale ground Corelle in its dreadful memory and spat her out like the seed of some bitter fruit. "It had to do with Arella."

"She loved you. I cannot imagine she betrayed you." Vamma frowned as she spoke.

"That she did not. Rather, I betrayed her. The Guildmeister from Ryl, Krage, forced himself on her."

Vamma looked at her in horror. "I have heard this name before, I think."

"You may have overheard Synna or me mention it. I do not know. Krage stayed at the farm a year ago, and I allowed him to escape, curse me."

"I understand why you wish vengeance on him, though I confess I fail to see how you betrayed Arella in this."

Corelle could not face her and stared down at the pommel of her saddle. "She became with child. Krage's child." Vamma's sharp intake of breath stabbed Corelle's conscience, sharper than any Guild dagger, but she could still not face her. "She learned I had been shrouded and wished to spare my life. She urged me to flee, and I begged her to come with me." She paused, the conversation as fresh in her mind as if it had taken place yesterday. "She would not come with me, and I could not understand why, though I now know. She could not flee across the land because of the unborn child she had concealed from me at that time. Rather than fall into the Guild's hands and be forced to have Krage's child, to be chained to him for all her days, she begged me to kill her."

Vamma gasped again. "You could not kill the woman you loved, could you?"

Tears from Corelle's eyes splashed onto the worn leather of the saddle. "I killed her, Vamma. I slit her throat, and I ran." The words travelled on so faint a breath, she did not know for certain Vamma had heard them. If she had, would she turn her horse and ride back to Yerrsun? Who could blame her if she did? Who could find fault in a woman who refused to ride further with a lover who confessed to the murder of the woman she loved, and a child with her?

Vamma gave a soft cry, but Corelle's shame would not allow her to look at her. They rode on, both in tears. The sun sank low in the sky ahead of them. No further words passed between them, but Vamma's resolute horse plodded onward beside Corelle's. She had not turned back. As the sky darkened, Corelle glanced sideways at Vamma. She rode upright, her head high, and she stared forward across the head of her horse. Tear stains tracked through the dust of the road down her cheeks, and she wiped at her nose often with the back of a hand. Still she did not speak, and they came to the village and reined in their horses before the Belram's Shadow.

"We should spend the night here." Corelle muttered the words, afraid to speak, afraid of the consequences. "In the morning, I will ride on. You may wish to return to Yerrsun. I would not blame you."

A lengthy silence followed. Corelle did not wish to break it; if she did so, she would destroy all that had existed between her and Vamma up to the moment she confessed she had killed Arella.

At last, Vamma gave her answer. "I cannot turn back. I think I love you."

CHAPTER 12
CORELLE

Corelle sat on the bed in their room in the Belram's Shadow, and Vamma stood before her. Anxiety consumed Corelle, and she balled the blanket in her fists as they talked. Vamma's confession had stunned her. Three women had said those words to her before, and they had all died. She did not wish another death on her conscience but could not return the sand now it had fallen. The words had been said, and nothing could change that.

Vamma seemed disappointed by Corelle's initial reaction. "I thought you would be happy to hear it."

"Why would you love me? You did not wish to commit to one person the last time we were together."

Vamma could not explain it, so she said. Corelle had never been out of her thoughts for long throughout the time they had been apart, and when she had appeared in the market in Yerrsun, Vamma had been ecstatic to see her again.

Once they had reached the room, Corelle had reminded Vamma of the three women who had said those words, and how they had brought about the deaths of all three. Vamma claimed Corelle saw their deaths in the wrong light. They had died not because they loved Corelle, rather they had lived and loved a magnificent woman and had met early deaths.

"Because of me. I even killed one of them, and her unborn child along with her."

Vamma objected. "You did not know about the child."

"I do not see a distinction. I killed the child, whether I knew of its existence or I did not."

Vamma glared down at her. She stood with the shuttered window at her back, hands on her hips. "I will take my chances."

Corelle sighed, exasperated. Vamma had missed her point in the last conversation they had held about this matter, and she missed it again now. "You may take your chances, but if you die, I must live with the horror of a fourth life taken because it became embroiled in my own. I cannot stand that."

Vamma tossed her head, and her brown hair flew back away from her face, where it had fallen as she gazed down on Corelle. "You are not the only person whose fate is important, though you try to make it so. I cannot choose whom I love. I love, and that is not for me to control. I may live for all the years to come and never die, despite your opinion to the contrary. Would you be content to spend the rest of your life without me?"

Corelle bit at her lower lip. She cared for Vamma and might relish a simpler life; the two of them in a small house where they could work on the stall together through the day and spend their evenings in the warm sunshine. They could chat about small things that had turned during the day, the nights filled with the scents and sounds of their passion. At the same time, Corelle longed to return to the sea, and if she did, Vamma could not accompany her. Corelle's violent life had destroyed all it touched and left her afraid to dream any longer. Desperate to relieve the tension, Corelle tried for a jest. "Will you say my Sending, if you plan never to die?"

"That I will. I have already composed it. 'Farewell Corelle, or

Jorinda. You were an acceptable lover, and as stubborn as the last leaf of the wet season that clings to the tree and pretends it is still summer.'"

Corelle smiled. "An acceptable lover?"

Vamma licked her lips, sensuous, provocative. "Prove me wrong." Her breaths heaved from her as she slid her hands up toward her breasts.

"This stubborn woman you describe might refuse." Corelle's sex grew hot with lust. Her tremors of passion strengthened as Vamma's nipples hardened under her own fingers.

Vamma's sensuous whisper stoked the fires of Corelle's desire. "Jorinda might refuse. Corelle would not." She still stood, but she moved closer and lifted her tunic as she guided an erect nipple toward Corelle's mouth.

Corelle reached around her and pulled her forward. She stroked Vamma's buttocks and sucked on the nipple. Her tongue flicked at it as Vamma gasped in delight.

Vamma wrapped her hands around Corelle's head. "I wish you would let your hair grow out again. I long to run my fingers through it rather than scrape them on this stubble."

"Enough complaints." Corelle pulled Vamma toward her and kissed her, her tongue thrust deep into Vamma's mouth.

It took more than an hour for them to sate one another. They lay in each other's arms on the bed, naked, and their hands still explored each other's bodies, tender kisses exchanged now and again the only sound. After some time, Vamma flopped onto her back and Corelle kissed one of her ears before she asked, "You are content?"

"That I am."

"I am not so stubborn, after all else. You will need to change my Sending."

Vamma laughed and made no immediate reply. She placed an

arm behind her head and stared up at the ceiling for a time. "And the third?"

"The third?" Corelle did not understand.

Vamma moved to lie on her side again and propped her head up with a hand, her elbow on the blanket. "The third woman who died. Arella and Deineike are two. Who is the third?"

"Pettra. Raolos's wife."

Vamma's eyes widened. "Raolos the Bailiff?" Her voice grew louder.

"He had not become the Bailiff then. Well, he might have. It is complicated."

"You stole the Bailiff's wife from him? Tell me the tale, or I swear I will hold my breath until I die."

Corelle laughed. "I doubt it is possible to do so. I did not steal her, in truth. I did not wish her to travel with me, but she insisted, as did her husband."

Vamma slapped at Corelle's arm. "You lie to me. He urged you to take her away with you? Did the three of you…?"

"That we did not. As I have said, we found ourselves in a complicated situation. Pettra had suppressed her desires through the years as she stood by his side, and he rose through the ranks until he became Bailiff. She wished to eat a different fruit, and I became that fruit."

"How did you come to be available? What of Deineike?"

"She had died. In truth, to my shame, this turned mere days after Deineike's Pyre."

Vamma knitted her eyebrows, and her mouth skewed. "I am not sure I approve of that part of the tale. Go on with it, nevertheless."

"There is little more to tell. The Duke banished me, and Pettra and I sailed to Vyrrmod. She died, and I returned to Dur after I heard Wilash's wife had been killed."

Vamma nodded and seemed to revisit the tale as though she

looked for some morsel she might have missed. "How did she die?"

Sharp tears of shame welled up in Corelle's eyes. Vamma reached up and wiped at them with a thumb. "She killed herself. Threw herself from a balcony."

Vamma sat up and pulled Corelle upright also. She spread her legs either side of Corelle and took Corelle's face in her hands. "That is terrible. Why did she kill herself?"

"She had desires I could not sate. She craved violence and pain when we made love. I could not indulge her, so she found pleasure with another, a man. He hurt her one night; far beyond what she desired, I fear. I had left her alone to track down Glailam, the former Bailiff. When I returned, I found her dead on the floor."

Vamma's eyes filled with sadness. "That is tragic. Did the man receive appropriate punishment for his treatment of her?" Corelle said nothing, but her lips tightened, and Vamma must have seen something in her eyes. "You killed him." It had not been a question. Corelle drew in a deep breath, then exhaled it in a long, slow sigh. "Then she did not die for love of you, Corelle. She died because she desired violence and went too far. That guilt is not yours to carry."

"I carry it, regardless. She suffered, in her mind, and I treated her in a shameful way. I loathe myself for…" She could not go on. Her guilt and shame choked the words off in her throat.

Corelle lay down on the bed again. Vamma sat back and bent one leg upward, the knee pointed to the ceiling. She rested her chin on the upraised knee and twirled the fingers of one hand through the stiff hair of Corelle's bush, casual, distracted. After long moments, Vamma spoke again. "I no longer think it."

Corelle had all but dozed off, and the words startled her. Through sleepy eyes, Corelle stared up at her. "Think what?"

"That I love you."

Corelle closed her eyes and ran a hand up the shin of Vamma's crooked leg. "What is scribed, must be." She laughed.

Vamma wrinkled her nose at Corelle's amusement. "What is funny?"

"Deineike hated it when I used that phrase."

The day's ride and the emotions of the evening bettered Corelle, although she battled her tiredness. She thought Vamma lay down beside her as sleep washed over her.

When she woke, night still covered the Eastlands. No light crept round the shutters. She shook Vamma awake and shushed her grumbles with a kiss. "We should make an early start. If we ride hard, we may come to Eastort tonight and avoid another night at an inn. There is one small inn between here and Eastort, but I would rather not stay there."

They had paid for the room the night before, so they left with no inconvenience to the innkeep. The front door of the inn had been locked, but they turned the key and walked out into the chill of the pre-sunrise air. They saddled their horses and set off.

Vamma had said little after Corelle had woken her, and when she had, she had railed against the early start. As the sun rose and the day warmed, her mood improved, but she still complained about the hour they had set off. "Why must we start so early to save a little coin?"

"I avoid it not because of the coin, in truth. Raolos funds the trip, and the inn costs little enough. It is owned by a man whose daughter cannot speak. They communicate with her by gestures. She is a sweet girl."

Vamma turned her head. "So far I have heard nothing to explain why we do not spend the night there."

"The innkeep has two brothers. Wait, that is no longer true. He had two brothers, but one died. Now he has only one."

Vamma slapped at her thigh, and the horses skittered. "Now all is clear. I would not stay there either, if the innkeep has a brother."

"If you will permit me to finish, you may understand the situation better." Her inadequate explanation frustrated Corelle as much as Vamma's jest at her expense. "I met the three brothers last year, and they irritated and aggravated me more than anybody I have ever met in my life. I named them Bushy and Sparse, for their beards."

"You named all three Bushyandsparse?"

Corelle glowered at her. "I meant the other two were named Bushy and Sparse."

Vamma frowned. "There were five?"

Corelle slapped herself on the forehead. "I am not even with them, and they still drive me to the limits of my sanity. They are… painful."

"You have said this already." Vamma wore a wicked smile.

"Now you irritate me." Corelle kicked her horse forward. To her annoyance, Vamma kicked her own horse to match her pace. They rode on in silence while Corelle battled her frustration. "The innkeep had no beard. I named his brothers Bushy and Sparse. They all chattered without end and laughed at every word any of them said."

Vamma laughed, then apologised. Corelle felt her cheeks burn and her ire grow. "Go on." Corelle thought she detected mockery in the invitation.

"That I will not. I despise them."

"I see this." Vamma seemed to struggle to suppress her laughter.

Corelle stared at her with narrowed eyes. "I hope you fall off your stupid horse."

"Now you blame my horse for these brothers? That is cruel." Vamma stroked her horse's neck and spoke to the animal in a tone of reassurance. "There, there. She does not mean it. She is irritated, nothing more."

"Go ahead—laugh. I should make you stay at the inn and rope you to their table. You would not mock me then, I promise you."

Vamma's entire body shook as she fought her amusement, and

she lost the battle. She burst into uproarious laughter that brought tears to her eyes. They rode on, the flat, featureless Eastlands landscape sundered by Vamma's loud, uncontrolled mirth. Corelle could not resist for long and joined in. Their laughter rose to the sky, carried by the wind to bring their amusement to any animals and plants close enough to hear.

CHAPTER 13
CORELLE

As the day headed into early evening, they passed The Eastlands Inn. Corelle pointed to it as they rode by. "There is the inn, curse them."

Corelle started as Vamma shouted. "Curse you, Bushy and… the other one."

Corelle raised a finger to her lips to urge Vamma to silence, and whispered, "They may come out to investigate." She kicked her horse forward.

When they were well clear of the inn, Corelle asked Vamma why she had said, "Bushy and the other one."

"I forgot the other's name." They both burst into uncontrollable laughter again.

Darkness fell, and they still had some distance to travel to reach Eastort. They could either ride on in the black of the night or see out the night on the ground. Corelle cursed the lack of moonlight but felt she could remember the road well enough, and it had been in good enough condition. To ride on should pose little danger. Nonetheless, they slowed the horses to a careful walk and stared ahead, hopeful they would spot any trouble before they reached it. Corelle knew the risks, but she had no desire to sleep on the ground.

She heaved a sigh of relief when a light appeared before them, and before long they rode into Eastort. The hour had grown late, and few lights showed from windows. Most had been shuttered and allowed no more than slivers of illumination into the street. They found a darkened inn, but they could not raise the innkeep when they knocked on the door. Corelle muttered about ill choices thrust on her by ill-bred men, dismounted, and searched for the stable. Once she found it, she pulled the door open, and they led the horses inside. They tied them to a ring affixed to a wall and pulled some loose hay together to fashion a makeshift bed. Exhaustion took them, and they fell asleep in each other's arms soon after they wrapped their blankets about them.

The stable boy woke them early in the morning. He stood and stared at them for a time, then shook his head and left. Within moments, the innkeep arrived in the stable and demanded to know why they had slept in his stable. Corelle explained they had arrived late and could not raise anybody to let them into the inn. She showed him the letters from Raolos and told him they travelled on important business. He remained unhappy they had slept for free in his stable but waved his arm and stomped out of the barn. He may have been intimidated by the prospect of further argument with an emissary of the Bailiff.

They mounted the horses and rode out of the stable. Vamma gave the stable boy a warm smile as they left, and he blushed bright red. They turned toward the river and allowed the horses to walk at a slow, steady pace. They would return Corelle's horse to the stables she had rented it from and leave Vamma's horse there for a time. Vamma suggested they could sell it, but Corelle had reservations about its sale when no decision about the future had been made. She said the horse mattered the least if Vamma's life lay in a new direction. The stall and her home must be far more important. Despite obvious reluctance, Vamma agreed.

Once they had stabled the horses, they carried their packs to the jetty. No passengers waited for the rowboat, and Corelle could see it tied to the jetty. Neither the rowers nor the steersman sat in it, but a man sat nearby. Corelle asked him when the rowboat would next leave for Ort. "It will not, not for some time."

"Why is this?" Corelle worried about how they would cross the river if the rowboat had been damaged.

"Two or three days ago, three large southern ships appeared in Ort." Corelle saw nothing unusual in that but kept silent and reasoned more of the tale would be revealed. "Peculiar ships they were. I never saw their like before, nor the men who spilled out of them. Two of them made straight for me. They carried swords and wore leather clothes. Strangest thing I ever saw. 'What are you about?' they asked, so I told them I steer the rowboat. They made it clear it would be unsafe to operate the rowboat again until they sent word to Eastort. Strange men with odd accents. I had never heard those accents before."

Corelle frowned and tried to fathom what lay behind the strange ships and the apparent threat to the rowboat operators. "How many men came off these ships?"

"More than I have fingers to count. I cannot count beyond ten, and I do not guess at numbers any larger."

Corelle battled her impatience. "Please guess this once. Double your fingers? More?"

"Fivefold my fingers, my guess, at the least. A number so large I could not reckon it."

Fifty men? Why would fifty southerners appear and order the rowboat not to operate? It baffled Corelle. "Did they fly a pennant on the ships?"

When he confirmed the ships flew a pennant, Corelle asked for a description of the sigil on it, and the man described it as red other than a white eye in the middle, a stylised tail, or tear, hanging from the eye.

Corelle turned to Vamma. "Qagrue. I have seen their sigil before. Why do they come to Dur?"

"Could it be linked to the death of the boy?"

She had been wise to lower her voice, Corelle guessed. It would serve no purpose to let other ears hear their conversation. "I know not, but I must see what turns. I must get across the river."

"This need not concern us, need it? We can ride back to Yerrsun and live there together, unconcerned by the deeds of these southerners."

"I have a responsibility to report the death of the boy, and I have not abandoned my plans to return to sea. I did not agree to a life in Yerrsun. I agreed to accompany you to Alcmouth and from there let the dice fall as they may. Now it seems I am unable to cross the river. I must know why." Vamma seemed taken aback, and Corelle apologised. "I am sorry, I had no cause to speak to you that way. I will not abandon you, not here, but I need to know what turns. The more is known, the stronger the knowledge."

Vamma looked at her in confusion. "Do you mean '*the more is known, the better the decision?*'"

"That may be how you say it in the Eastlands." Corelle felt the heat rise to her cheeks, embarrassed she had misremembered the phrase, something she had once been so excellent at. "In Ryl, we say things in different ways."

Vamma nodded in sympathy. "I see this. In Ryl, you say things in a way that makes no sense."

Vamma toyed with her again. "You are worse than Deineike. Curse my luck. I always fall in with such women."

Vamma's face contorted with suppressed laughter, and Corelle despaired. She could see no way to emerge from the battle of words unscathed, much less victorious. She prided herself that she knew when she had been bested, and on her reputation as a good loser. She poked her tongue out at Vamma, who burst into laughter. "That is an attractive look." Vamma gasped the words out between peals of laughter.

Corelle turned again to the boatman. "Would you rent me your rowboat for an hour or two?"

He looked her up and down, seemed unsure. "Can you even row?"

"That I can. Better than most, I warrant."

He squinted at her. "The boat is not permitted to travel to Ort."

"I will not go to Ort. Not to the docks, at the least."

"Then where will you go? What will you do with her?"

"I wish to catch fish." Corelle did not hesitate. She had not lied, though she wished to fish for information rather than the creatures that swam in the river.

He appeared unconvinced. "Fish, is it? Where is your pole?"

"I need no pole to fish for what I seek."

He tapped his fingers on the log he sat on, rhythmic, like a drumbeat, as he stared at her. At last, he responded. "Two regals."

"You misunderstand. I wish to rent the boat, not buy it and another like it." Corelle's anger flared, outraged he had attempted to charge so much.

"One regal. Final offer. You will need to swim if you do not want the boat." He folded his arms across his chest in defiance.

Corelle sighed in acceptance. In truth, she had no other option. "One regal."

Vamma reached for Corelle's arm. "Can you row?"

"Better than I can ride."

"What do you fish for?"

"News." Corelle kissed Vamma's lips. "Take a room at the inn. I will look for you there later today."

"Be careful. Do not do anything foolish."

Corelle laughed. "You say you love a woman who has killed

one of her lovers and seen two others die because of her, but you warn me against anything foolish." Vamma smiled, but the anxiety did not leave her face, and Corelle heaved a resigned sigh. "I will be careful, I promise."

"Come back to me." Vamma stared deep into Corelle's eyes.

"I will."

CHAPTER 14
CORELLE

Corelle turned to the rowboat. The boatman had untied the rope and stood on the jetty with it in his hand.

Vamma tugged at her arm again. "I love you."

Corelle's mind raced for a suitable response. "I am very loveable."

"That you are." Vamma kissed her, and Corelle turned toward the river.

Corelle clambered into the rowboat and pushed out the oars. The rowboat had been moored bow in, and she rowed the boat away from the jetty then swung north. As she rowed northward, Vamma gave her a small wave. The wave seemed sad somehow, as if Vamma believed she might not see Corelle again.

Corelle had no preference for north or south, but the tide flowed from the south, and it would be easier to row north with it. She meant to make land on the western bank some way from the docks, in a more residential quarter. With luck, she would find someone there with more information about the inexplicable turn the boatman had revealed.

Corelle had never thought of the rowboat as large even though it had taken four oarsmen to row, but it required substantial effort for one person to row without a steersman, and she sweated and panted as she forced the boat to cross the river rather than drift upstream with the current. She turned to peer ahead and scanned the bank. Something to do with the comparative effort required to pull rather than push required rowers to face backward, and in a vessel with other crew members, that had always been fine. Other eyes could search for danger or places to land as she rowed. Now she must do both, and it tired her. She saw a jetty with a small boat moored to it ahead of her and guided her rowboat toward it, keen to make land before she became too exhausted to control the boat.

As she came in, she shipped the oars and allowed the rowboat to glide to the jetty. She picked up a rope with a loop at one end from the bottom of the boat and made a good throw to one of the pilings of the jetty. She had not expected to miss, and she did not disappoint herself. Once she had made the little boat fast, she clambered out onto the jetty and looked around.

It had been built at the bottom of an expansive garden behind a large house. The size of the house suggested she had landed in the wealthy quarter, but Corelle knew she had not, as Raolos's house lay in that quarter, up the hill and away from the river. She imagined she had landed at the northern end of the better quarter and the owners had enough wealth to have a large house that allowed them to live on the river. Anybody so wealthy might take a dim view of strangers who moored at their jetty and wandered through their garden, but nobody challenged her.

She passed the side of the house and came to the front gate. The rear garden had been enclosed behind high hedges, but the smaller front garden had a well maintained white wooden fence all around it. Corelle muttered to herself, "Minarko should see how a real fence ought to be." A gate opened into the garden, covered by a white archway from which hung colourful flowers, and insects flitted about them in the warm sunshine of a perfect summer morning.

Corelle pulled the gate open and peered up and down the street. She saw nobody, but she pulled her fan out of her boot before she stepped out of the gate. She opened the fan's folds and waved it before her face to cool herself. Ever cautious, she turned south and walked toward the town square, mindful of her surroundings. As she walked, she strove to appear as though she might be nothing more than a local out for a stroll, although her clothes did not match the quarter. She hoped anybody who saw her might believe she had taken a walk as some respite from work in her garden.

She turned a corner and spotted a group of men in the street some way ahead of her. Even from a distance, she could see they wore the emblem of Qagrue on the front of their tunics, and they were armed. She wondered why they stood in the street. They could be patrols, or guards, but that made no sense. If guards were needed, why would Ibie's men not provide them?

One of the men pointed toward her. Another turned his head to stare at her. He held a long pole with a fearsome pointed tip. She had seen something similar at the Ducal Highhome. It looked more ornamental than functional. As more heads turned in her direction, she walked forward, calm and unconcerned to all appearances. When she passed a gate in the fence of a house, she pushed it open, entered the garden, and tried to look relaxed. She did not wish to attract any closer attention from the Qagrue men.

Corelle had entered a much smaller garden than the one with the jetty, and the house did not seem as impressive, but the garden had been tended with care, and the house maintained with equal diligence. The paint seemed intact, and the walls were clean and undamaged. She spotted movement in a window at one end of the building, and an older woman peered out at her. The woman seemed anxious, and Corelle gave her a cheery wave and moved toward the door.

She heard movement within the house, but the door did not open. A woman's voice called out from behind the door. "Who is there?"

"My name is Corelle. I am Durfolk, like you. I have returned from a journey to the Eastlands, and I find our town filled with strange folk. I would like to learn what has turned in my absence."

A brief silence followed, then a bolt slid back with a metallic sigh, and the door opened a crack. The old woman peered out at her. Men's voices came from the street, a language Corelle could not understand. She reasoned the Qagrue men had moved forward, either out of routine or curiosity about her.

The door opened wider. "Hurry." The woman ushered Corelle inside, closed the door behind her, and slid the bolt back into place. "Come in, away from the front windows." The woman's voice was urgent, insistent as she moved down the narrow hallway. She moved at a pace that belied the grey hair and wrinkled skin of an old woman. At the rear of the house stood a delightful scullery, a small stove built into the fireplace. Bunches of herbs hung on the walls, and some pans hung above the mantle, all shiny clean.

"Sit, please." The woman gestured toward a wooden chair, one of four arranged around a neat little table with a dainty cloth in the middle. "Would you like anything to eat or drink?"

"Nothing, my thanks. Who are these men?"

"That much I do not know. They arrived four days ago, a day or so either way, at the least. They seem to be everywhere. If you go for a walk, they stop you and ask where you are headed. I hear they will not let anybody near the square."

Corelle's heart sank. She could not seek answers from Ibie if she could not reach the square. The woman shifted from foot to foot, nervous. Corelle gave her a smile of reassurance, and the woman pulled open a drawer in a low cupboard against one wall. She took out a parch and held it toward Corelle. "Tore this off a tree yesterday. They had pinned it there. I saw them."

Corelle took the parch. It read, "By order of Sisnop, the Duke's Bailiff, the former Portreeve of Ort has been called to answer for treacherous crimes against the Duchy, and Gillar has been appointed the new Portreeve." She stared in disbelief at the parch, unable to believe Ibie had committed any crime against Dur, but the names Sisnop and Gillar confirmed her worst fears. The Guild had returned, and they lay behind all that turned. She looked up at the old woman, despondent. "If Sisnop is the Bailiff, then what of Raolos? What of Ibie?"

"I do not know, in truth." The old woman shook her head as a dejected tone came to her voice. "A neighbour told me he had heard they hanged Ibie."

Corelle's head swam at the words. She grasped at the edge of the table and dropped the parch to the floor. She concentrated on the cloth in the middle of the table, fearful she might faint. Ibie had been hanged? On what pretence? What turned? This must be another of her nightmares. What else could explain it?

"Are you all right, dear?" The woman's voice oozed compassion.

Speech had deserted Corelle. Her heart pounded, and her blood roared in her ears. She gave the old woman a wave of reassurance, but the woman took a step toward her, her eyes filled with concern.

If they had killed Ibie and announced themselves as the new leaders of the land, then Raolos might have been killed, along with the Duke. Wilash and Synna too. All dead? She could not bear it, and she threw her head back and howled her grief and her rage. How had so much turned since she had left Alcmouth? Could it even be possible? She tried to calculate how long she had been away. She had sailed north for five days, ridden for three days, stayed… what? Three days in Yerrsun? Two days back. That took her to yesterday, so another day to account for today. In two seven-days, Krage and the Guild had taken over the Duchy. It could not be possible. "Do you jest?" Corelle kept her voice quiet but fierce.

"That I do not. I do not understand it any more than you."

The woman had the right of it. She did not understand the grief that crushed Corelle, to think her friends might all have been killed, the land given over to the man she hated, a man who would kill any who questioned anything he told them to do. Dur had been destroyed. She must leave at once; take Vamma and flee.

How could she leave unless she knew what had turned? That had never been her way. She wondered if the old woman might have the story wrong somehow. A trade deal may have been struck with Qagrue. Qagrue had never traded with Dur as far as she knew. These men might have come as emissaries.

Corelle laughed at her naivety. Sisnop declared himself the Bailiff and named Gillar as the Portreeve of Ort. Ibie would not have stood for it for a heartbeat. Something terrible had turned while she chased a dead boy with a misspelled message carved into his back. She would have been dead also, had she stayed in Alcmouth. If she had returned to The Salty Home and sailed with the cargo to Steinlund, she would have learned nothing of these horrors.

She needed to find out more of what had turned. "Is this the only road to the square?"

The woman held out both hands as if to hold Corelle in the chair and whispered, urgent. "You must not go to the square. They will arrest you, or worse."

"Please. If I do need to get there, is there another way?"

The woman shook her head, and Corelle's hope collapsed within her, but it turned the woman had not shaken her head to indicate no other way existed. "This is madness, but there is a path. It runs along the river to the docks. From there it might be possible to use back streets if you know Ort well. You might come to the square that way. I fear you will die if you try."

Corelle nodded, grateful for the information. "I know Ort well enough, and we all die."

The woman's grey hair moved a little as she shook her head in sadness. "We used the path as children, but I do not think it has been used for many years. Everybody uses the street these days. So many more houses out here now. So many more horses and fancy carriages than in my childhood. The path might be overgrown."

Corelle grew impatient but did not wish to snap at the old lady. She clenched her teeth for a heartbeat, then forced a smile to her lips. "How might I find this path?"

The woman stared at her for a moment. "Use the front gate, turn left and you will see a narrow lane to the left. Follow it until you see the river. It is not far. The path will be on your right, if you can find it. Be careful, dear."

When she left the garden, Corelle would walk toward the men who had been stationed in the street for a time. Risky, but she had to know more. "You also. Do not leave the house alone."

The woman snorted. "They do not frighten me. Bullies never have. My husband tried to bully me, and I blacked his eye. He never tried again, through the long years of our marriage." She gave a sad smile and Corelle opened her mouth to speak, but the woman interrupted her. "Dead, dear. Three years now, my guess. I am glad he did not live to see these days."

The midday approached, and Corelle decided to search for the lane to see whether she could reach the square. She thanked the woman for the help and asked if she could keep the parch. The woman gave a dry laugh and said she would tear another from a different tree.

Corelle left her, this resolute, brave old woman who would not be cowed by southerners with their swords and ridiculous long weapons, not their tunics nor their aggression. She would be herself and curse them back to where they came from. Corelle turned left onto the street. The men still stood where she had first seen them, and she walked toward them. She soon saw the narrow lane and turned down it, glad to be out of sight of the men again. The overgrown jumble of hedge would hide any sign of the path the woman had mentioned, and she had to search for it. She pulled her fan out of her boot in case she needed a blade to cut away any part of the hedge.

As she peered through the hedge at what she thought might be the start of the path, she heard a gruff, accented voice. "What are you about?"

Corelle snapped her fan open and fluttered it before her as she turned to face the voice. The man wore the tunic of Qagrue and had his hand on the hilt of his sword, which dangled in an ornate leather sheath attached to his belt. How had he got so close, but she had not heard him? Had a year at sea dulled all her old skills?

Corelle kept her voice cheery, friendly. "I live nearby. I walk here every day. This old lane is used so little these days, and the solitude helps me reflect."

He looked her up and down and seemed thoughtful. He had a short, thickset stature with dark eyes and thin lips. He wore a round leather hat atop long black hair. He had dark skin, but Corelle's may have been darker thanks to her exposure to the elements this past year. "You not look if you live here." His voice sounded gruff, almost a growl.

His Dur left something to be desired, and Corelle did not grasp his meaning. "What do you mean?"

"You dirty with dust, dress like urchin. You are—garsheek— what is word? Dark. You are dark. These Durs hide from sun. You come with me, we find out you. What is called?"

She found his mangled Dur difficult to follow but guessed he had asked her name. "I am Pettra. I live in that beautiful little house behind you." She pointed past him toward the end of the lane.

He turned to look back, and she lunged forward. When she sprang the blade from her fan, it faced the wrong way. She had not yet grown accustomed to it and had held the fan upside down for a right-handed person. The blade had only one sharp edge and would be difficult to reverse and swipe along his throat, so she drove it into his neck with all her might. He cried out in pain and grabbed at her arm. She raised her other hand to the fan and sawed at his neck. She twisted the fan so she could work it across his neck.

He cried out again in his own language, but her fan found its mark. It sliced through his vein, and dark crimson blood spurted from his neck. His struggles grew weaker as his life ebbed away, and he collapsed to the floor as his blood pooled around his head. Her blade came loose as he fell, and she bent to wipe it clean on his tunic. He had not even had time to pull his sword from its sheath. It had proved as useless as she had expected in close combat and had not served him well.

She had no time to wonder where he had come from. His blood covered her, and she could not afford for his colleagues to see her. Her legs and arms pumped as she ran back to the large house, down the garden and along the jetty. She untied the rope, leapt into the rowboat and struggled against the tide as she rowed back to Eastort. The heat of the midday sun soon had her drenched in sweat as she hauled on the oars against the strong tide with a grunt at every stroke. At length, she turned her head and saw the jetty at Eastort. The trip across the Alc had been disastrous, and she needed a new plan.

CHAPTER 15
KRAGE

Krage had only been to Alcmouth once, many years ago. He had been born in Ryl and had left his home city no more than a handful of times before he met Styrrach. The pair had met in one of the less reputable taverns of the little city, where Styrrach had spread the word that he sought men who had the courage to join him in an enterprise as lucrative as it would be despicable. It had fascinated Krage, and Styrrach invited him to work with him almost as soon as they met. Whatever he had seen in Krage had convinced him.

Krage did not kill often. He recruited with care and attention. The deadly work the Guild performed would see them hanged if they were caught. Styrrach introduced the Portreeve into his scheme, but despite his eagerness for the coin, the Portreeve made it clear from the outset he would not hesitate to hang any who were foolish enough to be caught.

Krage snapped out of his reverie. He did not recognise the buildings on the bank of the river. He knew they had come to Alcmouth, but the city skyline did not spark any memories from his sole visit. His excitement increased, and he paced the deck, unable to keep still as he shook with anticipation. His hour had arrived, and he would soon have accomplished something even Styrrach would not have had the imagination to conceive, much less bring to fruition.

His mind flew back to a time a year ago when all seemed lost. The men he had sent to Alcmouth had been gone a pass or more when Gillar returned to the farm with the news Krage's trusted friend Priu had been captured and handed over to the Bailiff. Others of his men had been killed. The story had bewildered him, and he could not understand how they had allowed the plan to turn so awry until Gillar spat out a name. Corelle. She had come out from whichever stone she had hidden under, and she had thwarted all their plans.

Krage's plan had been for her to take the bait he had dangled in front of her when his men kidnapped the woman in Alcmouth. She would be captured by his men and handed to him at the farm. Instead, she had killed or captured half of the men sent to apprehend her. Priu would be dead by now, hanged by the Bailiff, who had Corelle's whispers in his ear.

Priu's death infuriated Krage, and he threw a chair across the room and ranted at Gillar for his failure to act. He had fled at the first sign of trouble, saved his own skin, and abandoned four good men to die. How had one woman brought such ruin on their plans? When he calmed down, he had insisted they leave at once. Corelle's well-known brutality might have persuaded some of the four to speak before they died, and she would be certain to ride to the farm ahead of a large force, determined to kill them all.

Sisnop had argued against it and pointed out nobody could reach the farm for many days. Carshan, who had once been the Portreeve in Yerrsun, had said Corelle could not land a large force at Eastort, and to ride north from Eastport would take a tenday at the least. They may not even know of the farm's existence.

Krage and Sisnop had bickered back and forth about the right course of action for two days. Krage wanted to leave. Sisnop did not and would not permit his men to accompany Krage. That would leave Krage almost unguarded, since Priu and the two men he felt he could count on had now been killed. Caught between doubt and uncertainty, he saw no way to leave unless he could persuade Sisnop and his men to go with him. He still had Ifor, but the man seemed slow and withdrawn, and he wanted more blades to guard him, after all else. He owed Corelle two lives now—his child and Priu. When Styrrach sent a letter to tell him Arella carried his child, he had been shocked. Before he could even come up with a plan to claim her and raise the child, Corelle had killed them both and fled. He yearned to repay those debts, but not at the expense of his own life.

He had argued with Sisnop for two days when a Portreeve's man from Yerrsun arrived at the farm with news Corelle and another were in the town and had asked about the farm. Krage cursed himself. He had stayed and argued with Sisnop about the right course of action until his ruin arrived on his doorstep. He urged Sisnop and Gillar to leave the farm without further delay and ride with him to Eastport. They would sail south and live out their days in comfort and affluence. Sisnop became even more insistent they stay. Only the two had come to the town by all accounts, and the Guild outnumbered them. Let her come, Sisnop argued. Guild justice would be served on her. She had no hope of defeating such a large force. They doubled the guards at each door of the farm.

Krage battled voices in his mind that assured him she would not have come here to be hacked to pieces by his knife. She had some plan to take him—alive or dead, she would not care which. At the same time, he recognised the Guild had her outnumbered, and he might overpower her and serve up rough justice to her and whoever had arrived with her. The Portreeve's message had been clear. No men from Alcmouth had arrived with her apart from this other who travelled at her side. She had sought the Portreeve's help in whatever endeavours she had travelled to Yerrsun for, which included the use of his men if it came to it. That help would not be provided, of course, and Krage saw the chance to avenge his child and Priu. He could not persuade himself to leave, even as he believed it the safest thing to do.

He dispatched one of their men to town to bring back more information. If he had all the facts, it would aid his decision. He told Velbur to watch her but not to interact with her. "She is deadly. Do not fail me. I must know whether there are more than two of them."

Krage suspected she would play some game of double bluff, and he stood ready to flee at a moment's notice even as he hoped the news would be positive. Velbur had returned, anxious and afraid. "She knows of the farm. She lies with the woman who brings the cart out here, and she may have cultivated other local sources of information. She will kill us all."

Krage had scoffed at him and mocked him for his blind belief of all the tales of her prowess. He laughed at her reputation. "There can be nobody who is as capable as these tales suggest she is." Even as he spoke the words, they rang hollow in his own ears. They must flee, head south. They would lay low and plan their next moves.

Krage despised Velbur, who had allowed himself to be caught by Corelle, and gave him an unpleasant death through Guild justice. He had forced all the men to watch and hear the man's screams as he mutilated him. None of them would be in any doubt of the fate that awaited them if they did not please him. It had been a crucial moment. It established him as the leader of the group without the need to battle Sisnop for that honour. Even Sisnop himself turned as white as the purest cloud in the sky at the end as Velbur died. The horror on Sisnop's face satisfied Krage even though everything had turned awry.

Krage had never killed anyone in such a brutal manner before.

He and Styrrach had invented the threat of "Guild justice" to keep men motivated to serve them, but Krage believed his efforts at the farm must be the first time there had been any actual "Guild justice." If somebody failed them, that man would be shrouded. Guild justice served as a tale to keep the members loyal, and its effectiveness as a threat had been successful. The actual mutilation of Velbur served a far more powerful purpose, and Krage wondered whether they could have resorted to it earlier, had they known how successful it would prove.

Anxious Corelle might hinder their escape, Krage dispatched a man to order the Portreeve to arrest her and detain her while they rode for Eastport. He knew no charges would keep her for long, so he proposed she be arrested for deviancy. Then he might arrange to kill the woman she lay with. It would be the next best thing to the death of Corelle herself. He told the man to place a small food order and return to the farm as soon as possible. He ordered the man to ensure Corelle had been arrested before he returned.

The next day, the man returned to the farm and told Krage Corelle's companion had killed the Portreeve's son before the two of them rode off westward. Krage considered this news. They may have fled because of the death of the Portreeve's son, but with Corelle it did not pay to try to second guess her. Like as not, she would try to deceive him and bring a large force of Bailiff's men to the farm. He had delayed long enough.

Krage refused to listen to Sisnop any more and sensed his display in the barn had ensured the men would follow him rather than stay with Sisnop. His guess proved correct, and Sisnop, downcast, agreed to leave with them. They left two men behind to kill the food woman, with orders to ride hard and catch them once she had died, then marshalled the rest of the men together. They departed and rode east, then turned south toward Eastport.

They had ridden hard for many days before they reached Eastport. His two men did not catch them up and by the time they were at the docks, he had resigned himself to the fact Corelle had killed them. He hoped they had killed the woman before Corelle caught up to them, but he would not wait for them. If she had pursued them, she might not be far behind him. They took control of the first ship that docked and forced the master to sail south to Vyrrmod.

Eastport. A tragic little place in Krage's estimation. It would have been beneath Styrrach to use it for his scheme, but the southerners sailed here nonetheless, encouraged by this new Bailiff, it seemed. Did he intend to have every tiny dot on the coastline of the land become a trade post? Krage had laughed as he remembered his earlier thought that no man could have everything.

As they sailed, however, he questioned that belief. A man might have everything, if he had the ambition and talent to take it all. After Vyrrmod, they sailed further south to Qanti, and as Krage watched the swarthy mariners move about the ship, their strange language in his ears, he became obsessed with the thought it might be possible to have everything, after all else. What if these people could be persuaded to fight for him, to throw down the Duke and his Bailiff? Krage could take over and have everything.

Everything. The mere thought of it excited him. He could not drive the vision of himself in an ornate robe, with all subservient to him, from his mind. What would they require? How could he persuade them to loan him sufficient men to carry out his audacious plan? The answer seemed obvious when he considered it. Wealth. It drove most ambitious men, he thought. He would offer them a share of all the trade between Dur and the other nations. There would be so much coin for him, he could not spend it in two lifetimes, so there would be plenty left to reward those who helped him.

He wavered between two considerations. Either the plan represented the greatest idea he had ever had, or it had been the most ridiculous thought to have ever entered his mind. The scope of the idea seemed vast, inconceivable, but the prospect he might become the most important man in Dur appealed too much for him to resist, no matter how unhinged the plan sounded sometimes when he ran it through his mind.

He could not push the thought away. Dur had no more than a pitiful few men who could fight. The Bailiff and Portreeve in Alcmouth had men, as did the Duke. They would be little more than symbolic and not fighters, he guessed. If the Qanti sent even a hundred men who could fight, they would overpower any resistance with ease. Once he took Alcmouth, he expected little to no resistance elsewhere. It seemed so simple, and that simplicity gave him his greatest sense of anxiety. If it could be so simple, why had nobody ever tried it before?

He decided to talk to the master of the ship about it, to gauge how his people might feel about it, at the least. To his frustration, the master not only preferred the current system and believed all Qanti traders felt the same, he also said they had suffered horrific losses in a recent war with a land called Qagrue and would not risk more of their young men in a venture that would bring them little.

Krage did not understand the word "war." He had never heard it before and had never heard of Qagrue. The master explained that war occurred when two lands disagreed about something, and the disagreement became so vehement, each land sent its men to fight one another. Qanti and Qagrue had fought each other for many passes. Fierce resistance from the Qanti had turned the Qagrue back, but the losses had been terrible and had left no appetite in the land for another war, more so one that would benefit them little.

Krage had been amazed such a thing as war existed, but he soon came to see he had proposed a war of a kind. The Qagrue sounded like a violent, unpredictable people, so he decided to sail on to their land with his idea. He felt certain they did not trade with Dur, so any income from his plan would be additional to anything they earned today. It might be such a sum, they could rebuild their forces and renew their war with Qanti. Krage did not care if they all killed one another once he became the Duke in Dur.

To his frustration, Qanti and Qagrue had no trade relationship, and more of his precious coin and time were wasted on a return to Vyrrmod before he found a ship that sailed to Qagrue. The land lay south of Qanti, a place so hot, Krage thought his flesh might melt from his bones if he went out in the sunlight. It had no centralised leader such as the Duke in Dur. The land had been divided up between various tribes, and it seemed those tribes fought one another as often as they united to fight a common foe.

To Krage's surprise, many of the senior Qagrue spoke passable Dur. They claimed they had traded with Dur until Styrrach insisted on lower prices. They were not prepared to accept less profit under such a scheme, and had ceased all trade with the land as a result. They also spoke of a time when Steinlund and Dur spoke the same language; how the Dur language had changed over the years, but since they still traded with Steinlund, they could understand the modern Dur and speak it to some degree.

Such a violent, barbaric land had been incomprehensible to Krage, but he seduced several tribal leaders with his talk of great riches and principal rights of trade. After lengthy discussions, one of the leaders agreed to give him four ships and four hundred men for his takeover in exchange for vast amounts of coin and trade.

He lay on his bed that night, excited and ecstatic at the thought. Four hundred men, whom the Qagrue called soldiers, represented a formidable force, more than enough to crush any resistance from the Duke and his puppets. Krage would be the Duke, and nothing could stand in his way.

He sent three of his most trusted men ahead of him. All the Guild members gave their allegiance to Krage now they had seen his ambition, each anxious to be part of the wealth he promised. He told the three men to gather intelligence ahead of his arrival with the Qagrue ships; how many men served the Duke and his Bailiff, whether any influential Durfolk might be persuaded to join Krage and work to appease the ordinary folk. He also suggested they should sow any seed of disruption, division, and distraction they could dream up. Two tendays after they had left, he stood on the docks in Rhek-Bil-Okin, Qagrue's largest coastal city, and watched four hundred men board the four ships. He had never seen so many armed men in his life. They made a magnificent sight, their leather tunics emblazoned with the sigil of Qagrue, most with swords at their hips, some with long poles with ferocious serrated metal heads atop them. In truth, he disliked swords. They were unsuited for any of the work he had ever had to do, but he imagined they might be well suited to the combat in which a soldier might expect to find himself. He could see no purpose for the long poles, unless they were used to knock on a door from the opposite side of the street.

On the voyage north, he promised Gillar he would be Portreeve of Ort, and assured Sisnop he would be the Bailiff. Carshan demanded to be appointed Portreeve of Alcmouth. This surprised Krage, who saw the position of Portreeve in the same city where the Bailiff operated as unnecessary, but he allowed the man his desire. At first, Sisnop demanded to be the Duke, but it had been Krage's plan, and Sisnop now had no allies among the men. The tables had turned, and Krage told Sisnop he would as soon throw him over the side of the ship as make him Duke in place of himself. Sisnop muttered but soon appeared resigned to his future position as Bailiff.

They had arrived in Dur, at last. The four ships approached the docks, ropes were thrown around and the dockhands all wore quizzical faces as the soldiers walked off the ships and stood in rows on the dockside of Alcmouth. The leader of the Qagrue soldiers, a vicious-looking man with a large scar running down his right cheek, stood beside Krage. The Qagrue names were impossible for Krage to understand, but he had managed to memorise part of this man's name, Jakedian something. Krage reminded him of his orders. "Remember. Do not kill anyone who does not resist you. There is no need to cleanse the land of all its people. It will be nothing but a pile of useless dirt without the people. Any who attack you, you are free to kill."

Jakedian's face turned into a snarl, and Krage took a step back, but the Qagrue nodded. "Not kill the weak ones. Only the strong ones." He shouted in his guttural language, and the soldiers moved across the docks toward the city.

Krage turned to Sisnop. "So it begins. The jade thought she had destroyed us when she killed Styrrach and persuaded the Duke to make that buffoon from Ort Bailiff. They will all pay a terrible price, and we will restore all they sought to take from us. Styrrach's death must be avenged."

They followed the soldiers toward the square. They encountered bodies, almost all in the red or yellow tunics of the Portreeve or the Bailiff. There had been some resistance, he guessed, or the Qagrue's bloodlust could not be constrained. Either way, he felt confident the Durfolk could not match the Qagrue. His plan had been set in motion, and soon enough he would be the most important man in the land. He smiled to himself. Even Styrrach could not have dreamt of a plan so bold. Krage had earned the title of Duke. He congratulated himself for his genius.

CHAPTER 16
CORELLE

As Corelle struggled against the tide, she hoped there would be no repercussions against the residents once the Qagrue discovered the man's body. That would be unfortunate, but it could not be helped. She could not risk capture.

She reached the jetty, drenched in blood and sweat, and sat for a moment with her head bowed as she sucked air into her exhausted body. The man who had rented her the rowboat walked toward her and threw a line. She caught it and made it fast to the bow cleat. He stared in amazement at her, and she guessed he wondered where all the blood and sweat that covered her had come from.

She had the right of it, and he gasped as he sought an explanation. "What has turned?"

"An animal attacked me." The reply had some truth, after all else.

"An animal? What sort of animal? You are covered in blood."

She reasoned he might understand the sweat, which he had not mentioned. "A dog. A big one. I must go and clean up. My thanks for the use of the rowboat." Corelle strode away from the man, desperate to avoid any more awkward questions. She ran to the inn, where she met the same reaction from the innkeep. It took some time, but she persuaded him to tell her the number of the room Vamma had taken for them both.

She knocked on the door and called out to Vamma, who pulled the door open and stared at her wide-eyed, a hand over her mouth. "Are you hurt?"

"That I am not, do not worry. There are guards from Qagrue across Ort, and I met one of them. I must clean myself, and we must decide what we do."

"You met one of the guards?" Corelle nodded. "Is that his blood, then?" Corelle nodded again. "He is dead?"

She nodded a third time and splashed water on her face from the vanity bowl. Satisfied, she dried herself with her tunic and realised she had still not bought any others. Vamma pulled a pair of trousers and a tunic from her pack and Corelle pulled them on. They were an acceptable fit, though far from perfect. The two women were of similar height, but Corelle's breasts were larger, and the tunic felt snug across them. She looked up in distaste, but Vamma stared at her, her brow furrowed, and she seemed not to have noticed the ill fit of the tunic. "What is it?"

Vamma sighed. "What turns, Corelle?" She appeared distressed and fidgeted with the hem of her tunic as she shuffled her feet. "Four days ago, I thought myself nothing more than a simple stall-holder who drank a little more wine than she ought. Now a boy is dead, foreign guards stand on the streets of Ort, one of them is dead at your hand, and I am in the company of a woman who deals out death as a grandparent will hand out sweet treats to children."

"You are in no danger from me." Corelle must keep Vamma calm.

"I believe you. I think." Vamma blinked several times and Corelle feared she might lose control of her emotions. "Some purpose drives you, however, and death walks in your footprints."

Corelle weighed her answer with care. She had revealed much, and Vamma had not turned from her to this point. It seemed Vamma wanted the truth, but Corelle must present it in a palatable form that did not cause any further distress. "I tried to hide from the purpose that once drove me. I had not killed since you saw me kill those two men, until today. Whatever gnawed at me a year ago; whatever plan Krage worked on, it has come to fruition, and I do not know what to do."

Vamma pulled her close. "You will think of something." Vamma's voice soothed Corelle, but how had she soothed her own anxieties with such ease? "You should sleep for an hour or two. You are exhausted."

It could not be denied. Corelle had slept little the night before, and the tension of the encounter in Ort combined with the physical effort required to row the little boat against the tide had left her drained in mind and body. She lay down on the bed with Vamma beside her.

When Corelle drifted off to sleep, she stood naked before a reflecting glass. She gazed at her own reflection and saw pain in her eyes. To her surprise, Arella's face replaced her own in the glass. Sorrow lurked in Arella's eyes as she stared out of the glass at Corelle and whispered, "I love you." Deineike's face replaced Arella's and glared out at Corelle.

Anger flashed in the blue eyes Corelle had loved so much. "Did you avenge me?"

"That I did." Tears ran down Corelle's face.

Deineike also whispered, "I love you."

Pettra's face appeared in the glass now, still atop Corelle's neck and body. Raw, carnal need flashed in Pettra's eyes as she snarled, "Beat me."

"I cannot. Do not make me."

Pettra's jaw clenched, her lips thin and tight. "I love you." As she cried the words, Arella's face re-appeared.

Corelle sobbed, desperate for the faces to leave her alone. "What do you want from me?"

"My child." A blade sliced a vermilion ribbon across Arella's throat, and a baby fell out of the wound.

Corelle screamed, opened her eyes, and Vamma gazed down at her. She stroked Corelle's hair and murmured it had been nothing but a bad dream. Corelle slapped her hands to her eyes and cried out in frustration. She had killed again, and the nightmares had returned.

Vamma spoke in a soft, reassuring voice. "A dream, nothing more."

"I suffered from these dreams before. I have had none for many passes, but now they return. It is because I have killed, I am certain of it."

Vamma continued to stroke Corelle's hair. "Poor Corelle. Can I help in any way?"

Corelle lowered her voice to a whisper. She did not want death to overhear the confession she made. "That you cannot. Nobody can, it seems. I am frightened."

"What are you afraid of?"

"I am afraid you will enter my nightmares. I am afraid you will die because of me."

Vamma patted Corelle's arm as she whispered, "Hush, hush." She kissed Corelle's brow. "I will not die. You will keep me safe."

"How will I keep you safe?" Corelle pushed Vamma away so she could look her in the eyes. "I could not keep the others safe."

"I am not them. Things are not the same now as they were."

"Things are not the same? We do not know how things are. I cannot understand anything that has turned since I left The Salty Home in Alcmouth."

"Then we will leave. We will retrace our steps, head for Eastport. There we will take ship to some other land. You said yourself you might leave Dur."

"That I did. I said that before I realised Krage's plans might well have threatened or killed my friends. Gillar now calls himself the Portreeve of Ort. Ibie is dead, it seems."

Vamma stared at her, horror on her face. "I met Ibie and thought him kind. This is sad news."

"That it is, if it is indeed true." She reached down to her discarded trousers, pulled the parch out of the pocket, and handed it to Vamma.

When she had studied it, Vamma looked up. "Who is Sisnop?"

"He led the Guild in Torric. Now he names himself Bailiff, which could mean Raolos is dead." Corelle's voice broke as she spoke. The horror of the deaths of her friends weighed on her and stole her breath.

"Raolos, Pettra's husband? Is that correct?"

"That it is. Wilash might also be dead. Synna as well. Who knows?"

Tears flowed from Vamma's eyes. "How has Dur become caught up in these things? What will we do?"

Corelle took Vamma's chin in a hand and forced her to look into her eyes. "*We* will do nothing. You will return to Yerrsun and gather your belongings together. Then you will head for Dur City, or Solgarn. Somewhere you are not known, after all else. There you may start up your stall again and live a long and safe life."

Vamma fell silent. "And you?" The question had taken some time to arrive.

"I do not know." Corelle's sadness threatened to overwhelm her. "I could travel to Alcmouth to discover what has turned, or attempt to, at the least. I could head south and return to the mariner's life."

"Wherever you go, I wish to go also."

"Again you say this. Do not attach yourself to me. You said it yourself; death walks in my footprints."

"I will come with you. It is what I wish."

Corelle sighed in frustration. She had not wanted Pettra to

accompany her either, but for different reasons than the ones that drove her to warn Vamma off. Vamma's safety mattered first and foremost in this recent development, and moreover, Corelle had no idea what she would do. If she returned to sea, they would have to go their separate ways. The development in Ort had altered Corelle's plans, but uppermost in her mind she still wanted to leave Dur. If her friends had been killed, then they had been killed by forces too powerful for Corelle to defeat alone.

Vamma would not be dissuaded, it seemed. "The longer we debate this issue, the less time there is for us to decide on an effective plan."

Vamma's argument had merit, but Corelle had already had the germ of an idea, as risky as it might be. "I have a plan, of sorts, but it is dangerous, and I would prefer not to involve you in it."

"You will have little choice. I will dog your footsteps, like death itself."

"That is unfair. I become responsible for you for no reason other than your stubbornness."

"That it is. It is unfair. What is scribed, must be. I will not return alone to Yerrsun. I love you."

Corelle raised a finger to Vamma's lips, but the words had been spoken. "I do not love you." The words compounded her misery and condemned Vamma to an untimely death.

"I do not ask it. It is not an exchange, where one must attempt to outdo the other. Come, tell me this plan, at the least."

Corelle heaved a reluctant sigh but relented and explained her idea. The plan would be both dangerous and uncertain. Corelle still looked like a mariner. She would travel across the river under cover of darkness and come to the docks along the path the old woman had told her about. There she would pass herself off as nothing more than an intoxicated mariner who returned to her ship.

Vamma bit at her lower lip. "You are a woman."

"That I am. What of it?"

"How many women have you encountered who were mariners?"

"Many." Corelle had lied, and Vamma looked askance at her. "None. But I am a mariner, in truth. I will mislead them with my knowledge of the mariner's trade."

Vamma waited a few heartbeats before laughter burst from her. "That is a terrible plan. I have none better, after all else, so it must suffice, but it is the worst idea I have ever heard. I suspect they will cut us down as soon as they see us." Corelle agreed with her but said nothing. "Will some of those you know from the Guild not recognise you?"

"I look little enough as I once did, and the hour will be late. I believe I will be fine."

"Your eyes betray you. You are Corelle. Those eyes belong to no other."

Corelle laughed at the irony of Vamma's words. "These men have not gazed into my eyes much."

"That is their loss." The soft, warm smile that came to Vamma's lips spread to her eyes.

"I long for them to look into my eyes as I send them wherever they travel to afterward." Corelle imagined the scene in her mind.

Vamma nodded, resignation on her face. "When do we leave?"

"Now. I will borrow the rowboat again."

"That man will not be there at this late hour."

"I have never been above a little petty thievery. I will steal it."

"That you will not. You will pay for its use."

Corelle threw her hands up, perplexed. "How will I pay for it if he is not there?"

"Leave the coin with a note."

"A note? You wish me to leave coin and a note somewhere on the jetty and hope he finds it in the morning?"

"That I do. I have a scribing tool in my pack. You can scribe the note before we leave."

Corelle shook her head. She could not believe that in the face of all that seemed to have passed, honesty concerned Vamma most of all even as she stepped into the rowboat and headed for her almost certain ruin. "We should find his home and take his coin straight to him. We could bake him a cake as well if you wish."

Vamma ignored the sarcasm. "Do you have any parch?"

Vamma had ignored it, but the sarcasm had not left the room. "That I do not. I do have the cake, at the least."

Vamma looked up. "Are you annoyed?" Her eyes sparkled with mischief.

Corelle gasped in mock surprise. "Why would I be annoyed? All hangs in the balance, my plan is madness at best. My friends may all be dead, my own life might end at any moment, and I must scribe a note and leave payment for a rowboat my lover wishes me to use to spirit her across the Alc in total darkness. We are sure to hit a ship and drown. At least the rowboat owner will have a pleasant note to remember us by."

"Very well, we will leave no note. We will leave three regals on the jetty in payment."

After some moments, Corelle wiped at the spittle that ran down the side of her chin from her wide-open jaw. "Three regals? Do you want me to pay for the rowboat or a fleet of three-masted ships?"

Vamma's smile belied the shake of her head, as though the debate both amused and frustrated her. "Two regals then. Now cease this argument and let us be on our way."

Corelle shook her head. Why must all her lovers be so stubborn? She sighed. "Let us leave." Vamma had bested her. As they passed through the tavernroom, Corelle dashed behind the counter, found a small, half empty cask of wine, and dropped it into her pack. Vamma stared at her in surprise but said nothing.

Corelle muttered her frustration into the night air as she left two regals on the piling the man had tied the rowboat to. Vamma need not understand some of the ribald curses Corelle unleashed in the

Kuirbek language. She helped Vamma into the rowboat, no easy task. From the way Vamma struggled to board the boat, it was obvious she possessed neither the legs nor the ability to ride in boats. "Did you find it this difficult to board the last time you rode this boat?" Corelle stifled her laughter as Vamma fell face first to the bottom of the boat with a small grunt.

"Worse." Vamma crawled to the nearest bench with little dignity.

Corelle untied the line from the bow cleat and put the oars out before she rowed the boat out into the river. Faint moonlight glistened off the surface of the water in beautiful, jagged reflections. The moon cast sufficient light for Corelle to see that Vamma appeared unwell. "Are you ill?"

"I ate some cheese earlier. I think it had passed its prime." Vamma leaned over the side and fetched up.

Corelle smiled to herself as she felt some sense of revenge for the earlier banter about the note. "That it had."

Corelle tied the boat to the same jetty north of the docks, then endured a similar fracas as she helped Vamma onto dry land. Vamma sat on the jetty for many moments and drew in deep breaths as she attempted to calm her stomach. Corelle waited until Vamma stood and indicated she could proceed.

They crept forward through the garden and out into the street, slunk through the shadows, and turned into the small lane. The body of the Qagrue man had gone, which meant he had been discovered, and Corelle wondered what had been made of his death. They had no time to consider that issue now. After a lengthy search, Corelle again found what she suspected to be the start of the path the old woman had mentioned.

The path had become overgrown, as the woman had hinted. Corelle used her fan to cut back some of the growth so they could move forward along the long-abandoned pathway. At times they were forced to crawl beneath the more stubborn bushes, and they made slow, painful progress. They both cursed as various thorns stabbed them, stones tore at their knees, and malicious plants wrapped themselves around their legs and bodies.

At last, she saw an aura of light ahead that must be the docks. She paused, and Vamma cursed as she walked into her. Corelle whispered backward at Vamma. "We will pretend you are a courtesan. We will arrange your hair and clothes to make it appear we have lain together already." When she turned, Vamma's hair already lay in total disarray, her trousers stained by the earth and her tunic torn at the shoulder. She stifled a laugh. "No matter. You already look the part."

Vamma spat back her own ungracious barb. "As do you."

Corelle gazed on Vamma, her cheeks red, and her breaths rapid. Her hair lay about her face in utter chaos and her shoulder shone in the half light. Desire grew within Corelle as she looked at the stallholder. "You look wanton. We need not pretend we have lain together. Let us—"

Vamma interrupted her with a hiss that sounded like a cornered cat. "You would sacrifice Dur for a dalliance in the dirt?" Corelle did not reply. "Corelle?"

"Hush. I need to decide." Vamma slapped Corelle's upper arm. The blow stung, and Corelle guessed there had been little play and much anger behind the strike.

Vamma's earnest face moved closer to Corelle's own. "How long is the journey to Alcmouth?"

"Four or five days."

"Then we will have time enough to lie together on the ship, if that is the case. For now, we must move on."

Corelle laughed as she remembered Vamma's reaction to the rowboat. "You will not wish any intimacy on the journey."

"Why do you say this?"

"Have you ever sailed on a ship before?"

"That rowboat, three times. No other."

"You needed to fetch up as you crossed the Alc. This journey will take a heavy toll on you, I assure you."

"The cheese caused that."

Corelle laughed again. "That it did."

Vamma appeared thoughtful. "I will feel that way for the entire journey?"

"That you will. Deineike could not..." She did not finish the sentence, uncertain whether from grief at the memory of Deineike or some sense of guilt she discussed her former lovers with Vamma so often.

Vamma reached out and squeezed Corelle's arm. "I will bear it. If she could, I will also. Let us move on."

They pressed on until they had a clear view of the docks. Two three-masted ships and one two-master stood at the northern end of the dock. Beyond them, Corelle could see the dim shape of three more large ships, which must be the Qagrue vessels. "We cannot turn back once we leave this cover, but you can still turn back alone if you wish."

"I could not cross the Alc without you."

"There is an old woman nearby who would shelter you for the night. They will come in search of the rowboat tomorrow. They could take you back then."

Vamma nodded her head toward the lights of the docks. "Let us go."

Corelle reached into her pack and pulled out the wine. She took a drink, then spilled some of it down the front of her tunic.

Vamma hissed at her in the moonlight. "What are you about?"

"We must smell as though we have drunk wine if we are to pass ourselves off as inebriated." Corelle handed the cask to Vamma.

Vamma tipped the cask back, drank some of the wine, then threw the rest into the bushes. They stepped out onto the docks and staggered about as they moved forward. Corelle swept her eyes around the area but saw nobody. They had almost reached the first ship when two men came into view from behind some crates piled up near the edge of the dock. Both their tunics bore the Qagrue sigil, and they wore short swords at their hips.

One of them spoke in his own language, but Corelle did not understand him. "I do not unnerstan'." She slurred her words as she walked forward, an arm draped around Vamma's shoulder.

The other man held up a hand. "Where go?"

Corelle pointed to the ships but made sure her hand waved at every ship at the dock. "My ship. I take her aboard for some fun." She laughed and slapped Vamma's behind.

The two men spoke in their own language, and they sounded angry. It seemed they argued, and both pointed fingers at one another and at Corelle. Corelle could not understand the problem, and her heart raced. At length, one of them slapped down the hand of the other and turned to the women with a gesture they should proceed. Corelle muttered something she hoped they would take for inebriated thanks and pulled Vamma toward the first ship. Vamma whispered at her in anger as they walked up the ramp. "You will pay for that slap."

By good fortune, the ship belonged to Rakulaj, and she called for the master, showed him Rakulaj's button, which she had retained for over a year, and explained she needed to get to Alcmouth.

"We sail on the next tide, but we do not go to Alcmouth. We sail for Arkkyd."

Corelle sigh with disappointment. "Can you not put in at Alcmouth and let us off there?"

"Corelle of Dur, respect is due, but Alcmouth is not safe for you now. There is a new Duke, a new Bailiff, and the token is restored." He sounded unhappy at the news he delivered. Corelle guessed he had enjoyed Raolos's conditions of trade more than he would under Krage and Sisnop.

"What of the Duke and Raolos?" Corelle longed to learn of their fate

"I do not know this. I tell you no more than they told me when we arrived here in Ort earlier."

"How did Alcmouth seem to you, when you sailed past it?"

"It looked as it always does except one of these Qagrue vessels stood at the dock."

"You have heard nothing more, anything that explains what has turned?"

He shook his head in despair. "No." The strange negative response she had encountered in many of the lands of the Torr Sea still sounded strange in her ears. "I sailed here direct from Arkkyd, and I return there without delay."

Frustration drove a bitter tut from Corelle. She could no longer take Vamma to Alcmouth. The city would be too dangerous for her. She wondered whether they should sail to Vyrrmod on the ship. It would be safer for Vamma, but not for her. The master might know the answer, she hoped. "Would the Upholders be interested in my arrival in Arkkyd still?"

He shrugged his shoulders, noncommittal. "It is possible. I cannot say."

Corelle turned to Vamma. She saw an inquisitive look in Vamma's eyes, but Corelle had no good news for her, and she gave a defeated sigh. "We cannot sail on this ship." They walked back down the ramp.

CHAPTER 18
KRAGE

As Krage followed the shouts, screams, and clashes of steel, he spotted the three men he had dispatched to Dur ahead of his arrival. When they reached him, he greeted them like old friends, embraced them, and welcomed them to the new Dur. "What news do you bring?" He longed to hear what they had learned or done to make his ascent to power easier.

The men explained they had kidnapped Peben, the Duke's son, and framed it on Raolos through arguments about Ort, arguments they had learned of by threats against one of the Duke's closest staff members. The audacity of the plot amazed Krage, but it pleased him to learn the people were disappointed the Bailiff had allowed the son of the Duke to be snatched. "Where is the boy now?"

"We hanged him in the barn at the farm." The smugness in the voice of the man who replied shocked Krage, given the hideous crime he had admitted to. "The crime will further outrage the people."

Krage battled his smile, which threatened to become a frown at the news of the death of the boy. His own child had never been born, but he harboured resentment against Corelle, who took its life that day in Zhanghar. To kill innocents, children in particular, seemed cruel and unnecessary. If it ever emerged his men had killed the boy, the people's anger might turn against him. The unimportant masses of Dur did not matter, but unrest might threaten his income, and that mattered a great deal to Krage.

He studied the three men he had sent ahead of himself. He had thought he could trust them, but could they be trusted never to reveal their part in the death of the boy? Under some future duress, might they reveal it had been Krage who sent them to Dur to carry out their mission? Should he have them disposed of? He had shrouded men before, and this felt little different, but to kill them would leave him with fewer former Guild members he could depend on.

He could reward them, send them as Portreeves to various scattered, isolated parts of the land, but that could be even worse. It would look as though he condoned the murder of the boy and even rewarded the killers.

Krage cursed the politics he found himself involved in before he had even declared himself the Duke. He gushed his thanks and invited them to accompany him. He would decide their fate later. They should not have hanged the boy—even the Guild had standards, and the deaths of innocents had always been prohibited unless unavoidable. For now, he recalled some wise words he had once heard. *"Keep your friends close at hand and keep your enemies in your pocket."* He would keep them close until he decided on their fate.

They marched on toward the square and into the Portreeve's Offices, where the Qagrue brought a man before him. The man's arms were bound behind him, and two Qagrue soldiers dragged him between them. He stared at Krage with unbroken pride in his eyes as the soldiers held him upright. Blood ran from numerous cuts on his face, his nose askew as though broken. His tunic had been slashed at the shoulder and blood soaked the cloth.

Krage glanced around at the bodies on the floor, several Qagrue men among them. The Portreeve's men seemed to have defended him with determination. Against one wall, a man in the red tunic of the Portreeve sat on the floor, his back to the wall. He waved a dagger before him and spewed curses at the Qagrue soldiers who stared down on him in apparent amusement. The man's other arm lay across a terrible wound to his stomach. He could not survive such a serious wound and would bleed to death before long. Krage turned to one of the Guild members and nodded his head. The man stepped forward and grasped the wrist of the fallen man, which still waved the dagger, although with less gusto now. The Guild member leaned down and drove his dagger into the man's throat, who gurgled as he died.

Krage turned to the bound man, who stared at him in horror. "You used to be the Portreeve?"

"I *am* the Portreeve."

Krage gave a short laugh at the proud tone in the man's voice. "Are you indeed?" He ordered the Qagrue to hold the man, then turned to Carshan. "You are now the Portreeve of Alcmouth. Congratulations."

He turned and left the building. The shouts of protest from the deposed Portreeve rang in his ears as Krage walked toward the Bailiff's Offices and heard the unmistakeable sounds of combat from within. Metal clashed on metal, men cried out in encouragement or pain, and some screamed in agony. When Krage saw Jakedian nearby, he pointed to the Bailiff's Offices. More Qagrue surged forward and entered the building through the ornate Ortwood doors.

Sisnop wore his concern in plain view on his face. "Can we win?"

Krage reassured him, as a parent will calm a child afraid of the dark. "Of course we can, and we will. We have superior numbers, and the Qagrue are fighters, cruel and experienced. Soon we will have complete victory. Do not fret."

The sounds of combat receded until only the shouts and groans of men who cried for aid remained. A contingent of the Qagrue emerged through the doors, some bloodied and with wounds that dripped blood onto the cobbles of the square. Their leader came over to Krage and told him the Bailiff's Offices had been secured.

Krage's impatience to learn the fate of Raolos could not be kept inside. "Did you take the Bailiff alive?"

"Found him in his office but would not be taken alive. He dead along with many men. A good fight. I lost many soldiers. They died well."

Krage tutted, disappointed he could not hang the idiot, Raolos, who had been a thorn in his thumb since he threw his lot in with Corelle. Nonetheless, Krage had taken one more step toward success, and the Qagrue seemed unconcerned by their losses, as though they lived to fight. Krage smiled at Sisnop. "Congratulations. You are the Bailiff." Sisnop marched into his new Offices, and Krage ordered Jakedian to regroup his forces. They set off for the Ducal Highhome, Krage at the rear, impatient for this final step of his plan to be complete. It had been so easy, he felt almost disappointed in the Durfolk.

When they reached the Duke's Highway, a significant force had been assembled, armed and ready to defend the Highhome. Word must have reached the Duke's Offices. Many men in yellow tunics stood before the Highhome, and more red tunics than Krage had expected. Stragglers, survivors from the battles for the Portreeve's and Bailiff's Offices, he imagined. Many of them had crossbows, a weapon the Qagrue appeared to scorn. More defenders stood before them than Krage had anticipated, but the Qagrue still outnumbered them. He ordered Jakedian to attack.

The crossbows were cruel, and the barrage of bolts cut down

many of the Qagrue before they could reach the defenders. The fierce battle raged for some time. Although the Qagrue soldiers were well trained and used to battle, the stubborn resistance as men fought for their Duke and their land for the first time in their lives surprised Krage. The Qagrue's great numbers told in the end, but many had fallen before the last of the defenders had been put to the sword. The Duke's Highway before the doors of the Highhome ran red with blood, and the dead and dying of both sides littered it.

For the first time, Krage questioned his scheme. Had he been too ambitious? He had never seen such a fight between so many men, and he guessed the Qagrue might have lost a hundred men or more. He had four other cities to quash, and if the resistance in each of them proved this stubborn, four hundred Qagrue may be insufficient.

He ordered the Qagrue into the Highhome to sweep up any last pockets of resisters while he sat under a tree and brooded on his new-found doubt about the likelihood of success. As time went on, and the people saw him as a benevolent leader who only wished to improve the wealth of the land, resistance might crumble. He laughed to himself and wondered how well he could play the part of someone committed to the welfare of Dur rather than himself. More politics, he realised.

After a time, the Qagrue dragged a man in fine brocade clothing out of the building, bloody and battered, even though his appearance suggested he might not be much of a fighter. He yelled and insulted the Qagrue who pushed him before them as he demanded to know who had launched such a reprehensible attack on the Duchy. Krage took his time to rise as the Qagrue held the man upright before him. The former Duke of Dur, Krage's prisoner, whose life was about to come to an abrupt end.

"Who are you, you wretch?" Spittle flew from the Duke's mouth, his face bright red with anger.

Krage measured each word of his reply. "I am the Duke of Dur." He turned to his forces. "Somebody bring a stool or a chair, and some rope."

A large crowd had gathered, and they muttered in confusion. Some shouted insults as a Qagrue soldier brought a stool and placed it beneath the tree. No rope could be found for some time, and the crowd grew more restless. Some of the Qagrue menaced them with swords, which served only to stoke the fires of the Durfolk's ire. At last, some rope arrived and one of the soldiers fashioned a crude noose, which he placed around the Duke's neck. They pushed the Duke up onto the stool and tossed the rope over a branch. Several Qagrue soldiers held it and pulled it taut.

Krage leaned close to the Duke and whispered in his ear, so none nearby could hear his words. "Your son has been killed, I fear." He faced the Durfolk as even more people crowded behind to learn what turned. "The Duke has been found guilty of crimes against the Duchy. He stole coin from the people through an organisation known as the Guild. Its leader is now dead, and soon this traitor will be also." He faced the Duke again and smiled at his discomfort as he struggled not to fall from the stool and end his life before his tormentors chose to do so. "Where is Corelle?"

The Duke found defiance somewhere within and curled his lips in contempt as he replied. "Who?"

"You would defend a ruthless killer?" Krage could not believe the Duke had even pretended not to know her. He had nothing to gain from his ruse.

The Duke's defiant stare did not back down in the face of his imminent death. "I banished her. She will never return to Dur."

"That is not true. She has already been back, a year ago. I know this."

Hatred filled the Duke's eyes, and he spat in Krage's direction. The spittle missed and landed on the ground, but pride burned in the Duke's eyes as he turned to face the crowd. "People of Dur, it has been my greatest honour to serve—" Krage kicked the stool, and it flew away from him. The Duke fell toward the ground as the soldiers, caught unawares, struggled to hold his weight and keep him suspended in the air. The crowd cried out with one voice as the Duke choked to death. His legs kicked as though he tried to run, his body spun around, his face turned purple, and his eyes bulged. He gasped for breath and clawed at the noose, but his own weight held it too tight. It surprised Krage how long the Duke took to die, but at length his arms fell limp at his sides and his legs stilled. His body continued to spin, and it swung back and forth in the gentle breeze.

Krage sought out the Qagrue leader. "Bring me the former Portreeve. Let us see where his allegiances lie." The Duke's attempted defiant speech had caught Krage on the back foot. He had expected the man to cry, bleat, and plead for his life. Instead, he had begun a speech that might have started further unrest had Krage not ended it.

The soldiers dispersed the crowd, rougher than might have been necessary, but Krage ignored them and entered the Highhome. Some members of the Duke's staff stood at the entrance, and many of them cried and embraced one another. Krage snapped at them. "Take me to the Duke's office." One asked him to follow. The Guild members followed behind, but none of the Qagrue had entered the Highhome with him. He felt glad to be rid of them for a time. Sailing north for so long with them had been most unpleasant. They were vulgar and violent and often fought among themselves. They had a pungent aroma he found difficult to stomach. On balance, he did not like them, and he would send them back to Qagrue once he no longer had need of them.

Krage settled in the enormous chair in the Duke's opulent office and placed his feet on the enormous desk before him. He permitted himself a self-satisfied smile. He had done it, and in the end, it had been easy enough. Styrrach's limited vision could never have foreseen this moment. His smile grew larger, and he looked around the office in delight. He chuckled as he spoke his achievements aloud. "Krage, Duke of all Dur."

CHAPTER 19
CORELLE

Corelle and Vamma trudged down the ramp back onto the docks. Corelle headed straight for the two-master, certain any hint of indecision would attract unwanted attention. She whispered to Vamma, "This is a disaster. The Qagrue are here, and we must reason they have captured Alcmouth also. I cannot decide whether they have sailed further north. Curse you, Krage." She spat his name out like a bitter fruit. "This must have been his plan all along. I did nothing more than delay him when I chased him from the farm."

"Do not blame yourself." When Corelle did not reply, Vamma asked what they would do now.

Corelle's mind had wandered, lost in her hatred of Krage, but she dragged her attention back to Vamma's question. "We cannot remain in Ort, and we cannot go to Alcmouth. We must leave Dur."

"In that case, why did we not sail on that ship?"

"I am sought in Vyrrmod, where it sails. They never resolved the matter of Pettra's death, nor the man I killed in revenge, my guess."

"What of the other large ship? Or this smaller one?"

"This one will not sail beyond Dur. It is too small for the open sea. The other might sail for another land."

"Then we should have gone to that ship."

The truth in Vamma's words nipped at Corelle with sharp teeth of recrimination. "That we should. I have piled poor decision upon poor decision. I should not have involved myself at all." She rued the day she had overheard the conversation in the tavern in Alcmouth.

Vamma seemed to sense Corelle's distress, and she wrapped her words in a warm blanket of comfort. "Then we would not have been together." Vamma slid an arm around Corelle's own and gripped her forearm. "I am happy you made that decision."

Corelle flashed her a grateful smile. "We can either sail south and abandon Dur, or go north to Zhanghar, in hopes the Qagrue do not reach there before us."

"How will we decide?"

"We will not. The master of this ship will. Unless he sails to Alcmouth, we will go where he goes and—" She pulled Vamma into a tight embrace and kissed her as the Qagrue patrol walked their way. Corelle made a snap decision, pulled back from Vamma, and dragged her up the ramp onto the deck. She hoped the men would not follow them out of some curiosity over their apparent change of vessel.

She marched, determined, to the aft deck and asked the officer on watch to bring the master. She did not dare glance around in case she aroused the patrol's curiosity further. Vamma could not have known what had turned awry, but she tapped her feet and fidgeted as though she had picked up on Corelle's sudden anxiety. It seemed the master had been woken from his sleep, and he appeared irritated about it.

"I serve Raolos." Corelle regretted the words the moment she spoke them. Raolos no longer served as Bailiff, by all accounts. His word carried no weight anymore.

The master glared at her. "Do you serve him, or these others who usurp the Duke? Speak true now, or you will both find yourselves in the Alc with your throats cut."

The irony of the threat amused Corelle, but the master's words brought cautious optimism. She pulled Raolos's letters from her pack and showed them to the master. He nodded as he read them, then returned them to her. "Very well. How can I be of service?"

"Where do you sail next?"

"Zhanghar. I will not sail to Alcmouth, but they have not gone north yet. I fear it will not be long. They have been in Ort for four days, I hear. They will head north; I am certain of it. They were not in Ort when I docked here a tenday ago, but I went to Ryl, then Zhanghar and back here. I docked yesterday."

"You have a cargo for Zhanghar?"

"I have a cargo for Zhanghar, and on to Ryl, if that is what my cargo needs. Will you fight?"

Corelle chewed at her lower lip. "How many of them are there, these Qagrue men?"

"I have been told there are two hundred or more here. In Alcmouth, I cannot say."

"So many. How can Dur resist such a force?" Corelle looked down in despair.

"The Duke and Bailiff are gone. Some say they are dead. Somebody must ensure every man who is available and able fights back. They are two hundred, and you say that is too many. I guess many times that number of Durfolk are here in Ort, available to join anybody who will lead them." His voice and intense stare left Corelle in no doubt; he wanted her to be that leader.

"Why me?"

"Because you served him, if those letters do not lie. Who else?"

"I am a mariner. I do not know how to fight hordes of men."

He mimicked her, but his voice dripped with sarcasm. "I am a mariner." He adopted a firmer tone. "You are Corelle, or so the letters say. You are legendary. You brought an end to the era of the token. You killed Styrrach, who ruled us with that infernal device and made sure we earned a fraction of the coin due to us. You are more than a mere mariner."

She glared at him as she struggled to contain her embarrassment. "High praise from a man who threatened to throw me into the Alc moments ago."

He coughed and glanced at his feet. "My apologies. I would not have made that threat had I known who you are." He chuckled. "It would have been me and my crew in the water, my guess."

She returned to the matter at hand with a resigned sigh. "Nonetheless, I speak the truth. Stealth, surprise, deception. These are my strengths. I do not know how to organise large masses of men into some sort of force, then instruct them how to beat well-armed opponents.

"Others will help, others will know. The Zhanghar Portreeve will have men. Ryl also. Word can be sent to Torric, Dur City, Vjort, all the towns. Men will come. I am certain of it. If we… if you do nothing, each of those towns and cities will fall, isolated. Together, this is how we can fight."

She smiled at his words. "It sounds as though you should lead, not me."

He blushed. "I will do all I can. I have this ship, and a good crew. Both are at your disposal."

"Is Raolos dead? The Duke also?"

"I know not, more than rumours that sail aboard the ships, and they are more plentiful than the rats in the holds. The rumours say they have both been slain. The Duke hanged in public, I hear."

Corelle had expected the news, but it saddened her to hear it confirmed. "When is the next tide?" She longed to be away before they were caught.

"We will slip away at once. We are not truly safe here if we are about to take on this abomination who now sits in the Highhome."

Corelle muttered to herself. "Krage, I am sure of it."

The master must have heard. "I have not heard his name before. It will be poison on my tongue until you have spilled his blood."

She turned and gazed over the dock. "There are no dockworkers. Will you throw away your lines?"

He nodded, as though she had confirmed something with her words. "I heard you have some skills as a mariner. Is it true?"

She laughed. "That much I will admit to."

He studied her for a moment. "Bow line your speciality, my guess."

His perception amused her. "Stern. I never miss."

"We will test that claim in Zhanghar, then." He smiled at her, shared warmth in a difficult time. "As for your question, that we will. We have rope aplenty aboard to replace them." Under normal circumstances, the dockworkers would untie the bow and stern lines and throw them up to the ship. This night, the lines would be untied from the ship and left tied to the cleats on the dock so the ship could sail away into the river.

Corelle nodded. "I do not doubt it."

The master considered for a heartbeat, then offered his hand. "Tamgellan." She shook his hand. "A pleasure to have you aboard."

"The pleasure is ours. This is my companion, Vamma." Vamma had remained silent throughout the lengthy conversation, but she shook Tamgellan's hand and expressed her pleasure to sail on his ship.

Tamgellan snapped orders, and mariners ran to the lines, untied them and threw them over the side. Others pulled on ropes, and sails climbed the masts, billowed in the breeze. Shouts came from the dock, and the mariners shouted back a few insults in response. The ship headed north as its sails filled with precious wind. A few Qagrue gathered at the edge of the dock, swords in hand, but none had crossbows, and unless they could swim, they were powerless to attack the ship. They were away, and Vamma hung over the rail and fetched up.

CHAPTER 20
CORELLE

The voyage north to Zhanghar took little more than two days, aided by strong, hot winds from the south. Vamma remained ill for the entire journey and slept little throughout. By the time Zhanghar came into sight soon after the midday, the pale skin, the dark circles beneath her eyes, and the frazzled hair told the story of her exhaustion and misery. Corelle stood at the bow and peered forward in anxiety but saw no Qagrue ships at the dock. Relief flooded through her, but they still had no time to waste. Once the Qagrue took Zhanghar, they would control the Alc and would have access to most of the trade to Dur. Corelle had little doubt that the accrual of wealth lay behind Krage's scheme. It had always been more than vengeance against her; the entire land did not need to be embroiled in that, and there would be no reason for Qagrue to become involved in a fight between her and Krage. Great quantities of coin lay behind these developments, she had no doubt.

She urged Vamma to stay aboard the ship but understood when she protested she wished to stand on solid ground for a time. Vamma agreed to find a bench within sight of the ship and to be ready to board in a heartbeat should it prove necessary. As soon as the ramp had been secured, Corelle ran down it and headed for the square. She passed The Ship's Yard and slowed her pace to a walk, overwhelmed by memories of all that had turned there. Her happiness as her relationship with Arella developed, followed by the decline into dejection as the full magnitude of her impetuous decision to join the Guild sank in. The fateful night she snuffed out the life of the woman she loved with no more than a moment's hesitation.

Corelle shook the thoughts from her head and picked up her pace again. She reached the Portreeve's Offices a little over an hour later, and she slowed to a walk once more, the better to regain her breath for speech. A woman stood behind the counter in the lobby, and Corelle handed her Raolos's letters, which she had stuffed into the waistband of her trousers as she left the ship. At first, the woman appeared prepared to argue Raolos no longer served as the Bailiff, but something in the set of Corelle's jaw or the flash of urgency in her eye ended the argument, and she ushered Corelle through the doors and onward to the Portreeve's office. Corelle poured out a rapid explanation of the pieces of the puzzle she knew about. News of Alcmouth's and Ort's changes in situation had already come to the Portreeve's ears, and it did not surprise him Zhanghar might be next to see the Qagrue ships moor at its docks.

He appeared conflicted. "What do you propose we do?" The question suggested he needed guidance.

It seemed everybody looked to Corelle for leadership, but she had no plan and no desire to lead these people. "I doubt you can resist them, if they come." His head dropped, his shoulders slumped, and any pretence of stoicism fell from him at her words. "You can gather your men and sail to Ryl. A ship heads there as soon as you can be ready. Send word to Dur City and Torric, Vjort, Delcan, Yerrsun, any large town. Ask any who have the stomach for a fight to come to Ryl. If they come there, you might hold the Qagrue off."

"You mean we can hold them off, do you not?"

"You. We. It matters not. It is doubtful you will defeat them, after all else. I am sorry. I can give you no further hope than this."

A brief silence descended on the room before he spoke again. "What of my people? What of Zhanghar?"

A small shrug confirmed her uncertainty. "I do not know, in truth. Coin lies behind these events, I believe. Without the people, Dur would be naught but bare ground. Your people should not be hurt if they do not resist." She looked down, guilty she might have given him false hope. "I do not know the answer. I am sorry."

He sighed, a heavy sigh of resignation, defeat, and hopelessness, she thought. "Very well. I will come to the docks as soon as I can, with such men as will come with me. I will send word for as many of the citizens to meet us there as possible." She opened her mouth to object, concerned he meant to bring the entire population of Zhanghar with him, but he insisted. "I cannot abandon them without explanation. I must give them some hope."

Corelle admired his demeanour. All he had believed throughout his life had been torn asunder in less than a pass, and now he must abandon everything he cherished—his position, his people, his city. Yet he still considered those he served. How different a character from the likes of Gillar and Krage. "I will meet you at the docks." She headed back out of the building, across the square, and on toward the docks.

Corelle sat beside Vamma on the bench and watched the Alc flow past. It lapped at the hulls of the ships moored at the dock. Vamma's colour had returned, and the fresh air appeared to have rejuvenated her somewhat. She asked Corelle how the conversation with the Portreeve had gone, and Corelle explained all they had discussed. "Does that mean we sail for Ryl today?"

Corelle took her hand. "That it does. I am sorry. You must ride the ship again."

Vamma gazed at the ship for some time. "It could be worse. I could be dead."

A bell rang somewhere behind them, accompanied by a great commotion. They both turned to watch a large crowd follow the Portreeve and his men onto the dock. One of the men rang a hand-bell that looked heavy and had a loud peal. Corelle pointed the Portreeve out to Vamma, and they walked toward the throng. With some help from his men, the Portreeve clambered onto some crates and held out his hands for silence.

Curiosity and anxiety held the assembled crowd in its grip as he addressed them. "Citizens of Zhanghar, many of you have doubt-less heard rumours of great change that sweeps across Dur. Our beloved Duke has been replaced by an imposter." He paused for effect, but Corelle guessed many of the crowd were already afraid enough. "It seems trouble will come to our door soon, and as a city we are ill equipped to deal with it. It has been suggested we form a force to resist these invaders and assemble it in Ryl. Letters have been sent to the cities and towns not yet under the yoke of these foreigners. With luck, many of their inhabitants will join us there. I sail now with my men for Ryl. Will any of you join us? We may need to fight, but the future of our Duchy is at stake."

A loud murmur went up from the crowd as he ended his speech. They may not have understood all the words, but the message had been received. Corelle watched as small groups debated among themselves what the words meant for them.

Somebody shouted, "What of us?" A loud chorus of agreement echoed around the docks.

"We urge you not to resist when the southerners come. It is our belief you will not be harmed. Life will go on, up to a point, but it will not be as we knew it unless we can fight back and send these southerners home with their tails between their legs." They were powerful words, but they were empty. Corelle did not believe the Qagrue could be defeated by the limited numbers of untrained men and women who might be prepared to resist them.

Somebody else roared that the former Duke must be to blame, and others claimed the Zhanghar Portreeve should answer for this crisis. As the argument grew louder, some in the crowd pushed and shoved each other, and Corelle feared order would break down, but the Portreeve's man rang the bell again, and silence rippled across the crowd once more.

The Portreeve gazed around, then drew a deep breath. "Do not argue with one another. Do not lay blame at any door, I urge you. If you must blame somebody, then blame me, for we believe the Duke is dead, and we have lost a great man. Will any join us?"

Several men raised their hands, more than Corelle had expected. The Portreeve's men helped him down from the crates and they pushed through the crowd that now encircled him. Corelle shoved people aside and reached his entourage. "This way." She pointed to the ship. The men who had volunteered to travel with them followed the red tunics of the Portreeve's men up the ramp, and Corelle counted them as they boarded the ship. Twenty-six red tunics and eight other men. She thought that came to thirty-four, and Vamma confirmed it. Thirty-four, plus however many would fight in Ryl, against two hundred Qagrue. It would be hopeless, but they had no more unless more Durfolk came from other towns and cities.

Corelle doubted any from Dur City or any of the Eastlands towns would answer the call. They had little enough to do with the westfolk, and she felt Krage and the Qagrue were unlikely to show any interest in the east where trade would always be difficult and the people strange. Life need not change much for the Eastlands, and she saw no reason for them to aid the cause of Dur in such circumstances.

Corelle followed Vamma up the ramp onto the ship, and the

master made ready to sail. They had a favourable tide and would soon be out of the river and into the coastal waters of the Northern Ocean. She gazed over the crowd as sails were unfurled and ropes untied. The people stood around, reluctant to leave the docks yet, unable to believe all that turned in their land—talk of an invasion of southerners, the Duke killed, their Portreeve and his men gone from the city. As the ship slid out into the water and headed for the Northern Ocean, the crowd watched it go, and an eerie silence settled on them. To Corelle, it seemed as though they watched their own lives sail away to leave behind empty shells, leaderless and with no direction. Vamma clutched at her as the waves tossed the ship about, and Corelle guessed her stomach would suffer more once they reached the ocean, where the swell would be heavier.

Vamma ran to the rail and fetched up. On this journey, many of those who boarded in Zhanghar suffered with her, the Portreeve among them. It would be a difficult journey for them, and one with little hope in sight at the end. Corelle's own future had no more clarity than theirs. She did not wish to linger in Dur and pondered how she might sail away from Ryl and head south. She might take Vamma with her, for her own protection.

As they sailed along the coastline to the north of Dur, heavy seas in the Northern Ocean battered the little ship. Corelle sat at the bow most days, while Vamma either suffered in agony at the rail nearby or slept in their cabin. During her year on The Salty Home, Corelle had not sailed the Northern Ocean, and as they ploughed west through the swell, she wondered what lands lay to the north of Dur, if any. If the rumours about Ictharelian proved true, could they sail west from the mouth of the Alc and keep sailing until they came back to it?

It baffled her to ponder the matter, but it fascinated her too. The mass of lands around the Torr Sea might not be the only lands in existence, and the thought excited her. If other lands lay on the opposite side of a globe, were they always in darkness, or did it become light there during the black of night in Dur? If such lands existed, would there be any people there? How could they not fall off the land and end up in the sky? Corelle longed to return to sea even more as she wrestled with these thoughts during the voyage. She spent her nights in bed beside Vamma, but neither of them slept much thanks to Vamma's unsettled stomach.

Four days after they left Zhanghar, Corelle saw a city silhouetted against the horizon ahead of the ship. The skyline still looked familiar, even after so long. After six years away, Corelle had returned to Ryl.

CHAPTER 21
KRAGE

Krage leaned back and felt small in the oversized chair that in turn felt small compared to the enormous desk in the Duke's office. Previous Dukes must have been full of their own importance if the size of the furnishings in the office could be believed. The massive office made any house or rooms Krage had ever lived in except Estway Farm seem tiny. The farmhouse had been huge, but no room at the farm had been anywhere near the size of this office.

His head whirled. Some insignificant tally clerk bored him with stories about the revenue the Duchy could expect to generate, and the man had bleated at some length about the share of the Duchy's trade revenue Krage had agreed to give to the Qagrue. Krage stopped the man mid-sentence and asked if he would be poor. "That you will not, my Duke." The man sounded subservient, something Krage found he disliked. The man should be afraid of him, of course, but this sounded different, as if the man considered himself unworthy to be in the office of the Duke. What a strange affair, that the sheets the Duke had been sired between should be counted more than his deeds. He dismissed the man and watched with contempt as he turned at the door and bowed before he left.

Krage always kept one of the Guild members with him in the office. It had been two days since they had taken control of Alcmouth, and he did not know whether any resistance might be mounted. Better safe than sorry, he thought. Today's guard had once been a Torric member, one whose face Krage had come to recognise on the voyages south, then north again. He seemed careful, always alert, and he flicked his eyes around without end. Krage guessed he would detect any threat long before it could reach the new Duke. What the man would choose to do about that threat remained to be determined.

He studied the man, who was short and slightly built, with close-cut blond hair. He looked like most Guild members, in truth. A certain type appeared suited to the work, Krage thought, although he did not fit that type himself. He stood tall and more well-built than the typical Guild member. He had performed few gests himself, of course; a few in the early days, but he soon had others doing the deadly work on his behalf.

Krage had pondered the death of the Duke's son and what action he should take about it for two days. He studied the guard, then asked, "What is your name?"

"Ricrid, my Duke." Ricrid had picked up the designation from the Aides, Krage guessed, but he had none of the servile subordination in his voice. He served Krage, but his confident air suggested he believed he would emerge victorious from a fight with his Duke. He had no fear of his employer. Would he have been afraid of Styrrach? Nobody would ever know, thanks to the jade, Corelle, but everyone had feared Styrrach. How could this man have been any different from the other Guild members who had quailed before Styrrach's monstrous evil?

Krage respected Ricrid's forthrightness. "Did you hear the tale of the Duke's son?"

Ricrid's reply sounded guarded, as if he had many words to say on the matter but wanted to be miserly in their use. "That I did."

"What do you think of the deed?" Ricrid did not answer. He gazed at his Duke and seemed to weigh what response might be expected of him, so Krage encouraged him. "Speak your mind."

"It is possible the boy might have returned to Alcmouth at some later date, backed by powerful supporters, and lay claim to the Duchy through his bloodline."

Krage nodded at the studied reply. "I hanged his father for treachery. That betrayal sundered his bloodline, did it not?"

"That it did." Ricrid stood stiff and uncomfortable, as though he still held something back.

"But?" Krage pushed for whatever Ricrid kept from him.

No change to his demeanour betrayed Ricrid's opinion of his answer. "They hanged a boy."

Krage agreed. He had been a boy, nothing more. Members of the Guild became hardened to death and would kill almost anybody for the right price. Most, in Krage's experience, felt reluctant to kill children. Children were above the petty politics of coin or were innocents who played no part in any dispute with another party. Krage could not determine why this unspoken rule applied, but it did. Krage had been unhappy from the moment his men revealed they had hanged the boy, and Ricrid, a remorseless killer, appeared to feel the same. "You would have taken a different approach?"

A short, sharp intake of breath preceded his answer. "Who can say what they would do in a situation unless they find themselves in it? The man who tells you what he would have done is never wrong, for he did not need to act. I cannot judge all circumstances those men found themselves in."

The insight of the answer shocked Krage, and he fought to keep any admiration from his face. "And those who killed him. What of them?"

Ricrid delayed his answer so long, Krage wondered if he had

not heard the question. When he did reply, each word seemed slow, as though Ricrid dragged them over hot coals of caution. "My Duke, they are your men."

"You are from Torric?"

"That I am."

"You do not prefer to guard Sisnop?"

Ricrid gave a casual shrug, as though the question had been unnecessary. "He was my Guildmeister. You are the Duke."

The reply again sounded cautious to Krage. More had not been said than had, and he wanted to hear the full story. "You know him more than you know me."

At last, Ricrid abandoned some of his caution. "My Duke, Sisnop wished to reinstate the Guild. Under his scheme, I would be required to slink down the road in shadow and kill fat, unsuspecting merchants for coin. I would live in a room over a filthy inn. I would glance over my shoulder whenever I went outside. Instead, I live in the Ducal Highhome, and I walk down the street with pride. This tunic, as ridiculous as it looks, parts crowds. I walk wherever I will—in the sunshine if I wish, or in the shadow if I am hot. None pursue me; all respect me. That is the difference between Sisnop and you."

Krage agreed the tunics looked ridiculous. Bright yellow and ordained with fancy pieces of cloth, they were despicable. He had decided to retain them for now, to ease the transition for the Durfolk. Too much change and unfamiliarity might stir unrest, but he had dispensed with the foolish hats the former Duke's men had worn. They reminded Krage of a pitcher flattened on one side, and were undignified in every way. Krage returned to the original topic. "The men who killed the boy?"

How could every word Ricrid uttered seem devoid of any emotion, any judgement? "He was nine years."

The answer caught Krage off guard. "He was what?"

"Nine years, my Duke. That is what some of your staff tell me.

That is too young for such a harsh death. To hang a boy of nine years..."

He did not finish the sentence because he did not have to. "He can say nothing, at the least." Krage aimed to learn Ricrid's true thoughts on the matter despite the careful, neutral words he spoke.

"His body can. Any who can link it to you can. Who knows who will find his body? They killed him at the farm. Reckless." He paused, then added, "No more than a boy."

Krage nodded. He steepled his fingers, his elbows on the desk as he leaned forward. "Can you make them disappear?"

Ricrid's expression did not change, but he did not answer for some time. "All three?"

"All three." Krage accompanied his response with a sad nod of acknowledgment.

"Is that wise?"

"He was nine years." Krage tried not to think of the young boy, how he must have kicked and choked as his father had, as his life left him after so few years. Ricrid gave him a cursory nod and made no answer. "Let me know when it is done. You will be appointed Sergeant, in charge of my personal guard. No word of this conversation need be recalled by either of us at any future time." Another nod.

Krage felt satisfied with the way Ricrid had answered the questions and felt he would be a trustworthy man to keep close at hand. He had been neither pleased nor displeased with Krage's decision it seemed, but to kill so young a boy when other options had existed could not be allowed to pass without recrimination.

Krage heard a commotion outside the office, and Ricrid crossed the room to stand between Krage and the door, dagger drawn. Krage opened a drawer in the desk and took out his own dagger. Gruff-voiced Qagrue shouts came through the door, followed by a knock and an alarmed cry from one of his Aides. "My Duke."

Krage called out, "Enter."

The door swung open, and an Aide stood in the door, nervous and fidgety. "My Duke, the Qagrue wish an audience."

"Then send them in." Krage placed the dagger on his lap despite his bright, cheery reply. "They are our trusted allies. They are welcome here at any time."

He needed them, the simple truth. Once all Dur came under his control and any potential resistance had been quelled, they could return south. He was Durfolk, and he felt sure the people would not care which Duke sat in the enormous office as long as their dull lives continued as they always had and the Qagrue took their brutality back to their own land far to the south. Until that day, he had need of the Qagrue's numbers. The Aide turned, gave an exaggerated bow, then extended an arm into the Duke's office as an invitation.

Jakedian entered the office, accompanied by three of his soldiers. One carried a crossbow, and Krage smiled. None of the Qagrue had carried the weapon when they arrived, but they had seen its deadly impact outside the Highhome. They must have decided not to be outmatched by the terrible instrument again. Krage could not still not recall Jakedian's full name. The Qagrue had names longer than he had time to learn, even if his tongue had the ability to wrap itself around them. He beamed at them. "Welcome, my friends,"

The terse reply did not surprise Krage. These people were direct and to the point, after all else. "Men crave more."

Krage knitted his brows as he tried to fathom what more they wanted. It had been but two days since they arrived. They could not have supped all the ale and eaten all the food in Alcmouth yet. Women? There were plenty of those also, he felt certain. "I apologise, my friend. What do your men crave?" He kept his voice level and polite. It would not do to reveal impatience or distaste for these unusual, unpleasant men.

"Fights, cities. Want to take cities."

Krage had not expected them to become restless quite so soon. He did not want to send them from Alcmouth yet. There had been isolated reports of resistance. The Qagrue had put them down with a little too much enthusiasm, Krage felt, but without them, he would have no real force to resist any who were unhappy with the new order. "What of the resistance here?" He wondered about the wisdom of a move to another city so soon.

"We leave men here, kill resists." The leader's broken Dur often proved difficult to follow. "Take rest to next city."

Krage had planned to take Alcmouth, Ort and Zhanghar first. The bulk of the trade came to the capital or up the Alc to the other docks. Once he controlled the river, he would turn his attention to Torric and Ryl. He had little interest in the Eastlands. They could wait; a wretched place, like a piece of food cast from a dog's bowl the dog might scratch for if it grew hungry later. "Do we rush things a little?"

"Must go to new city. Men restless. Restless men dangerous. Drink, fight, could kill soft Durs."

Krage guessed that by 'soft Durs,' he meant the citizens. Blood in the streets of the capital city should be avoided at all costs. "Very well." He smiled and summoned false enthusiasm. "Let us press on. Take three ships to Ort. It is the next town north."

"Is not city? Is small?" He looked worried.

Krage laughed. "It is not a city, though it should be. It is large. You will not be disappointed. Gillar will accompany you. He will become the Portreeve there. Let us say you will take three ships tomorrow and leave some men here. Does that suit?"

"This very good." At their leader's reply, his men slapped each other on the backs. They must have understood enough to know they were about to leave Alcmouth.

"Remember, only kill any who resist you, please." Krage maintained a smile so broad, his cheeks ached. "Once Ort is controlled, leave some men with Gillar, and take your ships north to Zhanghar.

Send word when that is ours, and I may sail north and celebrate with you."

"You not celebrate with Qagrue. You soft Dur, celebrate with us kill you." Jakedian roared with coarse, gruff laughter.

"Quite." Krage fought to keep the smile on his face.

Jakedian turned to Ricrid, and a chill menace crept into his tone. "You best put away needle, soft Dur. I not take offence. Others not so care as me. Caution, little man."

Ricrid's eyes did not leave the leader's, but at once the atmosphere became charged with tension. Krage's hand slid to his own dagger. Ricrid's smile held more threat than friendship, but he slid his dagger into his waistband.

The Qagrue slapped him on the shoulder. "All friends again, Qagrue and Durs." He turned from the room. His triumphant roars, and those of his men, could be heard as they echoed down the corridors of the Highhome until they passed from earshot.

Krage released the nervous breath he had held as the situation between Ricrid and Jakedian had worsened. He muttered aloud to himself, "What vile creatures."

Ricrid said nothing in reply. He returned to his position near the door and turned to face his Duke.

"What a distasteful incident." Krage muttered to himself again as he reached for the bottle of wine on his desk and poured himself a goblet. "It is so difficult to be a leader." He took a gulp of the wine and wiped the sweat from his face with a sleeve. "So difficult."

CHAPTER 22
CORELLE

It had been more than a tenday since they arrived in Ryl, and Corelle had been busy as she contemplated how best to defend the city if the Qagrue came. She knew nothing of the tactics needed to fight in city streets, but she saw some places where a mass of men might be funnelled into narrow streets, so stout-hearted defenders could battle fewer of the enemy at the front of their mass. In addition, people positioned on rooftops could use crossbows to pick away at the men toward the rear of the Qagrue force.

Long hours passed as she taught men how to wield daggers, the vulnerable parts of the body, the quickest way to put your opponent down, to be always on the move to make yourself harder to hit. She urged them to keep their daggers razor sharp. Swords might be unwieldy, even the shorter ones the Qagrue carried, but if one struck a man, he would suffer severe damage from the weight of the weapon swung with all the strength another could muster. Such a wound might not kill at once, but the loss of blood would take its toll.

Corelle worked with those who showed the most promise and

taught them how to dodge so they were not struck. The hard work and long hours exhausted her. At the end of many days of training, the Qagrue ships had still not appeared. They had fewer than a hundred men available to defend the city; more if the citizens joined in, although they had no training. It would not be enough, she often reflected, certain she would find her ruin in the very city in which she had been born.

Her nights with Vamma were passionate. They made love as though no more days remained to them, which might be the reality when the Qagrue came. They had taken rooms in the area Arella had lived in when Corelle had first met her. Vamma would talk of her day after their desires had been sated, how she had wandered the city and encouraged any who would stop to talk to her for a few moments. Along with the Portreeve's wife and other women from the city, she had worked to establish a haven where men and women injured in any fight could be brought and treated with such care and attention as could be provided. For long hours, they tore up bedsheets the people brought to the aid station, to make bandages from them. The people also brought blankets they stacked up against a wall. One of the city's chirurgeons had told them a person who suffered a deep wound needed to be kept warm or their body could shut down.

Vamma doubted the story, but Corelle believed it. She had seen people shut down as soon as they became threatened, unable to react or even comprehend what turned, wounded or not. As an example, she told Vamma the story of how Wilash, Klordia, and Deineike had been in some sort of trance after she had killed the two men in the alleyway behind the Bailiff's Offices. She had heard it called shock, and people would stand open-mouthed, incapable of any action.

Four days after they arrived, a ship brought word; Zhanghar had fallen to the Qagrue. Krage now controlled the Alc, and it must only be a matter of time before he came for Ryl. Corelle reasoned he might send the Qagrue to Torric first, the more important trade point of the two. Ryl had no direct trade with the southerners, who sailed no further than Zhanghar. All goods that arrived in Ryl were brought from Zhanghar or Ort, and it seemed no more ships would sail to Ryl until the Qagrue came.

Why had Styrrach included Ryl in his scheme? He would have made profit on the goods he moved here from Zhanghar, and wealth aplenty could be found in Ryl, but it seemed unnecessary in the wider scheme of things. He could not have made as much coin as he would in Torric, Alcmouth or Zhanghar. Ort would have been more profitable for him than Ryl, Corelle guessed, but his schemes there were thwarted by a Portreeve whom he could not buy. Now that Portreeve had been killed, along with Corelle's other friends, and she suffered long periods of stressful sadness when she thought of the injustice of such good men killed by the heinous creature that squatted in the Ducal Highhome these days.

After several days, Corelle gave in to Vamma, who had pestered her to visit her parents. She stood some way from the shop for a while and made sure no customers were inside. Nothing had changed—the same pale blue shopfront, although it seemed to have been repainted in recent times. The windows gleamed in the sunlight, her parents' making displayed there on crude wooden figures meant to resemble people.

Corelle felt certain no customers were in the shop, but her feet were reluctant to move forward. She had resisted Vamma's pleas for days, worried her parents would be displeased to see her or would be so offended by any stories they may have heard, they would not even speak to her. Vamma had called the idea ridiculous, and Corelle had given in to the insistent suggestions.

She gazed on the little shop where she had learned her making skills. She imagined the Portreeve whose wife had taken the dress without any payment had been in thrall to Styrrach on the day he visited the shop. The thought of a corrupt man's wife who stepped from a carriage at city balls in Corelle's making angered her now, and she balled her fists. Determined, she walked forward and entered the shop.

Her mother concentrated on some making at her table toward the rear of the shop, and she glanced up as Corelle walked in, before she returned her attention to her work. Corelle stood in silence with the door at her back. Her mother stopped and looked up again, curiosity on her face. "Corelle?"

Tears welled up in Corelle's eyes. "You recognise me after all these years, though I must have changed beyond all belief."

Her mother stood. "You are my daughter. How could I not recognise the child I birthed?" She held out her arms. "Come to me, Daughter, for I have missed you every day, and wished for you to walk through that door and into my arms again."

Corelle ran forward into her mother's embrace, and they held each other tight and sobbed into each other's shoulder. Her mother smelled the same as she had always smelled—the restful smell of sweet flowers, fabric, safety, and simple food. Corelle doubted she smelled as pleasant in return, but her mother did not relinquish her embrace.

The rear door of the shop opened, and Corelle turned as her father entered. His mouth opened, and his eyes widened. "Corelle." The whispered word resonated with surprise and affection, and he ran forward to throw his arms around both women.

Corelle had left Ryl at least six years earlier and had scribed only one letter to her parents, but they showed no resentment. They embraced her and appeared delighted to see her again. They knew nothing of the life she had lived, and she reckoned they would not approve if they did, but here, now, in their arms, she felt comfortable and content. Her father kissed the top of her head and took a step back to gaze on his wife and daughter still locked in their embrace.

Her mother wiped at her eyes. "It is wonderful to see you again,

Corelle. It has done my heart good." She released Corelle and moved next to her husband. "You look so different these days. Where is your beautiful hair?"

Corelle smiled. "I cut it off. It got in the way."

Her father's curiosity showed in his face. "In the way of what?"

Corelle considered where to begin her story, and how much to reveal. "I am a mariner." She settled for a simple explanation, and the truth. It had been the reason she had cut off her hair, after all else.

"A mariner?" Her mother frowned. "Is it possible for a woman to do this work?"

Corelle smiled. "A woman may do anything she wishes if she is given the chance. It is the lack of the opportunity that holds women back from many things."

Her father's brow knitted. "It seems I made a similar argument to you once, but you would not hear it."

Her mother nodded in agreement and Corelle tried to form counter arguments in her head, then thought better of it. She did not wish to disrupt the joy of their reunion. "That is a conversation for another time, Father." It proved easy to smile her love at them, though it had not always been so. "Tell me how you have both been. How does our little shop fare?"

Her parents gave her a brief explanation of all that had turned. The shop had enjoyed great popularity thanks to the patronage of the Portreeve and his wife, but Corelle's elaborate gowns had been missed. Then a new Portreeve had arrived. Her parents knew little of why, only that the Bailiff had appointed him. He had been the Portreeve in Delcan before Ryl, it seemed. He treated them well, and her father still paid into the levies. Corelle reasoned the grand politics of Alcmouth had passed them by for the most part. They knew little of what had turned along the Alc, although stories had reached them of the defences that had sprung up near the docks. Corelle judged they would not be interested to learn all that had turned, nor care overmuch who served as Bailiff or Duke. They lived far to the north of the capital, and a rock cast into the river in Alcmouth became little more than a faint ripple by the time it reached the docks in Ryl.

They urged her to stay for a meal that evening, but she told them she planned to eat dinner with someone else. They pressed her for more information and seemed to suspect there might be some romance afoot. Her mother wanted to know more, so Corelle relented and told them she had become involved in a relationship with another woman.

She had expected a disappointed reaction—no grandchildren for them to fuss over, no strong man to care for their daughter and treat them with the respect grandparents were due. To her surprise, her mother gave her a wry smile. "But of course you have, my dear Corelle."

"You know I am not interested in men?"

Her father smiled, no judgement in his voice. "We have always known. You never once showed any interest in boys. You only ever seemed to take to that girl. What was her name now? Come, I forget. Somebody remind me."

Nobody could recall the girl's name, and Corelle guessed they meant the one who used to come to the shop with her mother. She shook her head in amazement. "I thought you would be angry."

Her mother reached out and touched her cheek. "Why would we be angry? We wanted you to be happy. Is the woman you are with here in Ryl the same one you mentioned in the letter you sent all those years ago?" The slavering beast of sadness dug its claws into Corelle, and it must have shown in her face. "What is it, Daughter? Tell us."

"The woman I left Ryl to be with..." She hesitated and searched for the right words. "She died, two or three years later."

"That is sad to hear." Her father's disappointment seemed genuine, but to Corelle's relief he did not pursue the matter.

Her mother's face brightened. "Then bring this woman for a meal with us. We would love to meet her." Corelle did not reply. It would bring her little pleasure to introduce them to Vamma. In Corelle's mind, the relationship did not extend to meals with her parents. She enjoyed her time with Vamma, but she would prefer to leave Dur and return to the sea, and Vamma had no place in that vision. Her mother seemed to sense her reluctance. "Never mind. Another time. Will you be in Ryl long? Have you come from your ship?"

"No ships sail to Ryl at this time, Mother. There is conflict in the land, and Ryl may be attacked by southerners at any moment."

Her mother covered her mouth with a hand. "Oh my, what in the Five Cities turns?"

"I do not know the full tale, in truth." They stared back at her in concern. They had never shown any open affection for her until today. They had provided for her, which may have been all they could do to show they cared through her childhood. Guilt stood before Corelle and mocked her. She needed to escape its gaze for a time. "I must head off. It has been wonderful to see you both. Stay safe. I cannot tell what will turn, but trouble may arrive in Ryl."

"Then you stay safe also." Her father pulled her close and kissed her cheek. "My thanks that you came to see us. You are welcome at any time, but next time bring your friend."

"Vamma." Corelle had replied before she even realised it.

Her father nodded and wore a faint smile at some unknown joy the sharing of the name had brought him. "Bring Vamma to see us, please." He kissed her again. "Be careful, Corelle. I love you."

Her father's words left her dumbstruck. He had never said he loved her before. She could not recall that her mother had done so either. They had always been affectionate and warm but had never expressed their love for her. She looked up into his eyes and saw a man who had cared for her the best he could, but either he had not wanted to give his emotions voice or had not known how to. Even when she had left with Arella, he had not told her they loved her. Her father had been disappointed she left the shop when they had so much work to complete, she seemed to remember.

She stepped back and smiled, uncertain of how to respond. She turned for the door, but her mother's voice stopped her in her tracks. "We both love you, Corelle. Stay safe, Daughter."

In her heart, Corelle knew she should tell them she loved them in return, if for no other reason than it was the truth. She should be delirious with happiness they had found the will to tell her they loved her after twenty-four years. Instead, dread filled her, and it chilled her heart. Those words had condemned three women so far. Had her parents written a terrible fate for themselves with the same three words? She could not bear to bring about the death of her parents for love of her. It would be too much. Tears ran down her face, and she pulled the door open. She took a determined step out of the shop but stopped and stared at her boots in conflicted misery before she half-turned to her parents. "I love you." She stepped into the street and hurried away without a backward glance.

Now, a tenday or more since she had arrived in the city, she stood on the dock and stared north-east. The Qagrue ships had not arrived. Why did they delay? Tamgellan had sailed toward Zhang-har, but had turned about and returned to Ryl when he had seen one of the Qagrue ships patrol the entrance to the Alc. His ship had been tied up at the Ryl docks since then as the preparations contin-ued, and all who awaited the arrival of the Qagrue became more irritable with each day that passed, unsure of their fate but anxious to learn it.

Corelle grew impatient. Tamgellan could not sail east, but she suggested he sail west and carry her with him. He did not wish to test his little ship in waters he did not know. Corelle could not help him with any navigation information, for she had never sailed the stretch of water to the north-west of Dur. She knew nothing of the

Northern Ocean between Ryl and Malkartas. Tamgellan would not risk his ship, and her frustration increased.

That night, she told Vamma she proposed to ride south to Delcan. She might learn something there that would aid them. She might even ride on to Ort. Vamma said Corelle should not leave Ryl and head for an unknown fate. When Corelle argued she had no better idea of her fate while she waited in Ryl, rather than in Delcan or Ort, Vamma insisted she would accompany her.

In truth, Corelle thought it unlikely she would learn anything useful, but she wanted to be active, to do something; anything to resolve the restlessness that festered within her. She had prepared the men here as well as she could and now wished to move on. To her surprise, she did not much care about what became of Dur. Her parents and Vamma might be the only people still alive in the land she cared about. Her parents had been so unaffected by all that turned, she had no concern for them. Vamma would also be safe enough in Ryl even if the Qagrue came. She cared for Vamma, but she did not love her and would not find it difficult to move on and leave her behind, and she refused to take her. They exchanged harsh words for the first time.

Vamma's words spoke of her pain at Corelle's decision. "Why will you not take me? I love you. I wish to be with you. You told me you could keep me safer than I would be if we were apart."

Corelle sighed. "That I did, but we were in the Eastlands then, and some time ago at that. I believe you are safe here, while my own fate is less certain whether I stay or leave."

"Corelle, I love you."

Corelle thought she detected sadness and desperation in Vamma's voice. "I do not love you. I have told you this."

"Do you not care for me?" Tears welled up in Vamma's eyes.

"That I do, and that is why I do not wish you to accompany me. I intend to ride into the unknown. You would be in danger. Here, I believe, you will be safest."

Vamma hung her head. "You believe you can unravel the meaning behind Krage's actions."

"I believe coin drives him. That is simple enough to understand."

"Then are you driven by a desire for revenge, for Arella, for Klordia?" Corelle did not answer the question, uncertain she could trust her voice to make a reply and unsure she knew how to respond. "You are so obsessed with what you pursue in the distance, you do not see that which is right before your eyes."

Vamma's misery-drenched words stung, but they told Corelle nothing she did not already know. "This has ever been true."

Vamma sniffed and wiped at her nose with the back of a hand. "Will you come back to me?"

"If I live."

"Then leave, but first take me to our bed." She placed a hand either side of Corelle's face, kissed her, and her tongue soon aroused Corelle's desire for satisfaction. Vamma knelt on the floor, unfastened Corelle's trousers, and buried her head in the hair at the top of Corelle's legs. Corelle parted them, and Vamma's tongue turned its attention to her hot sex. It flicked at the entrance to her intimate zone. Corelle threw her head back and gasped, as a flame spread up the inside of her body, and the tongue tantalised her and drove her passion higher. She moaned as every part of her body cried out to be taken to a peak, but Vamma pulled away, and when Corelle looked down, a wicked, provocative smile teased her.

Vamma's hand slid up Corelle's stomach, and her fingers awoke ripples of lust that flooded through Corelle's body. She took one of Corelle's nipples and rubbed it between her fingers until she had made it hard and proud. Corelle pushed at Vamma's head and tried to drive her face back between her legs. She wanted the satisfaction of release to tear through her body, but Vamma resisted and licked at Corelle's stomach and thighs. Corelle did not recognise the low, guttural sound that came from her own lips, and at last Vamma pushed her face into Corelle's groin and licked at her swollen lips before her tongue thrust itself into her and lapped at her juices until it took Corelle to the finish she had craved.

Corelle lay on the floor and pulled Vamma's head up her body, then thrust her tongue deep into her mouth, the taste of her own juices in her lover's mouth. She thrust a hand between Vamma's legs and coaxed a sigh from her as her fingers slid into her sex. Her fingers thrust in and out until Vamma cried out and shook as pleasure surged through her.

They lay in each other's arms as the darkness closed in outside the windows. When Corelle awoke, Vamma still lay on the floor beside her, and the dawn brightened the sky. Vamma stirred as Corelle kissed her. She decided she would enjoy the soft warmth of her lover's body a little longer before she rose and set off for Delcan and, in time, Ort.

CHAPTER 23
CORELLE

Corelle slung her pack over her shoulder and kissed Vamma goodbye. She had bought some spare clothes at last, and she had also made a tunic for herself in the down time in Ryl as she waited, impatient for something to turn. Vamma's sadness radiated from her, but Corelle had made up her mind. She walked to the Portreeve's Offices and requested an audience with the Ryl Portreeve, where she explained her intentions. He begged her not to leave and argued they needed her skills if the Qagrue came.

She pointed out the many hours she had devoted to training the men in the city, how they had blocked the wider roads. Her skills did not extend to brawls in the street. "Let me use the skills I have." She ignored his protestations.

She found a stable owner who loaned her a horse, and she picked a docile animal the owner assured her had plenty of stamina. It would need it if she did ride to Ort.

Corelle rode south on the road out of the city. Although she believed it continued all the way to Delcan, she did not know for certain. She reckoned it would take her around six or seven days to reach Delcan. If she learned nothing there, she would set off for Ort, which would take another eight to ten days. It might have only taken six or seven days to sail, but she could do nothing about the much slower journey by horse as no ship had arrived in Ryl since they had learned of the blockade of the river north of Zhanghar, and it seemed it would not be possible to take ship to Ort for some time.

She eased the horse into the journey. She let the animal walk much of the time, with the occasional rest break. It would not do to wind the horse, as they had a long journey ahead of them. Her mount grew fitter as they rode, and it could sustain a faster pace that allowed her to cover more distance in each day. She stayed at inns every night, more for the horse than herself, although her back thanked her. She imagined the horse would do better on a good meal and the attentions of a stable boy.

She reached Delcan late on the sixth day and trotted into the town as darkness fell. Although Deineike had told her a little about Delcan, Corelle had never visited the town before. She found a large inn on the square and handed her horse off to the stable boy. She contemplated an extra day in the town to give the horse a full day's rest, but she only took a room for the night and decided to evaluate the horse the next day and make her mind up then.

She ate a meal in the tavernroom and enjoyed two goblets of wine. Not much more than a year ago, she would have drunk a full cask of the wine, and more. Even though the ship's crew drank whenever they went ashore for a night, Corelle no longer craved vast quantities of wine. She stared into her goblet and wondered what had lain behind that phase of her life. It had started in Vyrrmod, and her unhappiness in the relationship with Pettra provided the initial reason, but it had so consumed her, she craved it almost every night for a time. It had been a strange time, and the wine had been the dominant force in her life, not her. When she went to sea, she had still yearned for it at first. Over time, she desired it less and less until she had arrived again at a point where she could drink as much or as little as she chose on any given night. The present balance felt more comfortable.

A shadow fell across her table, but she did not look up. She stared into the goblet and waited. If she spoke, the person who stood near her might sit, and there would be tedious chatter to make. If she ignored them, they might go away.

No such luck. "May I join you?" The man did, at the least, have a gentle voice, not gruff or bossy as men's voices often tended to be in inns and taverns.

She hoped to make him as uncomfortable as she could, so he would leave her alone sooner. "Why would I wish you to join me?" She kept her voice calm and friendly. His desire for her company irritated her, but he had not been rude or offensive, and she did not want to provoke an argument if it could be avoided.

"For my wondrous conversation, of course." The good-humoured reply might have been intended to put her at ease.

"Your conversation is already too full of fancy words for my tastes." Corelle took a sip of her wine and gazed into the goblet again. With luck, he might take the hint and leave.

"You are not from Delcan." Corelle could not deduce how he had arrived at the conclusion, and she had no desire to ask him. "You travel through the town, although where you go is a mystery. A woman who travels alone—this is a risky thing."

"I go where I will, and it goes ill with any who hinder me." She did not look up, angry at his speculation and at how he implied all women were helpless weaklings who needed men to protect them.

"Those are angry words to throw at somebody who wants nothing more than some company for the evening."

She sighed, bored and tired of him already. "I do not desire any company." This time she did look up at him. She saw a tall, slender man, his long hair coiffed to such perfection, she reasoned it must occupy half his day to attend to it. He had a square jaw and bright blue eyes. His clothes were of good making, and he held a goblet.

He smiled at her. "I will be honest with you. You are a traveller, and I seek news. If you have come from Ort, you may have heard of events there and I would like to hear of them, if you would spare me the time."

She stared at him and considered his words. There had been no sincerity in his explanation, and he could not have known she came from somewhere other than Delcan. Such knowledge could not have been gained from their short conversation. He wanted a dalliance; she did not doubt it. As she weighed her thoughts, he dropped into a chair opposite her, mayhap in the misguided belief she had hesitated, keen to press his advances. She motioned with her head, a suggestion he should stand again. "I did not invite you to take a seat at my table."

He made a face of mock horror. "That is cold, my dear. Are you always so unfriendly?"

"I would describe it as cool, no more. You would not wish to see me when I am cold."

"A frosty but feisty one, are you? That might appeal."

She glanced around the tavernroom. "Why did you set your eyes on me? Why not one of the other women here, or a courtesan, who might welcome your advances?"

"I have told you. I seek news—"

"Do not persist in this line. I do not believe it."

His smile faded and a hardness came into his eyes. "You have an irritable demeanour. I may be mistaken about you."

"That you are. I suggest you return home and enjoy the pleasure of your hand."

"My hand has more social graces than you and is more attractive." He leaned forward as if to menace her.

Her small laugh mocked him, and Corelle's words were no kinder. "You behave like a spoiled child. You should grow up."

"Shut up. Do not speak to me this way." His face turned red with anger, and his temples throbbed. He had closed his hands into fists on the table, the knuckles white as he squeezed them tight.

Corelle reached down and pulled her fan from her boot. "You show up at my table uninvited, and now you threaten me? Leave, while you still may."

He clutched at his heart, feigned terror, and wailed in mock fear. "Ooh. I am so frightened. You are barely tall enough to see over the table, woman. Do not spit orders at me." He stared at her, and his eyebrows raised. Corelle stared into his eyes, and her gaze never wavered. She did not wish to cause a scene, but he had pushed her ire, and she would do whatever she felt necessary. His next comment caught Corelle unawares. "You are a deviant. I see it now. The short hair, the men's clothes. You reject me because you lie with women." She brought her fan up, and distaste twisted his face into an ugly version of his true self. "What is this? Some trinket you think will disguise your true nature? Real women use fans, not deviants like you."

Her attempts to keep her temper in check had been more than reasonable, she thought. He had persisted and had now become so rude, it could not go unanswered. Styrrach had called her a deviant, or so Synna had said, and had called Deineike a deviant in the room of The Duke's Seat during the brawl that had brought about Deineike's death. With a snarl, she pressed on the rivet of the fan. The blade sprang out, her hand moved, as fast as a striking snake, and the blade cut him from his ear to his jaw. It did not cut deep, but the wound bled, and he pressed his hand to the side of his face as he cried out in surprise. Corelle pulled the fan close to her face, pushed the blade back into its guard, and flipped open the fan's leaves.

At his cry, everybody in the tavernroom glanced around. Their eyes settled on him first, and by the time they looked to Corelle, she had leaned back in her settle and waved the fan before her face as though she were hot, a concerned look on her face. He took his hand away from his face and stared at the blood on it before he pressed it back against the cut. "She cut me." He wailed like an infant as he pointed at her with his other hand.

Corelle slid down in the settle somewhat to make herself appear even smaller and opened her eyes wide in surprise. Several men came over and looked at his face. He repeated his accusation against her, and she maintained her look of innocence. Somebody asked what she had cut him with, and he replied, "Her fan."

She fluttered the fan more, for effect. Somebody laughed, and others soon picked up the laughter.

Someone cried, "Her fan?"

Her victim spluttered as he scrambled for his dignity. "It is not… it has a blade. A concealed blade."

The laughter increased, and Corelle held her fan before her. She turned it over in her hand and examined it as though a powerful sword might spring from it at any moment. She looked up at the gathered men. "I am barely tall enough to see over the table." The laughter increased.

Her victim shouted for silence and tried to protest, to ask them how he had been cut if it had not been her. She rose and slid out from the settle. "He had lost a fight with the husband of his dalliance, my guess." Corelle threw her head back and loosed a scandalised laugh. The other men laughed and talked among themselves as they dispersed. She leaned forward and hissed into his ear. "You are fortunate I did not slit your throat." She turned and walked out of the front door onto the street. It would not be wise to let him know she had a room at the inn. She would walk the streets for a while, then return to her room.

Outside, the night had turned cool, but the lights of the night sky shone above her, no cloud to obstruct her view of them. The summer waned, and the wet season would soon fall upon the land again. The cycle of life turned without end, it seemed, but that cycle had been broken for so many who had touched Corelle. Whether broken by her or because of her, it did not matter, she reasoned. What would happen to that cycle now Krage controlled the fates of the Durfolk? Whatever the outcome, it would be less favourable now than it had been under Raolos and the Duke with his many words and knowledge of the histories of the land. All memory of those histories had died with him, she imagined.

Anger welled up inside her. Corelle had not cared for the Duke and had made no secret of it. For all his faults, his absolute loyalty lay with Dur. He had preserved the histories and had doubtless studied them in great depth to learn all the lore he had known. That servant of Dur had been replaced by one who served only himself and would kill any who stood in his way without a second thought. Corelle would do all she could to bring about his ruin, even if it cost her own life. She had been ready to sail away and leave Dur behind not long ago, but as she recalled the Duke and his dedication on her aimless walk through the unfamiliar streets of Delcan, she grew so infuriated, she determined to avenge all those who had died because of Styrrach, Krage and all the others who ran the Guild.

The change of position surprised her. She owed Dur nothing; the land had been hard on her, in truth. The Duke had irritated her whenever she had spoken to him, but he had not deserved death at Krage's hands. It seemed no different from a shrouding. It could not stand, and she would not tolerate it.

Corelle smiled to herself. She grew up as a simple garment maker's daughter from Ryl, and yet she become a trusted companion to the most powerful and mysterious man in the land. How many of the residents of Delcan who passed her, cloaks pulled tight against the chill night air, would ever have met the Duke? None, she guessed. The thought amused her.

Two days on horseback had tired her, and nervous excitement had coursed through her throughout the incident in the tavern room and left her drained. She had little enough knowledge of the phenomenon, but a member of the Guild had explained it to her one night when she returned to the Guild building after a gest, shaken and weary. The body produced a substance in the face of danger, she seemed to recall, and it travelled in the blood. It provided both improved resistance to pain and increased strength in muscles and increased the heart rate, which had been why she always slowed her breaths in stressful situations. She must have misremembered; it seemed foolish now—a child's story.

It took some time to find the inn again. She had been so consumed with her thoughts, she had not bothered to note which turns she had made. Not once had she even attempted to throw loose any who might have followed her, and it seemed some of the skills of her training had waned in the year she had been at sea. She did not desire any renewed training to restore those terrible skills. They had already brought her pain enough for one lifetime, and she was not yet twenty-five years. At last, she saw the inn and entered with caution, her fan in her hand. The front door led straight into the tavernroom—a common feature throughout Dur in smaller inns. Four patrons remained, and the man she had cut seemed to have left. She sighed in relief and crossed the room toward the rear door that led to the accommodation.

As she passed the counter, the innkeep smiled at her. "Quite a disturbance earlier, young lady."

She gushed as she returned his smile. "My apologies. He had drunk more ale than he should, my guess." She walked on toward the door and hoped the encounter would end there.

The innkeep's response stopped her in her tracks. "He comes in here from time to time. He has an eye for the ladies, that one. I do not know how you cut him, and I do not wish to. He must have deserved it, from all I have seen. Good night to you."

"And to you." Corelle pulled the door open and headed for her room, where she collapsed onto the bed and fell asleep the moment her head rested on the pillow.

CHAPTER 24
CORELLE

Old nightmares plagued Corelle. Deineike's charred body walked through her sleep all night and told Corelle she had burned her alive over and over. Noises outside her door woke her late in the morning, and she felt no more refreshed than she had been when she retired the previous night. She dragged herself from the bed, weary and still dressed in the previous day's clothes, dusty from the road and doubtless with an unpleasant stench. Although she had considered an extra day in Delcan for the horse's sake, she decided she had had her fill of the place after all else. She recalled Deineike had not taken to the town and thought she could understand why.

She grabbed her pack and settled for the room and stable. The sun had already risen high in the sky as she rode the streets of Delcan toward the eastern gate and out onto the road to Ort. That road would take her past Taro's farm, and she must decide how she felt about all it represented in a life full of remorse. She shook her head to scatter the thought. Time enough for that when she reached the farm lane; she would not brood on it now while it still lay days away. Grey clouds skittered north and threatened to hide the sun later in the day, but no rain had arrived yet as her horse carried her through the featureless Northlands.

To occupy her mind, she spent some time on the consideration of whether she rode through the Northlands or the Ortlands. The trivial consideration helped her avoid any reflection on the sad realities of her life. From somewhere in her past, she believed the Ortlands lay more to the south than Delcan, but since she rode toward Ort, that did not make sense, she realised. That led her to ponder who decided what to call the various parts of Dur and why, and to her surprise, the sun had sunk low in the sky by the time she had finished her contemplation on why there were Eastlands but no Westlands. She reined the horse to a stop. "Am I mad, horse?" The horse lifted its head at the sound of her voice, then dropped it toward the floor and raised it again. The gesture looked to her like a nod of agreement, and she laughed and stroked its neck. "You are no less mad then, for you carry me." The horse snickered, and Corelle wondered whether it understood her words and had laughed. She giggled at the foolishness of the thought. "You are right. I am mad." She kicked the horse forward again.

She found a small inn in a village and stopped for the night, which passed without event. No nightmares assailed her, and she enjoyed a more peaceful sleep. The next day, she set out again. The land became less agricultural, with far more trees as she rode further from Delcan. People might not create farms further from the towns and cities, although her ride south with Deineike had not given her that impression. She abandoned the thought and resolved not to waste another day on futile reflections with no possible resolution.

As she passed through a wooded hillside, movement caught her eye, and she stared forward. A group of riders approached, headed for Delcan, she imagined. They were some distance away, but there were, at the least, five of them. She stopped her horse and frowned, anxious for some reason she could not determine. Any encounter with them might place her in danger, and she turned the horse from the road. Once she had ridden into the trees, she stopped some way back where she still had a view of the road. If they rode past and did not study their surroundings, they might not notice her. She wondered if they might be some advance party from Ort, Qagrue men sent to scout the situation in Delcan or some such.

She dismounted, tethered the horse to a tree, then crept forward. A large bush offered a place where she could crouch unseen and watch the road. Soon enough she heard hooves as they approached, and the riders came into view. In truth, they numbered six, and they looked exhausted, slumped in their saddles with reins held loose in their fingers. The horses almost moved under their own volition, it seemed, and an air of dejection lay over the entire party. She did not recognise the first three, but behind them rode Raolos, Synna and Wilash.

Her heart leapt at the sight of her friends, but she suppressed her immediate desire to rush out and greet them. Although the three who rode before them wore the red tunic of the Bailiff, she could not be certain her friends had not fallen under their weapons. All three of her friends looked terrible, grimy with dust and slouched in their saddles in apparent misery. Lines streaked Raolos's dust-covered face, from tears, Corelle thought. His right arm sat in a bandage wrapped around his neck, and another bloodied bandage wrapped his forearm. He held the reins of his horse in his left hand, which rested on his thigh. He had a small cut high on his forehead. Synna had a bloodied bandage wrapped around one of his thighs, and Wilash had blood on his tunic high on the right side. The three in the front looked worse for wear also, and Corelle felt certain they must be Raolos's men.

The risks would be great if she had guessed wrong, however, so she remained cautious. She crouched low, convinced she would not be seen, although she had glimpses of the riders through the foliage of the bush. She called out. "Synna."

All six heads snapped up and around in her direction. Synna pulled a dagger out of his belt and held it against his thigh. The three in front also produced daggers they pointed toward the trees as though they might pierce whoever had cried out. Synna's eyes raked the trees, but he did not spot her. He shouted. "Show yourself."

Synna had his dagger, which convinced Corelle the three friends had not been captured. Nobody who wished to hold Synna prisoner would leave him in possession of a dagger. They would not see the next morning if they did so. She stood.

Synna's eyes widened, and she heard a gasp from either Wilash or Raolos. She could not be sure which. "Corelle?" Shock and surprise filled Synna's voice.

She stepped forward to the road and stared from Synna to Wilash, then to Raolos and back to Synna. Happiness overwhelmed her, and she could not keep a huge smile from her face. "By the Five Cities, it is good to see you all alive. I feared the worst."

Raolos's small smile faded already, as though he lacked the strength to maintain it. "As we did for you. It gladdens me to see you, though little else brings me any joy at this time."

Wilash shook off his inertia. "What brings you to this road?"

Corelle gazed on a weary, broken man, far from the Wilash who had laughed and gasped at her stories the last time she met him. His hair appeared even greyer than when she had left Alcmouth around a pass ago. "I could ask you the same, although I can guess your reply. As for me, I ride to Ort, determined to do something to alter these ill fates that have been written."

"You alone?" Raolos sounded as though he could not believe what she had said. "What will you do?"

"Whatever I can."

Synna's tired smile grew wider. "That will be a great deal."

"What turned in Alcmouth?"

Synna's sigh almost shattered Corelle's heart, the sadness of a lifetime captured in one breath. "Four ships arrived in Alcmouth with large numbers of men in each. They moved through the city and killed any who dared to stand before them. They had soon taken the Portreeve's Offices, and they came to the Bailiff's Offices. We resisted the best we could. We were outnumbered and taken by surprise." He paused and slid his dagger back into his belt. "I saw their numbers would overwhelm us. I could not risk Raolos's life and persuaded him to abandon the building. We headed for the alleyway at the rear, but we met more of them on the way. In the fight, they struck Raolos, and he fell. He broke an arm, but I managed to kill his assailant before worse befell him. Only we six escaped. One of Raolos's aides sat at Raolos's desk as we left. I fear he gave his life to buy us some extra time."

Raolos sobbed again, and sorrow washed over Corelle. She saw it as a measure of how good a man and Bailiff he had been, his staff and men would make such sacrifices to keep him safe. "What of Raopul?" Nobody replied, but all looked down. It did not prove difficult to deduce the boy had died or been captured. Corelle shared the sorrow of Raolos and his friends. The boy, at the least, should have been left out of whatever scheme Krage had hatched. Two young boys now no longer breathed because of the Guild. Corelle swore to herself there would be justice.

Corelle stepped forward and laid a hand on Synna's leg. "You are hurt also."

He nodded. "A sword. Can you believe it? A sword slashed me in close quarters." He gave a dark laugh. "He who wielded it struck me once, and he struck low, I am glad to say. They do more damage than you would think, those things." His eyes clouded over as if he thought back on the incident. He seemed to realise he had drifted off and smiled down at her. "I am fine. We left the city and have ridden north every day since. We have travelled across country for the most part and avoided people wherever we could. We did not wish to come close to Ort. We cannot be sure they are not there also.

We make for Delcan. It is not on the river and will give us a chance to catch our breath, we think."

Raolos added to the story. "We must find a way to leave Dur, for now at the least. We hope the Portreeve in Delcan will be friendly to us still."

Corelle nodded. "All that has turned, it is Krage."

Synna objected. "That it is not. These men wore strange clothes and spoke a language none of us know. They are from the south, my guess."

"That they are. They are from Qagrue. I have seen the sigil they fly when I sailed there. Krage has brought them here somehow. He has declared himself Duke, and Sisnop from Torric his Bailiff." Raolos opened his mouth and seemed taken aback by the news. "Gillar is now the Portreeve in Ort. You made the right choice to avoid that town."

In a small voice, as if he feared to hear the answer, Raolos asked about Ibie.

Corelle hesitated, anxious not to add to his unhappiness. Too late, she realised her hesitation had told him the story without any words. Tears pooled in her eyes as she replied. "Hanged, by all accounts. I am sorry."

Raolos threw back his head and yelled his anger and grief into the air. Nobody could have watched the torment that took him and not suffer great sadness of their own, and Corelle wiped at her eyes with the back of a hand. Raolos stared at her. "Why? Why have they done this? How have they done this? How can every-thing we are, everything we believe in, be cast down with such ease? Why?"

Corelle had no reply other than her own opinions, and they would provide little enough by way of an answer. In truth, the events confused her. "Coin, my guess. Revenge also, but coin is behind it in some part, however small or large. He sees the chance to become even more rich and powerful than Styrrach. How he persuaded the Qagrue to assist him remains to be discovered. I ride to Ort in search of such answers."

Wilash spoke again, distressed and urgent. "You cannot go to Ort. You said yourself it is in their hands. It will be too dangerous. Come with us. There must be a way to leave Dur while we determine what can be done."

"I must go. I will kill them if I can. If not, I will die in the attempt." She turned to Synna. "I told you the death of Klordia meant more than you would allow."

"That you did." Synna's smile faded, and his head dropped.

She took a sharp breath and stood upright again, cast off the dejection that had settled on her. "Ride on to Ryl. It stands still—or at the least it did a sevenday ago. Zhanghar's men are there, and we hope Torric and Dur City will come. Other towns as well, with luck. You will be safe enough there, I think. You could find a way to flee Dur, if you wish. A ship stands there with a friendly master who may be persuaded to sail further than I could persuade him if he thinks he helps the Bailiff." She gave Raolos a smile and hoped it encouraged him. "Zhanghar has fallen, and the Alc is blocked. No trade ships travel to Ryl, but the Qagrue have not sailed there so far. They control the Alc, and with that, they control most of the trade in Dur. Without trade ships, the food supply in Ryl is unlikely to last long. The people need their Bailiff."

Raolos blinked, then a steely look came to his face. "Very well. We will ride on to Ryl. We will take as many men from Delcan as will come with us, and from every town and village we pass on the way. We will make as much of a stand as we can in Ryl. If Dur is to fall, they will be required to pay a terrible price for it."

Corelle smiled at him again. She did not doubt he could stir men into action. He commanded respect, and men were prepared to be loyal to him. He might offer some hope, after all else. "I will do what I can to aid you in Ort. I will discover as much information as possible and do all in my power to bring it to you."

Synna urged her to ride back to Ryl with them "You are worth five of these untrained men."

"Only five?" She had teased him, but she shook her head. "A brawl in the street against swords is not where I can help Dur the most. I go to Ort, where I will be death in the dark to anybody I can get close to."

Raolos seemed to have no end of questions. "Have you any word of the Duke, or his son?"

Once more, sadness overwhelmed her at the terrible news she must now deliver, and her shoulders slumped again. "I have heard no official word of the Duke. Rumours suggest he is dead." Raolos choked, but he did not interrupt her. "Peben is dead. I found him at Estway Farm, hanged. The Portreeve of Yerrsun gave him a Pyre and a Sending. I am sorry to bear so much ill news, Raolos."

Raolos gave a cry, and his eyes reddened as more water pooled in them. "All is dark, all is dark. Good men gone, children murdered. How have I brought all this down on the land I love?"

"You have not brought it. You fought the Guild, and you wounded them. I might have had them in Yerrsun, but I let them slip away like sand through my fingers. If anybody is to blame, it is me."

He stared at her. "I did this. I should have been firmer and not allowed the Duke to banish you. I should have refused to become Bailiff unless he pardoned you. Klordia need not have died. Vital time need not have been lost as we sent you letters, and you sailed back to Dur. My pride affected my decision, and the hurt I felt when I lost Pettra to you, and I allowed that to cloud my judgement. I am to blame for this."

How did he blame himself and claim to have permitted her banishment out of some jealousy when he himself had begged her to take Pettra away with her? That decision, of course, had brought his wife nothing but misery and death. Anger rose within her, but she fought it down. They must not be sundered by an argument, not at this terrible time. "Then let us both share the blame, and let us both do all we can to resolve this. Go to Ryl, marshal men there, and make them ready to fight. I will go to Ort and do all I can."

Raolos sat in silence and stared forward as though some thought tormented him, but Synna also had more questions. "What of Vamma?"

"She is in Ryl. She waits for me there. Find her, please. Tell her you saw me, and I am safe." Synna nodded his agreement.

"What do we restore?" Raolos seemed to speak to himself. "The Duke is dead, and his line is torn. Dur can never be the same."

A man could not be allowed to wallow in his self-pity, or he would become a shadow of all he had ever been, and Corelle straightened once more. "Dur still has hope while its Bailiff is alive. You can rally the people, throw down these usurpers and restore Dur. A new Duke will present himself, or a new Duchess. The Duke's wife might take the role."

Wilash shook his head. "There has never been a Duchess in Dur."

Corelle smiled even as she rebuked him. "No woman had served as the Senior Tally Master before your wife."

Synna offered to come to Ort with her, but Corelle insisted he had another role to play. "Stay with Raolos. He has need of you. This meeting has added hurt on hurt to all he bears already. Keep him safe. Keep yourself safe."

Wilash's eyes sparkled, a small reminder of the man he had been before disaster befell them all. "Is he not to keep me safe?"

"None care what happens to you." Corelle laughed as she teased him. "Synna needs no words from me to know he must keep you safe above all."

Wilash looked away and raised a hand to his eyes. "Take care, my old friend,"

Corelle sniffed. "And you, the three of you." She turned to the three Bailiff's men. "Your loyalty is appreciated. My thanks. Raolos is vital to Dur's future. Permit no harm to come to him, I urge you." They nodded at her and assured her they would protect him with their lives if they must.

She stood in the road and watched them ride away. As they seemed to grow smaller, she did not move. They turned a bend in the road, and she lost sight of them. She lifted her shoulders, dropped them again, returned to the trees, and retrieved her horse. She rode east once more toward whatever fate was written.

CHAPTER 25
CORELLE

Corelle rode onward toward Ort. Day after day, she stared forward over the ears of her mount as they bobbed before her, and Ort seemed no nearer. She spent the nights in inns, used a tub from time to time, and ached without respite from the rigours of too much time in the saddle. For the first few hours after Raolos and his men had ridden off, she had wondered whether Gillar might have moved into Raolos's house. She could see no reason for him to ignore such a magnificent residence, so she decided to watch the house for a time once she arrived to see if he lived there. At the least, she might see an opportunity to kill him and bring some vengeance for Klordia. She wondered how many Qagrue would guard him. No doubt he would be well protected. It would require all her skill to get to him. She hoped all her training had not deserted her.

A sevenday after she had met Raolos, Synna and Wilash, she met Taro's farm again. The lane appeared before her, and she moved her legs from the flanks of her horse, determined to kick it forward. To her surprise, she could not bring herself to do so, and she reined her mount to a halt and stared in dejection down the lane that held so many memories. Deineike's words flooded back to her. *"Nothing here can bring you joy, Jorinda. Do not ride down this lane, I beg you."* Jorinda had not listened to those words and had regretted it. Corelle must not make the same mistake. It might shatter her beyond repair if she rode down the lane and went up the stairs to find Taro's bones still in the bed he had shared with her, but she felt the pull of curiosity and more. Something else urged her to ride down the lane. Guilt? She could not decide.

She could not deny it; had she listened to Deineike that day, she might never have returned to Ort. Synna would have killed Pettra and Raopul, and Raolos would have died soon after. Styrrach would still rule the Guild, and Deineike would be alive. Pettra had died in any event, but so had her beloved Deineike, taken from her by Styrrach, never to return. Her guilt in Taro's barn a year or more ago had turned her back to Ort and everything that followed.

Taro's farm had brought Deineike into her life, and served to set in motion events that would take her from Corelle, who doubted she could ever love again. She had loved Deineike with all she was, all she would ever be, had used up a lifetime of love in less than two years. There could never be another love. There could never be another Deineike.

She pulled the reins, clucked her tongue, and kicked the horse forward along the road. She would not allow herself to succumb to her guilt again. It had cost too much the last time she rode down the lane to the farm, and she could not bear to pay that price again. She could not reach the inn with the squeaky sign tonight, so Corelle and her horse would enjoy the grass for a mattress and the lights of the night sky for a ceiling. She resisted the urge to look back and the stronger pull to turn and ride down the farm lane.

An hour or so later, she stopped near a small clump of trees. They would provide some shelter, and she clucked her tongue and rode the horse into the cover of the trees. With the horse tethered, she pulled her inadequate blanket over her and closed her eyes.

Road weariness soon took her, but sleep brought her no relief from her inner torment. Deineike rose out of the hay in Taro's barn, blackened, her features unrecognisable. Two black stumps of arms reached toward Corelle, neither of which had hands. They seemed to urge her to join Deineike in the hay, and she took uncertain steps toward her former lover. Deineike's stumpy arms embraced her, but instead of the familiar smell of her sweat and her hair, the smell of seared flesh filled Corelle's nostrils. Deineike's long black hair had all been burned away, replaced by a dark scalp. Deineike leaned forward, and her tongue forced its way into Corelle's mouth. It tasted of decay, like the taste she might experience in her mouth if she raked over old coals.

Corelle did her best to ignore the blackness and the smell of burned skin. "I love you."

"Yet you burned me." Deineike's emotionless voice ripped at Corelle's heart with jagged claws, a wild thing bent on her ruin.

"My love, I am sorry. Styrrach had killed you, and I had you placed into the flames. Forgive me." Corelle's tears etched tracks through the black soot of Deineike's skin.

"I forgive you. I love…"

Corelle raised a finger to Deineike's lips. "Do not say it. Those words took you from me once. I will not have them take you from me a second time."

Deineike's gaunt lips drew back. Corelle guessed it had been a smile, but so misshapen were her lips, it appeared more like a grimace. Deineike reached up and pulled Corelle's hand away from her own mouth. "I love you."

At that, she dissolved into powder. Corelle grabbed in desperation at the small particles of blackened ash as they drifted away from her, and she tried to catch as many as she could, to rebuild Deineike and ensure she never told Corelle she loved her again. Instead, the wind blew in through the open door of the barn and scattered all that had been Deineike about the building. Corelle wept, and her horse turned to face her. Tears ran down its own face, and it spoke in the Dur tongue. "I am sorry." Corelle did not doubt it.

Birdsong woke her, and she lay on the ground in agony, her back on fire from the night on the hard, unforgiving soil. She arched her back in a futile attempt to reduce the pain as the bird that had woken her continued to chirp its ballad to the morning from somewhere above her. Her horse snorted as though it wished to join the song, but between them, the two animals could not bring any succour to Corelle's shattered heart. With many groans of discomfort, she rose, gathered up the blanket, placed the saddle back on the horse, and mounted. She picked a careful path out of the trees and across the dewy grass to the road.

Corelle pointed the horse's head toward Ort, but stopped. She imagined Taro's voice as it called to her and begged her to retrieve his bones, to give him a Pyre and a Sending. She sniffed back her misery, but could not allow herself to turn and look behind. If she did, how could she resist the voice in her mind that beseeched her to return to the farm.

She kicked the horse forward and rode on but could not shake the thought of the ill fortune that had dogged her, and she decided Dur had been a terrible place for her to have lived. As soon as she completed this business with Krage, she would leave. She must come to some decision about Vamma, but whatever turned, she would not—could not—remain in Dur.

Later in the day, Corelle passed the road that led to Vjort and could not resist a quiet whisper to herself, "Road to Vjort." She smiled and rode on.

CHAPTER 26
CORELLE

The sun poked out from beneath the blanket of clouds behind her as Corelle approached the inn with the squeaky sign. She could continue into the night, but the dangers would be great, and she wanted to reach Ort hale and hearty, not with broken arms and weary feet if the horse fell, brought down by some unseen hole in the road in the darkness. Her back still ached from the previous night, so she stopped and took a room at the inn, which she now noticed bore the name The Ortlander. The innkeep gave her a room at the front of the inn, and she gazed in misery out of the window at the sign as it blew back and forth in the breeze. She frowned and stared harder at it but heard no squeak. Had they repaired whatever flaw had caused the squeak that so irritated her and Deineike the first time they stayed at the inn? She could but hope.

The sign rewarded that hope, and it made no noise all night. The nightmares stayed away, and she woke refreshed and ready to face whatever awaited her in Ort. She ate a small meal, readied her horse, and set off on the final part of the journey. Raolos's house stood in the wealthy quarter, not far into the town itself, but gates defended the town entrance from the Delcan road, and they must be guarded these days. If the Qagrue guarded the entrance, they would not recognise her, but if the Guild watched the road, that could pose the risk of a confrontation. The wall only extended around the wealthy quarter; the wealthy protected themselves while the rest of the town could not afford to. What the wealthy believed they protected themselves from in Dur had never been clear to her.

The midday had passed when the gates came into view, and Corelle did not wish to waste time while she rode around the outside of the town in search of somewhere with no gates. She stopped, tied the kerchief around her head, and pulled it as low as she dared over her eyes. The sun slid down the sky behind her, and she hoped she would not be recognised as she pressed the horse forward again.

Dust covered her from head to toe, and she slumped in the saddle as she had seen Raolos and his men do, another bone-weary traveller, exhausted from the road and desperate for a bed. As she drew near, she saw two men in the distinctive Qagrue tunics, one on each side of the gates, which stood wide open. They watched her as she rode closer, but they said nothing to her as she rode through the gates, and she passed them with a half-hearted wave, which they did not return. She had returned to Ort and would need to have her wits about her as she moved through the town, or she might be spotted by unfriendly eyes.

First, she must stable the horse. She chose the stables where she and Deineike had claimed the horses Raolos had provided for them when they left Ort together. She felt the horse deserved some quality treatment for a day or so after the arduous ride. The stables cost more than she would have been prepared to pay in normal circumstance, but in the wealthy district, if you could not afford the price, then you should not be here. She pulled her pack from the horse, slung it over her shoulder, and left the stable staff to remove the tack and groom the horse. At the prices they charged, she would make them do as much as she could.

As she walked the streets toward Raolos's home, she used great caution to ensure nobody followed her. Darkness closed in as she reached the street where Raolos's house had been built, and she paused on the corner where she and Deineike had turned to hide when they first saw Synna watch the house. She wondered how Synna had meant to gain entry to the house and kill Pettra and Raopul that night. She imagined he would have walked up the carriageway once darkness had fallen, knock on the door, and kill the servant before he dispatched Pettra and Raopul. He would not be recognised, of course. Corelle might well be—by Gillar if he opened the door, or by the staff if he had retained any of Raolos's servants.

In truth, she could think of no better way to gain entry. If Gillar opened the door, she would steal his life in a heartbeat and shed no tears. If one of the staff answered, they might be new, and even if they had seen her before, they may not remember her. It had been well over a year since she had last been at the house, she had become slimmer and darker and had the kerchief on her head instead of the long brown hair she had sported in those days.

If he had moved into the house, she needed to know whether any others were with him. If he had his Guild members there to protect him, that would create a difficult situation. Even if he had Qagrue men, her task would be no easier. He might also have visitors—friends or business acquaintances. She decided to wait until much later before she went to the door. There would be a higher chance the people in the house would have settled for the night that way. The fewer complications, the better.

If the staff opened the door, how could she persuade them to let her into the house? She had no quarrel with them and did not wish to harm them, but she needed to get into the house fast before they raised the alarm. If Gillar heard the knock at the door, he might come to investigate. More complications than she wanted.

She wracked her brain for a way to gain entry to the house. She recalled the last gest assigned to Arella. She had disguised herself as a high-coin courtesan to get into the merchant's home. He had been used to courtesans at his home, so it had been simple for Arella to gain access to him.

That night, of course, Arella had been a spectacular blonde woman in a beautiful dress. Intelligence had been done to ensure the part she played would give her the chance to kill… Or had it? Corelle knitted her brow as she tried to recall the night in question. The entire story could have been a fabrication; nothing more than an elaborate ruse to keep Arella and her unborn child out of the way while the Portreeve came for Corelle, who had been shrouded.

She chased the thought from her mind. It did not help her here, tonight. Whatever the truth of that night, Corelle did not resemble Arella. A short, muscular woman with a kerchief around her head, rough work clothes and dark skin, did not suggest a courtesan who kept her skin pale and powdered to make herself attractive to the wealthy men of Dur. While Corelle could make a dress that would pass, if she had the time, she could do little about the other difficulties.

Corelle walked forward along the street and hid among the same flowers in which she had fought Synna. As she watched the house, she continued to work on a reliable plan. Could she bluff the staff? She could represent herself as the sort of rough and ready courtesan Gillar preferred. She could try to pass herself off as a man, although her large breasts and short stature made that plan questionable. The foolishness of the last plan brought a laugh to her lips, though she took care not to allow the laugh to become loud enough to draw attention to herself. In the absence of anything better, she settled on the courtesan plan. For two sevendays, she had ridden toward Ort, and she had nothing better to try. Synna would doubtless have had some words to say about the frailty of the plan.

Bright lantern light shone from the house, occasional movement visible through the windows. Gillar might not live here at all, in truth, but she dismissed the idea as soon as she had thought it. Why would he not live in this large, impressive house, doubtless better than anything he had ever experienced in his life?

A carriage approached. Corelle watched as it came along the street and turned into Raolos's carriageway. It stopped when it reached the house, but nobody approached the door. The moments drifted past, then the door opened, and three men spilled out into the warm lantern light that shone onto the carriageway from within the house. They seemed unsteady on their feet and yelled nonsense at one another. Corelle guessed they were inebriated. They all wore fine clothes. Corelle had never seen Gillar, but of the three, one who stood shorter than the others looked to her eye like a Guild member. She imagined he was Gillar.

The men clapped each other on the backs before two of them climbed into the carriage with some difficulty. Gales of laughter erupted from the other two when one of them almost fell back out as he took his seat. The carriage moved forward, drove around the circle, and headed back down the driveway. It turned the way it had come and disappeared down the street into the night. Corelle thought she heard somebody from within the carriage sing, tuneless and unrecognisable. The short man turned and walked through the door. He bumped into the jamb as he entered and staggered inside with a shouted curse. Somebody emerged from the parlour and closed the door behind him.

It had to be Gillar, she thought. She had not missed her guess— he had moved into Raolos's house. He had drunk more than he ought, it seemed, which made him an easier mark if she could get inside. The man had been a Guild member, there could be no question. His height and slenderness, the way he moved even in his intoxication. Everything about him convinced her she had found Gillar.

She settled into a more comfortable seated position, eyes still on the house. The lengthy observation of the house brought her unexpected pleasure after so many years with no Guild work. One by one, the lights in the house went out until all the front windows turned dark. To Corelle's surprise, she could not see any guards at the door. That concerned her, as she had anticipated Gillar would be guarded. Had she been charged with his security, the door would be the first point of entry she would have posted guards at. He might have been complacent, but it might also mean eyes peered out from behind darkened windows, eyes that would see her walk up the carriageway long before she would see them. She could do nothing about it; she dismissed the thought.

She heard voices, and two men appeared to her left. They walked side by side along the road. Corelle remained motionless. If she ducked down, the movement might be spotted from the corner of an eye. That had been how she had noticed Synna. As they passed her, they both glanced at the house. One of them whispered something to the other, and they both laughed. The one who had spoken spat toward the house before they carried on their way. The new Portreeve may not be popular with everyone, it seemed.

Corelle judged it close to an hour since the last light had been extinguished, almost two hours since the men had left in the carriage. Gillar must have retired to his bed by now, so she rose from the flowers and walked up the carriageway without hesitation. If any watched, she did not wish them to notice any uncertainty in her actions. As she drew near the door, a faint light shone from an upstairs window. She had not noticed it from across the street, but as the entire plan had been nothing more than a gamble, she pressed on.

She stood before the door, her breaths controlled, her fan in her hand, and gave a soft knock. With luck, Gillar would not hear her.

No lights came on in the house, and nobody came to the door. She knocked again, a little louder. As she raised her hand to knock a third time, she heard footsteps within, then bolts were drawn, and a key squeaked in a lock. Raolos had never gone to such lengths to bar the door as far as she knew, but she reasoned times were different now.

The door opened wide enough for the person within to peer out, which allowed light from a lantern to spill out onto Corelle. A woman stared through the doorway at her, a cloak draped around her shoulders over a nightgown. She squinted out at Corelle. "Who comes here at this late hour?"

"Gillar has summoned me here to attend upon him." Corelle's words sounded insincere as they dripped from her lips, and she felt certain the woman would not believe her courtesan story.

At that, the woman gasped and opened the door wider. "Jorinda?" The woman must be one of Raolos's former staff members who had remained at the house in Ort and had recognised her. Corelle had anticipated such an outcome but could not guess how the situation would now play out. She judged it wise to keep silent and wait for the fates to reveal themselves. "What brings you here, in truth? Speak now. The hour is late, and the guards are alerted."

Disappointment fell on Corelle like a heavy stone she must catch before it destroyed her ambition. The guards stood ready, and she had lost her initiative and any element of surprise. "I am here to see Gillar." Although she always strove to ensure the best possible outcome, the chances she would lose her life increased by the heartbeat. She must press on with her plan, regardless. "I bear a message from Raolos." She embellished the truth and hoped any loyalty the woman might still harbour for her former employer would work in her favour.

The woman's eyes narrowed. "Gillar says Raolos is dead."

Her answer confirmed Gillar lived in the house, at the least. "He lies. Raolos lives." A faint smile sprang to the woman's lips. "I spoke to him not a tenday since. He is safe in Ryl."

The woman's eyes stared into Corelle's own, as though she searched for something. "I miss him. It gladdens my heart to hear he lives. This inebriated usurper is not half the man…" She paused, her breaths heavier. It seemed she weighed her words. Corelle thought it prudent to remain silent, so she waited for her to continue. "What of Raopul?"

Corelle now found herself in the same situation in which she had placed Raolos, Synna and Wilash when she had asked the same question. She heaved an unhappy sigh. "Dead, we think."

Tears sprang to the woman's eyes, and she swayed. Corelle reached for her, concerned she might fall, but the woman brushed the hand away. The woman fixed her with another earnest stare. "You can have no love for this new Portreeve. Do you mean him harm?"

Corelle rolled the dice. "I mean to make sure he never sees another dawn. He and others have taken control of our land. They have murdered children. I believe they murdered the Duke. I mean to restore the rightful Bailiff and return Dur to the Durfolk."

The woman did not reply for a time. Had Corelle rolled ones? With a sharp intake of breath, the servant lowered her voice before she continued. "There is a guard at the top of the stairs."

Corelle tutted. She had no wish to kill more people than she needed to, and the sound of any fight might alert Gillar. He might escape or summon other guards from elsewhere in the house. "Is this guard one of the Qagrue?"

The servant shook her head. "The Portreeve surrounds himself with Ortmen more and more these days, since the southerners sailed most of their number north. This man is from the town. I know him somewhat. He is a good man at heart, I think."

"I come for Gillar. I will not kill this man unless he attempts to stop me."

The woman chewed at her lower lip then appeared to reach a decision. She dropped her voice to a whisper. "Come inside but wait at the door." She opened the door wide enough for Corelle to enter, then closed it, turned, and left Corelle in darkness. The woman had carried away the lantern that had spilled its light out of the doorway. Corelle held her fan ready at her side, the blade already sprung. She had waited for the Portreeve in this house before but always in the parlour and never determined to end his life. She smiled to herself as she thought, *There is a first time for everything."*

CHAPTER 27
CORELLE

After some time, the woman returned with a tall, slender man with long blond hair that hung well below the shoulders of his red Portreeve's tunic. Corelle raised her fan, blade extended toward him. "Do not try to intervene. I have no wish to harm you, but I will if you do not stand aside."

He held his hands out. "I am no threat to you. I hear you wish to restore order in the land."

"If I can." Corelle relaxed a little but kept a wary gaze upon the man.

He spoke in a quiet tone but could not disguise his anger. "I knew Ibie. They killed a good man. They killed an Ortman. He deserved a better fate."

His words confirmed Ibie had died. They threatened despair, but Corelle could not afford the distraction of misery until she had completed her work in the house. "That he did."

The man gave a terse nod. "Go to the top of the stairs. The third door along. He is in his cups tonight, though he is a light sleeper as a rule."

Corelle could almost taste the vitriol in her words as they left her lips. "I intend for him to sleep for all time." The man nodded again and gestured for her to proceed through the parlour. Corelle had been lucky; they both wished to see Gillar dead. She could not expect such luck again, so she moved with great caution toward the parlour, and both the servant and the man stood to one side. With one eye on the man, alert for any treachery, she crossed the parlour to slip up the stairs, as stealthy as a cat.

Outside the third door, she paused to listen for any sound from within. If he slept as light as the man had implied, he might well have heard their every word and await her on the other side of the door, ready to strike her down. She crouched and placed a hand on the door handle. She turned it so slow, it appeared not to move. She listened for any noise to indicate he awaited her beyond the door.

Once the handle would turn no further, she paused. If anybody waited on the other side and had heard the handle turn, they would expect the door to open almost straight away. When the element of surprise has been lost, it is imperative to behave in a way people who anticipate action could not expect. She crouched still and silent for what seemed like an hour. She listened to creaks from the house, the sound of her own soft, measured breaths, the beat of her heart as the blood passed through the arteries close to her ears. No sound came from the room, so she opened the door a crack. Nobody pulled it open in response to the small movement. That might indicate nobody waited for her, but had she been in the room, Corelle would not have pulled the door open. That would give away her presence, and Gillar also had Guild training.

She gave the door a gentle push inward. It seemed slow to open, but she would rather complete the task than fall to Gillar's blade because of her own impatience. Raolos had been so wealthy, he could afford high quality fixtures in the house. Neither the handle nor the hinges of the door had made a sound as she had opened it.

The door had opened wide enough for her to enter the room, but the complete darkness within stopped her. Little enough light shone here on the corridor, but the interior of the room seemed so dark, it seemed she gazed into a cavern far below the ground where light could not reach. She could not close her eyes to allow them to adjust to the darkness; that could prove fatal, so she stood, pressed her body close to the door jamb, slipped into the room, and moved to one side of the doorway.

As she stood against the wall, she controlled her breaths while she waited for her eyes to adjust to the blackness of the room. She heard a noise, as though somebody had stirred in a bed, and she remained as still as death itself while shadows formed themselves into shapes before her eyes. Time passed, and she made out the bed. The room seemed enormous, and the bed must have been not less than five paces away from her—a substantial distance to cover when time might be against her. The person in the bed stirred again. She had no time to spare in case he awoke, and she crossed the room, as smooth and quiet as a shadow.

"Who is there?" He had awoken, to her disappointment, but he had spoken and betrayed the position of his head and his vulnerable throat below it. She covered the last two paces, then crouched beside the bed and moved closer to him. He sat up in the bed, no more than a shadow in her eyes, but the movement sealed his fate. He seemed to fumble for a flint. If he felt certain somebody had entered the room, he would have called out to his guard. He may not have realised Corelle was there.

The flint struck and light sprang from the lantern. Corelle lay on her stomach next to the bed. The light almost blinded her after the darkness, and she needed her eyes to re-adjust. He must suffer the same affliction, and she imagined he squinted around the room to convince himself nobody had entered. He would notice the open door soon enough, she thought. Time to act.

She sprang to her feet, the blade held out toward him. Fear clouded his face, and he gasped out one word. "You."

"Vengeance is claimed for Klordia and Ibie." She sliced at his throat as soon as she had spoken. He swayed backward and tried to avoid the blade's kiss but could not evade it, and it gashed open his throat. He suffered a deep cut, but not a fatal one.

He croaked in desperation. "Help." His hands went to his throat as though he might keep his life blood inside rather than see it pour out onto the blankets and bedsheets.

Corelle gave him a malicious smile, but at that instant she heard noise from behind her, and he flicked his eyes toward the door. Had she seen panic in his reaction? She would deal with whomever had entered the room behind her once he lay dead. She smiled again as she balled her fist into his hair and pulled his head toward her. Her blade slashed again, and fresh blood pumped out of his neck. His artery had been severed. His life gushed over the blanket, Corelle, and the floor. She released his hair, and he fell backward where his head struck the head of the bed with a thump. He stared up at the ceiling with eyes that saw nothing anymore.

A woman's voice came from behind her. "Raolos will be angry about that carpet. It came from Qanti and cost more coin than most people will see in their lifetime."

Corelle turned. The guard and several women stood near the door, grim looks on their faces as they watched Gillar die. Corelle laughed. "That he will. He may require me to replace it. Or he may understand."

The guard took a pace forward. "What will happen now?"

Corelle had not considered her next move. She had never believed it would be so easy to kill Gillar, but she had arrived in Ort a few hours ago, and he had already fallen to her. Krage lived in Alcmouth now, and it would not be so simple a task to kill him. She wondered if they could reclaim Ort. The bulk of the Qagrue must have sailed north to capture Zhanghar, and if the town could be roused to fight back, they might defeat the southerners. Too many Qagrue remained in Alcmouth and Zhanghar, nonetheless, and they would not stand for any rebellion. The price might be high for the citizens of Ort. "How many loyal men did this wretch have in his service?" She waved toward Gillar's body.

He pursed his lips. "He has around twenty Ortmen. Some may remain loyal to what he stood for, it is hard to say. There are many Qagrue also, although I do not know the exact number."

Corelle pointed at Gillar's body. "If all things were equal, I would like to replace this atrocity with a Portreeve who is loyal to Dur. I fear to embroil others in my actions, however. I have imperilled you all now I have killed him, in truth."

The man rubbed his chin and looked thoughtful. "If I flee Ort, the blame will fall on me. The staff slept, heard nothing, and found him dead in the morning. You need not be implicated. That would leave you free to do more, my guess. I will travel to Ryl and join Raolos there."

She disliked his plan, but it took her by surprise he knew Raolos had gone to Ryl. "You know he lives?"

"Merja told me." Beside him, the woman who had answered the door earlier nodded in agreement.

Corelle considered his suggestion. She believed she could do little more here. Gillar had been killed, but the Qagrue remained in control. While she might find another who would be prepared to take over as Portreeve, she anticipated it would be a short-lived job. Once Krage learned of the events in Ort, the new Portreeve would soon swing from the gallows. Worse, the false Duke might encourage the Qagrue to take additional payment from innocent citizens for the death of his friend. *"Better to walk out with coin than be thrown out without so much as a groat,"* as the old expression went, and the death of Gillar would serve as coin for Corelle. "Very well. I will ride to Ryl with you. There is little we can do here, after all else." She turned to the women. "Go back to bed. Rise as normal in the morning, when you will discover to your horror Gillar has been killed in his bed by his guard. Summon the Portreeve's men. We will rest here for a few hours then head for Ryl." She turned to the guard. "What is your name?"

"Parstic."

"Go now. Tell your family you must leave. Bring them if you fear for their safety."

He shook his head. "I am unmarried, and my parents are old. They cannot travel."

"Then at the least fetch your belongings. It is a long ride."

He gave a bitter laugh. "I have few enough belongings worthy of the effort."

"We will be long gone before they seek to pursue us. The southerners are unlikely to follow us far. They will not wish to leave the town unguarded to pursue the killers of a man they would care little about." She nodded toward the bed as she said it. "We will try to get word to somebody you trust to let them know change will come, and Raolos is still alive."

Parstic nodded, a grim determination on his face. "Leesant. Ibie seemed to hold him in high esteem." The women also nodded their agreement.

"Then let us get a few hours' sleep before we start. I am weary." The staff left her alone in the room with Gillar. She glowered her hatred at his pale corpse as she snatched up the lantern he had lit, then found an empty bedroom, careful to avoid the one in which Deineike had died. Exhausted, she fell onto the bed and soon fell asleep.

CHAPTER 28
RICRID

Ricrid had come from Torric with Sisnop, but he had watched as the power within the group of leaders shifted in Krage's favour. Krage's plan, to return to Dur with the Qagrue, had been inspired, and Ricrid had been content to throw in with Krage as one of his guards rather than Sisnop. Krage seemed to hold him in high regard for the first few days, even to the extent of the order to deal with the three men who had hanged the Duke's son. He had not killed them; they had made a mistake, nothing more, and he knew two of them. He told them they had fallen from favour with their new Duke and advised them to leave Alcmouth at the earliest opportunity, or their futures might not be guaranteed. Krage appointed him Sergeant once somebody reported the men had disappeared.

Ricrid did not care for the Qagrue. They did nothing to disguise their violent natures, which Ricrid found arrogant and craven. Any group of three or four men could wield their swords before a crowd of frightened citizens and feel themselves powerful. Ricrid fancied he could kill several of them before they could guess his intent. He did not boast of his prowess when he killed; he slid back into the shadows and returned to his life.

Krage changed before Ricrid's eyes almost at once. He drank wine all day long, and some days it proved difficult to fathom whether he had become more inebriated on the wine or the power he now wielded as Duke. It mattered little to Ricrid. He had his job, and he need no longer fear the hangman's noose. If Krage treated him well, he would remain content. It seemed Krage understood Dur should remain a Duchy, and the Qagrue would leave once they had served their purpose, which suited Ricrid.

Four or five days after they had arrived in Alcmouth, word came to Krage that the son of the deposed Bailiff had been captured by the Qagrue. At first, Krage showed no concern, but as the day wound down and his inebriation grew, he railed against Raolos, and against the son. Corelle had killed Glailam, they had learned, and Krage seemed to place some of the blame on Raolos. Ricrid said nothing, reluctant to involve himself in the politics of the Duchy.

Krage prepared to leave and head for the vast home he had taken for himself. Ricrid had stood guard through the day, but others would travel to Krage's home and watch for his safety through the night. Before they arrived, Krage wagged a finger toward Ricrid in an indication he wished his guard to approach him. Ricrid would have preferred to have been addressed by name, but he bit his tongue and stood next to Krage.

"The boy." Krage slurred the words. He had consumed more than one cask of wine today and had seemed unbothered by the news about Raolos's son until this moment.

"What of him?"

"Kill him."

Ricrid took a step backward and glared at the Duke. He could not mean it, could he? The wine spoke, not Krage. "You jest."

"He killed Styrrach, my oldest friend."

Ricrid took a deep breath as he tried to arrange his thoughts. "Corelle killed Styrrach."

"That she did, but at his behest. On the say-so of the boy's father."

Ricrid exhaled and glanced upward. Krage had either become more intoxicated than Ricrid had realised, or he had lost his mind. "Corelle killed him because he killed her lover."

"Her deviant." Krage snarled as he spoke and sprayed his desk with spit. "Kill him."

"My Duke, a few days ago you ordered me to deal with the men who hanged the Duke's son. Why do you now wish this boy killed?"

"That boy was but nine years. This is no boy. He is in his teenyears."

"My Duke…"

"You challenge my orders?" Krage glared at Ricrid with wild eyes.

Ricrid lowered his head. "It will be done."

At the end of his watch, others relieved him, and he left the Highhome. He searched for a way to avoid the death of the boy, and he turned to one of the Torric members he thought he could trust.

Denstal had not changed allegiance from Sisnop to Krage, and his reward had been the position of senior guard to the new Bailiff. Ricrid and Denstal had been close in Torric, and they had met in Alcmouth for an ale on two occasions since their return. Ricrid sought him out that night and told him of his dilemma.

Denstal offered him an opportunity to avoid the distasteful task. "I will kill him for you, if you have become squeamish."

"I would not say I am squeamish. I am content to kill, but children should not fall under our blades. Is this what we have become? Child killers?"

"Where is this lad?"

"The Qagrue have him in their accommodation, I believe."

"Then let us go and see him. Krage claims he is in his teenyears. If he is, he is no child."

With no better plan of his own, Ricrid trudged along beside Denstal to the large building the Qagrue used as the main accommodation for the soldiers they had left behind in Alcmouth. They demanded to see the boy on Krage's authority, and the yellow tunics they wore carried sufficient importance. The Qagrue took them to see the lad.

They had him chained to a heavy table. His bloodstained clothes and askew nose told Ricrid the Qagrue had already served him rough treatment. As soon as Ricrid saw him, he knew the boy had not yet reached his teenyears.

"How many years are you, lad?" He strove to keep his voice calm.

"Eleven." The boy kept his eyes downcast as he shook with fear.

Ricrid glanced at Denstal. "Eleven years. He is only a boy, and these… people have mistreated him."

Denstal stared at the boy. "That they have."

"He has done nothing. I will not do it. He is Durfolk."

"Then what? Will you defy your orders? You will find a rope around your neck if you do so."

Ricrid sighed. Denstal had the right of it, but he could not murder a boy of eleven years. "So be it." He turned to the Qagrue who loitered nearby. "Do you speak Dur?" The man shook his head and shrugged his shoulders. Ricrid barked out an order to fetch somebody who did with a wave of his arm.

The man shouted something in his guttural language, and after a short wait another Qagrue entered the room. "What is?"

Ricrid stood close to the man. "I will take the boy."

"You not take. Qagrue take. He ours."

Ricrid thrust his face into the other's. "I will take him." He pointed to his yellow tunic to imply he held authority here.

The Qagrue pushed his shoulder, but as quick as the blink of an eye, Ricrid had his blade at the man's throat. From the corner of his eye, he saw Denstal pull his dagger and point it at the other Qagrue. The Qagrue under Ricrid's blade growled, furious. "You be sorry."

"You be dead." Why Ricrid had spoken his own language in the same peculiar way as the Qagure, he could not decide. "Release him."

The man nodded, and Ricrid lowered his dagger. The Qagrue produced a key from a pocket and released the boy. Ricrid pulled the lad close, and they left the building. Behind him, Denstal asked the lad his name.

"Raopul."

Denstal guarded their rear as they walked away, but he asked what Ricrid planned to do next.

Ricrid had no more than a hint of a plan. "How much coin do you have on you?"

"Because of you, the Qagrue will kill me, then Krage will want to kill me again, and now you want to steal my coin?"

Ricrid laughed. "We have spent coin on less worthwhile things."

"That we have." Denstal sighed and handed Ricrid a pouch that jingled with coin. Ricrid also had a full pouch with him. Krage had paid him a handsome sum for the so-called death of the three men who had hanged the Duke's son.

They walked the boy toward the docks through the poor quarter. They questioned a few folks in the street until they found what they searched for, an old woman named Umester who lived alone and had no close family. They went to her home, a rough, run-down house in which she had a small, dirty room. They gave her the coin and told her to take the boy away wherever she could reach and keep him safe, then walked the two of them to the dock.

They found a ship that sailed to Ort. The new token guaranteed safe passage for the woman and the boy, and the master seemed intimidated by Ricrid and Denstal. They made their way back toward the square.

As they trudged along, Denstal muttered, "I would invite you for an ale, but I seem to have been robbed."

His jest convinced Ricrid beyond any doubt they had done the right thing. "As have I." They went their separate ways.

Ricrid turned to look back as Denstal did the same. Denstal gave him a wave, and Ricrid returned it. Denstal shouted, "Another time," and Ricrid turned to head home.

CHAPTER 29
KRAGE

Krage sipped at his wine. He drank more these days than he had ever done before. In truth, now he had become Duke, the job bored him. He sat, bored, in a meeting with his Senior Tally Master. The man told Krage how much coin poured in, but it did not interest him. As long as he had plenty of coin, it mattered little to him whether they told him this amount or that. He had more than he could spend, it seemed.

The three men who had hanged the Duke's son had disappeared. He had ordered them searched for when he heard nobody had seen them for several days, but no trace of them was ever found. Ricrid had performed well, and Krage paid him a handsome reward. As promised, Krage promoted him to Sergeant. Ricrid turned out to be a loyal, dependable man. Krage felt certain he would be a useful fighter if things became dangerous, but in truth, Dur continued as it always had before he became Duke. Little violence occurred, as had always been the case. At times, somebody would attack one of the Qagrue, but the attacker never lived long. Qagrue justice, while not as brutal as Guild justice, still meant the person who received it ended up dead. Krage turned a blind eye to such things.

Ricrid never mentioned Raolos's son, but tales reached Krage's ears the boy had been taken from the Qagrue by two men in yellow. Krage had to endure several meetings with one of the senior Qagrue soldiers before the man could be placated, and Krage did not ask Ricrid what he had done with the body. In truth, he felt guilty he had ordered the death of the boy, in his cups one day. Once written, fates could not be unwritten, and Krage went on with his life as Duke.

The Senior Tally Master talked more about coin and ways to increase the volume of trade Dur could do with other lands. Krage gazed out of the window to watch the clouds meander across the sky. He sipped at his wine and heard almost none of the man's words. The sky told of the end of summer and the coming wet season, he thought. The dark clouds threatened rain, and the temperatures had dropped over the last sevenday. At least this year he could afford the best cloak in the land. Krage laughed to himself.

A knock came at the door and an aide entered the office before Krage had summoned him. Krage knit his brow and stared at the man, who shifted from foot to foot, uncomfortable. Krage barked at him, ill-tempered. "What is it, man?" The Senior Tally Master had fallen silent. At the least, the aide had interrupted the dull flow of words and numbers from the coin counter.

The aide wrung his hands in apparent discomfort. "My Duke, a delegation from Qagrue awaits your pleasure."

The Qagrue never bothered him any longer. Their leader had sailed north and taken control of either Ort or Zhanghar. Krage did not care which. He had left behind a few menial soldiers who almost never came to the Ducal Highhome, so it surprised Krage some had called on him now. "The soldiers wish to see me?" He wanted to be certain he understood the man, whose face had turned pale, beads of sweat on his brow. Krage wondered what had made him so anxious.

"My Duke." Krage could not miss the apologetic tone in his voice. "These are not soldiers. They arrived today from Qagrue by ship."

Krage tutted. "How else would they arrive, man? Aboard a giant fish?"

"My apologies, my Duke." The man spluttered and wrung his hands even more. "There is a tribal leader at their head, it turns. My apologies—his name is quite impossible for me to understand."

Krage nodded. The Qagrue had lengthy, complicated names that defined their family lineage, or some such nonsense. Far more sensible to have one concise name. He sighed. "Then send them in. I will receive them. Show"—he could not recall the Senior Tally Master's name—"him out. Bring good wine and sufficient goblets." Krage noticed Ricrid slip out of his office. With luck, he would return soon in case the Qagrue caused any difficulty.

As the Senior Tally Master rose, he appeared pleased to be dismissed. He left with the aide, and Krage crossed the office to stand near the couches. The door opened again and several Qagrue entered.

They did not wear the same tunics the soldiers wore, but sported elaborate long tunics of fine making, adorned with beads and depictions of animals Krage could not identify. He recognised one of them as the leader of the tribe who had provided him with the four hundred soldiers with which he had toppled Dur and brought it under his own control. Krage forced an air of civility to his voice and demeanour. "Welcome to Dur. We were not informed of your arrival. Had we been, we would have arranged a suitable reception for you at the docks the moment your ship—"

The man interrupted. "It matters not." Krage could not believe anybody would deign to interrupt him, the Duke of all Dur, regardless of their stature in their own land. The man gave a dismissive wave of his hand in Krage's direction that inflamed Krage's ire even more. "I come to see new territory."

Krage could find no words to respond. His mind raced over the announcement. The man had spoken six words; short and succinct, but Krage could not understand them. The man must mean some nearby territory, he imagined. "Territory? You have taken some new territory near to Dur?"

"Not near. Here." The man spoke with a flat tone. He did not look at Krage as he spoke but gazed around the office, as though the Duke might be beneath him, a stain to be ignored.

Krage grew ever more confused. What in the Five Cities could the man mean? "This is Dur. You are our principal trade partner, of course. It is not a Qagrue territory, however."

The man raised his eyebrows, as though Krage's words surprised him. He gave a short laugh. "Is now."

Krage could feel the heat in his cheeks as his face reddened. His heart raced, his palms clammy with sweat. "Wait a moment, please, while I explain things. That is not what we agreed."

The man shrugged. "We make new arrangement. We take Dur as Qagrue territory." At last, he turned his gaze to Krage, contempt in his eyes, as though he addressed a child.

Panic clawed at Krage's heart, and he did not know what to make of the man's word. His mind raced through the absurd claims as he tried to make sense of them and formulate a rational response to an irrational statement. He decided it would be best to return to the start. "I apologise. There appears to have been some mistake. I am the Duke here. This is Dur. It is my Duchy."

The man frowned. "What is 'Duke?'"

Krage sighed. "The Duke is the leader of Dur." His heart threatened to leap out of his breast, and sweat streamed from his forehead. He blew some cool air from his mouth upward over his face.

"Then you not Duke. I am leader. I am Kandaltorq Sumbrid Akh Torq. I am tribal leader of men already here. I am tribal leader of those in other ships follow me here. I claim this territory for tribe."

Krage's legs threatened to give way beneath him. He could not believe this had turned. This man had the audacity to arrive and claim Dur for himself, to strip from Krage everything he had worked for? His rage increased as he fumed on the outrageous unreasonableness of it. "You are mistaken." He battled to keep his temper under control and his voice level.

Kandaltorq, or whichever of his preposterous names he went by, seemed unfazed by Krage's protests. "Not mistaken." He laughed. "I did not believe you could take entire land with four hundred men. Thought you…" He seemed to struggle for the Dur word and turned to the men assembled behind him. Krage thought he muttered, "*Sgurkachek.*"

One of the others smiled before he translated. "Deluded."

"Deluded, this is word." Kandaltorq turned to Krage again. "I wrong. My men took Dur, and now I claim."

Krage heard his voice rise to a near-shout but could no longer control his fury. "That they did not. I took Dur. Me. Do you hear me? They helped of course, and you will be well rewarded for that assistance. Dur is my land, not yours."

Kandaltorq ignored his words. "I like my office." He turned to his companions again. "Remove him. *Enik shtah heinte.*"

Two burly men stepped forward and took one of Krage's arms each. They dragged him toward the door, although Krage protested the entire time. As they reached the door, it opened, and Ricrid entered the office with five of his men, all with daggers drawn.

One of the Qagrue who held Krage roared in disdainful laughter. "You wish resist? You will die."

Ricrid snarled, his eyes fixed on those of the one who had spoken. "As will you." The man sneered but did not release Krage.

Ricrid's voice, calm and sinister, brought chill bumps to Krage's flesh even though the assassin was on his side. "Release him." At that moment, Krage had some insight into what it must be like to receive a visit from a member of the Guild who had been sent to end one's days.

"Take him." The Qagrue pushed Krage forward, then pulled their swords from their belts. Krage struggled to stay on his feet and might have fallen had one of Ricrid's men not grabbed at him. He turned to face the Qagrue. Seven of them, Kandaltorq included, but only the two who had dragged him away had their swords out.

He looked at Ricrid in expectation, but Ricrid shook his head and motioned for Krage to leave the office. Once he reached the aide's office that adjoined his own, Krage understood. Many more Qagrue soldiers in the familiar tunics stood there. Their numbers would have been too great for Ricrid and his men. They would have been cut down for certain.

Ricrid leaned close to Krage, his voice quiet. "Let us find somewhere safer where we can talk. We are in peril here."

Whatever had turned lay beyond Krage's capacity to grasp. His scheme had been so perfect, and it had gone so well. He had become the Duke and ruled Dur. He had glimpsed a future where he earned all the coin any man could ever wish for. What gave this ignorant southerner the right to sail here and claim the land, Krage's land, for his own? Krage followed Ricrid out of the Highhome, his heart a dead weight in his breast. As they walked along the Duke's Highway toward the square, he muttered more than once, "I am the Duke." Many more Qagrue soldiers filled the streets than before the arrival of Kandaltorq and his men.

"I am the Duke." He had lost count of how many times he had said it as they reached the square and approached an inn. Sisnop, Carshan and many of their men in the yellow and red tunics of the Bailiff and Portreeve stood around in the square, hesitant, but when they saw Krage, they rushed toward him as one, and they yelled and shouted all at once. It seemed the Bailiff and Portreeve had been thrown from their Offices with no more ceremony than Krage, who once again protested. "They have come to steal my Duchy. I am the Duke."

Somebody asked what they should do, and Krage considered their options. They might not be safe in Dur. He had not been threatened, but he did not believe the Qagrue would permit him to raise a rebellion, even if he could gather enough men to stage one. "We must leave Dur. We will head south." He saw no alternative.

Sisnop pushed his face into Krage's. "We have wasted much time and more coin. We have done no more than make back all it cost us." His curt tone implied he blamed Krage for all that had turned.

"You should have made coin aplenty." Krage's self-pity fled him, his anger rekindled. "What have you been about?"

"I have paid all these men to serve me, and little enough of the trade coin has accrued to me yet. It has been a disaster."

Krage waved a dismissive hand at him. He cared little about Sisnop and his coin. He had his own secreted in a nearby house, safe and sound. He had retained a large sum, enough to live on in comfort should he choose to do so. "These treacherous Qagrue. We will travel to Qanti and see whether they will support us in the reclamation of Dur."

"Reclamation?" Sisnop's temples throbbed, his face a bright red. He clenched his fists so tight, the knuckles turned white. "I have no interest in any reclamation of this wretched place. We must go to Ort and warn Gillar. He is my trusted aide, and my friend."

Krage waved a hand at him again. "There is no time to journey to Ort. Send letters. Tell him to join us. He will be safe enough, my guess. Their leaders have not travelled to Ort yet." Krage did not care about Gillar. He had never cared about him, and he did not intend to start now.

Sisnop yelled like somebody denied a treat, petulant and red-faced. "Join us where? Qanti?" His temper seemed as hot as Krage's own. "I want no more of your schemes. They have taken us nowhere. I should never have listened to your idiotic idea in the first place."

Krage narrowed his eyes and stared at him, this man who had ridden on the back of his own ideas to become Bailiff, now turned on him and dismissive of his idea like a child grown out of its favourite toy. "Then proceed to Ort, rescue your precious Gillar. I will not travel with you. I go south today. I will shed no tear if I never see you again." He glared at Sisnop in an invitation to challenge him. He would kill him, or order Ricrid to do so. Ricrid had his dagger in his hand, Krage noted. Two or three former Guild members had come out of the woodwork and offered their services since Krage became Duke, and he had accepted them into his personal guard. As a result, Sisnop had three or four former Guild men loyal to him at best, while Krage had six. Ricrid, the best of them, had changed allegiance and fought for Krage now. The Bailiff's and Portreeve's men would not back either of them if it came to a fight. Krage felt certain he held the high hand.

With a rasp of breath, Sisnop turned and stomped off, three men with him. Carshan lingered and gazed at Krage in obvious hope but found himself the brunt of Krage's fury. "I do not wish you with me, you disgusting little man. Go, dog. Follow your master."

As Carshan scurried after Sisnop, Krage turned to Ricrid. "Find a cart and meet me on Torric Street." He laid a hand on Ricrid's forearm. "Hurry." He chose three of the others to follow him. The other two he instructed to follow Sisnop and keep him safe. He set off for the house where he had stashed his trunks of coin. He had resolved to take his coin south, along with Ricrid and his men. He did not care if Sisnop, Gillar and the others lived or died. He did not care whether the Guild members kept them safe or not. He cared only about himself and his safety. The four he would take with him were more than competent to protect him, and he did not wish to split his wealth with more Guild members than he needed to.

He would take Ricrid and these three. His reign as Duke had been short-lived, thanks to the treachery of the Qagrue. He muttered from time to time, "Curse them." He maintained a brisk pace through the streets, his plans burned to ashes around him.

CHAPTER 30
CORELLE

A knock at the bedroom door awoke Corelle with a start. She slipped from the bed, her fan in her hand, skipped to the door, and stood to one side of it. "Who is there?"

"It is Parstic."

"What is the hour?" She pulled the door open.

"It is early. The sun has not risen. But somebody else has. A man who calls himself Sisnop has arrived at the house and demanded to see Gillar. They arrived an hour ago from Alcmouth. He seems distressed. He is the Bailiff, is he not? Do you know him?"

"That I do not, but I know who he is. He is a friend of Gillar's."

"That is a sorry turn, then." Parstic betrayed no hint of irony. "He travels with a fine dressed man and at least five others. Some of Gillar's men are with him also. I believe they brought him here. Sisnop's men have an air of violence about them."

Corelle muttered to herself. "Guild members." Parstic had the right of it. A sorry turn.

"Guild members?"

Corelle had neither the time nor the inclination to explain the

Guild to Parstic. "No matter. Can you tell them Gillar is out of town?"

"His men know that is not true. Besides, Sisnop seems insistent. Desperate, in truth. They are in the parlour as we speak."

Corelle considered the situation they now faced. Even if Gillar's men did not join in, five Guild members plus Sisnop, who may be a skilled fighter, would be too many for the two of them to take on. Gillar's men would not be aware of what had turned but could not be expected to stand by and do nothing if they saw the Bailiff attacked. The odds were stacked against them. They should flee, but she would like to learn why Sisnop had sailed all the way from Alcmouth when he could have sent letters. It had to be some significant development to have brought him here in person.

Corelle did not care about her own life, but neither did she want to jeopardise Parstic or the other staff. She wore her tunic, but nothing else, so she told Parstic to wait while she pulled her trousers and boots on and wracked her brain for some plan that might work. When she opened the door again, she asked Parstic to tell the Bailiff Gillar suffered the after-effects of an excess of wine the night before but would be down soon. In the meantime, did he have a message for Gillar?

Parstic scurried off and returned some moments later. Sisnop instructed Gillar to gather his coin and prepare to leave. They had been betrayed by the Qagrue and must flee Dur.

"Did he mention Krage?" Corelle longed to know what had turned down in the capital.

"That he did not."

A disappointment. Did Krage have some part to play in whatever betrayal the Qagrue had committed, or had he also been betrayed? The development fascinated Corelle, although she saw no benefit for Dur in the news unless she could exploit this turn of events to kill Sisnop. "You could tell him Gillar would prefer to receive Sisnop in his room. Alone, with none of his men. There, I could kill him."

Parstic looked thoughtful for a moment. "There is great risk in this. I do not doubt you could kill him if he comes to Gillar's room alone, but what of the others? They are too many for us. They are sure to intervene when Sisnop does not return."

Corelle hesitated, caught between doubt and uncertainty. "What do you know of Gillar's men, the ones with Sisnop?"

"There are four of them. Good men, I believe, who might join us if they knew the truth of the situation. They do not, and cannot stand by as we kill the Bailiff, I think."

Corelle nodded. He had repeated her own earlier thought, but she had no other plan, and no time to make one. "We will roll the dice. Bring him up but emphasise he is to be alone. Gillar would not wish any of the men to see him in such poor condition."

"I will do my best." A lack of conviction rang in his voice.

"Parstic, save yourself if things turn awry. Do not wait for me. You know this city better than Sisnop's men. Make your escape and head to Ryl."

He nodded, a grim expression on his face, and headed back down the stairs. Corelle ran to Gillar's room and pulled the blanket up over his head. Blood stains covered the room, so she blew out her lantern and left the shutters down. Darkness folded the room into its black mantle as the flame flickered out. She stood to one side of the doorway and felt around the door handle, where she found a large key in the lock.

Corelle had a fragile plan, and these might well be her last moments. She felt calm and relaxed at the prospect. She had earned an early death. Few would disagree if they knew of all she had wrought in her twenty-four years.

Feet approached the bedroom. She heard more than one person and hoped nobody but Parstic had come with Sisnop. The door opened, and lantern light spilled into the room. In a stroke of luck, it fell short of the blood-stained carpet around the bed.

"Gillar, get out of bed, you inebriate. We must flee." A figure walked toward the bed. The lantern stayed outside the room, in Parstic's hand, she hoped. She pushed the door closed and turned the key.

Sisnop let out a startled yell, but Corelle's eyes had already acclimatised to the darkness that fell on the room. She had her knife at his throat in an instant. "Do not make a sound"

"Who are… Corelle?" It seemed realisation dawned on Sisnop at that instant.

"That I am. Tell me more of this betrayal."

"Why should I tell you anything?"

"I will kill you if you do not."

"You will kill me anyway, whether I tell you or not." He seemed calm and unafraid. "My fates are written. I should have listened to Krage and sent letters."

"What of Krage? Is he with you?"

"That he is not. He has fled south like a whipped dog. He trusted the Qagrue to help him take Dur for his own, but they turned on him and seized it for themselves. Now my life is forfeit to you for the friendship I bore Gillar. Is he dead?"

"That he is. I have sent him wherever he travels to afterward. I avenged Klordia."

"Who?"

"Wilash's wife. Ibie also, the Portreeve of this town before that monster came to claim the town."

"I have nine guards downstairs. How many are with you? The imbecile with the lantern?"

He had, at the least, confirmed only Parstic waited outside the room. "I have more, but that is my knowledge alone. You have Guild members with you?"

"Five of them. They remain loyal to me."

"Then they are loyal to a dead man. Your friendship with Gillar has brought your ruin."

"Then strike, and be done with it. I tire of your conversation."

She felt a reluctant admiration for his stoicism in the face of death, but too many people about whom she cared had died because of him, Krage, and Styrrach. She pulled the blade across his throat, a deep cut. More blood gushed over her as Sisnop made a strange, gurgling sound before he fell face first to the floor with a heavy thud. She hoped those downstairs would imagine Gillar had fallen out of bed or some similar excuse for the sound.

She opened the door and Parstic stepped into the room. While she wiped Sisnop's blood on his own trouser legs, Parstic gazed down on his body. "What now?"

Corelle glanced up at him. "Go down to them, keep them distracted if you can. I need some time to think of our next course of action."

He appeared reluctant to follow her instructions, and she understood his hesitation. He might walk into harm, but if they had to fight all the men assembled downstairs, their chances would be improved if he stood among them. He could strike at them as she entered the room. Gillar's men would be unlikely to fight at the start and might not join in at all if the Guild members attacked an unfamiliar woman in their employer's parlour. She saw it as their best chance, although it remained a slim chance at best.

He went back down the stairs, and Corelle took a deep breath. Nervousness tried to shake her, to persuade her to turn and run, but she fought to control her emotions and her body. She reasoned another fight lay ahead downstairs. When she judged Parstic had had enough time to talk to the others, she crept down the stairs. As she reached the bottom of the staircase, she heard voices she did not recognise. They sounded angry. Someone asked Parstic what delayed Gillar and Sisnop, and he said he did not know.

One voice rose above the others. "We should go up there and check. If you lie to us…"

Another voice leapt to Parstic's defence. "Wait a moment. Parstic is a good man. It sits ill with us when you accuse him of falsehood."

"Do you lie?" A third voice dripped disbelief at whatever story Parstic had told them.

Corelle stepped into the parlour. Parstic stood to her left, near three men in the red tunics of the Portreeve. Another red tunic sat in a chair near the window. A stout man in fancy clothing sat on the couch she and Deineike had sat on the first time they came to the house. The five Guild men stood in a group in the centre of the room. She did not recognise any of them as she shouted words that stilled the arguments. "Leave your daggers where they are."

CHAPTER 31
CORELLE

All heads turned to her. What must they have thought when she appeared before them, covered in blood? The Guild men stared at her with disbelief in their eyes, open-mouthed. She paid no attention to Gillar's men. They posed no real threat, and if she must die, she wanted to kill as many of Sisnop's men as she could before they took her life.

One of the Guild men whispered in disbelief. "Corelle?"

She kept her gaze fixed on the Guild men as she spoke to Gillar's red tunics. "There is a new Portreeve in Ort. Gillar has left. Leesant is your Portreeve now." She hoped she had remembered the name from when Parstic had mentioned it last night. Her memory for words seemed somewhat diminished of late.

A Guild member spoke before the Portreeve's men could answer. "Left for where?"

Corelle ignored him. "Do you men stand with your new Portreeve?"

Parstic pulled out his dagger. "I do." He stood tall, proud and decisive. None of the others spoke.

Corelle continued to watch the Guild men. "You five. Take

Sisnop's coin and leave. You have not wronged me, and he and Gillar have no need of it where I have sent them."

They all pulled daggers from their waistbands or belts as one asked, "You have killed them?"

"That I have. The Qagrue have replaced Krage, and Sisnop and Gillar are both dead. You do not need to throw away your lives for a cause that is already lost."

One of them took a step toward her, menace in his eyes, a snarl on his lips. "We are five. You are one. Who is to say we will die?"

Corelle brought her fan into view from where she had held it close to her thigh. When she pressed the rivet, the blade whispered its deadly song as it sprang from the fan's guard. "I am. You may kill me, I reason, but most of you will die. Who wishes to taste my blade first?" Corelle had played the bluff before. She gambled none of them wanted to die so others could kill her, and they hesitated, as she had expected. "I have no argument with you. You are pieces in the game, as I am. Take his coin, leave, and live a good life. It is a better offer than Krage or Styrrach would have made you."

From the couch, the stout man yelled. "Kill her. She has killed your Guildmeister and his Senior Aide. Her life is forfeit."

None of the Guild men looked at him. The men in the red tunics had their daggers out, confusion on their faces as she glanced at them. They turned their gazes to Parstic often, as though they sought answers from him.

She turned to the Guild members again. "If you kill me and do not leave, the Qagrue will kill you in any event. There are too many to resist."

Some of the Guild members nodded their heads and mumbled words Corelle could not hear. The one closest to Corelle returned his dagger to his belt. "There is truth in your words. Dur will not now be the Dur we knew. They call it their territory."

Corelle gave a grim laugh. "That remains to be determined."

"You will fight them?" He raised his eyebrows in apparent surprise at her words.

She shook her head and held up a hand to indicate he had misunderstood her. "That I will not. They are too many. I will do what I can to help, but I alone cannot remove them."

One of the Portreeve's men joined the discussion. "What of our friends and family? Are they abandoned to these southerners?"

The man on the couch seemed angry. "Kill her, you rabble. Why do you wait?"

One of the Guild men turned to him. "Still your tongue, man. You have no say in these matters. Those you served are dead. You no longer have any authority here."

Corelle frowned at the stout man. "Who is this man?"

He answered for himself. "I am Carshan, Portreeve of Alcmouth and former Portreeve of Torric."

She remembered the name; Minarko had mentioned him in Yerrsun. The bitter irony of his words amused Corelle, and she snorted in derision. "You are Portreeve of nothing. Have you not grasped that? You served Krage and Sisnop. The Qagrue care nothing for your title and will throw you into the Alc without hesitation. You deserve little more. How many Guild members did you hang when Sisnop shrouded them in Torric?"

His mouth dropped open, and the Guild members looked puzzled. One of them asked, "Shrouded? What does this mean?"

So few who had served as Styrrach's justice seemed to have grasped the Guild's true purpose. Corelle gave a sad shake of her head. "You still do not know the game they played. Whenever they found it convenient to make a display of justice to appease the gentle folk of Dur, they chose one of us to be shrouded—given away to the Portreeve to be hanged. If we became an inconvenience, as I did in Zhanghar, they shrouded us. They used us to do their unpleasant work, then threw us away like a tunic that has reached the end of its days."

Carshan's face reddened, and he shouted, spittle spattering from his lips in all directions. "That is untrue. You try to save your own skin."

Corelle twisted her face into a mask of fury. "I care nothing for my skin. You should be more mindful of those you insult. I have done unbearable things and deserve whatever fates are written for me. As have you."

"You hanged a friend of mine." A Guild member had spoken in a quiet voice full of menace. "You caught him at the docks as he watched a tally house. You hanged him from the mast of a ship."

"Yardarm." Corelle had corrected him from some strange instinct, without thought. The man turned his head, a perplexed look on his face. "The bars you refer to, they are called yardarms, not the mast." Her cheeks warmed, and she wished she had stayed silent.

The man stared at her for a moment, then turned his attention back to Carshan with a slight shake of his head. "You hanged him from the yardarm. You did this at Sisnop's orders?"

Carshan looked terrified, and he mopped at his sweaty brow with a kerchief. He did not reply straight away, and Corelle could almost see his brain race about in search of an answer to appease his accuser. "I..." He held out a placatory hand. "Sisnop is to blame." The bluster had gone from his tone, replaced by a feeble, pathetic whine.

The Guild man's face betrayed no emotion. "Sisnop is dead. He has paid for his part in the deaths of our friends. It may be time for you to pay your debt to them." The man had a cold detachment as he talked of the payment of debt. Corelle guessed she herself had spoken in the same tone many times. It would intimidate any who heard it, and even though it had not been directed at her, it chilled the blood in her veins. She imagined those she had killed after such words had all died in fear. They had seen a monster before them, one whose sole purpose had been their ruin.

Carshan forced out a laugh, reedy, nervous. "Friends. Let us not be rash here. The woman has already said there is plenty of coin for us all, and Dur is now an unwelcome home for us. Let us part as friends and go our separate ways."

Corelle glared at him, angered by the way he had referred to her. "'The woman?' I should kill you myself and save these men the trouble."

He spluttered and turned desperate eyes to her. "Forgive me, please."

A strict, no-nonsense voice came from the hallway door. "Spill no more blood on my master's carpets." All turned to look at Merja in the doorway, her arms folded and a fire in her eyes. Nobody moved.

Carshan wasted no time. He seized on her words as some form of reprieve. "My thanks, good lady. You are wise and more level-headed than my companions, I see."

"Take him into the rear garden. There you may do with him as you see fit. Raopul and Pettra will await him wherever he travels to afterward. I doubt that meeting will be pleasant for him." She turned and walked into the hall out of their sight.

His eyes wide, he half rose, but one of the Portreeve's men pushed him back onto the couch. "You have killed Raopul?"

His pudgy face covered in sweat, he shook his head from side to side, terrified. "I do not know this name. I have only hanged those who deserved their fate, killers all."

The Portreeve's man shook his head as his face took on a woebegone expression. "I knew the child. I would not have thought any man capable of so heinous an act as the murder of a child."

Carshan spluttered desperate excuses he must hope might save him. "I did not kill him. Only the Duke's son has been killed, and not by me."

Corelle's heart leapt. Might Raopul be alive after all else? Had Krage kept him alive, some valuable piece to use in negotiations should he find himself in a tight corner? Had the boy evaded capture altogether? He had been a smart lad, and Corelle did not doubt he had the wit to hide and find some safe place. Hope remained that he lived, and Corelle determined she would hold onto that hope unless evidence proved it futile.

Close to Corelle, one of the Guild members seemed to come to a decision. "Enough about the boy. We will return to Carshan and his fate soon enough. The Guild can be rebuilt with you at its helm." He nodded his head at her. She opened her mouth to protest, but he shook his head to silence her. "Hear me out. The southerners are our enemies. We cannot match them for numbers, but we know other ways to plague their existence. They will become our marks, and they will pay a terrible price for their new territory."

Murmurs of assent rose from the other four Guild men. One muttered, "A good idea."

Corelle shook her head. "What of those who cannot kill from the shadows? What of those innocents whom the Qagrue will hang unless they reveal the location of this new Guild? What of them?"

One of the red-jacket Portreeve's men joined in. "They would not dare. Gillar said it more than once. Without the citizens, the land would be nothing more than a patch of dirt he and the new Duke would not be interested in. The Qagrue must feel the same, my guess."

Another concern weighed on Corelle's mind. "You have hunted me for more than three years. Now you wish me to lead you? This makes no sense to me. Why would you wish this? Why such a change of heart?"

"We hunted you on the orders of those who no longer live." He wore a resigned look on his face. "Like you, we have few skills other than death. This is our one way to fight back. Although we hunted you, we did not catch you. Who better to lead us? You are formidable, we all know this. None wished to encounter you, although we acted as though we wished you brought to those whom you have now killed." The others all nodded at his words. "What else can we do?"

Corelle managed a smile amid such a tense moment. The man did not know she possessed skills far beyond death. She had become a mariner, and she wished to return to that life as soon as possible. She had no desire to lead a version of the Guild, even one dedicated to a better cause than it had been under Styrrach, and she told them so. "What else can we do? Flee Dur. That is my advice, as it has been since before the sun rose this morning. Take Sisnop's coin and leave."

One of the others played on her earlier words. "What of those you mentioned before? What of those who cannot flee Dur? Is it fair for us to take the coin and leave behind those who cannot leave, those who cannot fight back?"

She sighed. His point had merit, but it had implications so serious, she did not wish to consider them. Whatever turned, she had no wish to lead the reformed Guild, and resistance would be futile, in truth. She turned to Parstic. "How many Qagrue remain in Ort?"

He frowned. "I have already said I do not know for certain. If I had to guess, I would say forty, more or less. Most of them took ship north—two full ships of them travelled to Zhanghar. We have heard nothing of what turned there thus far."

Corelle could not visualise what forty men gathered together would look like, and she wondered whether Parstic would either. He may have spoken in the old Dur way, to invent a large number when the precise numbers were not known. Either way, she believed they would be a large force, based on his reply. "They will have lost no men in Zhanghar. The Portreeve and his men left for Ryl before the Qagrue arrived. There they are gathered with Raolos, who lives yet."

The Portreeve's men looked brightened by this news, but one of the Guild members shook his head. "The Bailiff died in his office. I saw his body. I entered with Sisnop after the Qagrue had killed Raolos."

Corelle could not resist a small laugh. "You were deceived. Raolos escaped. One of his aides died in his stead, loyal enough to spend his life to buy time for Raolos's escape. I have seen him, outside Delcan, not a tenday since."

The man appeared impressed. "Loyalty indeed, to give your own life for a man whose life had been filled with wealth and power."

"Raolos is a good man. He is not like Styrrach. He commands respect and loyalty. He hunted down the Guild and its corrupt Portreeves out of a sense of outrage at the evils they had done." Corelle gave Carshan a contemptuous glance as she spoke, and he looked away, unable to meet her gaze. "Raolos now readies to make the stand in Ryl we could not in Zhanghar."

Parstic broke his lengthy silence. "Should we go there and make a stand with him?"

One of his colleagues gave a sad shake of his head. "That would leave Ort at their mercy. We cannot abandon the people."

The atmosphere in the room had become charged with a violent optimism, and another of the Guild men attempted to drive the conversation in the direction of resistance. "I count eleven here. Six of us are worth more than the dagger we carry against these southerners with their swords."

Parstic seemed animated by the way the debate had turned. "There are others who would join us, I am certain of it." The other Portreeve's men nodded.

From the couch, wide-eyed in amazement, Carshan decided to add his opinion. "You are all deluded. Even Krage recognised he had lost. He fled. You should too. We all should. They will kill us otherwise."

Corelle held up a hand to silence him. "None would shed a tear for you. Your opinion carries no weight here." She turned to the Guild member who had stepped toward her. "What is your name?"

"Denstal."

"If we kill the Qagrue here, they will send more. The price could be high. Do not place the innocent at risk here. Their safety must come first."

He nodded. "Raolos fled alone?"

The change of subject surprised her, and she thought something flashed across his eyes. More lay behind this Denstal, but the sand fell. "That he did not. Three of his men rode with him, and two of my friends, Wilash and another."

"The one who has helped you, he is the other friend?"

"Synna. A Guild member from Alcmouth."

"I did not know him. We are from Torric. We know Wilash. We rode with him the day he pulled Gillar from his horse in pursuit of you." He smiled.

She returned the smile. "He is a kind man, not a killer such as you or me. He tells me he only tried to stop Gillar, but he fell from his horse."

One of the others laughed. "That he did, in truth. Gillar never forgave him."

Corelle saw no humour in the incident given its tragic consequences. "Wilash's wife paid a terrible price for that small slight. It gave me pleasure to avenge her."

Denstal nodded his agreement. "If what you have said is true— this shrouding. If that is true, you have served us all."

Parstic's enthusiasm seemed to grow. "We can send letters to Ryl. We can tell Raolos we stand here. He could join us. They would not find Ort so easy to retake."

She shook her head. "The Alc is blockaded at Zhanghar by the Qagrue. No message would come to Ryl, I fear. To take it by horse would take so long, it would be useless."

Denstal sighed in resignation. "Then it is up to us."

Corelle shook her head in bewilderment. "This is madness." Why could they not see it would be folly to resist a force so large? "This is a fight we cannot win. We were never trained to fight these Qagrue in numbers. There are two ships of them in Zhanghar, and there must be many more in Alcmouth now if they have thrown down Krage. More ships must be there, or on their way. We cannot win here. They will crush us."

Denstal stared at her. He appeared sad at first, but a resolute expression came to his face, and he turned to the others. "Who will fight these southerners with me? I never believed the day would come I would best the famous Corelle, but it seems she lacks the appetite for this enterprise. I will fight. Will you fight with me?"

As one, they let out a roar, pulled their daggers again, and slashed at the air. Corelle felt dejected by their appetite for what must be an exercise in futility and would end with them all dead. She sighed and held up her hands for silence. As their jubilant yells calmed, she looked from one to the other. She saw passion in all their eyes, the Guild men and the Portreeve's men both. She sighed again. They were all fools, but they were also brave. She could not find it in her heart to abandon them. "Very well, I will die with you, if that is what you have set your hearts upon. You Portreeve's men; gather as many as will join you in this enterprise and meet us at the Portreeve's Offices at the midday. The six of us"—she gestured at the Guild members—"will separate into pairs, make our way to the square, and kill as many of these Qagrue as we can on the way. Hide the bodies if you can. Leave them if you cannot. Do it fast and quiet. Do not attract more attention than you must. Let us thin their numbers as much as we can before we charge to our certain ruin."

Parstic led the Portreeve's men out of the house. He left Corelle with the five Guild members and Carshan. The dice had been rolled, and she believed she had rolled ones.

CHAPTER 32
CORELLE

Denstal nodded in Carshan's direction. "What about him?"

Corelle turned steely eyes on the former Portreeve, who sat bereft on the couch and rubbed his palms together in nervousness. "He played a part in the deaths of people I care about." One of the Guild men agreed and said they had also lost friends to shrouding.

Carshan pleaded, desperate, his face soaked with sweat. "Wait, wait. I can help you. I can be of service to you in your plan."

Corelle saw no future for the former Portreeve. Guild members had killed without reservation for nothing more than coin. Now they knew the part Carshan had played in the betrayal and deaths of their friends, his fate was written. "That you cannot. You are nothing but a fugitive. Those who gave you your orders are dead. The Qagrue do not care for you, and neither do we."

A Guild member grasped one of Carshan's arms, but he swatted at the hand that tugged at him. Others joined in and pulled him through the house. He screamed in protest, but there were too many to resist. Corelle and Denstal followed behind.

The men dragged him through the rear door. Some of the staff followed them out, and Corelle watched from near the door as the Guild members threw him to the ground next to a large bush that showed no signs of its flowers as the wet season edged its way into Dur. Merja stood next to Corelle. "Will they kill him?"

"That they will."

Merja made no reply. Carshan tried to crawl away from the four Guild men, but one of them kicked him in the side, and he collapsed to the ground. Corelle thought she heard him sob, and he pleaded over and over, "Please, please." The men had made up their minds. One of them took out his dagger and crouched down to stab Carshan several times in his side. Another stabbed him in the back of his neck. He cried out in pain as the daggers sank into his skin. The one whose friend had been hanged on a ship leaned over Carshan, grasped his hair and pulled his head back. He leaned close and whispered something, then reached around and slit Carshan's throat. The man's cries ceased, and a pool of blood spread across the hard packed soil of the path his head flopped backward onto.

Silence descended on the garden. Corelle marvelled at the staff for their courage at what they had seen. People unused to violent deaths often lost control of their stomachs, but Raolos's staff gazed down on the lifeless body with no trace of any adverse effects. Corelle turned to Merja. "I will send some men to dispose of the waste that clutters the home." Merja nodded, turned, and summoned the other staff back into the house.

Corelle gestured at the man who had slit Carshan's throat. "What is your name?"

"Harvikah."

"We will go together and find more work for our blades. Let us make our way toward the square."

He nodded, and they walked around the side of the house, down the carriageway, and onto the street. Corelle turned left, determined to make for the western gate, the one through which she had entered the town last night. It had been guarded at night, and she guessed it would also be guarded today. If the plan went awry and she or the others needed to flee, this gate would not be guarded once she had done her work.

As expected, two guards stood together near the gate. One of them leaned on the wall of a building, and Corelle wondered if the building provided some comfort facilities to the guards. There might be more Qagrue inside, but the plan had always contained an element of risk. She explained her concerns to Harvikah, then made sure they each had a different target to attack.

She pinched at her cheeks to bring a bloody red hue to them, something men seemed to find attractive, then unfastened several hooks on her tunic and plumped her full breasts. Her mark leaned against the wall, and she walked toward him, her eyes focused on his, her gait sensuous, she hoped. Once he noticed her, he said something to his colleague, who turned to watch her. Harvikah walked at a brisk pace along the opposite side of the street, but Corelle did not take her eyes from her mark. She ran her tongue around her lips in a provocative manner, but he seemed not to notice as he stared at her breasts. She closed the distance between them.

"How fickle, how shallow they are, these men." Had the circumstances been reversed, a woman who exposed much of her breasts and strode toward Corelle would signal danger. That woman would find Corelle on the balls of her feet, blade sprung and ready by the time she reached her. This man seemed oblivious to danger, and he stared at her breasts as though he had never seen a pair before in his life. She held her fan pressed against her side, but she raised her left hand to fondle one of her breasts as she drew close to him.

The move, designed to keep his attention away from her fan, almost brought her undone. The man pushed himself away from the wall, doubtless excited and prepared to sweep her into his arms. He may have intended to pull her inside or behind the building for a dalliance. To Corelle's dismay, the move placed him behind his companion, far more difficult to reach than if he had remained against the wall. She risked a swift glance at Harvikah. He was still five paces from his mark. She must strike, nonetheless, and hope Harvikah struck down his own mark before the man could pull his sword and kill her.

Her mark spoke to her as they came together. She did not understand any Qagrue, so she gave him a sweet smile and slashed her arm upward at the side of his neck. He stood much taller than her, his neck at eye level for her. Her blade bit into his neck and drove deep into the flesh. The familiar union of Corelle and her victim through her blade sizzled along her arm. She raised one corner of her mouth in a half snarl as he screamed and reached up to the wound. In the corner of her eye, his companion moved, and Corelle guessed he reached for his sword. She tugged at her blade and pulled it free. Blood poured from the man's neck, and he clamped his hand over the wound, his eyes wide with surprise.

He had taken a step back the instant her blade had pierced his flesh, and that brought his ruin. He looked down at her, so his jaw protected his throat, but he had exposed his stomach. She jabbed her blade into his abdomen with all her strength. Wilash's blade suited a slash attack best, but it had a point wicked enough to pierce flesh, and she pulled it out and drove it in again. Blood poured from the wounds. It soaked his tunic, and his face drained of colour. He had managed to pull his sword almost out of his belt, but she thrust her blade into his stomach, out, then in again. He crumpled to his knees and looked up at her with eyes that seemed to ask why he needed to die.

Blood sprayed across her face, and she started. Her confusion disappeared when the other Qagrue pitched forward in the periphery of her vision. She wore his blood across the grim tautness of her lips; it dripped from the end of her nose onto the ground. She slashed her mark's throat, and he toppled backward, slow, his legs folded under him. Blood pooled around him until he seemed to be asleep on a bed of vermilion.

Corelle glanced down at his colleague. Harvikah had opened his throat from ear to ear with one stroke. His head must have been turned toward her, and Harvikah's blade had found an easy target. She nodded her head at the building, and ran to the door, where she listened for any sound of alarm. No sounds came from the building, so she pushed the door open.

The room, nothing more than a small storeroom, might have no connection with the guards at the gate after all else. She pushed the door wide open and ran back to the bodies. They pulled first one, then the other inside the storeroom and closed the door. They tried to kick dust over the enormous puddles of blood, but it proved futile. To her surprise, a woman appeared with a yard brush in her hands, then two more. They joined in until the blood had been covered with dust and stones swept from the area around the gate. Corelle nodded her thanks to them.

One of them replied, "Kill them. Kill them all, for Ibie." The three went off in separate directions. Corelle could not guess where they had come from. Had they watched the entire incident from their windows and decided to help cover the evidence in case a patrol happened by? Any patrol would realise something had turned awry, of course. The guards no longer stood at their post, and it would not take long to find their bodies. Every heartbeat gained by confusion and investigation would help if things went awry for Corelle and the others, nonetheless, so the women's assistance had been welcome.

As Corelle led Harvikah away from the scene, she fastened her tunic again but kept her fan in her hand. They strode toward the square and looked around for any further Qagrue as they made their way about the town. They saw none, and Corelle felt both relieved and disappointed. With the deaths of the two at the gate, they had set in motion forces that must lead to a conclusion one way or another. Either they must prevail against the rest of the Qagrue, or they must flee and leave the residents of Ort to suffer whatever consequences came to them once the bodies were discovered. She did not agree with the theory of the Portreeve's man who had claimed the Qagrue would not kill the citizens in revenge for their actions. They might not kill them all, but some would be put to death, she imagined.

The square lay ahead of them. There had been no cries of alarm, and no bells had been rung to signal danger. So far, things appeared to run in their favour, although Corelle regretted they had not had the chance to kill more Qagrue between the gate and the square. The fewer they needed to fight in open combat, the better. She had been surprised they had not spotted any of the Qagrue, in truth, but she reminded herself Gillar's death had not yet been uncovered.

As they approached the square, they heard a buzz of noise some time before they saw a large group of men outside the Portreeve's Offices, all armed with a variety of weapons, most of them crude. They carried daggers, axes, pieces of wood that would serve as a club, and even a sword. She could not imagine how the man who wielded the sword had come across it. He might have picked it up from a dead Qagrue as other members of the Guild did their deadly work. A man with that level of initiative would prove helpful.

Many of the men wore the red tunic of the Portreeve, but some were ordinary citizens of all ages. Some might be brothers, fathers, uncles, and friends of the Portreeve's men, she guessed. Others may have followed a crowd that grew as it moved and had become swept up in what turned. Some doubtless wanted vengeance for the death of Ibie and any others the Qagrue had killed. More had gathered than Corelle had expected, too many to count. They moved around in the square like birds at the docks when a ship laden with fish puts in to unload its bounty.

Corelle spotted Denstal and pushed through the throng toward him. He saw her and waved. An eerie silence descended on the crowd, and all heads turned to watch her, covered in blood, her face and clothes caked in it. She had no idea how she must look; a short woman with a kerchief tied about her head who wore a skin of blood. Parstic stood next to Denstal, and he smiled at her as she approached them.

Denstal wore a grim smile. "We have thinned them down a little."

She nodded. "The west gate in the wealthy district is unguarded, if we need to flee."

Parstic knew the city better than any of them, and he shared his knowledge. "They have a building four streets from here they use for accommodation. It used to be a large inn before they arrived. Doubtless they squat there in their southern filth." A murmur of angry assent went up around him.

Corelle yelled for silence. "We go now to kill the southerners. Some of us may not return. Even if we kill them all, more will come. The fate of Ort cannot be foreseen. They may exact revenge on innocents. When this day is done, you must look to yourselves to keep your families safe. If you wish to take no further part in this, leave now. None will judge you any the worse for it."

The assembled crowd roared their approval as they waved their weapons in the air. She had missed her guess earlier. Not all in the crowd were men. No fewer than four women stood among the throng around her. Not one person walked away.

Corelle continued. "If we encounter patrols along the way, we must kill them. Do not hesitate to strike. They will not, if you give them the chance." She turned to Parstic. "Lead the way." She began her breath exercises to control her heartbeat.

Parstic headed south. He cried out as he walked, "Stay together, in one group."

They walked along in near silence. The crowd had grown quiet, as silent as the darkness Corelle imagined some of them would soon experience at the hands of the Qagrue. She guessed nervousness had stilled their tongues now the moment had come rather than any concern to arrive at the building unheard. The shuffle of feet on the street, the clink of metal as blades touched, the occasional cough, but not a word, only these small sounds from so large a group of people. Faces peered out of windows, and doors opened. A few people joined them as they walked through the streets, doubtless folks who guessed what turned and wished to take part, faces resolute despite the fear and uncertainty in so many eyes. If she could have gathered a force this large, all trained to fight, she believed she could have repelled the Qagrue when they first arrived. She imagined they walked toward a victory sweet in the taste but bitter in the consequence. *"What is scribed, must be,"* she thought.

CHAPTER 33
CORELLE

Without warning, Parstic stopped and pointed to a building. A sign still hung outside. The inn had been called The Duke's Rest, it seemed, though Corelle doubted the Duke had ever so much as seen it, let alone rested his noble head there for the night. She recalled an inn in Alcmouth with a similar name—The Duke's Seat, where Styrrach had killed Deineike. She turned to Parstic. "Is there a rear door?"

"That there is. It is in an alleyway behind the inn."

Corelle told him to take ten men and make sure nobody tried to escape by that route once they entered. He argued and said he would not be involved in the attack on the building, but Corelle needed somebody she could depend on, and Parstic would be the best person to keep the rear entrance guarded. That entrance could undo them if some Qagrue fled through it, or if reinforcements entered through it once the fight began.

Parstic grumbled even as he took some of the men and headed off, and Corelle turned to Denstal. "I have no suggestions on how we might achieve success here. It is unlike anything I have ever done."

He looked thoughtful. "The six of us should enter first and kill as many as we can. The others can follow us and search in groups for any who hide."

She shrugged. "We may die."

He gave her a casual smile. "That we may."

She pressed the seriousness of their situation rather than feel guilty if all but her died. "It is almost certain we will die."

His smile broadened. "That it is. Everybody dies."

She gave one sharp nod of her head. "That they do."

Corelle had no plan of her own, so Denstal's must suffice. She explained the plan to those around her. She urged the others to stay together in groups and not wander off alone, then summoned the five Guild men to her side and approached the door. Parstic should have reached the rear by now, so she pushed the door open. It opened into the tavernroom. As large as the inn had been, it had no fancy lobby like The Duke's Seat in Alcmouth, and Corelle stepped into the inn, all brash confidence.

Four Qagrue sat at a table near the counter with cards on the table before them. To her surprise, she saw no others. She had expected larger numbers to be in the tavernroom as they helped themselves to the ale and wine. Had they already drunk it all? One of the men said something in his own language, and she moved forward. She tried to pass herself off as a courtesan at first, and she ran her tongue around her lips in what she hoped would be a provocative gesture. A courtesan covered in blood with a kerchief on her head, she realised. The four of them turned to face her, curiosity on their faces. When she reached the table, she slashed the throat of the nearest man. His blood sprayed out across the table and turned it, the cards, and their coin red. Speckles of his blood decorated the faces of his companions.

They seemed stunned for a heartbeat or two, and their sluggish reaction cost them. The other Guild members rushed in behind her, and all four Qagrue fell dead before they could shout in alarm to their colleagues. Behind Corelle the other Ortfolk poured into the building and spread out to seek other Qagrue. The six Guild members pressed on through the tavern room to the scullery beyond it. Dirty goblets, cups, plates, pans and cutlery lay scattered everywhere. The Qagrue seemed to lack the discipline to keep their residential quarters respectable.

Corelle stepped around a large bench that ran down the middle of the scullery, and a man who had crouched there leapt up, a large knife in his hand. He swung it at her head, but she swayed backward and heard the whoosh of air across its blade as it passed her face. As he tried to stop the motion of his arm and reverse his swing, she stepped close to him to hinder his ability to move his arm in the opposite direction. She jabbed the point of her blade into his stomach four or five times, and he groaned. He still struggled to slash at her with his knife, but behind him, Harvikah stabbed him in the back. His dagger must have pierced the man's lung, and dark blood ran from his mouth. He coughed blood over Corelle once, then slid onto the bench and scattered the filthy dishes with an arm as he fell from the bench to the floor. She smiled her thanks at Harvikah.

They found the rear door and pulled it open. Parstic and his men stood ready, and they followed Corelle as she turned back into the inn. Shouts and the sounds of men in combat from above suggested the majority of the Qagrue had been upstairs. They had not anticipated such an attack might take place and had been caught unawares.

They went up the stairs to find the fight had all but ended. Once the clamour died down, they had killed seven or eight Qagrue in the upper rooms, along with the five downstairs. The swords the southerners had carried had proved all but useless in the close confines of the inn's rooms, as Corelle had known they would. One of the Ort men had been killed, nonetheless, and two had deep wounds from which blood gushed. She sent some of the townsfolk away with the two wounded men to find healers.

Parstic tugged at her blood-soaked sleeve. "We have not found enough of them here. The others must patrol the town or guard the ship in the docks."

Corelle tutted her dissatisfaction. "That is a sorry turn. I would have preferred one fight, no more. It is hard to judge whether the death of one man and the injuries of two more will serve in our favour or not. It is difficult to maintain the enthusiasm of a large crowd at the best of times, and harder when they see the harsh reality of combat."

Parstic and Denstal agreed with her, but there seemed little else they could do but hunt down the remaining Qagrue. They gathered the crowd together in the tavern room and told them to split up into groups of five or six and search the town for other patrols. She thought some members of the crowd might have already left— it seemed smaller. More might have gone with the injured men than she had realised.

The Guild members split into two groups. Denstal led one, Corelle the other. She thought three would be safer than two, since the Qagrue might now be aware of what had turned. The day had progressed well past the midday, and they agreed with the crowd to meet at the docks by the sundown. Her group saw a patrol of two Qagrue stroll toward them. So much blood covered the Guild members, they had no opportunity for subterfuge of any kind. They ran hard toward the two men, daggers drawn. Corelle felt fit from her year as a mariner, but the men ran faster than her, and she reached the Qagrue last.

They both had their swords drawn, extended before them. They shouted in their own language, but Corelle could not understand what they said. The two Guild men moved to the side to flank the Qagrue while Corelle confronted them from the front. The Qagrue waved their swords in arcs around them as they sought to protect themselves from whichever assailant lunged at them first. Corelle watched the tactic with interest, but it would not help them. Guild members did not lunge. Guild members did not expose themselves to retaliatory attacks by rash charges. They did not brawl, but their training taught them to be aware of the risks in the vicinity. A lunge opened bodies up to counter thrusts, and the three assassins waited for one of the Qagrue to over-extend himself. The Qagrue appeared disciplined also, content to defend until attacked.

Behind the Qagrue, people came out of their houses and watched in surprise. The noise of the throng as it grew larger sounded like the drone of insects as they flew ever closer, and one of the Qagrue turned his head to glance behind him, enough to break the stalemate. Corelle dived forward under the wild swing of the other's sword and slashed her dagger across the backs of the legs of the man who had turned, then rolled forward to avoid his sword as he recovered his composure.

She came up into a crouch, and the man faced her, agony on his face, his sword toward her. One of the Guild men, who had run in as the second man had swung his sword at Corelle, slashed at his throat. The Qagrue collapsed to the ground even as the third Guild man stepped behind Corelle's opponent and drove his dagger deep into the Qagrue man's ribs. With a cry of pain, the Qagrue dropped his sword. Corelle danced forward and slashed his throat.

They wiped their blades on the clothes of the dead men and pressed on. They did not bother to hide the bodies. The crowd followed them and seemed to grow with each street they walked down. They encountered no more Qagrue, and as the sun sank, they decided to head for the docks. They had spoken little since the fights in the inn, intent on the task at hand. They reached the docks to find a large crowd gathered there.

Denstal told her the other groups had found and killed only four of the Qagrue, in addition to the two Corelle's group had killed. Another Ortman had been killed. Parstic felt sure more

Qagrue must be aboard the ship. There seemed to be no more plausible explanation, so they marshalled some of the armed townsfolk to follow the Guild members onto the ship. One of Denstal's companions bled from a cut to his arm, but he brushed off her concerns when she queried whether he had taken a bad wound.

They searched the ship from top to bottom. By the time they had finished, another six Qagrue lay dead around the vessel. As she had suspected, Parstic could not calculate how many had been killed, but one of the crowd, a tally worker, believed they had killed not fewer than twenty-eight Qagrue at a cost of two Ortmen dead. Parstic still worried they had not killed them all, as he had believed there were around forty of them. He admitted he had guessed, and Corelle imagined any who remained would either escape by road or try to retake the ship.

She believed it would suit the townsfolk to keep control of the ship, but the docks had filled with Ortfolk, and a cry went up to burn it. She could not prevail in her argument it might be valuable to them, and soon enough it blazed at the dockside. Corelle untied the ropes, and the ship drifted out into the river. Corelle watched in sadness as flames leapt high into the night. The hollow pleasure of revenge had blinded them to the usefulness of the ship to their cause.

The people drank ale and wine on the docks, a vast celebration of the defeat of the Qagrue. Corelle did not begrudge them their moment of joy, but she feared the repercussions of the day's actions. A band of minstrels appeared and struck up a song, and Corelle smiled as she watched the Ortfolk whirl each other around in gleeful time to the music. When she wandered closer, she saw Khittie among the minstrels, the woman who had sung Deineike's Sending. Pettra had once said the singer lived in Ort, although many of the things said to her over the last years were a blur, lost in the depths of her grief.

Corelle hoped Khittie would sing, and she did not have long to wait. She did not recognise the song, and if the people on the dock were unfamiliar with it, they did not let that mar their enjoyment of the moment, as ever more of them joined in the dances across the docks. Khittie's beautiful clear voice soared into the night sky. It touched Corelle again with the pureness of its tone and the emotion that seemed to drip from every word she sang.

> *"Never thought to believe I could be what you wanted,*
> *Nothing lasts for ever.*
> *Never thought to be hopeful, I just told you the stories,*
> *And we are still together."*

The melody entranced her, and Khittie's performance of the song captivated her. Corelle swayed in time with the beat the minstrels created, carried away by Khittie's sublime voice. All around her, people danced and smiled with happiness. At first, Corelle smiled at the joyous theme of the song, which she took to mean that people who loved each other could overcome any difficulties. In different circumstances, she and Deineike might have proved Khittie's song correct, but Khittie's voice pierced some deep, dark part of Corelle and transported her back to the Pyre ground, not far from these very docks where people danced and made merry. Tears ran down Corelle's face, and by the time the song had ended, misery had pulled her into its powerful grip. She longed for Deineike's touch. It did not matter how deep she buried the memory of her, a song, a word, any small thing could dredge her face up into Corelle's memory, it seemed. She stood alone, a small island of despondency in a sea of joy, and she hoped nobody noticed.

The song over, Khittie moved away through the crowds, and Corelle could not resist a desire to speak to her, to apologise for when she had all but ignored her at the Pyre. She pushed through the crowds around the docks, and once she caught up to Khittie, she tapped her on the shoulder. The singer turned. A gentle breeze meandered in off the river and blew her long blonde hair around her face, and she pushed it back with both hands. She held it at the nape of her neck as she smiled at Corelle but did not appear to recognise her.

Corelle shouted above the din on the docks. "I owe you an apology."

"I am sure you do not." Khittie smiled and seemed unaware of what Corelle referred to.

"You sang a Sending for my… a friend of mine. Raolos and Pettra arranged it."

"I recall it." The smile fled from Khittie's face. "I remember you now."

"My behaviour that day was atrocious. Your Sending song is beautiful, as is the song you sang tonight. Deineike would have adored both. My thanks, and my apologies for my lack of gratitude that day."

Khittie's blue eyes gazed into Corelle's brown ones. "You were distraught. The loss of a lover is a painful loss. No apology is necessary, but I appreciate that you took the time to offer it. How do you fare these days? Are you hurt?"

The blood must have created the impression Corelle had been injured, she reasoned. She felt the sting of tears in her eyes again. How could she explain how she fared? How could anybody be expected to understand the layers of emotions that made up Corelle's life? No words could tell the story of how she felt in a short, polite sentence to a stranger. On an impulse, she leaned forward and kissed Khittie on the cheek. The woman smiled and took Corelle's hand in her own. Compassion sprang to her eyes, but she said nothing.

"My thanks. I am unhurt. This blood came from others." Corelle pulled her hand free and turned. She pushed through the crowds, desperate to leave the square and the myriad bodies that bumped and jostled her as the celebrations continued. She did not look back. Once clear of the square, she took several deep breaths to calm her heart and her demeanour and reflected on the conversation. How had Khittie known Deineike had been her lover? Pettra must have told her, she reasoned, since Corelle could not recall she had said a single word to the singer at the Pyre. Khittie had not found her silence unusual or rude. She had recognised the abject grief Corelle had felt at the time. Corelle had fainted as the flames consumed the body of the woman she had loved more than life itself. Somehow, Corelle had lived on after the Pyre, motivated by revenge as much as any desire to live, in truth. Somehow, she had come to this day, still bereft and full of desolation. Much had turned since that day, and only Krage remained alive of those who had built the Guild that had cost Deineike her life.

Somehow, she would go on. She sighed and set off for Raolos's house. She would collect her pack and spend the night at Pettra's house. Tomorrow could take care of itself. Tonight, Corelle would sleep with Deineike, even if she slept with nothing more than the memory of the tall, kind woman whose love she had been fortunate to know for so short a time.

CHAPTER 34
CORELLE

The following morning found Corelle exhausted. She had cried herself to sleep once she had reached Pettra's house after she had resisted the exhortations of Raolos's staff to spend the night at his house. Sadness had wrapped her in its arms after Khittie's song and would not be pried loose, and nightmares plagued her throughout the night. When she woke, her eyes bored into one spot in the bedroom ceiling as she lay listless between the bedsheets and listened to the heavy rain outside. Though it took all her strength, she dragged herself from the bed with a heavy sigh. Yesterday's events had left the city liberated for now, and doubtless many of its residents with headaches this morning. The rain would bring no relief from the effects of the night's alcohol and would not wash away the reality they must now face. The Qagrue would be sure to retaliate for the death of their men.

Dressed in cleaner clothes, not drenched in blood, she walked to the docks, the feel of the rain on her skin some pleasure, as though it might cleanse her of the sombre mood that still lay upon her. The raindrops felt warm on her face, as they often did at the start of the wet season. The rain would turn chilly soon enough, and the cold season would arrive in two or three passes. A circle of seasons every year, but so unlike the southern lands, where the cold season seemed never to come. She hoped she would bask in that warmth before the cold season came to force the Durfolk into cloaks and fires and bitter cold nights.

A three-master stood at the docks. It had not been there last night, and Corelle wondered whether she should ask to join the crew. Things still lay undone here in Ort, she realised, and she had Vamma to think of. The ship flew the sigil of Corkannae, to the south-east of Dur.

She looked around the docks. Few people braved the rain; some dock workers who moved the cargo from the ship, a man, his clothes drenched by the rain, fast asleep on a large bale of cloth outside a tally house, two others who crossed the dock toward her, workers on their way to their employment, no doubt. No sign of the red tunics of the Portreeve, nor of Denstal. They had work to do, but they all lay tucked up in their beds. Their tardiness irritated her, but she could do nothing about it. They had made no firm plans, but some of the others should have tried to meet up this morning. She sat on a bench and watched the dock workers as the sky lightened over the Eastlands.

Denstal appeared first. He emerged from a tavern, dishevelled. He gulped large drafts of fresh air into his lungs. Even from some distance, he seemed unwell, and Corelle guessed he had joined in the celebrations with enthusiasm. She sympathised with him—she knew from bitter experience how terrible he must feel.

He gazed around, and she waved. He did not return the wave, but trudged toward her, heedless of the puddles of water he splashed through. He sat in silence on the bench beside her. She laughed at his miserable demeanour. "You look terrible."

"I feel worse than I look, I promise you. Ale makes us pay twice: at the buying, and at the waking up."

She hid her surprise at his insight behind a gentle jest. "That is wise, for a killer."

"If I had the strength to pull it, my dagger would put you in your place, or me in the flames. I confess I would be hard pressed to decide which I would prefer at this moment."

Corelle laughed loud, impressed by his spirit. She knew how atrocious he felt. "I have been where you are now. I sympathise. Will it console you to know you will feel better by the sunset?" He drew a massive intake of breath, lowered his head toward his knees, and appeared to concentrate. She imagined he tried not to fetch up. "That it would not, my guess. Still, there are decisions to be made, and things to do, and it falls to us, since no others have yet risen from their beds."

"You make the decisions. I lack the strength to argue or the wit to form a thought."

She pondered their options, and they were few. In truth, they had only two—to flee or fight. If the Qagrue sent two, three, or even four ships, there would be too many men for the townsfolk to resist. The repercussions for the ordinary folk of Ort might be extreme. As had been pointed out yesterday, not all the townsfolk could flee, and therein lay the dilemma. The fates were written now, and they could not be unwritten. The Qagrue had been killed, and they could not be un-killed.

At that, Corelle remembered she had not sent any men to remove the bodies of the three men who had been killed at Raolos's house. Parstic might arrange it with the Portreeve's men, but Corelle must not forget to ensure they were taken away. "We must send letters to Ryl by some means." She thought aloud rather than explained a well-conceived plan. "If the Qagrue come, and we hope to repel them, we will need the men who are there with Raolos. In truth, they may still be insufficient, but without them, we are doomed to be overwhelmed."

Denstal glanced up at the ship at the dock. "Send letters on that ship."

"It will sail south. In any event, the Alc is blocked. That is why I rode here. If it is not blocked, then either the Qagrue sail for here or Ryl. Neither outcome works in our favour, and we can now surmise that many more Qagrue are in Alcmouth and are sure to spread around the land soon."

"In truth, what choice do we have?"

Despite Corelle's initial resentment, he had the right of it. They had no choice. They must find enough coin to pay the master. "Where is Sisnop's coin?"

"In trunks on a cart, in a stable near where the ship docked. That way." Denstal waved a hand in a vague northerly direction. "Somebody has doubtless stolen it by now."

Corelle set off to find the stable at once. If somebody had stolen the coin, she would be disappointed, since she would need a large amount to persuade the southern master to sail out of his way to Ryl, if he could be persuaded at all. At the northern end of the docks, she saw a stable set back from the tavern next door. She opened the small door inset into the larger outside one and stepped over the threshold, glad for some respite from the rain. A young boy inside moved soiled hay with a pitchfork, and he looked up as Corelle entered.

"G…good mor…morning." The words seemed to take a substantial effort to form.

Corelle could not decide whether he felt nervous or had a speech issue. "And a good morning to you. I have come for Sisnop's cart and horse. We leave the town today."

The boy looked perplexed. "I do n…not kn…know this Sis… Si…name."

Corelle wondered if Sisnop had used a different name, or if they had supplied Carshan's name. "My apologies. I meant Carshan's cart."

"Ah, Car… Car…" He tutted, glanced away, and clenched his fists. "He does n… n… not own th… the cart. Two trunks are st… stored, that is… that is all."

"The cart is borrowed?" The boy nodded. "Can I borrow a horse to pull the cart down the docks to our ship?" She favoured him with a friendly smile.

A man entered the stable from the opposite end, and the boy watched as he approached them. The man addressed Corelle as he drew near. "My apologies for my son. He struggles with his speech. Names in particular."

"There is nothing to apologise for. We have had a most pleasant conversation." She smiled at the boy again, and he blushed. "I asked him whether I could borrow a horse and cart to pull Carshan's trunks along the docks so we can unload them. We wish to sail onward."

The man frowned. "Where is Carshan then, that he cannot collect his trunk himself?"

Corelle turned over her potential replies in the blink of an eye. "Dead, I fear. The Qagrue killed him after an argument over a card game."

The man rubbed his chin and seemed deep in thought. "Dead, you say? Killed by the Qagrue, and they are all also dead. That is most convenient."

Corelle thought an appeal to his loyalty to Dur might bring better results. "I serve Raolos. Do you wish to see the rightful Bailiff restored?"

He shrugged. "It makes little enough difference to me who is Bailiff—this man or that man. Horses need stables whoever professes himself Bailiff. The affairs of great men like the Duke and his Bailiff do not much concern me."

Corelle had believed the fates of everybody in Dur were written by whether good men or bad men ruled over them, but to the average person, it seemed, the offices of the great and the good made little difference. "Then what of rule by the Qagrue? Do you think your fortunes will be so little affected if they control the land?"

He laughed. "They are all dead, are they not, or sailed away?"

"Some are dead, those they left here. Others will come, and the consequences may be dire for Ort now we have killed these."

"We?" He knitted his brows.

Corelle had slipped up and needed to recover the situation. She had not intended to tell him of her involvement in last night's incidents. "That is correct, we. The people of Ort."

His eyes narrowed and he looked her up and down. "I have heard of a woman who took part in last night's events. She led those who struck down the southerners. I might have respect for that woman. A woman who attempted to deceive me out of the belongings of a customer, I would send on her way with my boot print in the behind of her trousers."

"Very well. You have unmasked me. I played some part in the events of last night. I would not go as far as to claim I led the others. We fought together, and some paid a high price."

"I heard two died, and I admire your humility if you are the woman you claim to be. But how do I know you are?"

She bent down to pull the fan out of her boot, then sprang the blade. She grabbed the boy's arm and pulled him close to her body, the blade at his throat. A silence cloaked the stable for four or five heartbeats, then she lowered the blade and tousled the boy's hair. "That I am."

The man seemed about to protest, but instead he pulled the boy close and held him for a moment. In truth, the boy smiled at Corelle and seemed none the worse for the experience. The man turned and walked toward a nearby stall. "I will hitch a horse to the cart."

While he worked, Corelle smiled at the boy. "I am Corelle."

He nodded as his smile grew wider. "I kn... know. Who else?"

Like an unwelcome travel companion, Corelle did not relish the fame that accompanied her. She longed to be a nobody, a mariner aboard a ship or a clerk in a chandler's shop who sold equipment to masters and owners of ships. To be somebody nobody recognised or feared; she wished nothing more from her life now. Reputations meant nothing to her, but reputations always last, as she had told the Portreeve's man who let slip Arella had been with child. That conversation seemed a lifetime past, and she yearned for freedom from the expectations that came with her fame, or infamy—she could not decide which.

The stable owner led a horse harnessed to a cart toward her. "Here are Carshan's trunks. I will send my lad with you to bring the horse and cart back."

Corelle took the rope he offered her. It looped through a circle of metal in the horse's bridle. She led the horse out of the stable and along the dock, where Denstal still sat on the bench, bent forward from the waist. Corelle could not tell whether he fetched up or had fallen asleep. Three other Guild members and two men in red tunics stood nearby. It relieved her there were some helping hands available—she had been unconvinced she and Denstal alone could lift the two heavy trunks from the cart.

Why had they stored the trunks under Carshan's name rather than Sisnop's? Had Sisnop been reluctant to use his own name? He had declared himself Bailiff and might have feared somebody would recognise it. She shrugged the irrelevant thought away and stopped the horse alongside the three-master. She beckoned for the men at the bench to join her and the five latecomers wandered toward her. Denstal remained on the bench. He had not looked up, and since she could not see any vomit in the vicinity, Corelle guessed he had fallen asleep.

She explained the decision she had reached, and the six of them soon had the two trunks off the cart and on the docks. She gave the boy a groat, and he smiled his gratitude at her as he led the horse and cart back toward the stables.

A large padlock locked each of the trunks. After a brief inspection, Corelle reasoned they would be easy enough to pick when the time came. For now, she would not place temptation in the way of her helpers. She turned to look at the ship. Mariners tidied away ropes and made the deck shipshape. From the way they worked, and the absence of any cargo on the dock near the ship, she guessed they would either sail home empty or the master would soon leave the ship in search of a return cargo.

She ran up the ramp onto the deck and enquired about the master's whereabouts. One of the mariners pointed to some stairs that led to the aft deck, where she found the master bent forward near the wheel. He used his body to keep the charts he studied dry in the steady rain. He looked up at the sound of her footsteps on the wooden deck. He straightened but said nothing as she approached.

"Good morning to you, master." A simple start to the conversation. Most masters would have a good grasp of the language of Dur if they sailed here to trade. "I wish to make you an offer that will be worth more than any cargo you will find here in Ort." He raised his eyebrows but said nothing. "I wish you to carry letters to Ryl. You must leave at once, deliver the letters, and bring back anybody who will return with you."

He made no attempt to hide his disdain for her as he gave a snort of derision. "Such a voyage would cost a great amount of coin."

"I have a great amount of coin."

He tilted his head to one side and frowned. "You do not have the look of one so wealthy, you could rent my ship for fourteen days, even if such a voyage were possible."

Corelle did not recognise the word "fourteen" in the context of the passage of time. She understood the concept, but not to hear "two sevendays" distracted her for several moments. When she concentrated on his words again, she focused on his comment about the journey. "Why would the voyage not be possible?"

"Because the Alc is blocked beyond Zhanghar, as I hear it. The Qagrue do not allow vessels to sail beyond the mouth of the Alc. It is not possible to reach Ryl at this time."

She could not consider an attack on the Qagrue in Zhanghar because their numbers would be too great, and it would take too long to deliver letters to Ryl by horseback. That left only one choice: to attempt to sail to Ryl. "I have more than enough coin to make it worth your while. What amount do you wish? Come. Name your price."

His eyes screamed his doubt, but he appeared to arrive at a decision. "In your Dur coins, I would require two thousand regals to make this voyage."

CHAPTER 35
CORELLE

Corelle's head spun. She could not grasp a sum so vast as two thousand regals. If the trunks even held that much, she could not count high enough to remove it, after all else. She tried to think of something that might help her understand how much coin he meant. "That is more coin than there are lights of the night sky."

"That is the fee. You are not obliged to pay it to me. I am content to find a cargo and return home to my wife. I wish some time off when I return."

"Why is it so much? How do you justify this sum, the likes of which nobody can ever have seen?"

He laughed. "If nobody has ever seen it, then I have not missed my guess, and you do not have it. Regardless, I do not justify it, I name it. You have a simple enough choice. You can accept, or you can decline. All I ask is for you to make your decision a quick one. I must find a cargo here before other ships arrive and compete with me for it."

Corelle's mind whirled. She must first find out whether the trunks even held that much, then make the decision on whether to pay such an outrageous fortune for an attempt to reach Ryl that might not even work. "I need an hour." She tried to sound unconcerned despite the despondency that threatened to crush all the breath from her. "I need to count my regals out with care."

He gave another disdainful laugh. "You will need some help to carry it. It will be too heavy for a frail woman such as you. You will need many pairs of arms."

Corelle fought to control her tongue before she spat out that she hoped the weight of the coin would sink his ship as soon as he reached deeper water, gave a non-committal nod, wheeled, and headed back to the docks. She summoned the assembled men together, more of them at the docks now; Parstic had arrived, and the last Guild member. Denstal had left the bench and sat on one of the trunks. Three other men in red tunics had also arrived. Plenty of arms to carry the master his two thousand regals, she reasoned, but the thought brought no satisfaction.

"He wants two thousand regals to attempt to deliver letters to Ryl and bring Raolos and his forces back here to Ort." She waited for the gasps of astonishment to subside before she continued. "There is a chance he might not get through to Ryl. The Alc might still be blockaded at Zhanghar. It is an enormous risk."

"And an even more enormous sum." One of the Portreeve's men had pointed out what Corelle had anticipated. A sum so large would require great character to relinquish on such a fool's errand.

Corelle glanced down but snapped her head back up. She must not let them see defeat in her eyes or body. "I confess I cannot count that high. I can neither imagine nor fathom how many regals that would be."

The man sniggered as he replied. "Around two thousand, I would guess."

She glared at him, and his laughter died. "I realise that. I meant to suggest I could not envisage how two thousand regals would look or how much space they would take up."

He looked at the trunks. "Most of one of these, my guess."

She looked at him in astonishment. "You mean to tell me there might be twice two thousand regals in these trunks?"

He corrected her, and for a fleeting moment, Klordia's face popped into her mind. "That would be four thousand. But it would depend. If the trunks are full of groats, then there will be less. If they are full of precious jewels, then many times that amount."

She shoved Denstal along the trunk and collapsed onto it beside him. "I cannot comprehend these numbers or the concept of so much wealth." Her bewilderment robbed her of her breath, a whisper all she could force from her lips. "I am a simple garment maker's daughter. A dress that costs fifty regals is beyond the reach of most of the people of Dur. These Guildmeisters each had more coin than all the lights of the night sky, and far more besides. It baffles me."

Denstal suggested they open the trunks and confirm how much they held. "Who has the key?"

Harvikah waved an arm toward the better quarter. "Sisnop, my guess. Doubtless it lies on the floor of the bedroom in his pocket."

Corelle snapped her fingers. "That reminds me. Can some of you please arrange to dispose of the bodies?"

A despondent wail came from one of the men. "All of them?"

Corelle huffed an impatient breath. "There are but three."

"That there are, in the house. There are thirty Qagrue to dispose of also."

She sighed and placed her head in her hands. "That there are. Can we rouse some of the citizens to help? The bodies at the house are the most important. The staff should not be forced to live with the rotten corpses of those whose lives had turned rotten while they still breathed."

Somebody offered to take care of the problem, and she looked up into the face of a man she did not know, dressed in a red tunic, black hair cut short, and intense green eyes that stared into hers.

Parstic introduced the stranger. "This is Leesant."

She nodded. Parstic had proposed Leesant as the next Portreeve. Time enough to deal with that later. "My thanks." She smiled at Leesant.

Parstic reminded her of their problem. "The key. We do not have it."

Despite his pale face and visible discomfort, Denstal spoke up. "Corelle can open the trunks. Any of us could, except me at this moment."

Corelle rose. "I need a dagger please." The Portreeve's men looked at her as though she had lost her mind. "My blade is not a dagger. It is not suited for this work." One of them laughed, but she shot him a vicious look. "It is suitable for the work I ask it to do, however." The laughter died on his lips. Harvikah handed her his dagger, handle first. She crouched at the lock of the trunk she had been seated on and swatted in frustration at Denstal's legs until he moved them clear of the padlock.

The mechanism of the lock looked straightforward enough, but she cut a piece of her tunic away at the hem and took some time to wipe the padlock. Somebody asked why she did so, and she pointed out Sisnop had owned the trunks. He would not have wanted his wealth stolen, so he might have applied some poison to the padlock in case of interference by hands not authorised to touch it. When one of the Portreeve's men asked how Sisnop would have opened it without the poison killing him, she held up the piece of her tunic as she focused her attention on the padlock. Of course, there might be some mechanism concealed in the lock that might injure any implement introduced into it other than the key.

Corelle studied the padlock, then pushed the tip of the dagger into the keyhole, satisfied the dagger would be adequate to turn the tongue inside the lock. She breathed a sigh of relief as nothing sprang from the padlock to shatter the blade, and she manipulated the blade for a moment until the padlock sprung open. The men gathered around her gave a few small cheers, and she looked up at them. What a sight they must make, she thought, here on the docks; a group of killers alongside the Portreeve's own men, and they all stared down at a shoddily-dressed woman in a kerchief as she picked the lock of a trunk that would contain more wealth than any gathered here could imagine. Worse, she intended to steal it all and give it to the master of a ship as inducement to undertake a task so hopeless, he would wave at them as he sailed south past Ort in four or five days, unsuccessful but rich.

Denstal still sat on the trunk, and she pushed at him to encourage him to stand up. She pushed harder than she intended, and he fell off the edge of the trunk. He landed in an untidy heap on the hard packed ground of the docks. The other men laughed, and Corelle apologised. He waved her apology away and did not attempt to rise. She took the front edge of the lid in both hands, looked up again at the faces that peered down at her, and exhaled long and loud before she lifted the trunk lid.

Silence. Not even the sound of a breath from any of those who stared into the trunk. Denstal dragged himself to his knees and peered into the trunk, then fell backward into a seated position. Corelle turned to look at him, a stunned expression on his face.

Someone asked, "How much is that?" Corelle looked up at him and felt she might cry. Coins filled the trunk to its lid—groats and regals, of course, but other coins, some she recognised from her voyages to various lands, and others she could not recognise. They saw gems and shiny golden pieces of jewellery as well. The trunk held wealth so far beyond her comprehension, she felt it might have been better had it been a few groats or some sum she could understand.

She looked up at Leesant, who had a hand over his mouth, eyes wide in surprise. "Are there two thousand regals here?" She spoke in a voice so small, even she could not be certain it had been her own.

He allowed his hand to slip down from his mouth. "Ten times that, or more. How did one man have so much wealth?"

Corelle knew only too well how they had all come by their vast wealth. "He served as Guildmeister in Torric, and doubtless this is his and Carshan's combined. This is the sum of their endeavours in the Guild down the years, along with whatever he earned as Bailiff."

Denstal whispered a reply but could not tear his eyes from the contents of the trunk. "I heard him say he had made nothing as Bailiff."

Corelle could not keep the bitterness from her voice, angry at how they had all been used to create trunk loads of coin and gems beyond her wildest imaginings. "We enabled him to accrue this wealth. Styrrach had a horde like this. We killed to remove obstacles that threatened the operation. We helped all this wealth to pour into his coffers."

"And some of our friends were hanged in the process." Corelle did not notice which Guild member had spat out the words.

She drew in a sharp breath. "We have a decision to make. Do we pay this master two thousand regals to try to deliver letters to Ryl? We must act now. Any delay increases the chance that, even if he gets through and Raolos comes, we may all be dead long before he reaches Ort."

Denstal held his head in his hands, either from the effects of the previous night or the effects of the enormous fortune he had seen that morning. "Pay him. That is the least of our worries. Of more concern is what we do with the remainder."

Corelle looked up at Leesant. "Leesant, can you count to two thousand?"

"That I can, in theory. In truth, I know not. I understand how the numbers progress. I have never counted that far, but I will try." He knelt beside her and pulled out a large handful of coins and gems. "Let us keep the gems out of it and hope there are sufficient regals between the two trunks. This way we avoid arguments about the value of this gem or that necklace."

He counted the first handful of regals until he had them stacked up in four piles, then asked Corelle to move the rest of the items to one side. He took another handful of coins out and counted those as well. Corelle soon became lost and had no idea how close he had come to the two thousand as the piles grew on the dock, spread all around him. When she glanced up, she saw two men push observers away. She worried word could spread, and the entire population of Ort would descend on the docks. The townsfolk might kill them and make off with the wealth from the trunks. She instructed the Portreeve's men to keep people away, and to send for more men to help with the effort.

Still Leesant counted as the rain dripped from him onto the ground. Handful after handful of coins, gems and other precious items came out of the trunk. A dagger with a brilliant gold handle set about with gems had lain unseen beneath the treasure trove, and she stared at it in wonder when Leesant handed it to her. Leesant suggested it might be worth two hundred regals, and she laid it in the pile of discarded items, afraid to hold it any longer in case she dropped and destroyed it.

When the trunk had been all but emptied, Leesant sighed and looked at her. "Two thousand regals."

CHAPTER 36
CORELLE

The piles of coin stood before them, spread out around Leesant. They covered so much ground, a tunic thrown over them might not have covered them. She picked up one of the piles, its weight so great, she doubted she could carry more than two or three of them.

When Corelle asked how they would carry the coin onto the ship, somebody suggested a flour sack and ran off to find one. He came back with several and dropped them next to the pile of coins. By the time they had scooped all the coins into sacks they could carry, five flour sacks bulged with regals. Five of the men carried one each while Corelle ran up the ramp to tell the master she had the coin he had requested. Surprise strove against greed in his expression as the men dropped the sacks at his feet. He peered into each and declined Corelle's invitation to count them. He shook his head. "I trust you." His expression suggested he had not believed she could raise the coin, and Corelle wondered whether he could have even counted them, had he chosen to. It crossed her mind he might regret the offer to sail to Ryl now the price had been met. He did not attempt to break his bargain, however, and asked for his instructions should he reach Ryl.

Corelle told him to make ready while she scribed letters, then scampered down the ramp and into the nearest tally house, where she persuaded a tally clerk to part with some parch and lend her a scribing tool. She scribed a short summary of what had turned in Ort and exhorted Raolos to sail to Ort aboard the ship that bore the letters as soon as possible. Their combined forces could then make a stand in the town before the Qagrue retook it.

She sealed the letters with the seal of the tally house but scribed her own name on the outside of the sealed letters. With a hurried, "My thanks," to the tally clerk, she ran back to the ship and handed the letters to the master. The ship had almost been made ready to sail, so she returned to the docks and watched as it moved out into the current and headed north along with such little hope as they had. She imagined their chances were somewhere between none and as close to none as made no difference, but she had tried, at the least.

As the ship grew smaller, she turned to Denstal and Parstic, who stood and watched with her. She breathed words that were little more than thoughts to which she gave voice. "If the ship returns in four or five days, they have not managed to pass Zhang-har. Until then, unless the Qagrue come in the meantime, we can do little."

Parstic sucked a long, slow breath through clenched teeth. "Will we prepare for the fight if they do come?"

"There is little enough point with the numbers we have here."

Denstal's afflictions did not keep a sharpness from his voice. "You give up at the slightest excuse. I would not be so hasty to dismiss what might be done."

She sighed. "Your enthusiasm for this defence is impressive but misguided. We have insufficient numbers here without Raolos and whatever forces he has gathered about him. Even then it may be too few. Our foes may have hundreds of men."

"If you lead the Guild, we can soon enough become a force to be reckoned with."

She fixed him with a cold stare. "I will not lead you. Have I not already said so?"

"That you have not. You showed little enthusiasm, but you did not refuse."

"Then I refuse now, as I should have made clearer earlier. Even if I led you, I would not suffer whatever organisation we might form to be named the 'Guild,' after all else. Too much misery is attached to that name."

He waved away her protestations. "Call it what you will. You must lead us. The others will follow you. If you do not lead, I fear they will drift away and Dur will be lost."

Her retort came without hesitation. "Dur *is* lost. You cannot see it, but it is. Even if Raolos comes, and I doubt he will, I have no confidence we can defeat these southern invaders." His unjustified belief that by some chance they could return Dur to the rule of the Durfolk frustrated her. For all she knew, the Qagrue might govern the land better than the Duke ever did. Although she knew Raolos to be a fair and honourable man, it might be time for the old ways to be swept away. She had seen other lands that had been governed in different ways to Dur, and the people there had been as happy as the Durfolk ever were under the Duke.

Denstal shook his head in anger as he turned away from her, his fists clenched at his side. He shook as though he tried with all his might to control his temper.

Parstic seemed to reach for a compromise to dilute the tension between Corelle and Denstal. "We could appoint a Portreeve."

Corelle nodded at his wise suggestion. "A good idea. Is Leesant still the one you favour?"

"I trust him. He fought with us, he handled the count of the coin, and the others will follow him. I see no better option."

It did not concern Corelle who became Portreeve. She neither came from nor lived in Ort, and she had no desire to stay longer than necessary. "Then it is decided. Another decision awaits. What will we do with the rest of Sisnop's coin?"

Denstal turned to her again, a look of curiosity on his face, but he said nothing.

Parstic did not hesitate. "You take it. It belongs to this Guild, and as I understand it, the coin and more are owed to you by them."

She shook her head. "The debt the Guild owes me is all but repaid. If I can feed Krage to the fire, then it is paid in full. Coin cannot calm my blood. Vengeance alone can answer for all they have done to me."

Parstic glanced down and muttered. "Boiling water scalds, but boiling blood scalds the more." He raised his head again. "What, then?"

"Let Denstal and the others take what they wish. Give the rest to Leesant to spend on Ort. I have no other suggestion."

Denstal seemed surprised by her reply. "You will not take any?"

"That I will not. I took plenty from Styrrach's trunks. I need no more." She had almost no coin at all, and none of the wealth she had taken from Styrrach's hoard remained, but Denstal need not know that. She had no more need of the Guild's blood-stained coin.

Denstal persisted with his foolish idea of a new Guild. "At the least, will you stay until we know whether Raolos comes?"

She sighed. Raolos would bring Vamma and the complications that would accompany her. It would be pleasant to say goodbye though—to Vamma first, but also to Raolos, Wilash and Synna. "That I will."

A nervous tremor in his voice betrayed Parstic's concern. "Will the Qagrue get here before Raolos?"

Corelle sighed inside. They all had big ideas, big plans, but they all relied on her to fulfil them. "I know not. Unless word of what we did here comes to the Qagrue in Alcmouth, they may not travel north in any hurry. I do not pretend to know what their goals for Dur are, so do not place great trust in my opinion of their actions."

The answer seemed inadequate for Parstic. "Then all we can do is watch for them?"

"You can arrange some defences, as we did in Ryl. Barricade some streets with carts, bales, trunks; anything you can spare. Drive those you fight through narrow streets where crossbows may wreak havoc on them, and numerical superiority will count for less. Train any who will learn how to use a crossbow. Little else can be done. Their numbers are sure to be irresistible if they do come."

Parstic agreed to arrange the defences and step up patrols on the docks if that would help.

Corelle thought it would. "They are unlikely to arrive by any other route. If the docks are watched, you will see them as they come. I am certain of it."

Denstal offered his support. "My men will aid you. We will train any who wish to learn how to wield a dagger to its best effect. Where to strike, that sort of training. Corelle will be here for some days, by her own word. She may help, I feel, out of boredom if nothing else." He gave her a small smile, as though he wished to suggest no ill will existed between them over her refusal to lead a new Guild.

The two men wandered away. Corelle sat on the unopened trunk until a cart appeared, and men loaded the two trunks onto it before they drove it away. Corelle moved to a bench, where she watched as dockhands delivered crates, bales, and trunks to the bottom of a ramp that reached up to a three-master that had arrived as they counted the coin. Mariners carried everything aboard. They cursed if somebody got in their way and laughed and jested among themselves. An unusual pang of jealousy gnawed at Corelle, brought a knot to her stomach. They would finish this hard, enjoyable labour, then make the ship ready to cast off. It would sail out into the middle of the river and on to another city. She longed for the open sea, blue giants that cavorted nearby, different lands with different customs.

The tasks required here in Ort did not suit her. She did not know how to defend a city or town, how to brawl in the street against men armed with swords. For years, she had killed, and she hated it. It had brought nothing but the death of innocents, and with their deaths the need for more death so they could be avenged, a vicious cycle she could not break. It would be simple enough to walk up the ramp and ask the master to take her onto his crew. She could sail away from Dur, never to return, and concern herself no more with politics or the murder of men. The idea tempted her, but she had said she would stay. To her surprise, she had risen and taken some steps toward the ship as the thought had occurred to her.

Corelle had told Parstic and Denstal she would stay, but the ship would sail away, and those to whom she had betrayed her word would never see her again. There could be no recriminations. After all else, had she not broken every vow she had made?

Some part of her screamed at her to stop, and she heeded it. The ship had come from Jaiselnia, a land to the south she had visited twice in her year aboard The Salty Home. *"Stay put, Corelle,"* she thought. *"There would be no recriminations, but there would be guilt, and I have endured guilt enough for countless lifetimes already. I can stomach no more."*

She returned to the bench and watched the mariners load their cargo, an ache in her heart. Rather than sail south with them, she would remain, and the Qagrue would come. They would care nothing about the deaths of Sisnop, Gillar or Carshan. The deaths of their men would be avenged, however. The Ortfolk may pay a terrible price. What if she could find some way to deflect the

Qagrue's anger to some other land, to claim men from a southern ship came ashore and killed all the Qagrue? She laughed out loud at the far-fetched thought and checked nobody nearby had noticed. Nobody glanced at her.

They could blame the deaths on Sisnop. They might say he and his men arrived, angry at what had turned in Alcmouth, and had slain all the Qagrue. She almost laughed again. Sisnop had arrived with five Guild men and Carshan. It would be farcical to suggest they could have killed thirty men. Gillar might have helped, she reasoned. His men might have helped Sisnop.

Corelle sat upright. Sisnop had only five men, but did the Qagrue know that? She could never know, and it would be a mighty bluff, but even if they were caught in a lie, their situation could not be made any more dire. They could say he brought twenty men with him, and Gillar urged his own men to help. They could claim the Ortmen had no wish to fight the Qagrue, who had been kind and generous guests in their town. A lie of course, but again she doubted the Qagrue would realise that. When the towns-folk saw Sisnop's men kill their guests, they turned on Sisnop and Gillar and killed them and their men at the cost of some of their own. The town sacrificed its men to the Pyre to defend the Qagrue but could not save them. The Qagrue's leaders might even be delighted and declare Ort some sort of special place. She laughed again—she had gone too far now.

Corelle thanked the fates Synna had not arrived yet. He would have torn her idea into small pieces, pointed out all its flaws, its slim chance of success, and that it would bring about their ruin. In truth, she wished she had his support and friendship. As soon as he had told her what a terrible idea she had come up with, he would commit himself without reservation to its success. Denstal did not have that quality, and she suspected something lay hidden within him, though she could not guess what it might be. His eyes told her his words were lies at times, sweet treats designed to lead her to a place where she might serve his own ends.

She stood and strode toward the square. She resolved to bring the idea to Parstic and Leesant, at the least. They could laugh it off as ridiculous, but it made sense for them to hear it. When she reached the Portreeve's Offices, she strode inside and called for Leesant. Soon enough she stood in the Portreeve's office with Leesant and Parstic as they hung on her every word as she outlined her idea.

She had considered they might agree to the idea in the absence of any other, since she felt her plan did nothing to worsen the precarious situation they were already in. To her surprise, they embraced the plan with enthusiastic smiles and gracious words. They threw their arms around her and each other as they congratulated her on such a brilliant idea. Once they calmed down, Leesant came up with a further embellishment to the story. He could send letters to Alcmouth, tell the Qagrue the story before they even sailed to Ort. They might not wish to send their own here to rule and might be content to leave him in the Portreeve's post, happy to collect whatever financial gain Krage had received from the town before.

Corelle suggested the Qagrue's plan might be to kill all the Durfolk and populate the land with their own kind, but Leesant dismissed the idea as unlikely. Corelle thought his opinion baseless and risky, but the entire venture had been risky throughout. She reminded them Raolos had been summoned to Ort, and he might have a different idea in mind when he came. Leesant would not be downcast, and said if that situation arose, they would change their plan to something more favourable to them. Corelle guessed he cared about the people of Ort, and she did not have the heart to argue the point any further.

The two men, smiles as wide as the Torr Sea, set to work on a plan of how to word the letters they would send. Corelle left them to it and walked up to the little tavern she and Deineike had frequented. Syme still ran it, and he still remembered her. He gushed over her as soon as she entered. He even remembered her favourite drink and brought her a goblet of red wine without any word from her.

He wanted to know everything she had been about since her last visit. Her stories of her time as a mariner enthralled him, although when he insisted she remove her kerchief, he did not care for her hair, even though it had grown somewhat in the time she had been in Dur. He brought a fresh goblet of wine every time she drained one and sat with her all night other than when he had to serve other patrons. He insisted she tell the story of the blue giants at least three times, even though she thought she might have told him the tale the last time she had visited the tavern. She could not be sure, however, and his delight in the story made the repetition worthwhile. A few of his patrons drifted over to hear, and after two hours, she had a captive audience of ten or so listeners who hung on her every word.

By the time she left and headed back to Pettra's house, she saw two of everything as she staggered along the streets. Two couples passed her, and she closed an eye to make one of the pairs disappear. She heard the man tell his companion, in a voice loud enough to ensure Corelle heard him, how sad he found it that she could not walk in a straight line. She stopped, leaned on a wall, and shouted after him, "I do walk in straight lines. The problem is, I walk in many of them at the same time." She laughed so hard at her own jest, she slid down the wall and ended up on the ground as hysterical laughter shook her body until tears of merriment streamed from her eyes.

Once she reached Pettra's house, she crawled up the stairs and fell onto the bed in her clothes and boots. She woke late in the morning and felt as terrible as she imagined Denstal had the previous day. It must be some sort of retribution for her amusement at his condition. She could not rise from the bed until close to the midday, when she pumped water into a pitcher and drank it in large gulps. She felt so atrocious, she had to lie on the couch for some time before she could leave the house. Outside, a bright sun shone, and the glare worsened her already terrible headache. She accepted the truth; her condition would not permit her to leave the house, so she climbed the stairs again on all fours before she fell into the bed with a wretched, mournful moan. A deep sleep carried her away from her suffering, and when she woke, the sun had already sunk low in the sky. Her head still ached, but her stomach felt steadier. Slow and careful, she descended the stair, a firm grip on the rail to assist with her balance. In the pantry, she found some cheese, so she sat in an armed chair, nibbled on it, and cursed Syme's wine. It had bested her, and the day had been wasted. Nobody knew she was in the house, so nobody would visit. At the least, that meant nobody could tease her about the disgraceful state the wine had left her in, the only bright spot in a miserable day.

CHAPTER 37
CORELLE

Corelle felt much improved the next day, and after a small meal of the remaining food, she made her way to the Portreeve's Offices to request an audience with Leesant. He told her he had sent the letters to Qagrue the previous day. She thought he had acted too fast and without enough thought, but it did not surprise her, in truth. By now, she guessed the excitement of the victory of three days ago had faded, and the Ortfolk worried about families and friends. It made sense, but she hoped it would not stir the Qagrue into action. They could not hope to defend Ort if the Qagrue came before Raolos. She doubted they could defend it even with Raolos, but she kept this counsel to herself.

She wandered down to the docks where a two-masted ship had tied up, and she walked aboard to talk to the master. He had sailed from Alcmouth and had no news that cheered her. Cargo still sailed north at the least, but the letters had not yet arrived in the capital. It would be many days yet before they saw whether those letters sparked any recrimination. The Qagrue might be delayed if they chose to debate the implications, but they might also sail to Ort sooner than they had planned. The dice had been rolled and the fates written. They could do nothing but wait, but since Corelle had little experience of these weighty politics, she grew anxious. She feared a poor outcome from the events they had set in motion, but even if it brought her ruin, it would be preferable to an endless wait with no idea whether she would live or die.

Each day, she walked down to the docks to watch the ships come and go, never more than a heartbeat from the walk up the ramp that would see her leave Dur. Sometimes she would see Parstic, and they would talk for a time. She saw Denstal only once. He sat and talked to her for a few moments, but she suspected he harboured resentment she would not join his scheme to rebuild a clandestine group to resist the Qagrue. She would not, however, change her mind only to spare his disappointment. The Guild had been destroyed in Dur, and if nothing else had been achieved, that at the least had been worthwhile. Too many had suffered at the Guild's hands, and its restoration would be too painful. Denstal must live with the consequences of his shattered, unrealistic expectations.

The little rowboat from Eastort resumed operations. They had found it, it seemed, but she stayed away from it lest the operators recognise her and cause a fuss. As she watched it plough its way across the Alc each day, she reflected that, to most of the folks of Dur, life continued, little different from all they had ever known. The Eastlands may not even have realised anything had changed in Alcmouth.

She knew nothing of how things were in the Five Cities, of course. For all she knew, those cities ran vermilion with the blood of the Durfolk, massacred in huge numbers by the Qagrue as they seized Dur for their own. She doubted it but had no way to know for certain. Her frustration grew. In truth, she had no idea what the Qagrue intended for Dur. They might stay here for ever or they might exploit all they could to their own gain and move on. It felt worse not to know anything than to know a terrible fate lay in store for her land.

If the Qagrue intended to stay, they must have had no wish for Krage to serve them in any capacity, or he and his allies would not have fled. That did not mean the invaders did not wish to work with any Durfolk, of course. They may allow Portreeves to remain to run the cities and towns and keep the land organised while the Qagrue reaped the rewards. That seemed a less realistic scenario to Corelle. She stamped a foot. All her thoughts amounted to nothing more than speculation. She knew nothing, and as it had in Ryl, her impatience grew, and she wished for action, no matter the cost. Her frustration mounted, driven ever higher by inaction and lack of certainty.

The ship had been gone for four days when she saw the pale sunlight of early evening reflect from a sail. Her heart sank. No ship had sailed south in the days since the letters had been sent, and she feared the worst as she peered forward to identify the ship. The day had been wet, but the clouds had cleared and allowed the weak sunshine to catch the sail far to the north. She stared at it, torn between despair and hope, and she could scarce bring herself to breathe. As the ship grew closer, she thought it a little small to be the Corkannae vessel, but she stared at it until she saw it had only two masts. She exhaled a lengthy breath. The ship that had borne her letters had not returned. The little two-master might bring news of Zhanghar or even Ryl.

Her hopes for some news were dashed. The ship did not move out of the deeper waters in the centre of the river and sailed past Ort, headed further south. Some mariners stood at the rail as they passed, and they gazed on the town. She waved and yelled for news, but if they heard her, no audible reply came from the ship, and she watched in sadness as it grew ever smaller until it disappeared in the gloomy twilight as more clouds approached from the south.

The next day, the fifth since the ship had set out, Corelle felt certain the ship must return if the master had been unable to sail beyond Zhanghar. All morning, hope rose within her with each hour the ship did not appear. If he had got through to Ryl, he might have arrived by now. Raolos might arrive in Ort before the Qagrue, after all else.

The clouds she had seen the previous evening had brought atrocious weather with them. The rain poured down without mercy all day and she shivered as she sat on the docks. She became saturated in no time, her arms wrapped around her body as the cold penetrated to her bones. When she grew so cold she thought she might die, she sought shelter in the Master's Offices, and he suggested she sit near his fire. She wondered about the man's title. A master controlled a ship, and a master also controlled the dock workers and movement of goods through the docks. Ship's master and dock master might be versions of a similar word, but it seemed peculiar to her.

Less than an hour after the midday, a man entered the Master's Offices to report sail had been spotted to the north, a two-master he thought. A flurry of activity broke out as the master summoned dockworkers from somewhere in the rear of the building where they had doubtless been huddled around a warm fire to play at cards or dice. They grumbled as they donned cloaks to protect themselves from the rain. Corelle ran from the building, down to the edge of the dock, then peered north. The ship had almost arrived and had left the deeper water. It made for the dock, and her heart leapt, certain she would learn some news at last. With bated breath, she waited, impatient, as the ship she pinned so much hope on grew closer.

CHAPTER 38
CORELLE

The little ship glided into the dock, and mariners threw ropes down. She watched the smooth approach and admired the master's skill. The mariners' proficient rope work impressed her, and the thought again flitted through the passages of her mind she should ask the master to take her aboard as one of his crew, though a ship that never left the coastline of Dur might not suit her.

Dockworkers pushed the ramp up to the ship's dock, then stood around in expectation. To Corelle's surprise, only one mariner came down the ramp. She saw no sign of activity aboard, as would be normal if they intended to offload a cargo, and nothing had been stacked at the dockside for them to collect. The mariner spoke to the dockworkers while Corelle wondered whether she should run up the ramp to find the master and press him for news from the north. The conversation between the mariner and the dockworkers did not appear productive. The dockworkers shrugged shoulders and pointed toward the town, and the mariner, who seemed frustrated, waved his arms about with vigour.

Corelle decided to see what caused the fuss. If she learned nothing, she could board the ship and seek out the master. She pushed her way into the middle of the men who debated whatever the mariner had said. "Greetings. What turns here? No cargo to offload?"

One of the dockworkers replied without a glance in her direction. "This ship has come from Ryl. This mariner seeks Corelle."

Her heart felt as though it had skipped a beat. "Why do you seek this woman?" The man did not seem to hear her as he continued his animated conversation with other dockworkers. She reached for him and pulled at the sleeve of his tunic until he glanced at her. "Why do you seek this Corelle?"

"Because I carry a letter for her. These men have heard of her, but none know whether she is still in the town."

Somebody suggested the mariner should take the letter to the new Portreeve. Another had a less helpful suggestion. "Throw it in the Alc and be about your business, if you have no cargo for us to offload."

Corelle wanted to know who had sent her the letter. "Who is this letter from?" It could only be Raolos, but what did it portend?

The man confirmed her opinion. "It is from Raolos, who used to be the Bailiff."

Some of the dockworkers had lost interest in the mariner. He had no cargo for them to unload, which meant they would earn no coin while they stood in the cold and rain engaged in a debate about where he might find Corelle. It did not surprise her some of them drifted away in the circumstances. Anxious now to get hold of the letter, Corelle told the mariner he had found the woman he sought.

The man looked at her, and Corelle could not miss his lack of conviction. "I have a description of Corelle, and you do resemble her. It is somewhat convenient, nonetheless, that you hear my tale and now profess to be the woman I seek. I would have taken you for a nosy courtesan."

She snorted and reached for her fan. "Wilash made this blade for me. He travelled with Raolos. I am friend to him, as I am to Raolos. Synna also, who travels with them. I killed Styrrach in Alcmouth. I am Corelle."

She stared into his eyes, and he blanched before her ferocity. "Wilash is a name I am familiar with, and the tale of Styrrach also." He hesitated for a heartbeat or two, then reached inside his tunic, pulled out a sealed parch, and handed it to her. "Here is your letter. Our obligation is ended. We sail for Torric."

"Wait." Corelle longed to ask him questions, but he scurried up the ramp and the dockworkers pulled it down as they muttered their anger and disappointment the ship had no cargo for them to unload. They untied the ropes and threw them up to the ship's deck without heed for how difficult they made life for the mariners who awaited them.

Corelle stared at the letter. It bore the seal of the Portreeve of Ryl. Raolos must not have had time to retrieve his own seal before he fled Alcmouth, or the letter did not come from him at all but bore ill news of his fate. Raolos would not have had time to send the letter in response to her own, as the Corkannae ship could not have made it to Ryl and back in the time that had elapsed. Raolos had sent the letter of his own accord. She ran to the shelter of an open tally house door and broke the seal, unwrapped the damp parch, and scanned the words scribed on it in Raolos's bold hand, hungry for news. What she read left her distraught.

The Qagrue had attacked Ryl, a sevenday ago, she reasoned. That would explain why ships sailed south again, she imagined, since the blockade would be lifted. There had been a desperate battle for the city, with many killed on both sides. Men had come from Torric, Vjort, Delcan, and many other towns to make a stand for Dur, but they had been insufficient in the end. Tears stung at her eyes as she read on. The Qagrue had outnumbered them, and despite the ferocity with which the Dur men had fought to defend their land, the Qagrue had prevailed through sheer weight of numbers. The Qagrue's victory had cost them dear, but it had cost Dur a great price also, with many of its citizens now gone to the flames.

Raolos and Wilash survived unhurt and would sail west with Tamgellan. They would take Vamma with them, since Dur would no longer be safe for them. They hoped if they sailed west, they might come to Malkartas. Raolos made a jest about his desire to see whether Ictharelian was a globe after all else, and Corelle found a weak smile, dragged it to her lips. He went on to hope she had been successful in Ort and suggested she leave the town as soon as she could. He had heard the Qagrue say their tribal leader sailed for Dur and would take Dur as their own once he arrived. He suspected Krage and his allies might be dead, killed by the Qagrue.

She paused and lowered the letter, relieved Raolos, Wilash, and Vamma were safe, but he had not mentioned Synna. With a heavy heart, she returned to the parch to read the last paragraph.

It confirmed her worst fears. Synna had been killed in the fight. The docks and tally houses spun before her as the news struck her like a punch in a brawl. Her stomach muscles tightened, her mouth ran dry, her heart became a rock in her breast. She staggered back into the tally house and almost fell. Somebody called out to check whether she needed aid, the cry nothing but some vague echo from the bottom of the crevice on the edge of which she teetered. Synna had died? It could not be. The sting of tears hurt her eyes, but she read on. He had been killed outside the doors to the Portreeve's Offices. He had put up a ferocious resistance. He wielded two daggers and had slain a great many Qagrue. When the Qagrue saw him kill so many of their own and heard him yell encouragement to his men, they thronged around him. He went down under so many sword blows, Raolos could not find a piece of his body the blades had not slashed. Even the Qagrue recognised his valour and allowed Raolos to give him a Pyre and a Sending worthy of the way he had fought. Raolos closed the letter with a tragic apology. "I am so sorry. I know the two of you were close friends."

Her legs refused to hold her upright any longer, and she slumped to the floor. She crumpled the letter into her face as she cried bitter tears. As she screamed all her agony into the air, two men stood over her and spoke to her, but she did not care to hear their words. Tears soaked the parch, and the ink ran in dark streaks over her arms and, she imagined, her face. She had abandoned Synna, and now he had been killed. Why had she not stayed with him? Her selfishness could not be forgiven. He had been a good man, too good to fall to a mass of killers, none of them his equal, their numbers the only reason they could overwhelm him. She hated herself. She had left him alone to die, but she hated the Qagrue who had taken his life.

One of the men reached down and pulled her arm. He asked if she needed aid, and she looked up at him and sobbed dejected words. "I abandoned him." They pulled her upright, somebody brought her a chair, and they insisted she sit. She slumped forward, head in hands, and cried until her throat became hoarse, her lips became dry, her heart became dust scattered around the land.

What turned around her, she did not know. Two men in red tunics came in, and she imagined somebody from the tally house had summoned them. They recognised her and asked what had turned. How could she explain what had gone so awry, or the wrongs she had inflicted on so many people?

She pushed away the hands that held her. "I am fine." Corelle stood and staggered out into the rain to make for the nearest tavern. She ordered a cask of wine and a goblet, paid for it in a daze, then found a dark corner where she could sit alone. As she poured the wine down her throat, anxious for it to dull the pain that ached in every part of her, she reflected on the lives spent because they were close to her. Arella and her child, Taro, Deineike, Pettra, Klordia, the Duke and his son, Ibie, and now Synna. Had any of it been worthwhile? She did not even know what they had all died for, so how could she decide whether it had been worth that terrible price? Why did they all have to die? Their only crime had been to know Corelle of Ryl.

The land had been lost to southerners, thanks in no small part to Krage and Corelle. They had all died for naught, every one of them, those she had killed since the day she moved to Zhanghar among them. It would have been better if Styrrach's attempt to shroud her had succeeded, she thought; better she had been removed from the future of all those who had died because she had not.

The next day, she woke up in Pettra's house with no recollection of how she had got there. She lay on the floor of the parlour and felt worse than she had ever felt before after a night's wine. Her heart felt as though it had turned to stone in her breast. Her clothes and the carpet already stained by vomit, she could not rise in time to reach the privy, and she fetched up on herself again.

She judged it well after the midday before she could rise from the floor. She crawled up the stairs, grabbed her pack and looked inside it. Deineike's sketches lay at the bottom, battered, torn, and ruined. She pushed her few items of clothing around with contempt. She changed her trousers and tunic; the ones she wore were stained with vomit and road dirt. Dejected, she took her small pouch of coin, pushed it into her pocket, and walked out of the house. She left the pack behind, locked the door, and placed the key in the pocket with the coin.

Corelle trudged down to the dock, as miserable a picture as any who passed could have ever seen. Her head pounded, and every step brought further agony. Her stomach roiled, and she did not know how she had not fetched up several times as she walked. Her eyes fixed on the ground, she avoided the eyes of everyone she passed, consumed with her own misery and guilt. The sigil of

Corkannae fluttered at the stern of a ship at the dock. It must have arrived last night or this morning.

She stood near the ramp of the ship for some time as she gazed up at the mariners who loaded a cargo of crates into the hold. She guessed the ship would sail soon. At once, filled with a melancholy she felt sure nothing could dispel, she walked up the ramp and asked for the master.

A mariner led her to him, and she mumbled at him. "I can work if you will take me on to your crew." She had dispensed with any formality or introductions. "I am a fine mariner."

He gazed at her in clear disbelief. "No woman serves as a mariner." He had a deep voice and a strong Corkannae accent.

She raised her head and snapped a proud reply. "One does."

"One did. They say she is dead."

They stared at each other, the master and the killer. She needed to leave, and only he could help her do so at this moment—she must persuade him. "Will you not give me a chance?"

He looked her up and down, and she guessed he did not like what he saw. He did not see her at her best today, and she struggled not to fetch up. *That would seal the deal,* she thought. He would not take a mariner who fetched up in the gentle swell of the docks. At last, he sighed. "Very well, I will give you a chance. If you are incompetent, I will drop you off in Alcmouth and let the Qagrue have you."

"I promise you will not regret your decision. You will have no need to put me off the ship."

He tilted his chin upward, and a question formed in his eyes. "Did you know her?"

The question confused Corelle. "Who?"

"The other woman, the one who became a mariner."

She nodded. "That I did."

"Is it true what they say? Is she dead?"

She looked around the ship. An officer stood nearby, a quizzical look on his face. The mariners closed the hold and made ready to cast off. Birds swooped around in search of any dropped morsel of food they might scavenge up. She gazed out at the Ort skyline, familiar to her, yet distant, like a picture half remembered from her childhood. She looked back into the eyes of the master. "That she is."

ABOUT THE AUTHOR

HAYLEY PRICE has always been a storyteller. Throughout her life, she has told her story through songs as the principal songwriter in several bands, most recently Adventures With Alice, whose songs feature in many of her books.

A New Zealander, Hayley currently lives in Canberra, Australia with her long-time partner and a grumpy, bossy cat called Rosie. She loves baseball and suffers eternal torture as a fan of the San Francisco Giants. Music has been a major part of her life, and outside her own compositions, she is an enormous fan of Christopher Cross as well as Daryl Hall & John Oates and underrated 80s UK prog-rock band Voyager, who once named her their #1 fan.

Hayley's first book, The Vermilion Ribbon, received an Honorary Mention in the 2024 The BookFest Award for LGBTQ Fantasy, a 2024 Indie BRAG Medallion, and was a finalist in the ABLE Golden Book Awards 2024. Her second book, The Vermilion Cross, won third place in the BookFest Awards for LGBTQ Fantasy.

ACKNOWLEDGMENTS

"Driving Route 288"
    Performed by Adventures With Alice feat. Catherine Porter
    Written by Debbie Rollason
    © Hand Elephant Records 2021
    Lyrics reprinted by permission

Cover by Adrian DSGNS

Torr Sea map by Lara Mitchell

Dur map by André Barbeto

SPECIAL THANKS

Ailsa. I would be nothing without you.

Jo & Rob, Wendy & Danny. Loyal supporters and valued friends.

Bec and Bianca. For believing.

The Beta Bunnies. Ailsa and Bec.

Christopher Cross. Your music touches and inspires me.

Rosie. We would be less of a family without her.

Everybody who reads my books. It staggers me every day I sell a book. Thank you for taking the chance.

LINKS

Here are some links I hope you will find useful.

My website: https://hayleyprice.net

Please leave a review for this book at: https://books2read.com/u/bPpZkA

ABOUT REVIEWS

HAYLEY IS an independent author, and to obtain any visibility requires a great deal of work. The big publishers have huge budgets and can smother the market every time they release a book. Against this, independent authors have to try to get their books noticed.

One way you can help independent authors is to leave reviews for their books on Amazon, Goodreads, or any other platform where you have a voice. On Amazon in particular, reviews help promote the books in the algorithm, which leads to more people seeing the book. It doesn't have to be a long review—it can be as simple as, "This was a good book."

Please consider leaving reviews whenever you read a book, especially an independent author's book. It helps us immensely.

Thank you for reading Hayley's book, and for any review you leave.